Lies, Damned Lies and History

JODI TAYLOR

Lies, Damned Lies and History

THE CHRONICLES OF ST MARY'S
BOOK SEVEN

JODI TAYLOR

Published by Accent Press Ltd 2016

ISBN 9781910939000

Acknowledgements

Thanks to Catherine Curzon and her excellent website for all her help with Caroline's efforts to enter Westminster Abbey.

Thanks to Jacquie for patiently answering my midwifery queries. And then answering all the questions I forgot to ask the first time round.

More thanks to Phillip Dawson, who advised me on police procedures.

Thanks also to Sally Mylles and Alex Mylles for setting me straight on the turd equation. Any subsequent errors are all mine. So hands off!

Thanks to my editor, Rebecca Lloyd, who never lets my perpetual failure to grasp the basic rules concerning punctuation, spelling, grammar, character development, plot structure and basic novel writing get her down.

Thanks to Hazel for the ham sandwiches, hot buttered crumpets and crispy fried beef. To say nothing of her generous hospitality.

Dramatis Thingummy

Dr Bairstow	Director of the Institute of Historical Research at St Mary's Priory. Hanging on by the skin of his teeth. Not a happy man these days.
Mrs Partridge	Kleio, daughter of Zeus, Muse of History. PA to Dr Bairstow. Usually quite cross with Max anyway, so nothing new to worry about.
Max	Chief Operations Officer. In even more trouble than usual.
Leon Farrell	Chief Technical Officer. Just as furious with Max as everyone else is.
Mr Dieter	Second Technical Officer.
Dr Tim Peterson	Chief Training Officer and potential Deputy Director. Also in deep disgrace.
Major Ian Guthrie	Head of the Security Section. Furious with Max, which is OK, but disappointed in Markham – which isn't.
Mr Markham	Guthrie's number two. Also in it up to his neck.

Dr Helen Foster	Chief Medical Officer. Always furious with everyone, so no change there.
Dianne Hunter	Chief Nurse and long-suffering recipient of Mr Markham's affections. Probably still speaking to him out of pity.
Prof. Rapson	Head of Research & Development. Not often quite up to speed on current events, so relatively neutral.
Dr Dowson	Librarian and Archivist. As above on current events.
Theresa Mack	Kitchen Supremo. Former urban terrorist, so tends to reward rule breaking with second helpings of gooseberry crumble.
Mavis Enderby	Head of Wardrobe. 'Not sure what it's all about, but look at the damage to this costume and it's so difficult to remove bloodstains.'
Rosie Lee	PA to the Chief Operations Officer. Doesn't care what's going on. Everyone else is an idiot anyway.
The History Department	Conflicted. Loyal to Max and Peterson, but horrified at what they have done. Concerned for the future. Makes a change from fretting about the past!
Gareth Roberts	Soon to be ex-historian.

David Sands	Keeping an eye on him.
Mr Clerk	Historian.
Paula Prentiss	Historian.
Tom Bashford	Historian.
Elspeth Grey	Unenthusiastic historian.
Mr Phillip Atherton	Pathfinder. Bemused but loyal.
Miss Elizabeth Sykes	Pathfinder. Ditto.
Miss Celia North	Pathfinder. Never bemused. Loyal for as long as it suits her.
Malcolm Halcombe	Possibly from Salcombe.
Lisa Dottle	A bit of a wet hamster.
Clive Ronan	Renegade historian and bad guy. Hasn't been seen for a while.
Chancellor and members of the Senior Faculty, University of Thirsk.	Nominal employers and purse-holders. All head-burstingly furious with St Mary's and out for blood.
Dr Kalinda Black	St Mary's liaison officer with Thirsk University. Keeping out of it.
Miss Lingoss	Former trainee historian in search of excitement. Transferred to R&D and found it.

Key historical figures

Caroline of Brunswick	Unofficial Queen and professional troublemaker. Fat.
George IV	Her even fatter husband.
Arthur, Dux Bellorum	Yes – that Arthur.
Old man in cave	Your guess is as good as mine.
John Lackland	King John. About to lose something in The Wash. Not a sock!
Herne the Hunter	Or not. Possibly an hallucination. Or not.

Also featuring besieged Britons, marauding Saxons, excited Londoners, supernatural apparitions, Rushford's finest, pickpockets, bluestones, thieves in the night, possible wolves, a clergyman with a high moral tone, a number of lightly damaged Time Police Officers, an unspecified amount of Turd Tumbler, and Oscar the Ringworm.

Prologue

I've never been one for rules. They don't really seem to apply to me. I can't begin to count the number of times I've had to stand in front of someone's desk while they talked at me, sometimes for some considerable length of time. The only good thing is that, usually, it's only me involved.

But not this time. This time I was in serious trouble. This time I'd done something really bad. Never mind that I thought it was for the best of reasons. This time I'd really gone too far.

I couldn't complain. Not long ago, Dr Bairstow, who always saw further than anyone else at St Mary's, had tried to warn me, saying, 'You need to take care, Max. Great care. You are beginning to tread the line between what is acceptable and what is not. From there, it only takes the smallest step to find you have stepped over that line and that you have done the wrong thing for the right reasons. I am warning you, in future, to be very, very careful.'

I should have listened to him and I didn't. This time, I'd not just crossed the line – I'd practically pole-vaulted over it.

And this time I'd involved Peterson – whose future at St Mary's was looking very shaky indeed.

And Markham who, thanks to me, would now probably never succeed Major Guthrie as head of the Security Section.

And that wasn't the worst of it. People had lost their jobs. Roberts, my youngest historian had given in his notice. He'd insisted on trying to take all the blame. There had been a brief shouting session with Dr Bairstow and then Roberts was gone, hurling himself through the front doors and crashing the gears of his car in his haste to get down the drive and out of the gates. With the state he was in, I shouldn't have let him go, but there was no holding him.

And David Sands – long-time friend and ally. He'd resigned, too.

And possibly the worst of all, the Chancellor of the University of Thirsk, Dr Chalfont, who had fought our corner on so many occasions – she was out as well. She'd stood her ground and argued for us – which was good of her because she'd been more furious with me than anyone else, Dr Bairstow included – and the knives that had been waiting for this opportunity for years came out. She'd been allowed to retire. Ill health, they said, but that was just for public show. I'd got her sacked as well. And Dr Bairstow was only hanging on by the skin of his teeth.

I've done some stupid things. I've been reckless, but never have I ruined so many lives or left such a trail of destruction behind me.

I suppose the story begins with Bashford's attempt to emulate William Tell.

Chapter One

'Right you lot,' I said, crashing through the door to the men's ward in Sick Bay, mug of tea in one hand, Accident Book in the other. 'What's the story here?'

They regarded me guiltily. Historians Bashford and Roberts were contravening rules and regs by sitting on the bed. Sands hung over the back of a chair. Miss Lingoss was perched in the window seat, giving us all a first-class view of today's hair extravaganza. A red, gold, and orange sunburst was exploding around her head. She looked like an exuberant cactus.

The villain of the piece – or the idiot responsible for this particular catastrophe, if you wanted to use Dr Bairstow's exact words – was propped up on his pillows looking interestingly pale, his left ear covered with a dressing, which was, in turn, held in place by a rakishly angled bandage.

Someone found me a chair. One of the few advantages of being pregnant: you're not allowed to stand up. God knows why. You're just as pregnant sitting down. Anyway, I made myself comfortable, put my feet up on Markham's bed, pulled over his fruit bowl, and helped myself to his grapes. He knew better than to argue. He was – they all were – in some deep shit here. Since this was something that happened on a regular basis, no one seemed that bothered.

My name is Maxwell, and I'm in charge of the History Department – or The Usual Suspects, as they're sometimes known. Everyone present belonged to me, with the exception of Markham – or The Patient, as he's sometimes known. Or, on one or two occasions – The Accused.

He was fussing about my boots on his bed.

'If Nurse Hunter comes in I'll get the blame,' he said.

That's another thing about Markham. He's as brave as a lion, gets himself shot at, blown up, set on fire, dropped or drowned far more often than is probably good for him, and it's all water off a duck's back, but one harsh word from blonde, fluffy Nurse Hunter and he looks like a puppy with a brick round its neck.

'The sooner I get this sorted, the sooner I'm gone,' I said. 'Who's going to start?'

I'm not sure why I bothered asking. No one at St Mary's is backward when coming forward to tell their side of the story. They all talked at once, of course, and it would have been sensible of them to have spent a little time first agreeing which was going to be the official version, but we got there in the end.

'William Tell,' said Roberts, and from that moment, everything was crystal clear. No reason why I shouldn't have a little fun, though.

It would seem that an argument – sorry, academic discussion – had arisen over various myths and legends, and someone had dragged in William Tell. From there, it was only a short trip to the story of Tell shooting the apple off his son's head. From there, it was an even shorter trip to the possibility of such a feat. From there, it was only a tiny step to them having a go themselves, and from there it was as inevitable as a politician cheating on his expenses claim that Markham would lose a body part.

Back in the 14th century, Switzerland was occupied by the Austrians. They set up a hat on a pole in the Altdorf marketplace and instructed the people to bow as they passed. William Tell refused. Tell was famous for his prowess with a crossbow and, displaying the sense of humour for which Austrians are renowned, they thought it would be a hilarious idea to place an apple on his son's head and challenge him to shoot if off.

Which he did.

Apparently, various historians had scoffed at this, one thing had led to another, and the next minute, half of St Mary's was outside with a crossbow and a bowl of fruit.

You do see where this is heading, don't you?

'Whose idea was this? I asked and the way no one looked at Miss Lingoss told me everything I wanted to know.

'So why was the apple on Markham's head and not Miss Lingoss's?'

'Oh come on, Max,' said Sands. 'Stick an apple on her head and you'd never see it again.'

True enough, I supposed.

'Who shot the bolt?' I demanded and, astonishingly, no one could remember.

I sighed and closed the book. The only reason we weren't shut down years ago by the Health and Safety Executive is that we only have to file official paperwork if someone is actually carted off to hospital. Since we have our own very well equipped Sick Bay, we're able to keep most things in-house. Although if anyone ever checks up on exactly how we manage to get through two Accident Books a month, we're in serious trouble.

'So what really happened?' I said, putting the book away so they knew we were off the record.

'He moved,' said Bashford indignantly.

'I did not,' said Markham, even more indignantly.

'For the love of God, I was only ten feet in front of you. I couldn't possibly have missed. You moved.'

'You couldn't hit a bloody barn door,' replied Markham with spirit. 'I told you we should have used a pumpkin.'

I enquired exactly what the damage was.

'Lost the top of my left ear,' he said proudly. 'I look like Spock. Not the baby guy. The other one.'

'Actually,' said Lingoss, whose fault all this probably was, 'we should do the other one as well. So he's balanced.'

'It'll take a lot more than snipping his ear to balance Markham,' said Bashford, who obviously hadn't forgiven him for the slur on his marksmanship.

'You don't think it's spoiled my looks, do you?' said Markham, anxiously.

'No,' he said. 'Nothing could.'

He brightened. 'Thank you.'

I don't think that was quite what Bashford had meant but, at that moment, Hunter appeared with a tray of instruments and a determined expression, and we all found good reasons to be somewhere else.

I had an excellent reason for being somewhere else. Dr Bairstow wished to see me. I suspected he was about to make a spirited attempt to reduce Markham's salary on the grounds that he was paying full whack for someone with two good ears, and suddenly he had a security guard with only one and three quarters.

As I said, my name is Maxwell and I'm Chief Operations Officer here at St Mary's, or the Institute of Historical Research at St Mary's Priory, to give us our full title. We observe and document major historical events in contemporary time. Calling it time travel incurs Dr Bairstow's displeasure and you really don't want to do that, which was why, as I trotted towards his office, I spent the time deleting some facts and rearranging others, so that I could present him with a coherent and, above all, very nearly accurate account of the events that had led Markham to shed yet another body part.

I handed Mrs Partridge the Accident Book and she waved me through to his office.

'Good morning, sir.'

'Dr Maxwell. Please sit.'

I complied, eyeing the two mission folders on his desk. This looked interesting.

He never wasted time asking me how I was feeling, which I always appreciated. There was no point. I had significantly failed to suffer morning sickness, swollen ankles, cravings for bizarre combinations of food or any of the symptoms typical of your gravid female. Occasionally I suffered a little absent-mindedness. Twice Leon, my husband, had found his beer under the bathroom washbasin and the toilet cleaner in the fridge, and if he wanted to put that down to baby brain that was fine with me.

'Two assignments. Both from the usual source.'

He was referring to the University of Thirsk. Our employers. Or so they liked to think.

'So what have we got, sir?'

The first is to observe the coronation of George IV ...'

'OK,' I said, mentally assigning that one to someone else. Anyone else.

'And the other is ...' he paused dramatically, because if he does have a weakness, it's to be a bit of a showman, 'Arminius.'

I was enthusiastic. 'Herman the German! Cool.'

He leaned back. 'Yes, but not for you. I'd like you to give Arminius to Mr Clerk.'

'What? But why?'

He raised an eyebrow.

'I'm pregnant, sir,' I said indignantly. 'Not diseased. Or incapable. Or deficient.'

He raised the other eyebrow, effortlessly indicating that, for me, it was possible to be all four simultaneously.

'That was the deal, Dr Maxwell. No hazardous jumps. If you decline the coronation, I can always send Miss Sykes. She needs the experience.'

'So George IV or nothing at all.'

'How quickly you grasp my meaning.'

'Being pregnant has given me superpowers, sir. Which you could use to the advantage of St Mary's by sending *me* to the Teutoburg Forest and Mr Clerk to Westminster Abbey.'

'I don't think you will find this assignment to be lacking in excitement.'

'But it's so ...' I paused.

He looked up. 'So ...?'

'So ... girlie, sir.'

He sat back and prepared to enjoy himself. I sometimes think winding me up is the one small daily pleasure he allows himself.

I gritted my teeth and persevered. 'The Battle of the Teutoburg Forest is the battle that halted the Roman advance across Germany. A key point in History, and as such, sir, you need an experienced historian to lead the mission and ...'

'Do you doubt Mr Clerk?'

'No sir, he's very competent. It's just that he's not ...' I paused to grope for a word, which was a mistake.

'Pregnant.' He finished the sentence for me. 'The deal was that you continue to jump as long as your health permits – and I have to say it is a pleasure to see you looking so well, if a little flushed at the moment – and that you avail yourself only of the ... gentler ... assignments. I have distinct memories of putting these terms before you, and even more distinct memories of your accepting them.'

He had me there. At the time, I'd been so grateful not to be removed from the active list that I would have agreed to almost anything, but to see the great Arminius – Herman the German – to be in the Teutoburg ... to witness the battle that turned back the Romans ...

'I don't think you will find the coronation dull, Dr Maxwell, if that is what is troubling you.'

'More or less dull than a full-scale military engagement, sir?'

He handed me the folders. 'I'm sure you will make something of it. Take Mr Markham with you. A full set of ears is probably not a requirement for this assignment.'

Markham wouldn't be happy either. A major military confrontation would be kicking off in the Teutoburg Forest and neither of us would be there. Life is very hard sometimes. Coronations are usually long, stately, majestic, and, above all, respectable affairs, full of pomp and ceremony, with everyone on their best behaviour. The worst thing that can happen is forgetting to go to the loo before the six-hour-long ceremony commences.

This particular coronation did have a couple of redeeming features. Namely, two of the most unattractive people on the planet. Let me introduce the protagonists.

On my right, ladies and gentlemen, George Augustus Frederick, former Prince Regent, now George IV, King of the

United Kingdom of Great Britain and Ireland and of Hanover. Fat. Debauched. Crippled by massive debts. Gambler. Drunkard. You name it – he'd bet on it, shagged it, drunk it, or sold it to the highest bidder. Oh, and he was illegally married to Maria Fitzherbert.

On my left, his legal wife, Caroline Amelia Elizabeth of Brunswick-Wolfenbüttel. Fat. Highly strung – all right, mad. Hysterical. Demanding. Bossy. Unhygienic. Promiscuous. Loud.

Really, you could argue that by taking each other out of circulation, they'd done the world a favour.

Anyway, the marriage was a catastrophe even by royal standards, where the bar is set pretty high for catastrophe. Apparently, George was blind drunk for three days before his wedding and spent his wedding night passed out in the fireplace where, according to her version of events, his new wife left him to lie. Rumour had it that this was the only night they ever spent together. Since nine months later Caroline gave birth to a baby girl, we can only assume he had the most determined sperm in the history of ... well, sperm.

Anyway, on the death of his father, mad George III – the one who mistook a tree for the King of Prussia (easy mistake to make I should think) and peed blue urine – George ascended the throne. His wife turned up for the coronation and had the doors of Westminster Abbey slammed in her face.

And that's what you're stuck with if you're a pregnant historian.

Everyone else was off to record the History-changing Battle of the Teutoburg and I get bloody Caroline of bloody Brunswick. I said as much to Leon, whose fault all this was.

'I blame you,' I said. 'It's your incessant demand for sex that has saddled me with the Daft Bat of Brunswick.'

'Really?' he said, maddeningly unmoved by my plight. 'I don't remember any objections. In fact, I seem to remember you being hugely enthusiastic at the time. You did the thing with the ... you know.'

'Yes, never mind that now,' I said hastily. The only way to deal with embarrassing truths is to ignore them. Like a politician. 'The fact is that I'm off to 19th-century London to watch a bunch of fat Germans shouting at each other, and I'm going to miss one of the most important events in History.'

'That was the deal,' he said, mildly. 'You can continue jumping but only the quieter jumps. I seem to remember it being your idea.'

'Yes, but only because the other option was no jumps at all.'

'Which we can easily implement, if you're unhappy with the current arrangement.'

I sighed. 'No, it's fine.'

'You sure?' he said, suddenly anxious.

I felt my usual pang of conscience. Poor Leon. He never complains, but things aren't easy for him, sometimes.

'It's fine,' I said, suddenly aware that it was.

Chapter Two

Although he succeeded his father in January of 1820, George's coronation wasn't held until 19th July the following year. It took him that long to plan it. I might have forgotten to mention he was vain as well. He wanted the biggest, most badass coronation ever. Bigger even than Napoleon's – and he was an emperor.

The sums he spent were colossal. Parliament voted him £100,000 – which is a lot of money even today – and then, when it was obvious that even that sum wasn't going to be anything like enough, another £138,000. A total of about £9.5 million in today's terms. He commissioned a new crown, rejecting the traditional crown of King Edward. He even acquired the Hope Diamond, previously looted from the French Crown Jewels. You only have to look at the Brighton Pavilion – George's modest little seaside residence – to see he didn't do things by halves. Sadly for him, despite all his best efforts, the one thing his coronation would be famous for was not the spectacle, or the extravagance, or even his gorgeous self – it would be for his wife, the ghastly Caroline of Brunswick, who would steal the show. And for all the wrong reasons.

The 19th July was a hot day. Just for once, however, fashion worked in the female favour. I wore a pretty summer bonnet, which I tied rather racily under one ear, and a high-waisted walking dress of light blue silk. Since I wasn't a young girl, I had sleeves and only a moderate number of flounces. The material was light and comfortable. No corsets were involved in any way.

Markham, on the other hand, was trussed up like a turkey in a dark green long-tailed coat and an exotically embroidered waistcoat. He wore an intricately knotted cravat that pushed up his chin for that authentic 'staring down your nose at the peasants' look, tight breeches, and boots. He was hot before we even started. I tried not to feel smug.

We met in Hawking Hangar, outside Pod Eight, my favourite. Yes, it was looking a little battered these days, but weren't we all?

Pods are our centres of operation; they're solid, apparently stone-built shacks, which jump us back to whichever time period we've been assigned. They're cramped, squalid and the toilet never works properly. Number Eight smelled as it always did – of stale people, overloaded electrics, unstable plumbing, musty carpet, and cabbage.

We bustled inside, depositing our gear in the lockers. The console sat under the wall-mounted screen, which currently showed us a view of scurrying techies heaving their kit back behind the safety line. The two seats bolted to the floor were lumpy and uncomfortable, but life's essentials – a kettle and a couple of mugs, were present and correct. Since this was my pod, there would be chocolate biscuits around somewhere.

Bunches of thick cable ran up the walls and looped across the ceiling. Lights flashed among the mass of dials, gauges, and read-outs on the console. The whole effect was shabby hi-tech. Dilapidated and scruffy. Just like us. Actually, just like all of St Mary's.

As Chief Technical Officer, Leon was checking over the coordinates. 'All laid in. And for your return jump, too.'

'Thank you very much,' I said, seating myself in the left-hand seat and giving everything the once over.

'Take care,' he said, as he always did.

'Of course,' I said, as I always did.

He smiled for me alone and disappeared out of the door, which closed behind him.

I glanced at Markham. 'All set?'

'Ready when you are.'

'Computer, initiate jump.'

'Jump initiated.'

The world went white.

There were many people on the streets today, but this was London and there were many people on the streets every day. Given that this was Coronation Day, however, there were not as many as there could have been. To distract the crowds from any possible scenes his wife might make, a whole programme of public events had been laid on away from Westminster Abbey. There was to be a balloon ascension from Green Park. Even a herd of wooden elephants were to be rowed up the Thames. Something I thought would be considerably more entertaining than watching Prinny and his fat friends.

At this early hour, I found the temperature agreeably cool. We stood for a moment, inhaling the pleasant smells of fresh bread and – for the first time that I could remember on an assignment – coffee. Oh – and horses, of course. Hot, excited horses always have a strong olfactory presence. The streets were already deep in muck. Crossing boys were everywhere, industriously sweeping paths across the road for a carelessly tossed penny. I was glad of my ankle-length skirt and sturdy half boots. No historian ever goes anywhere wearing inadequate footwear: it's just asking for trouble.

Towards Westminster Abbey, the streets were cleaner – they'd obviously been swept for the occasion – but more crowded.

'Keep your hand on your holiday money,' advised Markham, piloting me through the crowds.

'What?'

'Pickpockets.'

'Ah,'

I've always regarded Westminster Abbey as an old friend.

'I've been here before,' I confided to Markham, as we elbowed our way through the enthusiastic crowds to get a decent view. 'Eight hundred years ago. My first proper assignment. Peterson and I were here as the first stones were being laid. Just before the Confessor died.'

'Really?' said Markham, fending off a man who wanted to sell us a flag. 'How did that go?'

'Quite well, actually. A bloody great block of stone missed us by inches and Peterson peed on me.'

'A big success by History Department standards, then.'

Having achieved our objective, we stood quietly, waiting. I had my recorder to hand. A stun gun and pepper spray nestled in the pretty reticule dangling from my wrist. We were ready to go. And there was not as long to wait as I had thought. Possibly thinking a timely arrival might mean easier access, the queen had arrived early. A clatter of hooves and a coachman roaring to small boys to get out of the way, announced the arrival of her carriage. An anticipatory stir ran through the crowd, all of whom knew she hadn't been invited. This was going to be good.

Dear God she was fat. And what was she wearing? Thankfully, someone had prevented her from adopting her usual style of dress, because there were occasions on which she had been seen in public with her dress open to the waist. Presumably, in deference to the solemnity of the occasion, she'd toned it down a bit, but not by much.

She wore a voluminous white satin gown, gathered under her massive bosom and falling to the ground, ending in a demi train. Her dark hair – too dark to be natural, surely – was skewered to the top of her head with nodding white ostrich feathers. Corkscrew ringlets framed her already flushed face. A hideously ugly diamond necklace did nothing to obscure the huge amounts of chest on view. Equally ugly diamond bracelets cut into the mottled flesh of her plump arms. Various brooches were scattered across the vast expanse of white satin. I swear, if she had stood in front of a mirror and said to her maids, 'Just throw everything at me and pin it where it sticks,' she couldn't have made a worse job of it. It must have broken their professional hearts to send her out looking like that.

I had no idea what was keeping all that flesh from falling out of her dress.

'Blimey,' said Markham, beside me. 'You don't get many of those to the pound.'

She climbed awkwardly from her carriage – it took two stout footmen to assist her – paused for the gasp of astonished admiration from the crowd, which never came, and began to make her way towards the doors of the Abbey, still standing open as the last of the guests slowly filed inside.

As she approached, a number of enormous, ugly men, hilariously dressed as pageboys, barred her path. Her husband, expecting trouble and knowing his wife, had hired professional prize-fighters to keep her out, led by the famous Gentleman Jackson himself. Which in itself was a good idea, but dressing them as pageboys probably was not.

Whether they actually would have manhandled her in front of the crowd, we'll never know. The crowd, sensing drama, fell quiet. She stood before them, unaccompanied even by a single lady-in-waiting. I thought she looked rather small (although still extremely fat) and pathetic. Raising her head, she shouted, 'The Queen. I am the Queen. Open.'

To say that her voice carried was an understatement. No horses actually bolted, but flocks of pigeons took to the air, probably never to return.

The crowd roared its approval of the pre-coronation entertainment and took up the cry.

'The Queen. The Queen.'

Nothing happened, and the shouting died down again while everyone waited to see what she would do next.

I could hear quite clearly from where we were standing.

She said, in strongly accented English, but with enormous dignity, 'I am the Queen of England,' picked up her skirts, and tried to squeeze between two cauliflower-eared pageboys, each the size of the Colossus of Rhodes.

Somewhere just inside the abbey, an unseen official roared, 'Do your duty, by God,' and with an echoing boom that could probably be heard three streets away, the massive doors slammed shut.

The crowd gasped. It was an almighty insult. True, she hadn't actually been crowned queen, but she was the wife of the king and no matter how much they loathed each other – and they did loathe each other – it was still a dreadful public insult.

She should have left. She should have gathered herself together, returned to her carriage and driven away. If she had left then, dignity and health intact, she would have won the day. At this point, the crowd was behind her. Being Caroline, of course, she blew it.

She uttered a shriek of rage, flung her ostrich feather fan to the ground, picked up her skirts and showing scandalous amounts of chubby leg, she ran.

She didn't walk, stroll, perambulate, amble, saunter, pace, stride, or waddle – she ran, and this was not an age in which highborn women ran. And certainly not in public. Probably most of them didn't even know how. For a princess – a royal – to hoist up her skirts, publicly show her legs and run was unthinkable.

Except that it did happen. She ran. Well, no, to be accurate – she lumbered.

The crowd, eager to see what could possibly happen next, streamed along behind her.

'Come on,' said Markham, seizing my arm, and we went with them.

Actually, I worried for her. Even though it was still early morning, it was a hot day. She was upset. She was extremely overweight. And she was running. It couldn't be good for her. Tonight, she would be taken ill and three weeks later, she would be dead. She really shouldn't be doing this.

She ran around the outside of the Abbey, dodging startled pedestrians coming the other way, all of whom probably wondered what the hell was going on.

We knew she would head for the cloisters.

'Bloody hell,' said Markham, keeping a firm grip on my arm as people surged around us. 'Is she mad? They're never going to let her in. Why doesn't she just go home? There's going to be trouble.'

She tried the door to the East Cloister first, but someone inside had got there first, and that door was locked. She rattled

16

the door latch and pounded on the door, but it remained unopened. The Abbey reared above her, massive and silent.

For a moment she paused, and then, nothing daunted, she set off again. For the West Cloister this time. She was really determined to get in. I wondered what was happening inside. Could they hear the hubbub over the music? Were they all sitting inside in the cool, listening to the uproar work its way around the outside of the building?

She was equally unlucky at the West Cloister where she halted, red-faced, chest heaving. And trust me, there was a lot of chest to heave. Her feathers were askew and her gown so disordered that she was barely decent. Now, surely, was the time for someone from her household to approach, take her arm, and gently lead her back to her carriage. If she'd actually had any friends in this country, that's what they should have done. She stood, quite alone in a wide circle of people, all silently watching to see what she would do next. I wondered if it was at this point that she realised how alone she was.

On the other hand, she was her own worst enemy. Wheeling about, scattering members of the crowd who'd closed in behind her, she set off again. For Westminster Hall this time, the site of the coronation banquet and where, despite the earliness of the hour, a good number of guests were already assembled.

And this was where it stopped being funny and suddenly became serious. This was England. You can't buck the Establishment. You can't do it now and you certainly couldn't do it in 1821. It may be old, fuddy-duddy, self-serving, and self-perpetuating – well, actually, it *is* old, fuddy-duddy, etc., but it's the seat of power in this country. It moves as fast as an arthritic glacier, but it doesn't need speed. The Establishment simply reaches out and slowly, inexorably, crushes everything in its path. Inconvenient princesses do not cause it any sort of problem at all, and never have. An order was shouted. Soldiers stepped up and suddenly, everything went very quiet and very still.

They held bayonets to her face. And they meant it. Just for once, she stood stock-still in disbelief, sweat running through the paint on her face, and her hair dishevelled. The hem of her skirts and her little soft shoes were stained with dust and horseshit. Dark patches showed under her arms. We could clearly hear her panting in the sudden silence.

I felt so sorry for her, but on the other hand, she seemed to have no problem making a public spectacle of herself, and her voice could topple buildings. She definitely wasn't happy. And she hadn't given up.

We couldn't see the next bit because everyone else was surging about trying to get a good view, but I know that she ignored them all, still trying to force her way in. Her voice, shrill with hysteria, her German accent thicker by the moment, carried clearly to those of us who couldn't get close enough to see. The crowd's good will was beginning to fade and the whole thing looked like deteriorating into a public brawl, when the deputy Lord Chamberlain solved everyone's problems and once again, the doors were slammed in her face.

You'd think she would give up, wouldn't you?

Still nothing daunted, she picked up her skirts and ran again – again showing vast amounts of unattractive ankle and leg – back to the Abbey door in Poets Corner. Markham and I, knowing where she would go next, had already set off, and were in place when she turned up, purple-faced with the effort, her bosom escaping from her dress. She was followed by a jeering crowd who, although accustomed over the years to their royal family making arses of themselves in public, were not impressed at this very unroyal display. Caroline had crossed a line.

I felt for her, awful though she was. She'd been publicly humiliated in front of all London. This story would fly around all Europe. If she had lived, she would have been a laughing stock wherever she went.

Except she wouldn't. Tonight – this very night – she would fall ill. No one was ever sure quite what ailment she was suffering from, but in three weeks, she would be dead. She would claim that at some point today, she'd been poisoned, and interestingly, her deathbed would be very closely observed by a man named Stephen Lushington, who was in the pay of Lord Liverpool, the prime minister of the day. The really sad thing was that she might well have been murdered. We'll never know, and at the time, no one cared.

But now, in front of me, Sir Robert Inglis was quietly attempting to persuade Caroline to leave.

I began to ease my way through the crowd. Because there was something I wanted to see. Everyone's eyes were fixed on the princess. She was clasping both hands to her massive bosom, struggling to catch her breath. It was very apparent that she was never going to be allowed inside the Abbey. Sir Robert was speaking very politely and calmly, and while the prize-fighters and slammed doors had only made her more determined to gain entry, his respectful persuasion was beginning to have some effect on her.

But what had caught my attention was a small smear of bright red blood on the back of her white glove. It was tiny. You could barely see it. It might not even be her blood. She could easily have brushed against someone. Or someone brushed against her. But suppose it was her blood. And tonight she would fall ill. And in three weeks, this inconvenient princess would be dead.

I don't know what Sir Robert said to her. Perhaps she was already beginning to feel unwell. The fight went out of her. I saw her shoulders slump. Even the feathers in her headdress were drooping. Three rough-looking pageboys led her quietly past the jeering people, and she heaved into her carriage. Defiant to the end, she waved to the unimpressed crowd, and was driven away.

I couldn't help recalling an unkind verse that circulated about her.

> Most gracious Queen, we thee implore
> To go away and sin no more.
> Or if the effort be too great
> To go away at any rate.

Markham and I took a moment to pull ourselves together ready for the next part of the assignment. The king himself.

Markham wiped the sweat from his face. I checked my recorder and took some footage of the area around the Abbey. We found a reasonably good position at the West Door and waited patiently for the procession to make its way from Westminster Hall, because we knew the king would be late.

In the 19th century, there were no crush barriers or any form of crowd control and everyone just milled happily about, enjoying themselves. The streets were full of carriages trying to get past, cabs and carts tangled with pedestrians, harassed officials, beggars and spectators.

Drivers swore at the crowd, who happily swore back again. The hot day was filled with the sights and sounds of overheated horses and people. The smell was ripe to say the least.

The noise was tremendous – people shouting, carriage wheels rattling over the paving, a band playing somewhere. The crowd was too thick for me to see them, but I could hear dogs barking all around us. I made a note to check whether London contained packs of feral dogs during this time period.

Word went out that the procession had begun to make its way from Westminster Hall, and people around us began to stand on tiptoe and crane their necks.

We passed the time discreetly recording the important people arriving. Everyone looked hot and harassed. George himself had designed their costumes, which were based on Elizabethan and Stuart design. He'd missed his calling. Never mind being king – he should have been a party planner.

The procession was preceded by a group of young women with baskets and I was pleased to see they kept up the medieval tradition of strewing the king's path with herbs as a prevention against the plague.

We watched the Crown Jewels and all the coronation regalia parade into the Abbey. It was almost worth being here just to see the massively long Great Sword of State. A couple of bishops followed on behind. I had no idea which ones – one bishop looks very like another to me, but someone would be able to identify them.

There was a lull. All around me, everyone was straining for the first sight of the king. Word had got around that he would be late. Apparently, he tore something just as he was leaving and being George, he'd had a bit of a panic.

We were bumped and jostled a little, but everyone was very good-natured, and the air of anticipation was building.

Finally, here he came. Sumptuously dressed, obese and oddly impressive. Everything about him was completely over the top. His train was nearly thirty feet long with beautifully intricate golden embroidery. Tall, white feathers nodded in his hat. The crowd fell silent, craning their necks for a better view. Men removed their hats. Women curtseyed as he passed. He was fat. He was unpopular. He'd wasted a fortune on this day – but as he walked past them, the crowds fell silent out of respect. He was their king and, at this moment, he wasn't ridiculous at all.

I was hot in my skimpy summer frock. Markham must have been baking, and George, surely, would burst into flames at any moment now. To ensure everyone had the opportunity to admire his splendid get-up, the silly juggins had instructed his canopy to follow along behind him, so he was exposed to the full blast of sunshine. His round, red, jowly face was streaming with sweat. He carried a silk handkerchief in one hand, with which he alternately mopped his faced and flourished at the crowd. Even as I stared, an attendant whisked it away and replaced it with a fresh one.

It was quite sad really, because in his youth, apparently, he had been a bit of a poster boy. There was now no trace of the dashing young prince. Except in his own memory, anyway. I thought he looked like a petulant baby with his protruding eyes and tiny, rosebud mouth, but he was very good-natured. He turned and waved at the people, who, with typical crowd mentality, cheered and waved at the man they had previously hissed and booed on every possible occasion. He knew how to work a crowd and even I found it hard to believe this was the

21

man who had mistreated his wives, betrayed his friends, and been involved in every scandal imaginable.

He paused outside the Abbey. His pageboys – real ones this time – got his thirty-foot-long train sorted out. I could hear his oddly high-pitched voice instructing them to hold it wider so that everyone could see the exquisite golden embroidery, and then, to a fanfare of trumpets, and with one last wave to the crowd, he entered the Abbey, to be crowned George, by the Grace of God, King of Great Britain and Ireland and of Hanover.

Around us, a hush fell as the fanfare died away and the last of the procession followed him in.

'Well,' I said to Markham – and you'd really think I'd know better by now – 'that went well.'

Hardly were the words out of my mouth than a portly man, red-faced in the heat, and trying to attract the attention of someone I couldn't see, barged into me, and knocked my recorder right out of my hand.

Normally, I have it looped around my wrist, just in case this does happen. I don't know why I didn't that day. I heard it hit the cobbles.

I tried to see where it went. I heard it again – being kicked along the ground. It was only a matter of time before someone trod on it and then I'd be in trouble.

I thought I saw it and bent forwards, trying to peer through people's legs. The crowd was dispersing and everyone was milling around, collecting family and friends, and moving in a million different directions at once. Someone caught me a glancing blow and down I went.

I heard Markham yell, 'Max.'

I ignored the splendid opportunity for a closer inspection of the filth-encrusted cobbles and rolled into a ball as feet and legs jostled past me.

I heard him again. 'Where are you?'

'Here.' I was struggling to get up, ungracefully showing at least as much leg as the soon to be late Princess of Wales.

'Yes, that's very helpful. A little more information, please.'

'Now then, m'dear,' said a voice, and a large pink hand pulled me to my feet. 'Give the lady some room,' he roared and people did.

I came up, bonnet askew, dignity still in the gutter I'd so recently occupied. Smoothing down my clothing as best I could, and trying not to think of what Mrs Enderby would say when she saw I'd been sweeping the streets with her blue silk creation, I said, 'Thank you, sir. I am much obliged to you for your kindness.'

Markham arrived, flushed and breathless.

'Are you all right?'

I nodded. The large man, dressed in a blue serge double-breasted coat that made his broad chest look even broader, frowned severely in a way that implied Markham should be taking better care of me, touched his hat and departed.

'I've dropped my recorder,' I said, panicking like mad because it could be anywhere by now.

'Right,' said Markham, staring around. 'No one's likely to have seen it, let alone picked it up, so the worst that can have happened is that it's been trampled. Dr Bairstow will frown at you but nothing worse than that.'

'We must find it,' I said, barely listening.

'Yes, we must, but try to stay on your feet this time. People will think you've been at the gin.'

'Oh, if only.'

He took my arm firmly. 'You look left. I'll look right.'

'It's not here. I heard it being kicked along the street.'

The crowds were thinning slightly. The ceremony itself would last six hours so most people were disappearing in search of entertainment, refreshment and a quiet corner where they could have a pee. Public toilets hadn't turned up yet, so most people either splashed against a wall or crouched in the street. Where I'd recently been. I really wished I hadn't just thought of that.

We were both lucky and unlucky.

Lucky, because against all the odds, we found it.

And unlucky, because as we hastened towards it, some ten or twelve feet away, someone else got there first.

Chapter Three

He was hatless and his long, lank hair hung around his face. He wore some sort of full-length, greasy greatcoat that smelled musty even from here. As I watched, he bent over and picked up my battered but still intact recorder, turning it over in his hands.

I stiffened.

Markham let go of my arm and strolled towards him.

'Ah, sir, I see you have found it. My thanks.'

The man said nothing, staring at us suspiciously. Even though Dr Bairstow would kill me, I really hoped it was broken, because any moment now he would accidentally activate it, and we'd be projecting a ten-foot-high image of Princess Caroline's bosom across the nearest building, and that really would take some explaining away.

The man, showing bad skin and worse teeth, stared at Markham for a moment and took to his heels.

Bollocks.

'Go,' I said to him. 'I'll follow. Keep your com open.'

He disappeared into the crowd and I followed as best I could. I could hear Markham puffing and cursing as I eased my way through. People here weren't as polite as they had been at the Abbey. When I looked down, my lovely dress was smeared down the front with nasty-looking brown stains. With that and my tipsy bonnet, I probably looked like one of those Hogarth engravings depicting the working-class poor and their close relationship with the demon drink.

The crowds were thinning. They'd probably headed towards the river, because who wouldn't want to see a herd of wooden elephants being propelled up the Thames? I'd looked forward to that myself.

I set my back against a wall, fanned myself, got my breath back, and said quietly, 'Where are you?'

'I must be about a hundred yards ahead of you. He's turning into an alley. There's a barrowman selling something or other on the corner. I've got him now.'

'For God's sake be careful. Hunter gets really upset with me when I take you back in pieces.'

No reply.

Again – bollocks.

I set off, keeping my eyes peeled for trouble.

I found the barrowman easily enough, skidded around a corner, and stopped dead, because I'd just entered another world.

The wide streets, stone buildings, well-dressed people, all the signs of a prosperous metropolis, had disappeared as if they had never existed. Even the sunshine had vanished. The sights and sounds of this special day died away. Here was darkness and silence.

This little lane was no more than ten feet across at its widest point. Buildings – I couldn't call them houses – rose up on either side. They weren't tall but they leaned across the narrow space like old ladies putting their heads together for a bit of a gossip. They cast long, deep shadows across the lane, which despite the summer heat, was a quagmire. The ground had long since been covered over with filth, sewage, household waste, animal waste, mud and rotting straw, all of which had built up over the years, making the street level now considerably higher than the doorways. Every time it rained, all this evil smelling sludge must have run straight back into the houses again. Probably to a considerable depth.

And being upstairs wouldn't be much more pleasant. Few roofs were tiled and none looked waterproof. Or even safe. Windows were tiny and many were shuttered tight. There was no glass. The walls were covered in damp, slimy stains that streaked down from the broken gutters, with similar stains working their way up from the swamp in which the houses stood. When the two united, the buildings would probably fall down.

The smell was awful. Industrial London was just kicking off, but the infrastructure lagged far behind. Living conditions for the poor were appalling. There was little access to clean water and no sewers. The rivers of London ran brown with filth. For many people, disease, poverty, and despair were the only things not in short supply.

I heard a noise nearby, pulled my stun gun out of my reticule, and moved silently along one damp wall.

There they were. Two dim shapes struggling in a doorway. I opened my mouth to shout 'Hoi' and wade in to help – literally – when someone grabbed me from behind and tried to seize my reticule.

I said piteously, 'Oh pray sir, do not rob me,' spun around and zapped him.

I heard Markham shout, 'Max,' and then there was the sound of another body hitting the ground. I panicked all over again because although Hunter could get very nasty when I took him back injured, it was nothing to what she would do if I took him back dead.

I was worrying unnecessarily. He strolled out of the shadows, holding my battered recorder.

'Amazingly, it still works.'

I took it from him. 'Thank you. You all right?'

'Just a small knife wound.'

'What?'

'It's fine,' he said, breezily. 'It's literally just a scratch, and truthfully, Max, I'm wearing so many layers of clothing, you'd have to fire a siege weapon at me to penetrate this lot.'

He was bleeding from a long, shallow scratch on the back of his hand. I pulled out a handkerchief and bound him up, enquiring when he'd last had a tetanus shot.

'No idea,' he said, 'but Hunter's always sticking me with something, so I'm not too worried. Don't forget to tell her how heroic I was, will you.'

We emerged from the alley, straightening our clothing as we did so, and a passing clergyman in his gaiters and wide-brimmed hat got hold of completely the wrong end of the stick, threw us an accusatory stare, and slowed down. Oh God, we were going to be Saved.

We all stared at each other. I couldn't think of anything to say. The clergyman was rummaging through his pockets. Were we going to be Pamphleted as well?

It was Markham who, as he said afterwards, saved the day.

Thrusting me forwards, he said, 'Very nice girl, yer honour. Very clean. Very skilled. And, already up the duff, so no problems with any little members of the clergy knocking on your door in years to come, if you take my drift. Now then, sir, always happy to oblige the clergy, so for you today, special prices. For services involving manual dexterity and ...'

The clergyman's mouth opened and closed as he struggled to find words to describe our moral depravity and then, hearing more voices approaching and possibly afraid of people mistaking the situation for exactly what it was, he turned on his heel and strode rapidly down the street. Markham politely lifted his hat to his departing back.

I thumped his arm. 'You're pimping me out now?'

'Well, I did my best and actually, Max, I think I was winning him over at the end. If you'd just exerted yourself to look a little more attractive, we'd probably have some spending money by now.'

I hit his other arm. 'He's probably gone for the authorities.'

He sighed. 'Great. Another century I can never come back to. And look at the state of you.'

'We'll just say I fell down.'

'Yeah – because pregnant women falling over is never a cause for concern.'

'For heaven's sake – give over with the pregnant. It's a condition – not a disease.'

'Dr Foster's going to kill me.'

'If you don't stop moaning, I'll kill you.'

He sighed.

'Look, we need to get our stories straight. Don't say I fell down. Say I was pushed.'

'Yes, that hardly sounds as if I wasn't doing my job properly at all.'

'By the crowd, idiot. Say it was an accident. No one's to blame.'

'How does you rolling around in the gutter as a mob streams over the top of you make me sound good?'

'Oh, so that's what this is all about. You're just scared of what Helen will say.'

'Aren't you?'

'Dr Foster doesn't frighten me,' I said loftily, knowing full well I'd suffer for that if she ever found out. 'Look, we should get out of here. I can hear barking again and the last thing we need is to be attacked by some pack of rabies-ridden, feral dogs.'

'Let's go to the park' he said. 'They've laid on stuff to keep the mob happy. We'll stare at some flowers, and you can wash your face, straighten your bonnet, and regain your social status before we go back.'

So we did.

Just for once, neither Dr Foster nor Nurse Hunter were particularly interested in Markham's scratch – or *major laceration,* as he kept calling it. I think he was a little peeved at the lack of attention.

'Your blood pressure's elevated,' said Hunter to me.

I had to tread a little carefully because we'd told them I hadn't suffered any sort of peril or injury, and if they thought even a normal, bog-standard jump would raise my blood pressure, then I'd be grounded for the duration.

'Well,' I said carelessly, 'there might have been the teeniest, tiniest bit of an altercation.'

'Might have been?'

'There probably was.'

Hunter sighed and consulted her clipboard while Markham and I sat, feet up, swigging down our tea and waiting for her to finish with me.

'Are you eating at least five pieces of fruit and/or veg a day?'

'Yes, of course,' I said, wondering what this had to do with Caroline of Brunswick.

She ticked the 'no' box. I mean, why bother to ask?

'Are you taking at least an hour a day to relax and take things easy?'

A couple of hours ago, I'd been racing around Westminster Abbey in pursuit of an inappropriately active Princess of Wales. In the interests of peace and harmony – to say nothing of Markham's love life – I said, 'Yes. I've just had a pleasant stroll around the park in the afternoon sunshine.'

She sighed. 'When?'

'I told you. Just now.'

'I mean – what time period?'

'Oh. Early 19th century. It was actually very pleasant. No one died. Not in front of us, anyway. No one attacked us. There were no earthquakes.'

'So how on earth did the pair of you pass the time?'

I said, with dignity, 'It was a cultural experience.'

She made another note.

'Are you doing your pelvic-floor exercises?'

Markham blinked at her. 'Which one of us are you talking to?'

'Of course I am,' I said, with more speed than accuracy. 'Forty-five minutes with Chief Farrell and you have a pelvic floor that could crack walnuts.'

Silence.

Markham whispered to me, 'What's a pelvic floor?'

'Something you crack walnuts with.'

'I could do with one of those. Can I borrow yours?'

'I'm sure if you want your nuts cracked, Nurse Hunter would be more than happy to oblige.'

We were remanded for the statutory twelve hours, of which we only served six, because the Arminius assignment came back in a hurry and they wanted the beds. A grumpy Markham and I were expelled and forbidden alcohol. Seven days in his case – the rest of my life in mine.

Chapter Four

I debriefed the Arminius crew personally as soon as they emerged from Sick Bay and they were all discharged within hours except for Bashford who had suffered his customary blow to the head and was still recovering.

'I'm not sure I'd recognise him without concussion,' said Ian Guthrie, handing me his report.

'There's not a lot of difference,' said Sykes, grinning, 'but just for future reference, he is extraordinarily suggestible for several hours after the initial blow.'

We regarded her with some confusion.

'To the head, I mean,' she said indignantly, and we breathed again.

'Right,' I said. 'Let's get started. Mr Clerk, would you like to begin?'

They went suddenly quiet, then Clerk spoke. 'Well, I'll tell you something, Max. I wouldn't want to be caught in the Teutoburg Forest today, let alone in 9 AD,' and the others nodded.

'Quinctilius Varus must have been out of his mind to take his legions there. Dark, wet, and completely silent, Max. No birdsong, no small animals, no signs of life anywhere. God knows, it was spooky enough before the battle, and now there's the ghosts of twenty thousand dead Romans and their auxiliaries flitting through the glades.'

'I don't know what Varus was thinking,' said Prentiss. 'Not only did he act on dubious intel, but he didn't even send out any recon parties and he allowed his forces to become separated. They were easy meat. The slaughter was massive.'

'Where were you?'

'Mostly up a tree. You'll see though, when you read our report, that visibility was poor. Mist, fog, not a lot of daylight getting through the thick trees. Our recorders weren't a lot of use so mainly we had to rely on our ears.'

I imagined them, clinging to trees, balancing precariously on branches, as below them, an entire army was slaughtered. And not just any old army. A Roman army. *This* was what being an historian was all about – not chasing fat princesses around Westminster Abbey.

They talked on and I saw it all. The damp, dark forest. The narrow road – a hill on one side, a swamp on the other. The ferocious German tribes, united under Arminius. The increasingly desperate Romans. Some fought. Some fled. Varus fell on his sword. His second in command deserted, taking the cavalry with him.

The aftermath was no less bloody for the survivors. Some were sacrificed in religious ceremonies – their bodies cooked in pots. A lucky few were ransomed. Some were enslaved; most died horribly – and the Romans never crossed the Rhine again.

I talked to them all, collated their reports, watched such footage as they had, initialled everything, sighed deeply because I'd missed it, and took it all off to Dr Bairstow. Who wanted a word.

'Caer Guorthigirn,' he announced, passing over a file and two data cubes.

I brightened immediately. A British hill fort near the Welsh borders. This sounded considerably more interesting than watching the Royal Bosom come adrift from its moorings.

'Excellent, sir. Pre or post Roman?'

'Post,' he said. 'Mid-6th century. I require you to ascertain whether this particular fort was built for defence or some other purpose. Ceremonial, possibly. Whether it was refortified after the Romans left. This is the age of Saxon incursions after all. You will map and survey the site and its surrounding area. I would be grateful if you could settle, once and for all, the vexing question of revetments before the Professor and Dr Dowson actually come to blows. You may select your own team, but I would like you to include Dr Peterson.'

'Is he back on the active list, sir?'

Some months previously, Peterson had been injured in Rouen, 1431. Someone else had died. The Time Police had turned up and I had lied through my teeth to them. That's all I'm prepared to say about that particular assignment.

Peterson's wound had been severe and although he'd flung himself into physiotherapy and rehabilitation sessions (usually organised by Markham and therefore borderline illegal in civilised countries), he would never again have full use of his left arm. Since he was right-handed, he was insistent this hardly slowed him down at all. He still had bad days, however, when he had to wear a sling. Mrs Enderby had run up a few for him.

Black silk: 'For formal occasions,' Peterson said, messing about as he always did when something was serious.

A jaunty red and white spotted affair: 'For casual or sportswear.'

Blue, the History Department colour: 'For everyday use.'

And a wicked, rich, dark crimson silk: 'For romantic occasions,' he said. 'For when I want to impress Helen.'

I personally thought it would take a great deal more than a bit of red silk to impress Dr Foster and said so.

'It matches her eyes,' he'd said and I'd laughed with him. He looked exactly as he always had – tall, relaxed, grinning his lazy grin. Was I the only one who remembered him, white-faced and unconscious on the pod floor, as his lifeblood soaked into the carpet? Or saw him afterwards, lost in despair as he struggled to come to terms with his injury? To all intents and purposes, his recovery had been complete. Was I the only one who sometimes wondered if he was as all right as everyone thought? Well, if he was on his way to being back on the active list, then the answer to that would seem to be yes.

'That's good news, Dr Bairstow.'

He agreed.

'Is this assignment for Thirsk, sir?'

'It is. And now that the uproar over their recently discovered Botticelli paintings is dying down, they are eager for our next discovery.'

'They're insatiable, aren't they, sir. We've created a monster.'

'We have, but a benevolent one. They are very kindly disposed towards us at the moment, and I wish to bask in their approval for as long as possible.'

'I'll give the matter some thought, sir. How does Persepolis sound?'

'One assignment at a time, Dr Maxwell.'

'Indeed, sir, but as I'm sure you will have noticed, I am rather on the clock at the moment.'

'That state of affairs can easily be remedied, Dr Maxwell, should I learn from Dr Foster that you are overexerting yourself.'

In addition to Peterson, I selected Sands because of his interest in all things post-Roman, Roberts, for no better reason than he came from Herefordshire, and Markham, because, he said, someone had to keep an eye on us.

'Dear God,' said Leon, as we stepped into the pod. 'Peterson with only one and a half working arms, Sands missing a foot, Markham with half an ear gone, and Roberts still with no discernible facial hair.'

Roberts bridled indignantly, touching his upper lip, presumably in case something had sprouted in the last half hour.

'And what am I missing?' I said, quite offended over this criticism of my team.

'Nothing you need worry about, Scarecrow.'

I wore a soft woollen underdress, with another thicker one over the top. Both were in undistinguished shades of brown, but they'd keep me warm. I tied my hair up in a piece of linen and tucked in the ends. Quick and neat.

They'd given me a pair of soft leather boots that looked more badly worn than they actually were, designed to look unappealing to boot thieves. I've never actually been robbed of my footwear, but Bashford once told me that it had happened to him, and had been one of the most embarrassing experiences of his life.

'And if that wasn't bad enough,' he'd continued, 'not only had I to complete the assignment in my socks, but when I got back, Mrs Enderby stared at me reproachfully and you know what that's like.'

I did indeed know. It's very rare that any of us return from an assignment not liberally splattered with something. Mud, blood (ours and other people's), random body fluids, (ours and other people's), excrement (not usually ours, but always a possibility if the assignment becomes more exciting than normal), animal waste, bits of rotting vegetables – the list just goes on and on. And then we get Mrs Enderby's special reproachful stare. She never actually says anything, but somehow that makes it worse.We assembled outside Number Five, one of the bigger pods. I could hear Dieter and Leon inside, carrying out last-minute checks. We stowed our packs in the lockers, along with surveying equipment, recorders and torches. I myself had only recorders and a change of clothes. I'd been warned against trying to carry anything heavy, which suited me down to the ground. I didn't intend to lift anything heavier than a mug of tea. Sands seated himself at the console to scan the read-outs and I nabbed the other seat before Peterson could get there.

'Aren't I driving?' he said, hurt.

'No,' said everyone within earshot. Peterson tends to land his pods like a stone skimming across a lake. If he's really on form, you can end up a good half mile away from your landing coordinates. I don't know how he does it. I suspect he doesn't either.

And that was it. We were ready to go.

Not only is there a wonderful hill fort at Caer Guorthigirn, but the place itself is smothered in legends. Vortigern supposedly burned to death there – that's the High King Vortigern, not Mrs Mack's beloved kitchen cat, obviously. The Romans supposedly captured the famous King Caractacus nearby.

There's also a cracking cave, excavated by the Revd W. S. Symonds in 1871, which was discovered to be full of Neolithic remains – flint tools, together with the bones of mammoths, cave bears, lions, woolly rhinos, and other exciting animals. It's known as Arthur's Cave, although that doesn't necessarily mean a great deal. There are Arthur's Caves all over the place. He's a bit like Queen Elizabeth. Legend has it she slept in nearly every stately home in England and obviously Arthur wasn't constitutionally capable of passing a cave without nipping inside and getting his head down for eight hours either.

We were in a no-lose situation this time. If the fort was still inhabited, we'd have an unparalleled opportunity to observe and document life in an occupied hill fort; and if not, if the people had finally drifted away, then we'd not only be able to survey and map, but we could have picnics with some pretty spectacular views. Much of the 6th century was taken up with the British struggles to resist Saxon invasions, but this area had been comparatively quiet. We'd carry out a little light surveying. I'd sketch what I could. We'd take our time, complete the assignment at a gentle pace just for once, and be back in time for tea next Tuesday. Job done.

So, of course, we landed in the middle of a war. What is it with us?

We landed on a steep slope. A very steep slope. We tilted sharply and then two of the hydraulic legs activated to keep us stable. Stable being a relative term for a pod full of historians and Mr Markham.

'This isn't right,' said Sands, checking the console. 'According to the read-outs, it should only be about eleven in the morning. If that. What's going on? Why is it so dark?'

Markham peered at the screen. 'It's smoke.'

'Smoke?' I said. 'Is something on fire?'

We angled the cameras. The split screens showed people struggling past, all heading in one direction: uphill. Women were shouting and trying to herd children and livestock at the same time. Sheep scattered. Pigs refused to move at all. Some men were present, shoving people in the right direction, or helping push laden carts through boggy patches. Many had swords drawn and we didn't need the anxious glances they were throwing over their shoulders to tell us what was happening. This was an evacuation.

People were toiling uphill, backs bent under their loads, helping each other. Children frequently fell and rolled back down the steep slope until someone caught them and set them on their feet again. We angled the cameras again, trying to make out their destination, which was also ours. Caer Guorthigirn.

'Well,' said Peterson, looking at me. 'What do we do?'

The correct procedure would be to leave at once.

'We go and have a look, of course,' I said, mildly irritated that anyone would even ask. 'There's no record of any early 6th-century massacre here so we should be comparatively safe. And Thirsk won't be happy if we have to go back and start again. We have an excellent opportunity to observe a possible Dark Age conflict at first hand, so let's get some work done.'

All perfectly sound reasons for placing ourselves in harm's way, as I think everyone will agree.

We took a blanket each and some packs of those shitty high-energy biscuits that no one ever eats. They're about two inches thick and built of some material designed to be harder than teeth. You can mix them with water or milk and call them breakfast. You can dip them in tea and call them shortbread. You can hurl them at the enemy and be prosecuted under the Geneva Convention for subjecting your foe to cruel and unusual punishment. No one even looks at them until absolutely everything else has been eaten, and only then if we can't get rat.

We loaded up with water and sallied forth to see what we could see.

The pod was hidden in dense woodland. Tall, slender trees grew thickly, but not so thickly as to impede our progress. It was autumn and a thick carpet of golden leaves covered the ground. Others floated silently down to join them.

Smoke drifted up from the valley below. Smoke brought up on the wind. I squinted down through the trees. Here and there, I thought I could see small flickers of light. Homes were burning, but whether they'd been torched by an invading army or by their owners, I was unable to tell.

No one noticed us. People were joining the procession from all directions, all of them clutching whatever had seemed valuable to them at the time.

A man and a woman were struggling with an unwieldy handcart. We tossed in our bundles. Roberts and Markham put their backs into it and with a glooping noise, the wheel came free from the mud. We followed along with the others.

It wasn't an exodus because that implies running from something. These people were running to. Running to safety. To the hill fort which now, as I stopped plodding upwards and lifted my head to look, seemed a very long way away.

'Max,' said Peterson softly. 'You should go back.'

'I'm fine,' I said. 'There are other pregnant women here and you don't see them bitching about how steep the path is.'

We struggled on. The slope, steep to begin with, now became nearly vertical. I concentrated on putting one foot in front of the other and not losing my balance. I picked up an old branch and used it for support. I used undergrowth and low-hanging branches to pull myself up the seemingly never-ending hill. It wasn't a cold day and the wind had a soft drizzle in it. I could feel sweat running down my back. My breath rasped in my throat and I could feel my heart thumping, but I would not give in. I said nothing, gritted my teeth, and struggled on. One foot in front of the other. And again. And again.

The path steepened even further and for me, the last part was a nightmare. Why the bloody hell anyone would want to attack a hill fort was a complete mystery to me. Any warriors getting this far would be bent double, sucking in as much oxygen as they could get while wheezing, 'Just give me a minute, will you,' as the defenders peppered them with arrows and spears. As far as I was concerned, they could keep it and I'd live in one of the nice valleys below. The nice *level* valleys.

'Nearly there,' said Peterson, who was wheezing himself.

I said, 'You OK?' to Sands who was limping a little.

'Absolutely fine,' he panted, pausing to bend forward and rest his hands on his knees. 'Bloody hell, please tell me it's not much further.'

It wasn't.

At the very summit, most of the trees had been felled, giving any defenders a clear sight of approaching armies. Piles of stripped tree trunks lay around, carefully wedged.

'Neat,' panted Peterson. 'They knock out the wedges ... and the trunks roll down on top of anyone who hasn't already succumbed to ... some sort of cardiac event. They'd be travelling at some speed, too. Impossible to dodge. You can barely keep your feet here. And look.' He pointed. 'You have to come up this way because they've covered everywhere else with brushwood and felled branches.'

He was right. Using the natural slope and the materials to hand, anyone taking refuge here would be near unassailable. Looking ahead, I could see where natural rock outcrops had been incorporated into high stone walls. We were nearly there.

The track broadened out and became well defined. Potholes and ruts had been filled in with small stones. The way was still steep but much firmer underfoot. The area had been cleared of all obstructions and obstacles. This was where any invading forces would be forced to fight. Right under the walls of Caer Guorthigirn.

We retrieved our bundles from the cart, which could go no further anyway. The last I saw, it was being incorporated into some sort of barrier. We stepped aside as if to rest. I wanted some shots of the hill fort itself, together with some of the stream of people still snaking their way up towards it.

More smoke drifted on the wind, catching at my throat and mixing with the rich smell of earth and wet leaves.

'Wow,' said Roberts, struggling to keep on his feet in his excitement. 'It's so much bigger than I thought. I used to play up here when I was a kid. It was right in the middle of a conifer plantation then, so we never really got the full effect.'

Looking ahead, I could see two vast enclosures – one to the right and one to the left, both enclosed by revetments – dry stone walls. So that settled that argument. Although in whose favour I'd have to wait and see.

Between the two enclosures, the path became a passage and dipped sharply, exposing any attackers attempting to access the main gate to heavy fire from above. The passage was about twenty yards long, no more than a cart-width wide, and ended at a pair of heavy wooden gates.

A group of armed men stood there, urging people through as quickly as possible.

I had a sudden panic over whether we would be required to identify ourselves, but these were simpler times. Protection and shelter were offered to everyone.

They let us through and once inside we were ushered very firmly towards the right-hand enclosure. Along with civilians and other animals. They should have had a sign saying, 'Expendable people this way.' With an arrow.

Fighting men were mustering to the left, in the smaller and more heavily fortified area. I caught a quick glimpse of some thirty or forty thatched round huts before the pressure of people behind me pushed me away and into our enclosure. My guess was that in normal times, people lived in the smaller enclosure, and this larger one was used for working and keeping animals.

We paused just inside the entrance and looked around us.

'We need to establish ourselves some territory,' said Markham. 'A base for our possessions, such as they are, and a place to gather if we get separated.'

I glanced around. We stood in a large, open space, enclosed by a stone wall. Not as high as the other enclosure, but for anyone approaching up the hill, the wall would still be above head height.

'Not the front wall,' he said. 'That's just asking for trouble. This way.' We made our way across the grass to a quieter area near the back wall. From there, standing on tiptoe, we could look down an even steeper slope. All around us were other wooded hillsides, all in the russet and gold shades of autumn.

'If it wasn't for all the trees I reckon we could see my house from up here,' said Roberts, grinning. 'Or we could if it had been built yet.'

'Where?' demanded Peterson.

He pointed. 'Just over there. See that smaller hill? Somewhere in the middle but nearer to the left. The house will be there, facing towards us. To the left will be the two barns. Facing them are the cattle sheds and milking parlours. We have two. We will have two. The silo tower is over there.'

He paused, staring eagerly over the wall. 'I think my tree house is just ...' he sighted down his arm '... there. This is so cool!'

Peterson was amused. It's a bit of a rarity for any of us to have family. Especially family with whom we were still speaking. Or who were speaking to us. 'How many?'

'Oh, it's a big farm. Over two hundred animals all together.'

'I meant in your family, idiot. Why aren't you with them, riding the range?'

'Third son,' he said cheerfully. 'Surplus to requirements. And it's a hazardous business, dairy farming. Me mam was dead chuffed when I went off to seek my fortune in the gloriously dull world of European History.'

This statement was greeted with disbelief. 'You have a mother?'

'And two younger sisters.'

'Hazardous?' said Markham. 'You were a dairy farmer, for heaven's sake. What could possibly go wrong?'

'Have you ever seen the size of a cow? Up close? Right up close, I mean. I've been bitten – well, gummed and slobbered on – kicked, and crushed. My brother had a nasty chain-saw accident to his leg. You can roll a tractor – done that – me dad stayed the whole day at my bedside, waiting for me to come round and then tried to strangle me. There's chemicals that make your eyes drop out and your lungs burst into flames. Then there's the weather. Sunburn ...'

'Hold on,' said Markham. 'In Wales?'

'Well, all right. Exposure, then.'

'Can I just ask – what exactly does your mum think you do for a living now?'

'Sit in a library, thinking deep academic thoughts, and not, in any way, getting ringworm, or poisoning myself with pesticides, ripping myself to pieces on barbed wire and getting tetanus, or finding myself underneath an angry cow.'

There was a thoughtful silence.

'Actually,' said Sands. 'I think she might have a point. To the best of my knowledge, no historian has ever found himself underneath an angry cow.'

'Give us time,' I said.

'Here,' said Markham, bringing us back to the present and dropping his bundle. 'It's quiet and out of the wind. We'll camp here and the second they're through the gate – whoever they are – we're over this wall and down the hill back to the pod. No arguments. Right – what have we got in the way of weapons?'

We're not allowed to injure contemporaries – it's a capital offence – so whatever we carry is for defensive purposes only. We had the usual stun guns and pepper. And hairpins in my case. If none of that worked then we'd just have to rely on the historian's natural ability to cover vast distances very, very quickly.

Except that one of us had an artificial foot, one of us had a weak arm, one of us was missing a bit of one ear, one of us was pregnant, and none of us was very bright.

We made ourselves comfortable against the wall. From where we sat, we had a clear view of the entrance to the enclosure in which we were quartered. People were still hurrying inside, although the flow was much less now. Taking stock of our provisions, we had food for two days and water for about twenty-four hours.

'There'll be a supply of water somewhere around,' said Peterson, confidently. 'There must be, otherwise the enemy would only have to sit outside the gates and wait.'

He was right. There were two wells in our enclosure, both surrounded by muddy, churned up ground. One for animals and one for people as far as I could see. There were about eight or ten huts, clustered together around a large, barn-like structure in the centre, with haystacks and sacks of grain stacked against their walls. Across in the other enclosure, I could hear the ringing sound of hammers on anvils and there were two forges near us, as well. Away at the far end, about thirty greasy-looking sheep, a large number of pigs, and six small, skinny cows had been herded against the wall. Piles of brushwood kept them penned in. It's always a surprise to see how small farmyard animals used to be. Some of the sheep were no bigger than large dogs and the pigs – these pigs anyway – were certainly not the fat, wobbling monsters we were used to. The cows were mud-covered and bony. They all had horns and were about as far from massive, glossy black and white Friesians as I could imagine. But they seemed docile enough. They all got their heads down and started grazing.

'They seem very calm,' said Peterson, talking about the people, I assumed. 'There's no panic anywhere.'

No, there wasn't. People deposited their belongings and set about making themselves comfortable. Either the threat was small or they'd done this so many times that the fear had worn off.

'Or,' said Peterson, 'they have confidence in their defences.'

'Or rescuers,' said Markham.

'From whom? From what are they being rescued?'

They all looked at me.

'No idea,' I said. 'I know that after the Romans left, the country was vulnerable and defenceless. The Saxons are moving in, but that doesn't necessarily mean this is all about them. This might simply be some local dispute over a border or some stolen cattle.'

He nodded. 'True.'

I looked at the scene around us. People were greeting each other, unloading their small piles of belongings and setting up camp.

Such men as I could see wore coarse, woollen undershirts with long sleeves and woollen trousers. Most wore some kind of belted tunic over the top. No pockets, obviously, but their belts hung with pouches for those valuable and important items. Most wore swords. They all had a dagger at their belt. Most people wore shoes, too, seemingly made of one piece of leather with what looked like an extra piece added for the sole.

Women wore linen under-dresses, again with long sleeves and drawn tight around the neck. Their sleeves were tied with string or braid. A second outer dress was fastened at the shoulder with a clasp or brooch, Celtic knots seemed a popular design. They also wore belts and pouches. There seemed little difference between men's and women's shoes, but I did notice that some women wore woollen socks. As did I, so obviously women and their icy cold feet are not a modern phenomenon.

What struck me most were the colours. I knew they used vegetable and berry dyes, and everywhere I could see various shades of red, brown, and ochre, although there was very little blue or green. To my modern eye, all the materials were coarsely woven and looked very heavy. Practicality seemed preferable to fashion, with women's skirts finishing at the ankle to keep them out of the mud. Interestingly, not all women's heads were covered. I made a note to try to discover whether this signified their single state, or their religious beliefs. Head covering became more popular as Christianity gained ground and I wasn't sure how much ground it had gained in this area by the 6th century.

On our right, about fifteen to twenty feet away, a family with several children was unloading their belongings. Three loudly complaining chickens in wicker cages were carefully placed against the wall out of harm's way. They laid out their blankets, as we had done, unpacked a few pots and a precious metal skillet, and set about making a fire.

It was done in seconds. 'Wow,' said Peterson in admiration. 'Even Markham can't ignite something that quickly.'

'Bet I could,' said Markham. 'Shall I give it a go?'

'No.'

My heartbeat had returned to normal and it was time to earn our pay. I heaved myself to my feet. 'We should take a look around. We'll split into two groups and see what we can see. Markham, Roberts, and Sands, you head off that way. Peterson and I will try to get into the other enclosure. Where the soldiers are. We're bound to learn more in there.'

'Excellent plan,' said Sands, and it would have been if they had let us in. We were turned away, politely at first and then they shoved Peterson backwards and the message was clear. Soldiers only. Stay out. So we did.

We turned away and watched the gate guards urge the last stragglers through. They didn't close them, merely stationing themselves across the entrance, but there was no doubt they could be closed at a moment's notice.

Not that they would need it. Like all hill forts, it was a good position defensively. They could see any one and anything long before they were within striking distance. And, in my opinion, anyone making it to the top would need a good half hour's quiet sit-down – and possibly even oxygen – before even contemplating anything requiring any effort at all.

We wandered around, weaving in between the little camps that were appearing everywhere as women got busy. Children ran around getting in people's way. Many of the old men had gone to the front wall and were peering over the top, pointing and nodding. I wondered if they were reliving old battles.

I estimated there was just over one hundred people here, mostly women, children, old people, and their livestock. I had no idea of the number of fighting men and it clearly wasn't a good idea to try poking around. The last thing we needed was to be apprehended as spies.

After a while, my ears became attuned. There was a great deal of what I took to be an ancient version of Welsh, some old English, from which I could distinguish the odd word, and even after all this time, a little Latin was still being spoken. Indeed, when I first heard it, a woman was telling off two small boys. I assumed she was saying that if they didn't behave then they would be carried off by bears, but as we walked around, I heard it everywhere. Ursus. The Bear. Everyone was talking about

The Bear. I listened carefully, but couldn't make out whether this was a good or a bad thing. Whoever or whatever he was, he commanded some very healthy respect. It was only as I passed a large group of people all talking away at the tops of their voices that I got it. The pronunciation confused me a little at first, because they were speaking in Welsh and I was listening in English, and then suddenly, it hit me like a hammer blow.

They were talking about Arth.

Oh my God.

And now that I'd heard it once, variations of the word were everywhere. On everyone's lips.

Ursus.

Bera.

Arth.

Arthur.

I felt my heart pick up. It surely couldn't be ... There's no record of him fighting here ... We couldn't possibly be that lucky ...

Peterson gripped my arm. Hard. He'd come to the same conclusion.

'Max ...'

'I know.'

At the same time, I heard Sands say, 'Max ...'

And then, suddenly, something was happening.

A group of soldiers, armoured and armed, pushed their way in through the gate, split up, and started around the enclosure, pulling out people, apparently at random.

No, not at random. They were lining up the men. Men who could fight.

'They're conscripting all the able-bodied men,' said Sands. 'Looks like we're in the front line this time.'

None of them seemed particularly worried.

I was. 'You're not able-bodied. None of you is able-bodied. If we added you all together, you wouldn't make a whole person. You're all missing feet, ears, upper arm muscle.' I thought of Roberts. 'And facial hair.'

Now we were in real trouble. Not because of the actual fighting, although that would be hazardous enough, but because we're not allowed to kill contemporaries. Not under any circumstances. We've saved a few in our time – and don't think that doesn't lead to problems as well – but we'd never actually killed anyone. We'd never be allowed to get away with it. If History doesn't get us, then Dr Bairstow will. Even setting aside the question of 'who were we to decide who should live and who should die', History has very strong views about meddling historians. Terminally strong views.

On the other hand, we probably wouldn't live that long. A pitched battle was about to be fought and none of my boys were up to spec in the body-parts department. Apart from Roberts, of course, and even he appeared to have stopped developing around the age of twelve.

I ordered them back to our camp, and we all clustered together, watching what was going on. There was no escape. Nowhere to run. We could only stand quietly as two soldiers approached, gave us all the once over and jerked their heads in the direction of the group of men assembling near the gate.

I watched them being led away. There wasn't anything I could do and I didn't want to draw attention to myself. Around me, some women wailed, but the majority seemed resigned. One woman desperately tried to hold on to her two young lads, neither of whom looked above ten or eleven. Two men pulled her off, but gently. She stood, white and shocked, and was surrounded by other women who took her away.

I stood alone. Above my head, the warm wind tore the clouds to shreds, trailing them across the sky like tattered banners. I pulled my thick cloak around me, more for comfort than warmth.

I watched my team join the column of other men, all being herded towards the gate. Most of the conscripts were either very old or very young. One or two limped. I guessed these were second-rank fighters. The 6th-century equivalent of cannon fodder, possibly.

Peterson turned, waved cheerfully, and disappeared.

They'd gone.

I found I could barely breathe. They'd be at a huge disadvantage. What could they do? If they killed someone ...? History might not even allow them to defend themselves. And they couldn't run away – they'd risk being killed as deserters. And I could do nothing. There wasn't a single thing I could do to help them. I had a terrible vision of them being overrun by a horde of blood-soaked Saxons. Going down without a fight. Because that was the correct thing to do. The historian thing to do. I might never see them again. Any of them.

I stood, torturing myself with visions of them being hacked into pieces so tiny that bringing the bodies back to St Mary's would be an impossibility. In my mind's eye, I saw them fall, one by one, overwhelmed, unable to help themselves. I hugged myself even more tightly and struggled for calm, trying to think of something. I had wild ideas of escaping out of the gates, getting back to the pod, and going for help. Maybe returning with Guthrie and a security team and somehow getting them out.

Useless. The gate was guarded. No one in and no one out. Even if I managed to get out over the walls unaided, what could Guthrie do except risk more people?

I was so deep in thought that I realised afterwards I'd been hearing this lack of noise for a long time without any idea of its significance. A sudden silence around me – a sudden stillness as people listened.

There, miles away, on that faint line between actual sound and imagination, I could hear it. First a murmur, then a rumble, then a roar and then a beat as an unknown number of feet marched more or less in rhythm. I'd heard that sound before. In Colchester, as Boudicca's army approached, and now I was hearing it again.

This was no local squabble over stolen cattle or a disputed boundary. These were Saxons. Probably not an invading army, but a raiding party. Or possibly, given the noise and commotion below, several raiding parties. I tried to remember whether the Wye was navigable to this point. I imagined dragon-headed boats rowing up the river, silent except for the occasional soft creak of an oar. In my mind, I saw giant men, splashing to the banks, hoisting their swords and shields and setting off through the trees.

This was the classic approach at dusk – too dark for numbers to be accurately assessed. Night-time fears would double the number in the minds of the defenders and, then, a new day would dawn. The sun would rise, picking out men, armour, and spears. I've been besieged before. I know how quickly that feeling of security behind high walls can turn to a fear of being trapped behind those same high walls.

I blinked to clear my eyes, because the wind was making them water, and turned back to my suddenly cheerless and solitary camp. They'd left me a blanket and some rations, for which I was grateful. I wrapped myself up, leaned back against the wall, and closed my eyes.

I was roused by a shout and a poke. The correct response would have been to leap to my feet in an instant, assume a defensive posture, all ready to deal, effectively and efficiently, with whatever threat was being posed.

In reality, I thrashed around inside my blanket, unable to free my arms, and eventually toppled over. Suddenly, I was glad Peterson and the others weren't around to see that.

There was no threat. Unless you count granny, grinning gummily at me, and gesturing. The neighbours were inviting me over. There was granny herself, mum stirring something in a pot, and their indeterminate number of children who wouldn't stay still long enough for me to count them.

I shared their meal. They had hardly anything and yet they shared everything with me. We had some hard, flat bread, which I chewed very carefully, because it was full of grit from the millstones. We dipped this in some kind of hot, salty broth that could have been anything and I wasn't going to ask, followed by a heel of hard, dry cheese. There was no meat. I looked at the chickens who stared beadily back again. None of

51

the portions was very large and I saw granny give her cheese to the kids.

I crawled over to my bundle, pulled out a pack of the hitherto despised high-energy biscuits, and shared them out. They loved them, washing them down with some kind of fluid that looked as if it had been drained from someone's U-bend, so it was probably beer.

By the time we finished eating, it was dark. We smiled at each other and I curled up in my blanket and tried to sleep. Behind me, the chickens made the sort of noises that led me to believe they were contemplating suicide. I don't know why they were worrying. Chickens had value – even if it was very short-lived. If tomorrow went badly, we'd have even shorter anticipated life spans than the chickens.

I was lying on the hard ground, feeling the damp seep up through my blanket, when Peterson spoke in my ear. 'Can you talk?'

'Yes.'

'Don't worry about us, we're all fine. I don't think they were that impressed by us. We've been put at the back. We seem to be guarding some sacks of strategically important flour.'

'Really?' I said, relief temporarily overriding the damp.

'Yes. We don't even have weapons. Wait. Hold on.'

I could hear the sound of men's voices.

'Ah. As you were, Max. We've just been issued with three swordy-looking things,' said our on-site weapons expert.

'I thought there were four of you.'

'They've given Roberts a stick. I think they think he's a girl.'

I could hear Roberts waxing indignant in the background.

'Well, I keep telling you – grow some facial hair. It's not difficult. You just have to stop shaving for a couple of days. You still there, Max?'

'No. I got bored and wandered off. Of course I'm still here.'

'We're going to get our heads down now. Big day tomorrow.'

'OK,' I said, trying to sound cheerful. 'Try to remember to stay at the back.'

'We'll be fine. And you make sure you stay safe, as well. We'll need to brag about our exploits when we next see you.'

I snorted, but he'd closed the link.

They might have got their heads down. They probably did – Markham could sleep on a clothesline, but for me there was no chance. Apart from the depressed chicken noises, granny's snores could have woken the dead, and in our enclosure, smiths hammered all night long, working on weapons and shields. Men moved backwards and forwards, shouting instructions. In the distance, excited dogs barked, baying at a moon visible occasionally through holes in the shredded clouds.

I lay on my back and looked up at the cloud-cloaked stars. It wasn't cold. The air was warm and wet. I could feel rain in the wind.

I gave it up in the hour before dawn, sitting up and earning my keep by stirring their dying fire back into life. I could see bubbles of moisture on my blanket and clothes. I nibbled my last biscuit and then, just as the sky began to lighten a little in the east, horns sounded.

My first thought was that this was it – the fighting was about to begin – but there was no way an army could have snuck up on us unawares. Whoever it was, it wasn't the Saxons. I could hear the distant thunder of hooves. Shouts rang out. More horns sounded from the gates.

All around me, people sprang to their feet and ran, shouting, to the wall.

I followed behind them.

In my ear, Peterson said, 'Max, something's happening.'

'I know.'

I ran to the wall on legs that trembled with excitement. My heart pounded. I fumbled with my recorder with clumsy fingers. Because if this was who I thought it might be... I elbowed myself a place at the wall, stood on tiptoe and peered down the slope.

They came fast, their big, powerful horses thundering uphill, manes flying, and hooves kicking up great divots of mud. About thirty of them. A horn sounded – a long musical note. A greeting. From behind me, up on the ramparts near the gate, another horn responded. A low, rumbling tone, dark and dangerous. Then, a great noise of them all together, returning the greeting. I felt the short hairs on my neck stand up on end.

They galloped out of the early morning mist like avenging gods. All foam and fury. A long banner snapped behind them. As a contrast to the skinny, underdeveloped livestock, which was all we'd seen so far, the horses these men rode were good – very good – their muscles bunching and flexing as they galloped up the hill. These were warhorses that had been taught to fight and maim and kill.

Their riders were equally tough. These were not the chivalrous knights of legend. These were hard-looking men; swords and battle-axes hung from their saddles and their shields were slung across their backs.

The excitement around us was intense. People jostled each other for a good view. Children were lifted up to sit on top of the wall and wave. All around us, people cheered. The word Arth was everywhere.

Remembering I was supposed to be on the job, I activated my recorder, saying softly, 'Sleeveless jerkins. Coarse shirts. Trousers. Leather boots. About thirty of them. Good horses. Stirrups. Ten spare horses at the rear. Three baggage horses. Assorted grooms. Blacksmith. Armourer. Maybe a medical man. Hard to say. No religious symbols visible.'

The gates opened. People streamed out to greet them, cheering and shouting. Granny grinned her toothless grin at me.

I was close enough to see the splattered mud on their boots, make out the coarse weave of their trousers, see the sweat stains under their armpits. I fixed my gaze on the man riding under the banner, watching his tangled hair lifting and falling in time with his horse's stride.

Then, just as they breasted the rise to approach the gate, in one smooth movement, they drew their swords. I stiffened, but it was a salute, not a threat. This was friend, not foe. The guards at the gate returned the salute, roaring a greeting as with scarcely a pause, the riders swept into the fort.

In my ear, Peterson said, 'Someone likes a dramatic entrance.'

But this wasn't just any someone. I knew who this was. I'd seen the banner as it swept past. I'd seen the Red Dragon, blazing fire and fury.

This was Arthur Pendragon.

Chapter Five

I've been so lucky. I've seen more than my fair share of heroes. I saw Hector and Achilles fight at Troy. I watched Henry V prevail at Agincourt. I even witnessed Leonidas's stand at Thermopylae. I've seen legends come to life in front of my very eyes and now, if I'd interpreted things correctly, I was about to see the biggest hero of them all.

Everyone around me was shouting, 'Arthur', or one of the many variations of his name, and jumping up and down as if just his presence was enough to win the day and, for all I knew, it might be. All around us, unseen dogs howled hysterically, the noises filling my head until I thought it would burst. I leaned against the wall for support.

In my ear, Peterson said, 'Max,' very faintly, but I wasn't in any condition to respond. Because it was *him*. It was *Arthur*. Riding under the Red Dragon of the Pendragons. His own personal emblem.

I became aware I was clutching at the wall so tightly that two of my fingertips were bleeding. I smeared the blood across the stones for luck, because this was an age when stones demanded blood, and historians need all the luck they can get.

Someone must have thrown a bucket of water on the dogs, because the noise subsided and I could hear myself think again.

I pushed myself off the wall and watched people begin to move away, returning to their little camps, talking excitedly. Boys picked up sticks, using them as swords, pretending they were Arthur. I heard the word everywhere and now he was here and I'd just seen him. Up close. Nearly close enough to touch him. The real Arthur.

Forget the High King of medieval legend. Forget the myths and fairy stories. He didn't found Camelot. Or the Knights of the Round Table. He didn't search for the Holy Grail. He didn't kill dragons or rescue damsels in distress. He didn't have a magician named Merlin. Those are just pretty stories. He didn't do any of that.

What he did do was fight. He was a war leader. A Dux Bellorum. And, by the looks of him, a bit of a bastard. Forget the tall hero with long, golden hair. The real Arthur was a stocky man, broad-shouldered and short-legged. Long, dark hair hung in greasy snarls around his face. His bare arms bulged with muscles. Later, when I was able to observe more closely, I would see he wore two golden arm bracelets, each depicting a dragon eating its own tail. No beginning and no end. Was this the origin of the legend of the Once and Future King? They were his only ornament.

Much is made of Arthur carrying the image of the Virgin on his shield. On other occasions, he may have done so. Or that story might simply be Christian embellishment. Today however, his shield bore the device of the Red Dragon, as did his standard. He was distinguished from his fellow riders only by a matted pelt which I assumed to be made from bear, which hung around his shoulders. More likely, it was just wolf, but it was a nice bit of PR, just the same.

There has always been a theory that there was more than one Arthur – a number of chieftains scattered around the countryside, leading the struggle against the Saxons and somehow they all merged into one mighty legend, because, physically, one man and his army couldn't possibly have fought at all the battles with which he is credited, but here was a very likely explanation. This is how he managed to be at so many battles at so many different places around the country. He commanded a portable army. A small, highly organised mobile cavalry unit, working out of bases scattered around the land, and able to cover long distances very quickly, bringing reinforcements and much-needed professional assistance to beleaguered Brits in their struggle against the invaders. He had arrived at the best possible moment, skidding in under the very noses of the approaching army. Making a spectacular entrance.

58

Raising morale. Because everyone knows the cavalry always arrives in the very nick of time.

I looked up. The sun had risen, but the sky was still dark. The smell of smoke was everywhere as the valleys burned below us.

Staring over the wall and through the thick trees, I could just make out an approaching mass of men. Torches flickered in the gloom. The sound of drumbeats floated on the wind.

They weren't marching – there was no ordered tramp of feet, just a long, unbroken rumble of sound. Occasionally, a voice would be raised in command, shouting words I couldn't make out. I tried to estimate numbers, but they were a continually shifting mass in thick woodland.

The day was overcast. Wisps of mist lay in pockets between the trees. A light drizzle fell. I smoothed the moisture off my sleeve and wondered how safe we were up here. I was wet. The grass was wet. There was mud. How easy is it to run uphill, sword in one hand, and shield in the other? With a hail of missiles raining down from above? With bloody great tree trunks rolling down towards you, bouncing over the rough ground? Uncontrolled and uncontrollable. Crushing everything in their path. How easy to slip on the wet grass, or in the mud? Or become entangled in the brushwood? Or impaled on sharp branches? How would they get up the hill? In attack formation? Or would they just grit their teeth, lower their heads, and charge?

I would soon find out. Time to earn my entirely inadequate pay.

I've watched many battles. It's my job. And we don't hang around at the back, either. Peterson and I were up with the archers at Agincourt. The Battle of Bosworth was practically fought around Markham and me. Being in a battle, surrounded by men with no thought other than to slaughter each other as quickly as possible, is terrifying. But not half so terrifying as having to sit, helpless and listen to one happen around you. Not to know what's going on outside, or what's happening to your friends. To listen to the war horns, the cries, the clash of swords, the shrieks of the wounded and dying. To be blind, vulnerable, powerless ... I really don't recommend it. I particularly don't recommend the part where you sit helpless, locked in a hut for your own safety, listening to blood-crazed Saxons scrabbling at the thatch overhead, shouting to each other in anticipation of the treats in store for them – women, plunder, feasting – knowing that if they are here now, then it's because everyone else out there is dead, or dying, or driven off; that the day is lost and the winners are here to claim their prize. That's really not a good feeling at all.

First things first, however.

I turned my attention back to what was going on around me. As discreetly as I could, I recorded the enclosure, the people crowded at the walls, and got the best shots I could of the forces below us, still partly concealed in the morning mist.

I was certain that all the interesting stuff was happening in the other compound, but Peterson and the others would have all that under control. If they could spare the time from guarding all that strategic flour, of course.

On the ramparts, the big horn sounded again. Not in welcome this time. A warning. The mighty note rumbled on and on, deep and menacing in the mild, early morning air. At the same time, they ran up the standard. With a snap, the banner unfurled, revealing the Red Dragon, fluttering defiantly, and a roar went up around the fort.

We cheered too, our women and children's voices pitched high over the masculine bellow as we shouted to give ourselves courage.

I know I'd speculated about the Saxons' ability to fight after that long struggle up the hill, and I had looked forward to seeing it, but the chance came more quickly than I expected, because with a suddenness that took everyone by surprise, Old Faithful, that big, deep horn, rumbled again, and over the dramatic echoes a single voice was raised in command. The gates crashed open and the cavalry exploded out through them, headed by Arthur himself, bear pelt flying out behind him, wielding a sword in each hand.

The speed of the attack took my breath away. Whether the Saxons had reckoned on a moment or two to get their collective breath back was now unimportant, because they weren't going to get it. They lifted their heads to see a wall of horses and swords thundering down the hill towards them.

For a moment, I wondered why on earth Arthur's men would sacrifice the safety of the fort to engage the Saxons face to face, but it actually made perfect sense. Of course, Arthur couldn't afford to be penned up inside a remote hill fort for weeks. That wasn't his style. He moved fast – always appearing where and when least expected. Building the legend. He would never lose the initiative to the Saxons. He would take the fight to them. Of course he would.

He had the advantage of shock and awe. His horses had the advantage of a steep slope in their favour. They smashed into the Saxons at full speed. Men disappeared under hooves or were tossed aside by the impact. Those that didn't fall under the horses were cut to pieces before they could get their shields up.

Arthur fought like a lion. Or a warrior. Or a hero. He fought with both hands, striking to the left and right simultaneously. When one sword shattered on a helmet, he pulled out his long-handled axe and continued to lay about him like a demon. His horse fought too, all red-rimmed nostrils and blood-flecked foam. Giant metal-shod hooves rose and fell as he kicked and trampled those around him.

The charge inflicted massive damage. In its wake, a small force of infantry followed on behind, mopping up the few who had survived that initial charge. With the Saxon army strung out down the hillside, the odds were in the defenders' favour. A great hole opened up in the Saxon ranks.

Their momentum carried Arthur's men straight through. For one moment, I thought they would be carried away, victims of their own speed and weight, but I had underestimated them. A horn sounded and they dragged their horses to a halt. Some nearly sat down in an effort to stop in time. As one, they turned, reformed their line, and charged again. Back up the hill this time. Caught between the cavalry and the foot soldiers, the Saxons wavered.

Another group of men issued forth from the gates and a hail of arrows darkened the sky still further as archers on the walls shot continually into the Saxon wings. Hissing death dropped from the skies. Men went down like trees. I looked at the slaughter around me and took a moment to wonder. This was not one of Arthur's famous twelve battles against the Saxons and yet the ferocity was massive. Whatever must Mons Badonicus or Camlann have been like?

I'd underestimated the Saxons, however. Arthur was not the only man on the battlefield with a grasp of tactics.

The Saxons were splitting up, dividing themselves into smaller groups, thus forcing the riders to split up too, which considerably diminished their effectiveness. Arthur still had a fight on his hands. And these Saxons were the ancestors of those who would hold the shield wall at Hastings. This was not just a minor skirmish. This was going to be bloody.

Small bands of Saxons, moving in tight-knit groups, were forcing the defenders to engage on their terms. A larger group of about twenty or so put their heads down and headed for the open gate. Voices shouted a warning and Arthur moved fast to engage. He was hampered by a force of seemingly suicidal Saxons who sacrificed themselves in vast numbers to ensure their fellows reached the gates. Their casualties were enormous, but the objective was gained.

The men at the gates put their shoulders to them, struggling to get them closed before they were overwhelmed, but too late.

The Saxons burst through, big men, red mouths open wide, blood-splashed, full of fighting frenzy. I could feel the blood pounding inside my head. We were about to be overrun. Was this why no record of this battle survived? Was this the one that Arthur lost? Was this the battle that was quietly forgotten? Because it was the one that didn't build the legend.

The few men in our enclosure left the walls and began to force us women and children towards the big central barn. I stood quietly at the wall and hoped to be overlooked, but there was no chance. A man pulled me away and shoved me along with the others. Everyone was being pushed into the barn. For our own safety. I hoped.

I spoke softly. 'Tim? You OK?'

'Don't worry about us, Max. We're still on the Dark Age equivalent of potato peeling and latrine digging. You?'

'About to be herded into a big hut, along with the other non-combatants. In order of importance – livestock, children, household implements, miscellaneous tat, and women.' I paused, struggling with a sudden lack of words. 'Look after yourselves.'

'You too.'

'Tim ...'

Silence.

I tried again. 'Tim ...'

His voice wasn't quite steady. 'I have to do this, Max. I have to prove to the world, and to myself, that I'm not completely useless.'

I knew it. I knew he wasn't as OK as everyone thought he was. I *knew* it.

'Tim ...'

'Yes?'

'If you had no arms at all. Or legs, either ... Or even if your head dropped off ... you'd never be useless to me.'

Silence.

Just as I was about to close the link, he said, 'Or you to me.'

Then the link went dead.

I didn't know how much to protest and I didn't want to make myself conspicuous. All around me, women were gathering up livestock and children impartially and pushing them towards the big, central barn. It made sense to get us out of harm's way. To clear the decks for action. I allowed myself to be driven along with the old, the young, and the four-legged.

They pushed us inside and slammed home the bars. We were locked in. Whatever was going to happen, there wouldn't be a thing I could do about it. I know it was for our own safety. The fighting was only yards away, on the other side of the wall, but every instinct I had was telling me not to be trapped in a building with no way out. I couldn't help remembering the Temple of the Divine Claudius at Colchester. The Romans bundled their families inside for safety and they were fine until Boudicca sent her men onto the roof. To prise away the tiles. To drop down onto the helpless people beneath. To indulge in an orgy of slaughter until the floors ran red with blood, and no Roman, man, woman or child was left alive. A whole city died that day.

I tried to peer through a chink in the door. As far as I could see, peering from side to side, there were just two guards out there, standing swords drawn.

I stepped back thoughtfully. Two guards were a complete waste of time. Should the Saxons come boiling into our enclosure, what good could two men possibly be? And then it hit me. They weren't to keep the Saxons out. They were to keep us in.

I looked around me. It was a bit of a squeeze, but the barn was large enough to house us all fairly comfortably. I could smell hay, dust, animals, and earth. There were no windows, but light filtered through chinks in the pitch walls. Looking up, the roof was supported by sturdy beams, over which had been layered brushwood and then the thatch, all supported by four central pillars set in a square. The floor was of beaten earth with a stone threshold. It was a good barn. Sturdy, well made and mostly weatherproof.

A pile of hay stood against one wall. Not a huge pile – I suspected it was the end of last winter's store. The sheep were already making inroads.

People got themselves organised. Elderly people sat in the middle with the smaller children on their laps. Older children and some women chivvied aside the sheep and sat themselves down on the pile of hay. Worryingly, all the children were very quiet. Big-eyed, they sat listening. We were all listening, because in the time it had taken to get us all inside and for us to sort ourselves out, things had gone very quiet outside.

What was happening? Had the Saxons withdrawn and gone home? Unlikely. Or were they preparing themselves for an all-out assault? Much more likely.

The silence was unbearable. Not knowing what's happening is a bugger. I looked at the wooden door and pushed gently. It gave a fraction, but only a fraction. There was no way out.

I suspected, however, that there were many ways in. In my mind, I saw big, blond men tearing aside the thatch and jumping down, swords stained with blood. Or using their weapons to force their way through the mud walls, to fall on us in a blood lust.

Which just goes to show there's something seriously wrong with my imagination – it was probably on pregnancy overload, or something – because there was nothing to stop them killing the two guards outside, lifting the bar, and just strolling in through the door.

Yes, there was. There was us.

I stared thoughtfully at the door and then looked around to find Granny doing the same. I suspected she'd had exactly the same thought.

We tend to think of people in the past as less intelligent than us because they can't drive cars or understand computers. Actually, that applies to me as well. On both counts. But Granny, who was probably only in her forties, although she looked much older, had almost certainly done this several times in her life. Looking around the barn, a good number of them had probably been in similar situations before. These were turbulent times. The departing Romans had left a vacuum, which the Saxons were determined to exploit. Arthur would fight his famous twelve battles all over the country, before dying at Camlann.

I looked around me. In these days, women did not fight, but we could defend ourselves. We did not have to sit, helpless, waiting for whatever came through that door.

I think the same idea had occurred to several other women as well.

We formed a small group by one of the central pillars. There was always the language barrier of course, but I'm pretty good at conveying my meaning through the medium of mime. There were some sacks of something stacked in the corner. They'd been there for some time by the looks of things. I think they contained grain of some kind maybe, carelessly stored, and the rats had got at them, but they were heavy and the door opened inwards. They were a start.

I pointed at the sacks and then at the door. They nodded.

There was what looked like the remains of an old plough – we could use that to wedge the door – and a pile of stones. I had no idea why someone would want to store rocks in a barn, but we could certainly throw them at anyone we didn't like the look of.

Several women brought up tools of some kind. No scythes or sickles, sadly, but the old wooden handles could be used as staffs. Even buckets can be nasty weapons if wielded with malicious intent. And we intended to be very malicious.

We set to work building our barricade. As barricades go, it wasn't that brilliant. I suspected it would hold them for five, possibly six seconds, but it gave us something to do. Anything was better than sitting passively waiting for whatever was going to happen to us. It gave us at least the illusion of control, and best of all, it took our minds off what was going on out there. Of husbands, fathers, brothers, colleagues, all of them fighting for their lives. And ours.

Sadly, it didn't take our minds off things for very long.

Astoundingly, I had Peterson in my ear. 'Max what's happening?' He sounded breathless but intact.

'Safe. We're all together and guarded.' Probably not a good idea to tell him it was just two men. 'Where are you?'

'Still safely at the back. We're the reserve. No cause for concern. We're all drawn up ready to go. Just awaiting the word.'

The noise around him increased to a deafening clamour. The Saxons must be almost on top of them. Shouts rang out.

'Shit,' said Peterson. 'This is it, Max. Talk to you later.'

They would fight. It was useless to expect them not to. And they would almost certainly die. Either at the hands of the Saxons or History itself, and if they tried to save themselves by refusing to fight then the British would kill them out of hand. And Peterson – looking for an opportunity to prove to himself and the world that he could still function. How long would he last? How long would any of them last?

Hard on this thought, I heard Peterson, breathless and jerky. 'Heads up Max. Coming your way.' The link went dead.

They were indeed coming our way. I could hear shouting and the clash of metal on metal drawing ever closer. A ripple ran through us all. People instinctively drew closer together.

Something crashed hard against the door. People jumped in shock and began to back away. In my mind's eye, I saw our two defenders being cut down as a horde of Saxons burst into our enclosure and encircled the hut, roaring, clashing their swords on their shields. Looking for the way in.

Around me, children whimpered in fear. We drew closer together, clutching our pathetically inadequate weapons. Even the sheep had stopped eating.

I'd found myself a piece of wood about the size and shape of a rounders bat. God knows what I thought I'd do with it – I was crap at rounders at school, but it was probably much easier to hit a big Saxon than a small ball. Or so I told myself. And of course, in rounders, the balls don't usually come at you with homicidal intent. That's hockey.

We stood in silence. I could hear people around me. I could hear their breathing and the occasional rustle of their clothing. I heard someone sneeze in the dust.

Granny stood facing the door. I stood with her. What would you have done? I couldn't not fight. It just wasn't in me. Maybe if I just hit them very gently, History would let me get away with it. Other women joined us, their faces grimly determined. The smaller children and babies had been hidden under the hay.

In the silence, we could hear the Saxons as they circled the barn. I'm not sure how many there were, but not more than six or seven, I was sure. The vast majority were still slugging it out elsewhere.

We turned slowly, listening hard. No one made a sound. Even the babies were quiet. Everywhere, women tightened their grip on whatever weapon they had found and prepared to defend themselves and their children.

I was so tempted to call up the others, even if only for reassurance, but if they were safe then they would call me. And if they weren't safe, there was nothing I could do to help them. The last thing they needed was me distracting them.

We waited.

But not for long.

Chapter Six

I think, actually, that a full-scale assault, full of sound and fury, would have been less terrifying than standing helpless, listening to them whisper to each other as they circled the hut.

They weren't sure what was inside. They suspected we'd been shoved in here for safe keeping, but they weren't certain. For all they knew, they could open the door and twenty or so fully armed warriors would burst out and cut them to pieces. So they crept around and around the hut. I could hear their quiet footsteps, the murmured comments. I could hear them dragging their hands across the mud walls, looking for weak spots. Chinks of light shone through the door and occasionally, one would be obscured as someone cautiously tried to peer in. They were unlucky. It wasn't light outside, but it was considerably gloomier in here, and they could only risk a very brief glimpse. No one wanted a sword through their eye. The battle still raged in the distance, but all their attention was here.

I was proud of us. No one screamed. No one panicked or tried to run away. We were all frightened. I could hear our gasping breaths in the silence, but other than that, no one made a sound. Not even the babies. Everyone knew that once the men on the other side of the wall realised we were just an undefended group of women and children ... with the added bonus of livestock thrown in ... We wouldn't stand a chance.

Someone tried the door. I heard the bar scraping in its holders. Heard it placed softly against the wall. Someone pushed very cautiously. I saw the door move an inch or so but no further. Our barricade of heavy sacks held.

They tried again. I think more of them must have pushed this time. One or two of the sacks moved but nothing serious.

I heard a thump and then a series of thumps as they put their shoulders to it, but the barricade held.

Turning back to the other women, I nodded encouragingly. Every second the barricade held was another second nearer rescue. We had only to hold on until Arthur triumphed.

We all stood motionless, inadequate weapons raised and ready. I wiped my sleeve across my forehead. It was a muggy day. There were a lot of us in this enclosed space. The air was stuffy. And I was shit-scared. Just to be clear.

The silence seemed to drag on for a very long time. Had they given up and gone away? Had they gone to re-join the others? Or had they just wandered off to look for easier pickings? Unlikely. We were the easiest pickings.

I stood motionless, eyes fixed on the wooden door, waiting for just the tiniest movement that would tell me they were still there.

And then, behind me, someone knocked something over. I don't know who or what it was. Something wooden clattered onto something else. Not a loud noise, but it was enough to give us away. Now they knew we were here.

I heard a lot of whispering and then a strange, scraping noise against the wall. For a moment, I couldn't think what on earth it could be and then something floated down from the roof.

A stir ran around the barn as, simultaneously, we all realised what they were doing. They were climbing the walls. They would come at us through the roof.

I looked up. There were the four central pillars, supporting the timber beams. They'd laid brushwood over those to support the thatch. Everything was loose. It wouldn't hold them for long. They would pull away the thatch and drop through. And we were trapped.

The same thought occurred to all of us. Women threw themselves at the barricade, heaving sacks aside. We had to get out. We were no safer outside, but at least there would be room to move. To run, maybe, or find somewhere to hide until this was over. Because Arthur would win, I was sure of it. The only question was whether we would be alive to see it.

Old people began to yank children out from under the straw. Babies were securely tied to their mothers who herded themselves into a tight group, clutching their pathetic weapons. They were terrified. Many of them were crying. Tears ran down their grubby cheeks. Their eyes were distended with fear as they stared wildly about them. But they stood their ground.

Because there's something in the female genes. Something carried down from the dawn of time, maybe, from when we were bottom of the food chain and everything was a threat. Something that, despite overwhelming odds, makes us turn, stand at bay, teeth bared, weapons raised, and defend our children.

More straw and dust floated down. I looked up. A face appeared, long hair hanging down around it. He stared for a moment and then shouted something over his shoulder. He was pushed aside and another face appeared in his place. There was the sound of laughter.

Another hole appeared. Large lumps of thatch fell around us.

I looked behind me. Three women and an old man were struggling to heave the sacks aside. A group of women and children clustered behind them. Around me, some half dozen women, single, like me, I guessed, stood looking up.

The only thing that bought us a little time was that they'd made their holes in the highest part of the roof. Too high to jump and risk a broken leg because, looking at the faces around me, no mercy would be shown to any man unfortunate enough to be unable to defend himself.

Two men tried to lower another. He hung for a moment, legs kicking, still too high to drop. I had a sudden idea, ran to the pile of stones, and began to throw them. Others had the same idea. I'm a good shot. Suddenly, this wasn't somewhere he wanted to be. He shouted to be pulled up. His mates, laughing their heads off, let him go. He fell heavily. An old man pushed us roughly aside and stood over him with a rock. There was a nasty sound.

And now, we had a sword.

The old man, one-eyed and heavily scarred, picked it up, hefted it expertly, sighted down the blade and grunted in satisfaction.

Over our heads, they'd stopped laughing and were furiously excavating. Even more lumps of brushwood and thatch fell around us. Surely now, they could safely make the jump. The roof sloped – where the roof met the walls was not that high above our heads. But they didn't. They cleared the roof, tossing everything down into the barn with us. I could see the sky, hear the sounds of battle around us. But they didn't jump.

It was the old man with the sword who understood first. Turning his head, he shouted. The women at the door redoubled their efforts to pull the heavy sacks away. And then I got it as well.

They were going to burn us.

They would drop lighted torches down on top of us and this barn, full of hay, straw, wood, and thatch would explode into an inferno. And they'd wait outside the doors to cut down anyone trying to escape. We had to get out now. Or we would burn.

I could hear men shouting all around us. There were a lot of them. They began to scramble down off the roof. Obviously they wouldn't want to be caught up there when the torches were dropped.

More shouting. And now, the clash of swords. There was fighting. Were we being rescued? We couldn't see a thing. We had no idea from which direction the most peril would come. Were we now safer inside or out? I made a mental note never ever to be caught like this again, and then the little voice inside me, that one gives me such a hard time in the small hours when I can't sleep, said, 'You should be so lucky.'

A movement caught my eye. I looked up. I saw a flicker. The next moment, a lighted torch dropped through the roof, trailing a stream of black, oily smoke, and landed squarely on the biggest pile of bone-dry brushwood.

I ran towards it, hoisting up my skirts and began to stamp out the flames as best I could, cursing the fact I'd left my blanket out there somewhere. Others joined me.

I stamped and kicked and scuffed and made no impact at all. The fire was spreading.

Someone must finally have got the door open because suddenly a great blast of warm air blew around me. The small fire became a major conflagration. Flames roared hungrily, feeding on the oxygen. Someone grabbed me from behind. I could see sparks flying heavenwards through the hole in the roof. Terrified livestock were stampeding past me. I was knocked over by a sheep. Not what you want on your death certificate. Trampled by sheep. I could hear men shouting. Someone heaved me up, lifted me off my feet and ran. I was being rescued. I hoped.

After the heat of the barn, it seemed very cool outside. The breeze was welcome. Someone laid me on the ground. Granny's face swam above me. She held something to my lips and I may have inadvertently drunk the devil's urine. Or beer, as the brewing industry would probably like me to refer to it. It didn't matter. I was temporarily lost in the hazy euphoria of smoke inhalation and not being dead.

I thought I'd only closed my eyes for a second, but when I opened them again, I was wrapped in my blanket, and Peterson was there.

'Well,' he said. 'This brings back memories. You unconscious on the ground and showing your knickers.'

I gazed up at him. 'You've peed on me again, haven't you?'

'Not this time,' he said happily. 'With increased age comes increased bladder control.'

I always thought it was the other way around, but he seemed so cheerful that I let it go. 'Where are the others?'

'Safe and sound. Everyone has exactly the number of body parts they started with.'

'Where are they?'

'Clean-up duties. Yes, the warriors get the beer and women, but they also serve who do the clearing up afterwards. At least, that's what I told them.'

I clutched his arm. 'You didn't kill anyone?'

'Of course not,' he said indignantly. 'We *are* professionals, you know.'

I let that go. It wasn't the day for an argument.

It was obvious the battle had been won. The Red Dragon still streamed overhead. The dead had been cleared away. Wounded people were being ministered to. There was an air of bustle and purpose.

The barn in which we'd hidden was smouldering. The roof was mostly gone but the walls were intact. Livestock grazed quietly back in their makeshift enclosure.

It was quite a pleasant post-battle scene. I've seen worse.

He helped me sit up. 'Everything OK?'

I looked down. 'I think so. Scorched skirts. Correct number of limbs. Young Farrell kicking like a madman and a slight headache, but otherwise fine.'

He passed me some water and I washed away the taste of the beer.

'So come on, tell me. What happened? How did you all manage to survive both the Saxons and History?'

He looked smug. 'Max, we were magnificent.'

'I don't doubt it for a moment, but how did you actually manage it?'

He grinned at me. 'We fought ourselves.'

'What? You're kidding.'

'Well, there weren't any badges or distinguishing features, and no one knew us from Adam, so we just turned and engaged each other. I took on Roberts, and Sands and Markham engaged in what must have looked like a death match. We all hammered away at each other. There were lots of flourishes and shouting and wild slashing, just to make it look good. Occasionally one of us went down and sprawled on the ground for a bit of a rest. We swapped partners every now and then, or had a bit of a mêlée when we got bored, and it must have worked because everyone left us alone to get on with it.'

I stared at him in admiration. 'Tim, that's brilliant. And don't tell me it wasn't your idea.'

He contrived to look brilliant and modest at the same time. 'Well ...'

I wanted to ask how his arm had held up but at that moment, with an overwhelming aroma of beer, the others turned up, each clutching a jug of something unspeakable.

I sighed. 'I see Mr Markham has still managed to get himself injured. Did you hit yourself over the head again?'

'No,' he slurred with great dignity. 'Been hearing about the barn. Did you really burn it down?'

'No. Actually I was trying to put it out. I gather we were rescued in the nick of time. Are you lot drunk?'

'To the victor the spoils. Big party next door. Came to get you. Just remembered you can't drink.'

'Too late,' I said, remembering Granny and the beer. Peterson helped me up. I wrapped my blanket around myself and we followed our meandering guides into the other enclosure where I was finally able to look around.

It was much smaller than the other and there were far more huts scattered around. The place was packed and everyone was having a great time. Something was roasting on a spit and smelled really good. I suddenly realised I hadn't eaten for hours. Rough tables were set up with jugs of something awful. Piles of fresh-baked flat loaves were stacked in baskets, together with what looked like some sort of cake, dripping with honey. I helped myself to a large portion and immediately became smothered from head to foot in sticky stuff. Unsecured objects began to stick to me in large numbers. Leaves, fluff, dust, flying insects, Mr Roberts – even my fingers were gummed together.

We found somewhere safe to sit down – before three-fifths of our happy little band fell down – and tucked in. I still remember the damp grass, the smell of roasting animals and baking bread, the excited talking, laughing and shouting. Mini battles were fought again so men's families could admire their skill and daring. Young boys practised with sticks, showing off for their fathers. Even the dogs were back, barking and howling in the distance. Someone must have shut them up somewhere and the smell of meat was driving them frantic. All around us, everyone was having the Dark Age equivalent of a Great Day Out.

Two small teams were engaged in a tug-of-war over a fire. They strained happily away to shouts of encouragement from their quaffing friends, and then the fire burned through the rope and they all went sprawling, to huge hilarity.

As a further demonstration of muscle and futility combined, a number of young men were engaging in trials of strength. Stripped to the waist, they were heaving rocks around. I turned my back because it was difficult enough to concentrate as it was.

There was wrestling and it was hard to say whether it was friendly or not. Even as I watched, two men crashed to the ground. Impressively, neither of them spilled a drop.

At the centre of a very wide circle, another young man was juggling with knives. It should be said that he was very, very drunk, which was probably why he was able to get away with it.

Everywhere was exuberance and fun, shouting and laughter, excited children, and very apprehensive sheep.

We met Granny's son. Ulf something or other. I couldn't make it out. He was younger than I thought he would be, a pleasant-faced man with wide gaps between his teeth, and who seemed to be wearing all his children at once. One sat on his shoulders, one hung off his back, one was clinging to one leg and the last was freelancing around his ankles. His wife beamed silently at his side. He seemed to have escaped completely unscathed. Granny's pride and relief rolled off her in waves. She kept gesturing to me. I think she was telling him about the barn. He smiled and nodded and said something to Peterson which, he later claimed, was an offer to buy me.

And all the time, some kind of music played, some people sang, an awful lot of people quaffed, and we had the sort of good time you can only have when you suddenly and unexpectedly find yourself still alive.

We should have left. We should have quietly packed up our gear and departed. But we didn't. It wasn't often that we actually had the opportunity to observe the aftermath of a battlefield. Most of our assignments ended with us racing back to the pod and shouting for emergency extraction. It was very pleasant to sit for a few hours with friends.

Arthur had scrubbed up well. Gone was the sweaty, muddy warrior. His hair had been washed and combed, although it still wasn't golden. More a kind of light brown. He wore it loose around his shoulders. Interestingly, he had no beard.

'Ha,' said Roberts. 'Well, if Arthur hasn't got one then I'm certainly not going to bother.'

'Like you have a choice,' said Sands, grinning.

He was an affable leader, submitting to being led around the enclosure. A number of men were presented to him – I assumed they'd distinguished themselves during the battle. There was a lot of laughing and hand clasping. And he was approachable. Small children milled around his feet and he seized one and hoisted him onto his shoulder. His progress was easy to follow – like royalty today, he wore bright colours so he could easily be identified. His appropriately royal-blue cloak fastened at his right shoulder with a Celtic knot clasp. Beneath, he wore a red tunic which fell to mid-calf.

'Are you getting this?' enquired Peterson, softly.

'You bet.'

He didn't come anywhere near us and I wasn't sure whether to be sad or glad. Duty done, he seated himself on the ground along with everyone else and got stuck in.

I have to say I caused a small sensation when I split open my loaf and stuffed a thick slice of roast mutton inside. I rather think I might have anticipated the invention of the sandwich by a thousand years and more, and cursed myself for not having thought to patent it. If I'd had my wits about me, we could all have been scarfing down ham maxwells. Or indulging in a crispy bacon maxxie. There would be toasted maxwells, open maxwells, maxwells with the crusts cut off, the king would entertain his guests to cucumber maxwells ... I surfaced to find everyone watching me with some concern. Peterson leaned over and gently removed my cup of beer and I think we were all relieved about that.

Just as dusk began to fall and I was thinking about chivvying them all back to the pod, a man walked quietly to stand by the fire. At once, everyone fell silent.

He wore a simple white robe, spotlessly clean. A stool was brought for him, which he politely declined. He carried a hand-harp, which he strummed gently.

Lifting his head, he sang. I have no idea of the subject, I didn't understand the words, but the tune carried a strange, halting rhythm. Sometimes a note was held just for a fraction too long, or an unexpected pause broke up the expected sequence of notes. And at the end of every phrase, a long, sliding note dragged at the heartstrings, and tailed into nothing. People stopped drinking. The dogs even stopped barking. I felt the tears on my cheeks. This was grief made tangible. A song to those no longer in this world. The last note died away. There was no applause.

He began again and this time there was a different rhythm. A dancing, skipping, insistent beat. I felt my feet tap in response. This tune could raise the dead and make them dance. For no reason at all, I thought of giant stones, dancing their way across the country, defying the laws of physics. I saw them slotting smoothly into place, as meek and obedient as sheep. To stand forever, black against the sky. I remembered the old name for Stonehenge was the Giant's Dance; remembered that according to legend, the wizard Merlin spoke the words and the stones danced to his bidding.

Believe it or not, I've never visited Stonehenge. Not in any time. But I could. My last jump was coming up. I could visit Stonehenge. I could touch the stones. Walk among them. I could see them when they were young.

He started another song. It was very dark by now. The juggling and other activities had halted. I looked around. Everyone was standing or sitting in a large circle, listening. His voice was liquid gold. We swayed gently in time to the mesmerising rhythm of the music. He sang softly but clearly, and the words mingled with the smoke and sparks from the fire, and rose slowly towards the stars.

I don't know for how long we sat there, just listening. Eventually, the words dwindled into silence. Now the people applauded. The musician stood, slim and tall, head bowed, accepting his due. I wiped my eyes and when I looked again, he had disappeared.

People sighed, shook themselves, and refilled their mugs. Now things grew rowdy. Songs grew bawdy and suggestive. All around, people were disappearing into the darkness. I could hear a lot of laughter and shrieking.

Eventually, Arthur stood up, seized two laughing girls, and disappeared into the hut set aside for him.

Markham, Sands and Roberts, their arms around each other – although whether as a demonstration of affection or much needed support I had no idea – set off in search of more jugs. Tim and I sat quietly. He drained his cup.

I grinned. 'Now we know what puts the pee in Peterson.'

He snorted.

To fill the silence and with some trepidation, I asked, 'How did the arm hold up?' My fears were groundless; he answered quite normally.

'Quite well. I don't think I'll ever be able to wield a sword as well as I used to, but I was able to use a spear as a quarterstaff. If I can use both arms, then I'm not too bad. I'm going to get some practice in when I get back. Quarterstaffs are pretty lethal, you know. And their reach is much greater than that of a sword.'

I waited.

He turned to me and in the light of someone's fire, I caught a glimpse of his crooked grin. 'I'm not so useless after all.'

'That'll come as a surprise to the rest of us.'

He put his hand on my arm and I covered it briefly with my own, searching for the words to ask him. He'd once told me he wanted to ask Helen a Special Question. He'd never mentioned it since and I didn't like to ask. Now, I wondered if he'd put off asking her until he'd regained his faith in himself. I opened my mouth to frame a tentative question, but then the others came back with more jugs and the moment passed.

Roberts retracted his undercarriage and collapsed beside me, grinning all over his face. He waved an arm to embrace the socially disintegrating scene around us. 'Bloody hell, Max, we really are the dog's bollocks, aren't we?'

I grinned and nodded.

He waved his arm again. 'We saved them. Well, Arthur did a bit, of course. All these people. Max, I keep thinking, somewhere here tonight there might be some of my ancestors.' He waved his arm yet again.

'What – in amongst the sheep? That would account for a lot.'

'No, sorry – my arm went the wrong way.' He giggled. 'Gotta say though, the one on the end looks pretty good to me.'

Markham watched him in tolerant amusement. 'That's an actual girl.'

He squinted. 'I knew that.' He began to make preparations to heave himself onto his feet. 'I might go and say hello.'

Markham pushed him back down again. 'Yes, and find yourself looking down the wrong end of her father, three uncles, eight brothers and seventeen cousins. Stick to the sheep. They might find your lack of facial fleece oddly alluring.'

Sands twisted round to look at him. 'He can't possibly be from around here. Everyone's got a beard. You could lose a small horse in the one on that bloke over there. There are six-year-olds with more facial hair than you. The goats have beards. Even some of the women have beards.'

Roberts struggled indignantly, failed to gain control of his outlying regions, and collapsed again. Seconds later he was snoring.

Markham stared at him. 'No beard. Can't hold his drink. No way this boy's Welsh.'

We briefly discussed lugging him back to our campsite but no one could really be bothered and so, in line with the prevailing 'sleep where you drop' culture, we did the same.

Chapter Seven

We awoke at dawn, chilled and damp. Early though it was, most people were already up and moving around, stirring the fires back into life. A very wobbly Mr Roberts found us some stale bread. None of them fancied the beer. Peterson and I grinned at each other.

It's a strange thing, but the sky was still dark and it wasn't all smoke from the bonfires. I sat in the warm, wet wind and looked around me. Yes, Arthur would hold the Saxons for a while, but he would die at Camlann if all the legends were true, and then they would return in force and then there would be no one to hold them. I looked up. Dark clouds gathered overhead, and in the east, a dim light glimmered. For the time being.

Peterson nudged me back to the present. Something important was happening.

Arthur emerged from his hut, still wearing his good clothes. He carried a sword in his outstretched arms. Every historian present automatically reached for their recorders. Markham rolled his eyes.

At once, silence fell. I had no idea what was going on. The presence of the sword seemed to preclude this being some sort of religious ceremony. I know Christianity wasn't yet fully established across the country – if in fact it ever was. I once read that during the Second World War a number of churches removed their altars for safe keeping and that buried beneath some of them were old pagan symbols – people hedging their bets, I suppose, just in case this new god didn't make the grade. It would be interesting to know whether the pagan symbols were replaced under the altars after the war was ended.

This, however, was not a religious ceremony. A group of men – leaders of the community, I assumed, lined up behind him.

Behind them, in neat lines, Arthur's own men. Behind them, a great mass of everyone else, all jostling and pushing for the best view. We grabbed our stuff and joined them, and the procession set off, out through the gates and down the hill. The ground was badly churned up and there was still the odd piece of Saxon lying around, but Arthur marched steadily onwards.

'He's going to the cave,' whispered Roberts, behind me. 'He's going to Arthur's Cave.'

I suppose, if you thought about it, where else would he be going? But why? Some historian sense was telling me this was important.

We wound our way down through hazel, beech, hawthorn and oak trees. There were even mighty yews here, ancient and venerable, sweeping the ground with their branches.

And there it was: a large rock formation loomed through the trees. We halted outside a double-entranced cave that opened into darkness. Other than the occasional murmur, the crowd was completely silent. I gazed about me. The rock was green with moss and ferns. Ivy scrambled everywhere. Generations of dead leaves carpeted the ground. The area in front of the cave had been cleared, but trees grew from above and their overhanging branches obscured the two entrances. Possibly because of that we didn't see where he came from but, suddenly, he was there.

A collective gasp went up from the people – including five historians and a security guard, it should be said. Those at the front stepped back.

Arthur, however, stood firm.

'Who is he?' murmured Peterson. 'Is he a Druid?'

He stood tall and straight, with a great beak of a nose protruding from the mother of all beards. Long, grey hair streamed down his back, almost to his waist.

For a few seconds, no one moved. If I close my eyes I can still see the scene today. The glowing colours of autumn. The crowd of people gathered around the cave entrance and standing amongst the trees, all still and silent and watching. Arthur, deliberately vivid in his red and blue, offering up the sword in his outstretched arms.

I had no idea what was going on here, but whatever it was, it was very, very important.

Arthur spoke. I couldn't make out the words, but his voice was deep and solemn. He was taking an oath over the sword.

The old man, clad in dingy white robes and none too clean himself, stepped forward, and with great reverence and honour, accepted the sword.

A kind of sigh went up from those around me. A covenant had been made.

My mind was racing. Arthur had presented the people of Caer Guorthigirn with his sword. Well, *a* sword, anyway. Maybe he did this after every battle. As a symbolic gesture of his protection. Was this how the legends of Arthur's mighty sword were born?

I strained for a glimpse of the sword itself. I couldn't see clearly, but this was no Excalibur. This was an ordinary broadsword, tapering to a point. Peterson's the weapons expert, but I could see it was modern in design with a pommel rather than the old-fashioned, washer-style handle. The handle looked golden, but I was willing to bet it was gilt. It wouldn't be gold if he was handing them out all over the country.

Arthur bowed, although whether to the sword or the old man was not clear. Maybe both. The old man raised up the sword, holding it above his head where everyone could see it, flourished it three times, and then, still without a sound, turned and, I supposed, re-entered the cave, although a long curtain of ivy obscured him somewhat and when I looked again he was gone.

'Where did he go?' whispered Roberts. 'I've been inside this cave. It's quite shallow. Doesn't go anywhere.'

'Maybe not in our time,' said Peterson. 'Today though, I think I could believe anything.'

We'd had the forethought to collect our gear. No one had fancied struggling back up the hill again. As the crowd dispersed, we made our way slowly through the woods, back to the pod.

In the distance, I heard a thunder of hoofs. The great horn sounded again – in farewell, this time. Had Arthur already been called away to fight somewhere else? Was he, at this moment, riding hard into that faint light in the east? To his next battle?

We returned to the pod to find someone had already stacked a pile of logs against it. A tribute to the genius design, I suppose, but a bloody nuisance to have to clear away.

Our return was uneventful. We touched down gently and I operated the decontamination system. No one had been injured. Well, no one had been badly injured. Just for once, we could exit the pod, intact and successful.

I smiled reassuringly at Leon, who grinned back, and we all traipsed off to Sick Bay to listen to Hunter giving Markham a hard time about something. I spent the night sorting through our material and writing my report. Out of consideration to Dr Bairstow, some parts of it had to be quite carefully worded. Reading it through, I was rather proud. Without actually saying so, I'd managed to give the impression that I'd spent the day sitting in a well-appointed barn, completely divorced from whatever nastiness was going on out there. I deflected him further by spending a considerable amount of time describing the sword and recommending the location be passed to Thirsk for them to investigate further. Imagine if it was still in there somewhere. Arthur's sword! I stuck my initials all over everything, bundled up my report with everyone else's and sent it off to the Boss. Who requested the pleasure of my company first thing the next morning.

When I arrived, he had my report open in front of him. Some parts were highlighted. I thought I would pre-empt the inevitable.

'I was never in any danger, sir. I was in the second compound, which never actually came under any attack at all. We all sat quietly and were rescued.'

He refused to be deflected.

'You were, nevertheless, involved in a 6th-century conflict.'

84

'Only very peripherally, sir. In fact, I wouldn't dignify it with the word "conflict". It was more of a 6th-century scuffle.'

'Despite scanning your report very carefully, I seem unable to locate your reasons for not immediately returning to St Mary's the moment it became apparent you were about to be involved in this ... scuffle.'

Well, that wasn't surprising because I hadn't given any. The opportunity had been too good to pass up. And we'd seen Arthur. And his sword. I did think he was being just a little ungrateful. It seemed safer, however, not to mention this.

'Well, we didn't know that at the time, sir.'

'So, the panic-stricken populace fleeing for their lives in terror, the burning buildings, the assembled soldiers – all that passed you by? Should I recommend you to Dr Foster for an eye test?'

Shit. That wasn't good. I've never said anything, but sometimes, when I'm a bit tired, I can't always make out small print. Or really, any print at all. Long sight was no problem. I would easily be able to see the bus that would run me over. I just wouldn't be able to make out the number and route. You can't wear spectacles on assignment and so I'd been telling myself it was just a side-effect of pregnancy. Inconvenient but temporary.

'Thank you, sir. I shall avail myself of the opportunity as soon as it is safe for me to do so.'

He looked up. 'I had not realised that eye tests could be so hazardous.'

'Only to the pregnant, sir. The … emissions … from the … light box can be detrimental to the well-being of the foetus. Sir.'

Well I didn't see why I shouldn't play the pregnancy card once in a while. It was stopping me doing all the interesting stuff like drinking, stuffing myself sick on chocolate, getting the good assignments and so on, so I thought I'd use it to my advantage for once.

He raised a disbelieving eyebrow. 'Emissions?'

I replied with conviction. 'Indeed, sir. I'm certain you will agree one cannot be too careful.'

He sat back and prepared to enjoy himself, handing me a metaphorical spade to facilitate the hole I was digging for myself. 'I struggle, Dr Maxwell, to reconcile your reluctance to undergo so hazardous an experience as an eye test, with the apparent enthusiasm with which you hurled yourself into a potentially fatal Dark Age encounter.'

'Perhaps sir,' I said cunningly, knowing he'd never in a million years authorise the expenditure, 'the acquisition of some sort of protective garment would considerably lessen the risks involved.'

'For whom?'

'Well, me, for a start, sir.'

'I quite agree,' he said. 'Let me do what I can to lessen your concerns. I shall immediately commission Professor Rapson to design some sort of lead-lined wigwam, which I'm afraid I must insist you wear, Dr Maxwell, to mitigate the potentially fatal results of a modern eye test. In addition, I shall ask Dr Foster to provide a visual record of your compliance, the unit-wide circulation of which will, I think, go a long way towards allaying any similar fears your colleagues may be experiencing.'

He took advantage of my speechlessness. 'Dismissed, Dr Maxwell.'

The next thing, of course, was for him to alert Thirsk to the possible existence of Arthur's sword. '*One* of Arthur's swords,' I kept saying, and no one took a blind bit of notice.

Thirsk were ecstatic at the prospect. As well they should be. As usual, we'd done all the work and they would get all the glory. We'd get the cheque, of course, which would keep Dr Bairstow happy for a day or two.

The Chancellor was particularly excited and I received a personal message from her, thanking me and the other members of the team. She'd never done that before. This was going to be big. Everyone was very happy.

As was I, because it was an opportunity again to shelve the longstanding problem of what to do with Elspeth Grey. Don't get me wrong – she's one of the nicest people on the planet but she was the fly in my department's ointment.

Over a year ago now, we'd rescued two stranded historians – Elspeth Grey and Tom Bashford. They'd been snatched by that bastard, Clive Ronan, and stranded in Roman Colchester, just as Boudicca attacked the town. We'd got them out by the skin of their teeth, but there was no doubt it had been a traumatic experience for them both. Bashford not so much, because he'd been semi-conscious throughout most of it – it had been Elspeth who had battled to keep them both safe – but while Bashford had resumed his duties with enthusiasm, Grey had not. I'd given her the time I thought she needed, but her first assignment – to Ancient Egypt – had not gone well. Not well at all.

I honestly didn't know what to do with her. Firstly, she was a fully trained historian and I was reluctant to part with her. Secondly, if she left, Ian Guthrie might well go with her and that would be a huge loss to St Mary's. I often wondered if he wasn't moving in that direction anyway. He'd named Markham as his number two and I often saw the two of them together these days. Was Markham shadowing Guthrie in preparation to take over the Security Section? It was very possible.

However, Arthur's sword offered a reasonable compromise. Miss Grey had represented St Mary's on the expedition to recover three missing Botticellis. She was the obvious choice for this assignment as well. It was a win-win situation for everyone.

I briefed her – she accepted the assignment – and disappeared off to Thirsk the very next day. I heaved a sigh of relief at having deferred the problem yet again and got on with things.

Six weeks later, unbelievably, they found it. They found Arthur's sword.

And then the shit really hit the fan.

Chapter Eight

I honestly hadn't been sure they would find it. I knew the cave had previously been excavated and although they hadn't been looking for Arthur's sword at the time, I myself was convinced it had been discovered hundreds of years ago and was quietly residing in someone's private collection. Or that it had been hidden so completely that no one would ever find it. Or even that it was no longer of this world. You can blame pregnancy fantasies for that last one.

It turned out to be none of those. They went over every inch with metal detectors and there it was. They had to chip it out of the surrounding rock, but it was still there, wrapped in layers of desiccated leather.

The Chancellor sent me another personal message together with a series of images. I stared at it – remarkably well preserved and exactly as I remembered it. If I closed my eyes, I could still hear Arthur's deep voice filling the silence around us. I could still see the old man's gnarly hands reaching out to take it …

We were heroes. Everyone loved us. Especially the Chancellor who, apparently, had been having a bit of a rocky moment, politically speaking, and this was just what was needed to enable her to put the academic boot in. Or in her case, of course, an expensive but elegantly understated court shoe.

We basked in that almost unheard of phenomenon, Dr Bairstow's approval, because our funding was secure for the foreseeable future. The word on the street was that he was carpeing the diem by compiling a wish list the like of which had never before been contemplated, let alone submitted. The rest of St Mary's regarded us with awe and admiration. I'd like to think.

'Arthur's sword!' people kept saying.

'*One* of Arthur's swords,' I kept saying back, trying to keep a sense of proportion.

No one was listening and after a while, neither were we.

Did we get big-headed? Did we walk around thinking we were the dog's bollocks? Of course we did. Anyone would. It was Arthur's sword, for God's sake. *The* Arthur and very nearly *the* sword. And we'd found it. Well – we'd enabled it to be found. Of course we got big-headed.

And then things started to go horribly wrong.

Not a huge thing to begin with. I thought afterwards it might have been a warning shot.

I don't normally watch the news. The last time I bothered was when, yet again, they reopened the controversy over Richard III's final resting place, with the City of York waging war on the City of Leicester, and Westminster Abbey poised to engage the winner.

It was Peterson who drew my attention to it this time. A factory had closed. Not something that would normally interest us, but it was situated only a couple of miles from Caer Guorthigirn.

'I think we might have walked past the site,' he said.

I watched the screen. The company had, quite suddenly, declared bankruptcy and closed. They had been the major employer in a predominantly rural area.

'A financial disaster for the region,' declared the newsreader.

Roberts looked gloomy. 'Half my family worked there,' he said. 'The half that doesn't work on my dad's farm, anyway.'

'Bad luck,' said Peterson, sympathetically.

He nodded and walked away.

Then, things went even more wrong.

The first I knew was when Roberts found me in the Library.

'What's the matter,' I asked, in concern. His face was blotchy. Surely, he hadn't been crying.

He laid a local newspaper before me. 'My mam sent it. Look what's happened.'

I folded back the page and peered at it. The word catastrophe leaped out at me. Shit! I read more closely. A heavily laden lorry had careered down the hill, failed to negotiate one of the bends, and smashed into a pub's car park. Two parked cars had slowed it only slightly, and the whole mass of tangled metal, still travelling at some speed, had crashed straight into the crowded pub itself. Fatalities were high. Casualties even higher.

'Gareth, I'm so sorry. What a dreadful thing to happen. Did you know any of them?'

He swallowed and nodded, unable to speak for a moment.

'Do you want some time off? Go and visit your family? Everyone must be devastated.'

'No, I've spoken to them on the phone. They're OK. Well, reasonably OK. The thing is, Max ...'

'Yes?'

He fiddled with the paper, making a big thing of folding it neatly. 'You don't think ...? After what happened with the factory as well, you don't think this has anything to do with Thirsk taking the sword away, do you?'

'I'm not with you.'

'It can't be a coincidence, can it? The sword is removed – Arthur's symbol of protection – and suddenly, bad things start to happen. Suppose it's like the London Stone – you know, "So long as the Stone of Brutus is safe, so shall London flourish." Or the ravens leaving the Tower means the Crown will fall and Britain with it. Suppose it was left by Arthur to keep the people safe and by removing it, we've laid them open to ...'

He was beginning to gabble.

I said gently, 'It's a coincidence. A dreadful one, but just a coincidence.'

'These are not coincidences. These are disasters. First the factory closing. And now – this.'

He was more agitated than I could ever remember. I couldn't blame him.

'These things come in threes, Max. What next?'

'Nothing comes next. Yes, it's a tragic coincidence, Gareth, but nothing more than that. Look, it says here that the brakes failed. It was a mechanical rather than a supernatural disaster. Nothing to do with us. And certainly nothing to do with you.'

He so desperately wanted to believe me.

'Do you think so?'

'Yes,' I said firmly. 'I really think so. I don't think removing the sword was in any way responsible for the factory closure or the accident.'

He picked up the paper. 'OK. Thanks Max,' and he trailed back out of the Library.

I watched him go, turned back to my data stack, and stared at it for quarter of an hour, seeing nothing.

He was back the next week. My office, this time. He burst through the door without knocking. He looked dreadful.

'Max!'

My assistant, Rosie Lee, was making tea in the corner. We have an arrangement. She makes me a cup of tea – I allow her a comfort break. It's a system that works well for both of us. Given that she's usually as hospitable as cholera, I expected her to invent an excuse and sweep from the room, but not this time.

I got him sitting down and she put a mug of tea in front of him. *Then* she swept from the room. I probably wouldn't see her for the rest of the day, but I didn't have time to worry about that now.

I didn't mess about. 'What's happened?'

He could barely speak. 'You remember? Do you remember?'

I tried to calm things down a little. 'Remember what? Tell me what you're talking about.'

'I told you. I told you it was all connected. You didn't believe me, but I told you. That these things come in threes. And now it's happened again.'

'Oh my God, not another accident?'

He shook his head, suddenly unable to speak. I keep a little something in my bottom drawer for this type of emergency, and added a tiny drop to his tea. Just a tiny drop because Dr Bairstow has strong views on drinking during office hours.

I made him take a few sips and then said, 'What is it? Tell me what has happened.'

He gulped. 'Oh, Max.'

'What?'

'Foot and mouth.'

'Where?' I said, knowing the answer.

'My dad's farm. They've set up a temporary control zone. The farm's all shut down. And probably the neighbouring farms too. Everything's stopped. No one can move their stock. There are restriction orders everywhere. I know they have to do it, but it doesn't take long for a field to be grazed out, but you still can't move the stock, and you have to bring in fodder, and the field gets wetter and muddier, and there's shit everywhere, and you can't keep the hay clean, and the animals can't move in the mud, and there's nothing you can do about it. And it's my dad's dairy herd. Three generations to build. We've won prizes. They're not numbers – they have names. He knows them all and they'll all be destroyed. On the farm. In front of him. His life's work. And then they burn the carcases. He'll never be able to replace them. Maybe he won't want to.'

'Is it definitely confirmed?'

'No, not yet. But it will be. I know it.'

I switched on the screen and together we watched the pictures of barriers, restriction notices, disinfectant baths, and anxious faces. They pulled back to show images of the wrecked pub, followed by the closed factory gates with a few men standing around looking lost. Even the newsreader was commenting on the extraordinary run of bad luck that in less than a month had brought a prosperous community to its knees.

Roberts turned to me. 'In Arthur's day it was the Saxons. Today it's ...' he gestured at the screen. 'This.'

'Gareth ...'

'Suppose it doesn't stop here, Max. What's next, do you think?'

He almost ran from the room.

I called Sands and directed him to keep an eye on Roberts.

'Already on it,' he said. 'We're in the bar.'

I frowned.

'I can hear you frowning,' he said, 'but it strikes me that this might be the best thing. If he's as pissed as a newt, then he's not going to be able to dash off and do something stupid.'

'Is he talking about doing something stupid?'

'Oh yes.'

'Do *not* let him out of your sight.'

'Copy that.'

That done, I called Peterson, thought for a moment, and called Markham as well. So that the three of us could talk about doing something stupid.

It seemed disloyal, somehow, to plot treason under St Mary's roof and so, that evening, we all changed into civvies and convened a meeting at the Falconberg Arms – the pub in the village.

Markham got the drinks in and we settled ourselves in the furthest, darkest corner of the lounge bar, surrounded by hunting prints and horse brasses.

'Well,' I said, kicking things off. 'The usual rules apply. Only one person speaks at a time. Everyone gets to speak. No interruptions. No violence. We all know what tonight's topic will be. Mr Roberts, will you go first?'

We all knew what his opinion was, but it seemed wise to let him speak first.

'I think we did it,' he said in a low voice. 'Well, not us specifically, but I think we initiated the events. We – Thirsk – moved the sword. It was put there to protect the people and we took it away.'

He sat back, indicating he had finished.

Peterson stirred. 'You can't possibly know that.'

'I can,' he insisted. 'I do. There's no way my dad's farm can have foot and mouth. It's just not possible. There's not been any new livestock – he hasn't even been to the livestock markets for a few weeks. Not Monmouth, nor Abergavenny. It's a prize herd. He looks after them far better than he ever looked after us. And streets ahead of how he looks after my mam. According to my mam, that is.'

'It's a highly contagious disease,' said Peterson. 'Vehicles, people, equipment, other animals – it could have come from anywhere.'

'All right,' he said hotly. 'What about the lorry crash? Vehicles go up and down that lane all day long. Nothing like that has ever happened before. Why now, suddenly? And what about the factory? It was fine. They're not some fly-by-night operation – they make agricultural equipment. They're a family firm established for the last thirty years. Their order books are full, Dad says. Why now do the banks suddenly decide to pull the plug? I tell you – it's the sword. They took away the sword and suddenly everything starts to go wrong.'

Silence.

'Surely you can't deny it?'

'It does sound a little far-fetched,' said Sands, mildly.

Roberts took a pull on his pint, set the glass down carefully on his beer mat, and said quietly, 'Events are escalating. Who wants to speculate on what will happen next? Anyone?'

Silence. We all looked at our drinks.

'Well, let's have a think, shall we? What about a fire at the infants' school? How many would you like to see die before you consider that I might be right? What constitutes a tragedy? Five? Twenty? Would they all have to die before you can accept what's right in front of your faces?'

He was beginning to shout. I put my hand over his and said, 'Hush.'

He jerked it away angrily, and went to speak again but Markham said, 'If Max says to hush, then I really think you should hush, don't you?'

He subsided into his pint.

'Right,' I said. 'Everyone just slow down and take a breath. Stop and think for two minutes. Then we'll go round the table and listen to what everyone has to say. Everyone gets to speak.

No interruptions. Questions and discussions at the end. Starting now.'

We picked up our drinks and no one spoke for two minutes while we marshalled our arguments.

As you can imagine, everyone had a great deal to say. Two more rounds of drinks materialised. I made several trips to the facilities. Eventually, it all ground to a simmering halt.

'Right,' I said. 'We put it to the vote. 'Who agrees with Mr Roberts' theory? Peterson?'

He put down his glass and said, 'I think there might be something in what he says.' Which was as big a surprise to him as to us, I think.

'Mr Sands?'

He shook his head. 'No. Sorry mate – but no. I think it's just an unfortunate coincidence.'

'Mr Roberts?'

'It's the sword.' He stared us down, defiantly.

'Mr Markham?'

He sighed. 'I don't know. I really don't know, and because I don't know I'm saying horses, not zebras.'

He meant – if you hear hooves, think horses, not zebras. The most obvious explanation is usually the right one, and the most obvious explanation was just simple bad luck.

'Two each,' said Peterson, downing the last of his pint. 'It's up to you, Max.'

It wasn't yet too late. Even at this stage, we could step back from the brink. And I did. I stepped back. I said, 'I agree with Sands and Markham. Coincidences. Tragic, unfortunate coincidences.'

Roberts wasn't happy, but he'd agreed to abide by the decision. We made our way back to St Mary's in unaccustomed silence. We parted company in the Hall and worn out, I went to our room, where Leon greeted me with the news that as they were shutting down the dig at Arthur's Cave, part of the trench had collapsed, burying two Thirsk archaeologists, one of whom had not survived.

Twenty-four hours later, we were assembled in my office. Rosie Lee, protesting violently, had been evicted. This time we had a plan.

'We take back the sword,' said Roberts before anyone else could say a word. 'We take it from Thirsk, we go back to the hill fort and we replace it in the cave. We have to. Before anyone else dies.'

'The cave is the first place they'll look for it,' objected Sands.

'We'll work out that detail when we come to it,' said Roberts. 'Let's start with actually stealing the sword.'

'No,' said Markham firmly, from his moral advantage as our resident criminal expert – from the criminal's point of view, of course. 'You always plan your exit strategy first. Never mind how we get in – how do we get out?'

'Out of where? Where is it being kept, exactly? It's a big campus.'

'The sword is currently located in their Archive and Museum,' I said. 'In a small workroom off the Zetland Library. The one that houses the Byland Bequest.'

'That's on the Northallerton campus.'

'Correct. And all the better for us because Kal works in the main admin building on the St James campus in Thirsk. With luck, she can't be implicated.'

'Neat,' said Sands, admiringly. 'How did you find that out?'

'I emailed Thirsk and asked them.'

'And they told you?'

'Why wouldn't they? We're worshipped as gods at the moment.'

I stood up and locked the door.

'Before we go any further, there are some points to bear in mind. If we do go ahead and do this – take back the sword, I mean – we cannot possibly hope to get away with it. Even if we're not caught in the act – which we probably will be – everyone will know it was us. We'll be seen on campus. CCTV cameras will have us racing up and down motorways all over the country. Everyone should be aware of this. We have not yet reached the point of no return. If anyone wants to back out – now is the time to do it.'

'Have we considered ...' said Sands slowly, 'just going to the Chancellor and asking for it back again. You never know.'

'It's Arthur's sword,' said Roberts, in despair. 'They'll never give it up. And once we raise their suspicions, they'll put it somewhere else, and we'll never be able to get to it.'

'Besides,' said Markham. 'It's always better to seek forgiveness than beg for permission. Trust me.'

We devoted as much time and effort to this assignment as we would to anything that had come down from Thirsk. More, in fact. We had to do this the low-tech way, so there was transport to think of, routes to plan, and driving schedules to allocate.

Peterson caught my eye and raised an eyebrow. I shook my head faintly. We would not be taking Leon's pod. We weren't going to get away with this and I didn't want him implicated. It's not good for a kid to have both parents in prison.

We broke off at lunchtime – anyone missing meals at St Mary's is automatically under suspicion of something or other – and reconvened afterwards. We pulled up maps and diagrams. We discussed routes, balancing the advantages of motorway speed and convenience against the ever-present surveillance systems. We thrashed out a plan for getting in, and another one for getting out. We discussed how to avoid any restrictions in the Caer Guorthigirn area. The only thing we didn't talk about in any great detail was how we would dispose of the sword. Because we didn't know.

Obviously, it had to go back into the cave, but how would we conceal it? We discussed it for ages, getting nowhere, and eventually decided we'd wing it once we got there. Which is pretty much the History Department's motto.

'And how are we to steal the thing, anyway?' said Sands.

'Leave that to me,' said Markham. 'You just get me there. I'll do the rest.'

'We can get in on our St Mary's credentials,' I said, 'that won't be a problem. But the workroom we want won't be open to non-essential personnel.'

'Kal can get us keycodes and passwords.'

'No,' I said firmly. 'We don't involve anyone else.' I looked around. 'We all need to be very clear about this. We are breaking the law. We are committing a crime. I have no illusions that we will get away with this. I have no idea what the consequences will be, but I think we can rely on them being severe. At the very least, we'll be sacked. We may go to prison. Academic disgrace is a certainty. No one should be regarding this as a romantic adventure. Or a crusade. We are stealing something that doesn't belong to us.'

'As did they,' said Roberts, hotly. 'It wasn't theirs to take away. It was given to the people of Caer Guorthigirn. It belongs to them, regardless of who found it. Or who owns the cave. It belongs to the people. We're not stealing it – we're taking it back.'

Well, if that was what he wanted to tell himself ...

'That's as may be,' I said, 'but everything stays in this room. We don't involve anyone else. Not Kal, not Rosie Lee, not Hunter, not anyone. We don't take anyone else down with us.'

Peterson looked at me. 'Not Leon?'

My heart thumped unpleasantly. I kept my voice steady. 'Especially not Leon. He's Dr Bairstow's number two. We'd be putting him in an impossible position. Agreed?'

They all nodded. 'Agreed.'

Peterson and Roberts would share the driving. Roberts would provide the transportation. 'Sands, you stay with the car while we're inside,' said Markham. 'There's nothing more embarrassing than erupting from a building clutching your loot only to find the car's been clamped. Or towed. So your job is to ensure our quick getaway.'

He nodded.

Markham would do the actual thieving.

And me ...?

I was fighting off attempts to make me stay behind. Which I managed to do very successfully by simply ignoring everything Peterson said.

'You're pregnant, Max.'

I was making a list. 'And we won't want to hang around at service stations so we'll need sandwiches and water in the vehicle. I'll organise that.'

'It's too risky for you.'

'Mr Roberts, please make sure your vehicle is fuelled and serviceable.'

'Suppose someone gets hurt? You, for instance.'

'I've done the staff work – here are our routes. This one's from St Mary's to Thirsk, and this one from Thirsk to Caer Guorthigirn. Refuelling stops are marked. No one drives for longer than two hours.'

'Max, you can't go.'

'I've prepared a cover story because we'll need a reason to be in the Zetland Library.' I passed over sheets of paper.

'Max!'

'And I've already done the groundwork by telephoning the librarian with queries as to the availability of some volumes.'

'Are you even listening to me?'

'No, of course not.'

'Look ...'

'And all the reservations are in my name so if you don't take me then you won't even get in, let alone get anywhere near the sword. Do you still want to leave me behind?' and swept on before anyone could say yes. 'The biggest problem is going to arise when we reach the cave.'

'Bigger than actually stealing the thing?' asked Sands.

'Oh yes,' said Markham. 'That's the easiest part. Max is right. We have to decide what to do with the damn thing once we've got it.'

'Put it back in the cave,' said Roberts, impatiently. 'Surely that's the whole point.'

'And that's it?' demanded Sands. 'We just wrap it in a blanket and lay it down in the cave somewhere? Because no one's going to find it there, are they?'

'We bury it somewhere,' said Roberts.

'Yes, because geophys will never be able to detect such a sophisticated hiding place. Max, we need to think about this because we could be wrecking St Mary's and ourselves for nothing. There's no point in us doing it if less than twenty-four hours later, the sword's back at Thirsk again.'

Silence.

'And,' I said, 'there's the problem of actually getting to Arthur's Cave. It's a quarantine area. We're going to have to conceal the car somewhere and walk across country. We can't afford to be irresponsible. We mustn't carry infection in and we certainly mustn't carry infection out. Someone needs to steal a couple of cans of the antibacterial stuff we use in the pods. Enough to spray us and the car.'

'I'll do that,' said Markham.

'We should take a pod,' said Roberts. 'We could do the whole thing in minutes.'

'Thus implicating everyone at St Mary's,' said Peterson. 'No. When the manure heap collides with the windmill, it needs to be very clear that we acted alone.'

'We'll find a way,' said Roberts, with confidence.

'You don't know that.'

'Yes, I do. It's Arthur's sword. It was left by him for the people of Caer Guorthigirn. The sword will find a way.'

An even more sceptical silence this time.

I think the only reason no one argued was that, actually, we never thought things would get that far. In my mind's eye, I was already seeing high-speed motorway chases, police helicopters swooping down on us, stingers, arrest, disgrace, me giving birth in prison ...

Afterwards, Peterson and I walked slowly around the gallery together.

'I think we've done everything we can, don't you?' he said.

I nodded. 'Yes, I think so.'

'As I always say – whatever the task you're about to undertake, you should never neglect the basics. Doesn't matter what you call it – staff work, advance planning, spadework, foreplay – a little effort at the beginning always pays dividends in the end.'

'Does Helen know you refer to your romantic interludes as spadework?'

He looked over his shoulder. 'You're not going to tell her, are you?'

'Depends whether you make my silence worthwhile.'

His smile faded. 'If we get this wrong – if we're all banged up, then it won't matter anyway.'

I stood still. 'Tim, we're not going to get away with this.'

'I know. Max, have you thought of persuading Dr Bairstow just to ask Thirsk to give it up?'

'To give up Arthur's sword just because a couple of historians with over-active imaginations say so? You think they'd do that?'

He sighed. 'No, you're right.'

'And as soon as we ask, we've tipped our hand. They'd never even let us on campus after that.'

'Just a minute.' He stopped, pulled me down and we sat on the stairs – often a traditional historian debating position. 'Why do we do this?'

'You mean all this?' I gestured at the activity in the Hall below.

'Yes, but specifically, why do we unearth artefacts? Why do we dig them up? Don't you ever think we should just leave well alone?'

I nodded. He had a point. I've sometimes thought this myself. It happens with mummies. They're removed from their final resting place and displayed in a public museum, or shut up alone in dusty storerooms. Does the fact that they were buried thousands of years ago make it right? When you think of all the love and reverence with which Egyptian mummies and their possessions were carefully buried. Images of loved ones, favourite pets, texts for future guidance, everything carefully placed to ensure their safe entrance into the next world – and then along we come. Well, not necessarily us, but someone. I'm not very religious, but other people are. I often wonder if we've screwed someone's chances of an afterlife by disturbing what was supposed to be their final resting place and scattering their personal treasures as if their former owner has no more use for them. How many souls have been condemned to a kind of limbo, spending eternity in the cold and dark, and all because we took away the treasured possessions with which they had so carefully provided themselves?

I shook myself mentally. There would be plenty of time to debate the moral position with myself when I languished in a prison cell.

We settled on the next Friday. Not a lot happens at St Mary's on a Friday. We had no trainees so there were no exams to set up. The afternoon would be devoted to the weekly Friday afternoon confrontation between the Security and Technical Sections on the battlefield – sorry, football field – followed by a lengthy session in Sick Bay for their wounds to be treated, followed by an even lengthier session in the bar while inquests were held and everyone blamed everyone else. We'd have a long day, but it was possible we'd be back before anyone noticed we were missing. Well, before everyone else was missed. I had the misfortune to be married.

There's a downside to being married. Actually, there are several but they mainly involve who ate the last biscuit, who left his boots just where anyone could fall over them if she wasn't looking where she was going, and inappropriate places to put ice-cold feet just as someone's dropping off to sleep.

The really big downside to marriage concerns the inexplicable need of half a married couple to know, at all times, exactly where the other one is. I mean – what's that all about?

I had two choices. I could lie or I could tell the truth.

I don't like lying to Leon – I could if I wanted to, he would believe anything I said, and that's why I don't lie to him. I just told him I was going to Thirsk – God knows he'd find out soon enough anyway. He nodded absently, and continued staring at his data stack. I stared at his bent head for a few minutes, wondering if this was the last time I'd ever see him as a free woman – me, I mean, not him – and took myself off for an early night.

Chapter Nine

I don't want anyone to think we just breezed through this with no thought of the implications. We all knew what we were doing and what would happen to us, and we went ahead and did it anyway.

We assembled an hour before dawn in the car park. Roberts was already in his car, waiting for us. I guess that, just like the rest of us, he hadn't had much sleep. Markham had a backpack. Roberts and Peterson had the maps. Sands and I had sandwiches and enough water for an expedition to the Antarctic.

'One final thing,' I said, as we stowed our gear. 'We all need to be perfectly clear that this was my idea. I compelled you to carry out my instructions. You were given no choice.'

'No way,' said Roberts, indignantly.

'Yes way,' said Peterson, heavily. He looked at me. 'Are you absolutely certain?'

'Yes. I'm thinking of St Mary's. When we are caught, you will all need as much plausible deniability as you can muster. I'm head of the department which means I'll go down regardless, so I'm ordering you to save yourselves. God knows how much shit will hit the fan, but you're all key personnel and St Mary's can't do without you. Your instructions, therefore – and you will follow them – is to blame me for everything and save yourselves.'

'Dr Bairstow won't believe it for a moment,' said Sands, shoving his bag in the boot.

'No, but it will enable him to save you by sacrificing me.'

'It should be me,' said Roberts.

'No, it shouldn't. Your family is dealing with enough shit at the moment without you making things worse for them. You will comply, Mr Roberts, or you don't come with us.'

Reluctantly, he nodded.

We drove slowly down the drive, tyres crunching on the gravel. There was little traffic in Rushford. We picked up the motorway and headed north. No one spoke.

Now that the moment had come, I was really regretting I'd ever agreed to do this. I never asked, but I wouldn't have been the slightest bit surprised to find the others felt the same. If there had been roadworks, or heavy traffic jams, or anything really, we would quite happily have turned around and returned to St Mary's. Sadly, the roads were clear and we were making good time. It's typical, isn't it? Where's a bloody contraflow when you need one?

We left the Great North Road at the Thirsk turn-off and cruised into Northallerton around mid-morning.

Sands parked us behind the former prison, now the Zetland Library.

We'd argued long and loud over whether to wear the formal St Mary's uniform, which would undoubtedly facilitate our entry to almost wherever we wanted to go, against the charge of publicly bringing St Mary's into disrepute. Bearing that in mind, we wore civvies, but smart ones.

Sands stayed in the car. The windscreen was pebble-dashed with the appropriate permits, parking tickets and passes, but as Markham had said, you don't take any chances with your getaway car.

I know the Boss always carries on as if Thirsk are the devil's representatives on earth, but they were lovely to us. One of the librarians had ready all the volumes I'd requested. A quiet table had been reserved for our use. They'd even laid on tea after our long journey. I felt terrible. So, by the looks of them, did everyone else.

We thanked the librarians politely and made ourselves comfortable. From where we were sitting, I could see the unobtrusive door on the back wall that led to the working areas behind the library. There was a keypad attached. Fortunately – for us that is – it chirped musically as each key was pressed. Markham propped a book in front of him, stared unseeingly at the pages, and hummed the notes to himself, jotting things down on a scrap of paper.

I opened a few books myself, took out my scratchpad, logged into their system, and began to work. Everyone else did the same. Four hardworking academics dedicated to their task. Mr Roberts twitched occasionally, but librarians are always convinced that everyone finds old books as fascinating as they do themselves and, in an environment that frowns even on heavy breathing, silent twitching is excitement made manifest.

Lunchtime came. Most people disappeared. Standing as if to relieve my back, I could see just one member of staff quietly shelving books down at the far end. No one else was in sight. There would never be a better opportunity.

Markham closed his book and pocketed his piece of paper. 'I've got it.'

'Really?'

'Easy. Just a tip, Max, always have a silent keypad.'

We made our way separately, each of us holding a book or scratchpad as camouflage, and silently converged on the door.

Roberts, despite his objections, was to stand guard and fend off anyone looking for us. He stationed himself in the Religion and Ritual section and opened a book at random.

'Suppose there are cameras?' he hissed. 'Should you cover your faces?'

'For God's sake,' said Peterson. 'One pregnant woman. One midget with mange. One incredibly handsome man. Who else could it be but us?'

'You're not that short,' said Markham.

'Just shut up and do the thing with the door.'

Markham took a deep breath, hummed a series of notes under his breath, and stared at the keypad. 'The first key is always the shiniest,' he muttered, flexed his fingers like an internationally renowned classical pianist, and then in one swift, confident movement, tapped in the code, twisted the handle, and stepped back to allow us in.

We found ourselves in a large, open workspace. Various tables were dotted around. Computer monitors stood on every flat surface. Map cabinets were ranged against the far wall. But artefacts – none.

'This way,' said Peterson, and we strode confidently across the room to another door. A long corridor stretched before us, with two doors on each side, helpfully labelled A45, A49, B15 and M400. I hoped their artefact classification system was a little less random than their door numbering.

The secret is not to creep. To look as if you have every right to be there. I was at the front, holding my scratchpad, cover story prepared, but we never needed it. The place was deserted. I probably shouldn't say this, but anyone wishing to break into a major academic establishment could do worse than consider a Friday afternoon. If challenged, our story was that we were lost and once we identified ourselves as St Mary's, no one would doubt it.

We worked our way down the corridor. We would tap at the door, receive no reply, and slither inside. Markham would keep watch while Peterson and I worked our way around the room, scanning the classification labels.

The last door was locked.

'Aha,' said Markham. 'A chance for me to demonstrate my talents again. Out of the way, Max. Let the dog see the rabbit.'

I stood nervously while he did whatever he needed to. There was no camera coverage in this corridor, but should anyone challenge us, our 'lost and confused' story wasn't going to account for Markham's obviously criminal activities. The one advantage, however, was that the fire door was right opposite, should we need to get out in a hurry.

More quickly than I could have imagined, there was a slight 'snick'.

'God, I'm good,' he said, stowing something away in his pocket.

Peterson and I surged forwards.

'Hang on,' he said. 'Seriously, you two shouldn't be allowed out on your own. If the door is locked then it's probably alarmed as well.'

'It's not the only one,' muttered Peterson. 'I'm bloody terrified.'

Markham had pulled out a tiny torch and was examining around the doorframe, muttering to himself. He inspected the handle closely.

'Well?' said Peterson, 'is it?'

'Don't know. Probably.'

'How can we find out?'

'Open the door and if a bloody siren goes off then yes, it is.'

'Can't you fix it?'

'No.'

'What's happening?' said Roberts in my ear.

'Technical discussion,' I whispered. 'Just keep your eyes open. And be prepared to move fast.'

Markham took hold of the handle. 'Do you know what you're looking for?'

'Yes,' said Peterson with confidence.

'I think so,' I said, with marginally less confidence.

'Right,' said Markham. 'On three.'

'One.' He opened the door and pushed us in.

'You said three,' I said accusingly.

'I lied.'

'What?'

'I've just broken into a top academic facility. On what grounds did you expect me to be truthful as well? Now get on with it.'

'The alarm didn't go off,' I said. 'That means we're OK.'

He looked at me pityingly. 'Ever heard the words "silent alarm"?'

'Oh.'

'Just bloody get on with it, will you. I'll watch the door.'

We found ourselves in a large room with floor-to-ceiling wooden drawers. Some were shallow. Some deep. Some were long and flat. Others tall and thin. Some were tiny. Some were glass fronted, displaying artefacts. The old wood was darkened with age. The brass handles gleamed. All the joints were beautifully dovetailed. It was a work of art in its own right. I would have given anything to be able to examine it at leisure. I sighed. It seemed very likely that after today, none of us would ever have that opportunity.

Our computer talks to their computer. We had the classification number. This should be a piece of cake.

'Right,' whispered, Peterson. 'It's a sword. Look for drawers that are long and flat.'

We divided the wall between us and began, as quietly as we could, to scan the labels. Being Thirsk, of course, they hadn't made it easy. Many of the labels were handwritten and had faded over time. I began to fret again.

I needn't have bothered. Peterson found it almost immediately. Lying in a specially constructed case, there it was.

This was really going well.

I crossed the room to look over his shoulder. The sword seemed – diminished – somehow. Pitted. Rusted. Old. Somehow sad. I remembered the images the Chancellor had sent me. How could it deteriorate in such a short time?

'Brilliant, Tim,' I said. Stepping aside, I opened my com. 'Roberts, Sands. We've found it. We just have to get it out now. Keep your coms open and be ready to move quickly.'

'This is encouraging,' said Markham, doing the finger-flexing thing again. 'I can't see any sort of security tags. I should just be able to lift it out. We'll leave the case. I know it's probably sacrilege, but I'm going to shove it down my trouser leg and we'll just walk out. We'll tell anyone who asks that we're going for lunch and just never come back. And it's Friday – we might have the whole weekend before anyone realises it's gone. They might not even connect the theft with us. I rather think we might get away with this after all, don't you?'

Gently, he reached out to touch the sword and with an ear-splitting shriek, every alarm in North Yorkshire went off.

'Bollocks,' said Peterson. 'No time for finesse,' and he yanked out the sword and handed it to Markham who pushed us out through the door. We didn't bother with the corridor, heading straight for the fire door, which Peterson kicked open. We raced down another hot, dry, dusty, dead fly-filled corridor lit only by a dingy skylight, burst through another fire door at the other end and erupted out into some sort of loading area.

We paused to get our bearings and make ourselves look respectable.

Both Sands and Roberts were jabbering away in my ear. In stereo.

'It's all gone tits up,' I said. 'Mr Roberts, please make your way back to the car. Standard procedures.'

By which I meant, don't draw attention to yourself. Don't catch anyone's eye. Don't keep looking over your shoulder. Most importantly – don't run.

'This way,' said Peterson. In the role of concerned colleague, he took my arm, presumably in case being pregnant had caused me to lose all sense of direction. Which, of course, implied I had one in the first place.

'Just a word of warning,' I said. 'If the going gets tough I intend to faint. Watch out I don't drag you down as well.'

We made our way slowly around the side of the building, back towards the car park.

Roberts said, 'I'm being evacuated out of the building. I've told them you'd gone for lunch. No one's looking for you.'

Yet.

'I'm nearly at the car,' he said. 'I can see Sands.'

Markham said, 'When you get there, stay there. No matter what you see or hear.'

'Copy that. Did you get it?'

'Course we did,' he said, cheerfully, ignoring the screeching alarms, the running people spilling out through the gates, the confusion, the chaos ...

I was familiar with this procedure. The alarms go off. People know it's only a fire drill or a bomb scare or something. Section heads have to cattle prod everyone out of the door because they're all shouting, 'I'll just finish this spreadsheet.' Or 'Are you kidding, I've waited all morning for access to this database,' or 'Wait, I need to go back for my shopping/handbag/shoes/whatever.' No one knows what's going on. The fire marshal is tearing her hair out trying to get everyone to congregate at the official assembly point AWAY from the building, people! The security people are trying to get in to see why the alarms have gone off. The fire brigade turns up, fruitlessly looking for someone who knows what's happening. Librarians have stopped to gather important documents. Members of the public try to drift away, not realising they need to be accounted for and the whole thing is just chaos.

We're St Mary's. We can do chaos.

We slipped quietly through the milling crowds, through the ornate gates and into the car park. We walked very slowly, stopping every now and then to have a good gawk at what was happening, because that was what everyone else was doing.

A car pulled up beside us and I very nearly had a heart attack, but it was Sands. Very pale, but quite calm. Roberts was with him. We climbed in, Markham very carefully not impaling his important bits on an even more important historical relic.

Sands drove very slowly through the crowds. No one spoke. People had milled out into the road outside. Pupils from the nearby school, for whom it was also lunchtime, had stubbed out their cigarettes and come to see what was happening. Council staff, streaming down the High Street had become embroiled in the confusion. If we had planned it, we could not have done better.

We drove slowly towards the roundabout just as a couple of police cars flashed past, lights on, and sirens blaring.

'Just keep going,' said Markham. 'If we're stopped, I'll throw the sword out of the window and we'll come back for it later.'

'No, we bloody won't,' I said, outraged. 'That thing's priceless and I'm not having you flinging it willy-nilly into ditches.'

We turned left at the roundabout and set off out of Northallerton. I twisted around and looked back over my shoulder. I very much doubted I would ever see the place again.

'Right,' said Peterson, unfolding his map. 'Head south if you please, Mr Sands.'

Now to the problem we hadn't really discussed because, quite honestly, we never thought we'd get this far.

'I've been thinking,' said Sands, as we skirted Leeds. 'It shouldn't be a problem. They'll never think to look in the cave. Why would they? They'll just assume some collector's stolen it and it's in a private collection somewhere.'

'Not as soon as they see it was us, they won't. They'll go straight to the cave.'

'No,' I said, heavily. 'We tell them we sold it on.'

'What?'

For an historian to steal a priceless artefact is bad enough. There are no words to describe one who would do it for money.

I took a deep breath. 'We tell them we were approached by someone whose identity we can't possibly divulge, and they offered us a huge sum of money to steal the sword, and it's already out of the country by now, and there's nothing they can do about it.'

The car was full of a stunned silence.

'What's the problem?' I said.

'Actually,' said Peterson, 'it's a very good idea. But what happened to the money?'

'They'll never know and we're not saying.'

'Bloody hell,' said Sands.

'Bloody brilliant,' said Markham.

I fell asleep in the car, which given my habitual insomnia was surprising, but the warmth, the silence, the hum of the tyres – I was out like a light.

I woke up as we slowed to exit the motorway and turn right for Herefordshire.

'Not long now,' said Roberts, passing me some water.

No one replied.

'Has anyone tried to contact us?' I said.

'We've switched our phones off.'

So far, the weather had been with us, dry and clear, but as we neared our destination, I could see wisps of something sitting in low-lying areas and occasionally trailing across the road.

'Bugger,' said Roberts. 'Fog.'

'All to the good, said Peterson. No one will see us.'

'True, but it's going to slow us down.'

The fog thickened. Sands switched on the fog lights. We slowed down.

'Told you,' said Roberts. 'We wouldn't have had this problem with a pod.'

'Turn left here,' said Markham, flapping the map around and nearly taking my eye out.

'I thought men were supposed to be able to fold those things. It's the universe's compensation for not being able to do anything else properly.'

I was instructed to do it my bloody self.

'This,' said Sands, 'is as close as I care to get. We're just outside the quarantine zone. There's a B&B over the road so with luck, everyone will think the car belongs to their guests.'

Markham flourished the map again. 'We cut across country here. Emerging ...' He stabbed the map with his finger, '... Here.'

No one moved.

'It's still not too late to turn back,' said Sands.

'Yes, it is,' I said, opening the car door. 'The moment we decided to do this, it was too late.'

'We need to stick together,' said Peterson, as we unpacked our boots, sprayed them yet again with our antibacterial stuff, and then gave them a good squirt of strong disinfectant just to be on the safe side. Sands sprayed the car tyres as well.

I looked around us.

The world was white.

I'd forgotten the smell. Wet leaves and earth. The distant smell of smoke. The muggy warmth. I looked again at the beads of moisture on my sleeve and for a second I was back in the 6th century as the Red Dragon snapped in the wind. I wondered if it was always like this in this area. As if, somehow, it had never escaped its own history and stood always, one foot in the here and now and one in the past. If I closed my eyes and listened, I could hear the movement of people all those long centuries ago. Hear their panting breath, the creak of the handcart. Or possibly it was just the wind in the trees.

Except there was no wind today. The world was close and still. We were the only things moving.

To begin with.

At least we didn't have to go all the way to the top this time. Arthur's Cave was on the hillside to the south east and the path was clearly marked.

We picked our way carefully, our footsteps quite silent in the fallen leaves and muffled by the fog.

Behind us, something moved.

I stood still and stared into the white depths.

'Deer,' said Roberts and why he was whispering was anyone's guess.

Then, another movement. Slightly closer, this time.

We stared around us. I could hear the gentle pattering of water on leaves. And, if I listened very hard and used my overheated imagination ... I could hear ... breathing ...

I tried hard not to think of tales of the Wild Woods. When things moved among the trees. When things stalked unwary travellers and led them astray.

Somewhere, a dog barked and another answered. The spell was broken. People walk their dogs in all weathers.

One of us laughed nervously and we picked up the pace.

I stumbled.

Markham took my arm. 'For God's sake, Max, be careful.'

'I'm fine. I had no idea you were such a wuss.'

'I just don't want to have to explain to Chief Farrell why you gave birth halfway up a Welsh hillside.'

'Are you scared of Leon?'

'More scared of him than I am of you.'

'Months to go yet. Stop panicking.'

A cool breeze dried the sweat on my face. The fog began to break into tendrils, which drifted, ghost-like across the path. I could see the wavering outline of trees, appearing and then disappearing again. I was conscious of an air of unreality. In this fog, nothing seemed real. Had I, in fact, woken up? Was I sleepwalking? Perhaps I was just tired.

Then, suddenly, we were there – the twin entrances just ahead of us. Two dark holes in the fog.

Not much had changed. Ferns and flowers still grew from the rocks, watered by the moisture running down them. The entrance seemed smaller somehow – fallen leaves and soil had built up over the centuries and we had to climb to get near. The trees seemed closer. Behind us, something moved in the undergrowth. We spun around, staying close together. I peered into the shifting fog, trying to make out shapes. A woman appearing along the path with two Labradors at her heels would have been a very reassuring sight, but there was nothing and no one.

We approached in silence, standing at the entrance to the cave, wondering what on earth to do next. Water dripped somewhere, otherwise the world was completely still. Did time actually pass here?

I don't know what made me do it. I turned slowly and got the shock of my life.

He stood behind us.

He hadn't changed. Not one bit. He still looked exactly as he had the last time we saw him. When Arthur handed him the sword. He was still wild-haired and dirty. Still with the tangled beard. Still wearing the same robe. Still with the same forbidding expression.

I dragged my eyes away and pulled at Peterson's arm.

'What?'

I looked back and he was gone.

'He was here.'

They turned. 'Who was?'

'The old man. He was here. Standing on the path just there.'

The path was empty.

We looked around – as much as we could in this strange white mist.

'Well, he's not here now.'

We turned back to the cave and there he was again. Standing between the twin entrances. Like the doorways to heaven and hell.

Roberts drew in his breath with sharp hiss.

No one moved.

We stood looking at each other for a very long time. I was conscious of a definite reluctance to get any closer. There was danger here. None of this was for us. We shouldn't be here.

Markham, who, thank the god of historians, had had the sense to pull the sword out of his trousers before attempting the long trek, handed the sword over to Peterson, who passed it to me.

I seriously thought about passing it to Roberts – he was the local boy after all – but I was head of the History Department. This was my responsibility and this was what I was paid for.

The old man's eye's followed the sword's every move.

He didn't move. Could he move? I don't know what put that thought into my head.

I took one small pace forwards, and when I survived that, another. Then another.

By now, I was only an arm's length away.

I offered up the sword.

His eyes were dark and deep. I couldn't look away.

He took it in silence.

We looked at each other. I could not have spoken to save my life. My throat had closed and I could barely breathe. Things receded. Bloody hell, surely I wasn't going to faint. Not now ...

I felt myself sway. The fog swirled closer. Someone grasped my arm, steadying me. My head cleared. When I looked up, the old man was gone.

'Where did he go?'

Roberts turned around. 'Back into the cave, presumably. Anyone want to go in to look?'

There was no reply. No one moved. I personally wouldn't have gone in there to save my life. I remembered that no one had entered the cave when the sword was first presented. Not allowed in then – not allowed in now.

The white mist swirled. Water dripped. We stood at the entrance to another world ... To linger would not be wise.

We ran. Well, as best as one pregnant woman, one man with a weak arm, one man with a bionic foot, a perky-eared security guard, and a beardless Welshman can run.

The drive back to St Mary's was accomplished in silence.

We were met by Major Guthrie who arrested us.

Chapter Ten

The gates were already open as we approached. We did not make the mistake of assuming this was a welcoming gesture.

We crawled slowly up the drive, listening to the loose stones bouncing off the bottom of the car, and pulled into the car park. Roberts switched off the engine and we sat in the sudden silence.

'Now what?' said Sands.

The question was answered for us.

Major Guthrie appeared and he wasn't alone. Evans, Cox, Gallaccio, and Keller were with him. None of them looked very friendly.

On the plus side, there was no sign of the police.

'Come on,' said Peterson. 'I'd rather go to him than have him come to us.'

We set off across the car park to where a bleak-faced Guthrie was waiting.

We stood before him in silence.

Finally, he said, 'You are all under arrest.'

We nodded.

'My first choice was to march you all through the building in handcuffs, but I have been instructed to tell you that if you give me a promise of good behaviour, then you will be spared that particular humiliation.'

I said, 'I agree.'

'What about the rest of you?'

'Max speaks for us all,' said Peterson quietly.

Never had Dr Bairstow's office seemed so far away.

We were walked through the building.

Through Hawking, where expressionless techies watched us go by. I couldn't see Leon anywhere.

Down the long corridor, passing from patches of bright light to deepest shade, it struck me suddenly that my whole life had been like that.

Past the kitchen, where Mrs Mack and her team clustered in the doorway as we passed.

Past Wardrobe, where people stuck their heads out of doors as we approached.

Through the Great Hall, where silent historians were lined up to watch us. Clerk and Prentiss stood together, saying nothing. Sykes looked distressed. I guessed she'd been yelling at someone, but whether she was for or against us was anyone's guess. Atherton sat quietly at his data stack, his face giving nothing away. North straightened up, folded her arms, and glared at us. We climbed the stairs, our footsteps sounding very loud in the unaccustomed quiet. Nobody said a word.

We walked past R&D where a troubled-looking Professor Rapson opened his mouth as if to speak and then closed it again. Someone plucked at his sleeve, Dr Dowson was my guess – and he turned away.

Past what wasn't going to be my office for very much longer.

Past Peterson's – ditto – and, finally, to our destination. Dr Bairstow's office. Major Guthrie tapped once and went in.

We were made to wait.

We lined up in Mrs Partridge's office, waiting to go in. No one spoke. I could faintly hear voices in his office. Mrs Partridge busied herself at her desk and ignored us.

I looked at us all – exhausted, muddy, thirsty, shocked – and made my voice as firm as I could.

'We expected this. We went into it with our eyes open. There's no choice now but to accept whatever comes our way.'

They nodded.

The door opened. Major Guthrie jerked his head, indicating we should enter.

We entered carefully and he closed the door behind him on his way out. I could feel my heart knocking against my ribs. It was evening by now, and the curtains were pulled across the window. The overhead light seemed dazzling. I trod across the familiar faded carpet and stood in front of his desk. His old clock ticked away in the corner as we waited for him to end our time at St Mary's.

It seemed an age before he spoke. 'Explain your actions.'

I gave it to him briefly, not bothering with excuses or justifications, taking full responsibility for my team's actions.

When I'd finished, he said nothing, his face expressionless, gazing at each of us in turn. I swallowed hard and forced myself to stare back again.

Roberts was visibly shaking. Nerves. Emotion. Fear. The effort of keeping it all inside. I don't know.

'I understand you regard yourselves as a team. Very well. I shall deal with you as such.'

Roberts stepped forwards. 'You should blame me, sir.

'I do blame you, Mr Roberts. I blame all of you.'

'It was my fault. It was my idea. I made them do it.'

'I recognise your attempt to save your colleagues, Mr Roberts, but it should be said that St Mary's can well do without senior officers who allow themselves to be so easily persuaded to show such poor judgement.'

'It wasn't poor judgement,' he said hotly. 'It was the right thing to do.'

'You stole a priceless artefact and ...'

'It wasn't stealing. It didn't belong to Thirsk.'

'No, it belonged to the owners of the cave, who happily loaned it to Thirsk for investigation and verification. Has it not crossed your mind that you have caused the university considerable embarrassment? What can they tell the owners who entrusted it to them?'

'They're not the owners. The sword belongs to the people to whom it was given.'

'Who are long dead.'

'Then it belongs to their descendants. Just because a person's dead doesn't mean their possessions automatically go to Thirsk for them to pick over like vultures over a carcass. I'm surprised at you, sir. You've always said that whatever we discover remains the property of the country in which it was discovered. You've always insisted upon it. What's so different about this? Is it the money? How much did Thirsk pay you to ...?'

At this point, both Peterson and Sands said, 'Shut up.'

He wasn't listening. The tears were rolling down his face, which was red with emotion. He looked even younger than ever. 'You're so caught up in its value and prestige that you've forgotten what it means. And the purpose for which it was given. You had no right to take it. You have no right to keep it. You're no better than looters.'

The silence in the room congealed into something unpleasant.

'Mr Roberts – you are dismissed.'

To this day, I'm not sure what Dr Bairstow meant by that phrase. Did he keep it deliberately ambiguous? It didn't matter because Roberts said, 'No I'm not. I resign,' spun on his heel and slammed the door shut behind him. Two seconds later, I heard Mrs Partridge's door slam as well.

Sands spoke into the silence. 'I resign as well. My notice will be on your desk in thirty minutes.'

He turned to us. 'Max, Peterson, it's been an honour and a privilege,' and then he too left the room.

The pain in my chest told me I'd forgotten to breathe again. My instinct was to fly after them, but neither of them would have thanked me. Roberts, I think, was too emotionally involved to think clearly, but Sands knew exactly what he was doing. Dr Bairstow could now legitimately say that two members of staff had been dismissed over this incident and that those remaining had been appropriately disciplined. It now remained for us to discover what form that discipline would take.

He started with Peterson.

'I see very little point in continuing to prepare you for the position of Deputy Director. I suppose I should be grateful that your unsuitability for the position has become apparent before either of us has wasted too much time on what has turned out to be a pointless exercise.'

Shit. Shit, shit, shit. I turned my head to stare at Peterson. He'd never said anything about this and he must have known what would happen. Wisely, he did not attempt to reply, just staring over Dr Bairstow's shoulder at the curtains behind him.

On to Markham. He sighed heavily. 'My fault, I suppose. I was aware of your criminal record when I employed you. I may as well tell you now that Major Guthrie is deeply disappointed by your behaviour. As am I. At his request, I have cancelled his recommendation that I regard you as his imminent successor as Head of Security.'

I'd thought as much. Guthrie had been planning to leave. To be with Grey. And now he couldn't. Someone else's future ruined.

Dr Bairstow paused. Because it was my turn now. I lifted my chin and thought furiously about not crying.

'How could you do this, Max? After everything I said to you last year – how could you do this to St Mary's?'

I hoped to God that the question was rhetorical because I didn't have an answer and, even if I did, my voice had fled. I fixed my eyes on him, felt a hot tear run down my face, and somehow croaked, 'I apologise, sir. I'm truly sorry.'

His face was cold. 'I wish this repentance had occurred before you actually perpetrated the crime. Before you dragged the professional reputation of St Mary's through the dirt. Before you jeopardised the future of an organisation to which I have devoted my life. Before you let down your colleagues and disappointed me.'

I was unable to speak.

'You are no longer my Chief Operations Officer. In fact, you are no longer an historian at all. All privileges are revoked. You may consider yourself grounded for life. You have made your last jump.'

For one mad moment, the world swirled around me. Behind me, Peterson put his hand in the small of my back. Support and comfort.

I swallowed so hard I hurt my throat and opened my mouth.

'No,' he said, as I made to speak. 'You will not resign. You will remain here – partly because St Mary's has invested a great deal of money and effort in you and I am reluctant to see it completely wasted – but mostly because you need to learn a lesson. There are consequences to each and every action. You will remain here and endure the consequences of yours. You will observe, at first hand, the unfortunate repercussions of your ...' he gritted his teeth, '... actions and their effects on others. Because of you, Dr Peterson is grounded until I deem otherwise. Mr Markham has lost all seniority and will be replaced as Major Guthrie's second in command. Mr Roberts and Mr Sands have each lost their jobs.'

He stopped again and began to align the files on his desk, his hands not quite steady.

'You have jeopardised the future of your colleagues. You have irreparably damaged the hard-won reputation of my unit. You have no conception of the lengths to which I have had to go over the years to convince various bodies that History is not a resource to be plundered at will. Only to find my senior staff have broken into an academic establishment and stolen a priceless artefact.'

He paused and I knew something horrible was coming. The only sound in the room was his ticking clock and my pounding heart.

'You should know that the only thing standing between all of you and a very long prison sentence was the Chancellor.'

Peterson said hoarsely, '*Was*, sir?'

'Heads had to roll, obviously. Despite making her and her university look ridiculous, the Chancellor fought our corner. Long and hard. She was, to some extent, successful. I am still here. However, as you yourselves are so fond of saying, "There's always a price to pay" and the Chancellor is the one who has paid it. They have forced her out. They are calling it retirement on the grounds of ill health, but she is out. To expect the new regime to regard St Mary's in a positive light will be unrealistic. At the very best, there will be rigorous scrutiny at every level. I am expecting them to establish a permanent presence here. At worst they will close us down.'

I could feel the sweat trickling down my back. Half of me was hot – the other half ice-cold. I would have given a very great deal to be able to sit down.

He pulled himself together. He hadn't finished with me.

'Since your actions have almost certainly compromised our future funding, you will devote such time as you have remaining here to finding alternative methods of raising the money we will soon be desperately short of. An appropriate wage will be paid to you, along with all maternity benefits you have accrued, but you will not return to St Mary's after the birth of your child. I leave it to you and Chief Farrell to determine your future. Furthermore, since your recent actions have demonstrated that you are not to be trusted in any way, you will ensure all work passes my desk. You will not, under any circumstances, initiate any action – any action at all – without written permission from me or a senior member of staff. Is that clearly understood?'

I nodded.

'I don't care where you work, but it will not be anywhere near the History Department. You are no longer an historian. Obviously, there will be occasions when interaction is unavoidable, but you will keep these instances to a minimum. The same goes for all other departments. You will report to me and to me alone. Kindly indicate your understanding.'

I nodded again.

'Having said that, I would be grateful if you could ensure your new duties keep you out of my office as much as possible, Miss Maxwell.'

And there it was. I was no longer a head of department. I'd lost my academic title. At St Mary's, only chief officers retain the courtesy of their academic titles. I was back to being Miss Maxwell again.

'In fact, I think it would be better for all concerned if I did not have to look at any of you for quite some considerable time. Dismissed.'

He opened a file and began to read.

I don't think any of us drew breath until we were safely on the other side of the door.

Mrs Partridge looked up. 'There will be an all-staff briefing in one hour when these staff changes will be announced,' she said. 'I am instructed to inform you that your attendance will be required.'

Shit. He was going to do it in public, in front of friends, colleagues … husbands …

We nodded and left.

Peterson led us to a quiet corner. I don't think any of us could face the world at that moment.

Markham took my arm. 'You all right, Max?'

'Fine,' I said, lying my head off.

'What now?'

I took a breath and tried to think. 'I have to see Roberts.'

'Best be quick, then. He won't be hanging around.'

He wasn't. He was hurtling around his tiny room, slinging his belongings into a sports bag. A closed suitcase stood by the door. A bulging bin bag was filled with stuff he wasn't taking with him. Posters had been ripped from the walls, bringing down lumps of plaster with them. They'd been savagely crumpled and most of them had been flung into the waste bin. Several of them had missed. He was crying with anger and frustration.

I tapped on the open door.

'Fuck off,' he shouted, without even bothering to turn around.

'Hey,' I said softly, stepping into his room.

'Max. Sorry. What happened? Did he sack you?'

'Death by inches, I said, easing my way around the bin bag. 'Replaced as head of department, grounded until the day I die, and not to bother coming back after maternity leave.'

'Oh God,' he said, sitting heavily on the bed. 'I'm so sorry.'

'Not your fault,' I said. 'We all agreed to it.'

'Peterson?'

126

'Still with us – just grounded.' I didn't mention he'd lost his chance at Deputy Director. The whole point was to calm Roberts down a little.

'And Markham?'

'Again, still with us. Reduced to the ranks, which won't bother him in the slightest.' I paused. 'Sands resigned.'

'What?'

'Voluntarily. There was no coercion. He's doing the grand gesture thing.'

'So who's left?

'Oh, he's got plenty of historians. Clerk will be the new head of department, I expect, and there's still Bashford and Prentiss. And Sykes, North and Atherton, as well. And Grey.'

'Three of them are still Pathfinders. Grey's not … well, we know what Grey is. He has only three historians. He can't possibly operate with just three. He'll have to reinstate you and Peterson.'

Now did not seem the moment to tell him I'd be extremely surprised if the History Department was allowed to operate at all, let alone with only three historians.

I tried to get him to wait at least an hour or two. Maybe to have something to eat and calm down a little before roaring off into the night, but he couldn't wait to get out. I made him promise to drive carefully. 'Please, Gareth. I can't take any more grief today.'

He stopped, took a deep breath, and threw me a wobbly smile. 'I will. I promise.'

'I mean it. I don't want you being the next piece of bad news.'

He shook his head. 'The sword's back where it belongs. That's all ended now. You wait and see.'

I hoped to God that his quiet confidence wasn't misplaced. If we'd done all this for nothing … I shook myself and said briskly, 'Very possibly, but it doesn't mean you're bloody immortal. Just go carefully is all I ask.'

He nodded, and at that moment, someone said, 'Knock-knock,' and Sands came in, followed by Markham and Peterson.

I said, 'David, what are you going to do?'

'Oh, I've got one or two ideas. Don't worry about me.'

'But I will.'

'You haven't heard the last of me, I promise you. And Rosie will keep you in touch.' I'd forgotten about him and Rosie Lee. Was this the end for them as well? How much damage had we done today?

'We'll walk you out,' said Peterson, and we did.

We walked them down the stairs, striding through the Hall, where people were beginning to gather for the meeting. Silence fell whenever people saw us. There was no sign of Clerk or Prentiss, both of them tactfully absent. People stood back from us, unsure of what was happening.

Markham stiffened.

'Not their fault,' muttered Peterson. 'Keep walking.'

We stood outside on the steps. The night was cold and there was rain in the air.

'Why have we come out of the front door?' I said. 'The car park's round the back.'

Sands let his bag drop. 'An act of defiance,' he said. You never creep about when you're in deep disgrace. Heads up. Look them in the eye. Leave by the front door.' He turned to us. 'You should go back inside. You don't want to be late.'

'It makes very little difference now,' I said quietly, and for a moment, his mouth twisted. I put my hand on his forearm and he turned away.

Roberts brought his car around. We stowed their gear and then stood awkwardly.

'Well,' I said, 'since Dr Bairstow wouldn't say it, I hope you will accept it from me. Mr Sands, Mr Roberts, St Mary's thanks you for your service.'

'Very acceptable,' said Sands. He shook my hand. 'It's been an honour and a privilege.'

I nodded, too choked to speak, suddenly realising I'd never hear another 'knock-knock' joke from him again. Never again would I tease Roberts about his bum-fluff.

Roberts shook my hand, tried to smile, failed, and climbed into the car.

We watched them drive away. Roberts spraying gravel and crashing the gears in his haste to get out of the gates.

'Sands will pull him over in the village,' said Markham, confidently. 'He's just letting him have his big exit.'

'You sure?'

'Well, that's what I told him to do.'

I tried not to think about what an excellent head of Security he would have made had he ever been given the chance.

The three of us looked at each other.

'Well,' said Peterson. 'We'd better go and face the music, I suppose.'

We had the sense to sit at the back and St Mary's had the manners not to turn around and stare at us as the announcement was made. I could see the back of Leon's head as he sat next to Guthrie in the front row. Clerk sat on his other side. Where I used to sit. I wondered what he was going to say to me. Leon, I mean.

The briefing finished and we left as soon as we could.

'Right,' said Peterson. 'I don't know about anyone else, but I could really do with a drink.'

'Give me a moment,' I said. 'I want to shower and change.'

'Me too,' said Markham. 'We'll meet in the bar in twenty minutes to discuss things.'

'What things?'

'Survival strategy. The coming weeks are not going to be pleasant.'

He was right. They weren't, and it was starting now, because Leon was waiting for me.

'It's your own fault,' scolded my inner voice, not so active these last few years, but now back with a vengeance. 'To put yourself in a position where the good opinion of one person is so important to you. What were you thinking? How could you be so stupid? To leave yourself vulnerable to the opinions of others. Of one person in particular. And now look what's come of it. He's unhappy, so you're unhappy he's unhappy. What sort of idiot are you?'

A very good question.

'Before we start throwing the furniture around,' he said, 'I have something to say.'

I folded my arms. 'Go on.'

'As Chief Technical Officer I am angrier than I can possibly say. That you could do such a thing beggars belief.'

I unfolded my arms and prepared to disembowel him.

He continued. 'As your husband, I am mildly exasperated at your inability to stay out of trouble. At this particular moment, I am this unit's CTO. Later tonight I will be your husband. All right?'

Somewhat deflated, I nodded.

His first question was mild enough. 'So, what's this all about?'

I remembered what Sands had said about never creeping about when you're in disgrace and came out swinging.

'You know what it's all about. Don't tell me you and Dr Bairstow haven't spent hours discussing this and agreeing on appropriate punishments.'

He said quietly, 'I think you sometimes forget that until Peterson takes over as Deputy Director, I am second in command of this unit.'

'Well, that's not going to happen now, is it?'

He stiffened. 'Are you suggesting I've been personally motivated in all this?'

I don't know if this happens to anyone else, but when I'm hurt and angry and ashamed and guilty I feel the need to lash out and damage someone else.

'Well, of course you are. You have exactly what you wanted. I'm out of St Mary's without you even lifting a finger. And Peterson won't be superseding you as second in charge. You'll have the little wife at home doing little wife things in the house with her baby and you'll be a proper number two, won't you?'

'I'm making allowances for you at the moment because you're upset and when you're calmer you'll know that none of that is true.'

'Really? Well, I'm sure you think you're right.'

'What's got into you?'

I whirled around. 'I've broken the law, lost my job, lost others their jobs too, ruined the career prospects of my two best friends, and wrecked our funding opportunities for the foreseeable future. What the hell do you think has got into me?'

There was a ringing silence and then I slammed into the bathroom. I threw my clothes around the room and climbed into the shower. After two minutes, an arm appeared around the curtain with a mug of tea. Drinking tea in the shower isn't easy, but I appreciated the thought and gave it a bloody good go.

He was gone when I came out.

Fifteen minutes later, I strode into the bar full of wrath and rebellion, fully intending to break a few more rules – mostly the ones concerning pregnant women and the levels of alcohol deemed appropriate by those who take it upon themselves to deem such things. Typically, once I got there, I found I'd lost the taste and had to make do with a rebellious tonic water instead.

I wondered if I would ever grow accustomed to people falling silent whenever I walked past.

Peterson and Markham had already bagged a table and I joined them. Judging by the number of glasses on the table, they'd been there for some time. I raised my glass.

'*Illegitimi non carborundum*, guys.'

'Actually,' said Markham, turning his glass around on the table, 'I thought that could have gone much worse.'

We regarded him in astonishment.

'Did you miss the bit about Roberts and Sands resigning?' demanded Peterson. 'Or Max being demoted and being made to stay and face people every day?'

Typically, he didn't mention his own ruined chances.

'No,' said Markham quietly. He leaned forwards and so did we. 'But I did miss the bit where Dr Bairstow demanded to know the whereabouts of the sword so that it could be returned to Thirsk.'

We sat back.

'So did I,' admitted Peterson.

I nodded in agreement, turning over the implications. That should have been the first thing he asked. Should have been his main priority. Returning the sword to what the world considered to be its rightful owners would have gone a long way to making things right again, and for some reason, he hadn't done so. Hadn't even mentioned it. Was it possible ...?

'Doesn't mean he won't have us back again tomorrow and start pulling out our fingernails,' said Peterson, gloomily.

'And even if he doesn't, tomorrow isn't going to be good for us,' said Markham. He looked at me. 'How are you doing?'

He meant Leon.

'He's oscillating,' I said. 'One minute I'm being blamed for everything under the sun and the next minute he's shoving a mug of tea under my nose. I'll get through it.'

'We all will,' said Markham. 'Just a few suggestions. We stick together. Not necessarily physically, although I think that's a good idea, since we're social pariahs at the moment, and likely to remain so for some time, but we should eat together at least.'

'Agreed,' I said. 'And we never look downcast, or miserable.'

'Or guilty,' added Peterson. 'That's important.'

We nodded.

'And we don't discuss anything with anyone. I'm afraid that includes Leon and Hunter.'

Markham and I agreed. He looked around the room. The way people were ignoring us was making us the centre of attention. 'The next few days are going to be a bitch.'

Back in my room, the Chief Technical Officer had disappeared and my husband sprawled across the sofa in jeans and a dreadful old sweater he wouldn't throw away because it was the one he had been wearing when I appeared in his workshop. He regarded me somewhat warily. 'Who am I talking to at the moment?'

'Both of us,' I said, wearily, plopping down beside him. 'The ex-Chief Ops Officer and your wife, and both of them are very, very sorry. Leon …'

'No,' he said, pulling me onto his lap. 'Don't say anything. Not tonight. Tomorrow the Chief Technical Officer will shout at the ex-Chief Ops Officer who will probably throw her boots at him, but tonight, right now, you are my wife, and you're unhappy and tired, and more than a little frightened of the future.'

I nodded. No point in denying it.

'Could your husband have a word with his wife?'

'Wife speaking – go ahead.'

'There's a small cottage available for twelve month's rent. Down in the village. Do you know the one?'

'Dark green door almost opposite the pub?'

'That's the one.' He groped in his pocket and fished out a crumpled piece of paper. 'Two beds. Kitchen, living room. Breakneck staircase. Small garden at the front. Yard at the back. Nice views over the fields. Recently modernised. Semi-furnished. What do you think?'

'It sounds ideal. When's it available from?'

'Now.'

Silence.

'Only, I was thinking, there's no reason at all why we couldn't move in at the weekend. We sign a contract, hand over the deposit and Bob's your uncle.'

He was offering me a face-saving way out. By this time next week, I could be gone from St Mary's. I was eligible for maternity leave. Whatever Dr Bairstow had said, I could – if I wished – leave at any moment and start my new life. I had visions of a cosy cottage, a crackling fire. Me sitting in the garden, painting, with a gurgling and unrealistically clean baby at my feet. I was so far lost to reality as to imagine savoury smells issuing from the kitchen where something tasty nestled happily in the oven and Leon looked on in astonished admiration.

Sometimes I think I'm my own worst enemy. This sunny picture was replaced by a vision of Markham and Peterson sitting alone forever, while I waltzed off and played Happy Families. I couldn't do it to them.

I smiled at him because I appreciated the offer, and said, 'Thank you. It sounds just what we were looking for. Sign a contract by all means, but if it's all the same to you, I'll finish my time here. I've always said I'll work until just before my due date, and that's what I'd like to do.'

I held my breath in case he took it badly, but he said, 'I thought that's what you'd say.'

'Are you annoyed?'

'Not at all. I'm just relieved you haven't suggested installing the other two misfits in the spare room.'

'Oh no. I'd never do that. I was thinking of the garden shed.'

Silence. I stared at my hands.

'Leon, I …'

'What?'

'I was just thinking …'

'What?'

'That I'm lucky. Because things are much easier for me. All I have to do is believe in you implicitly, and that's easy because I know you will never, ever, let me down.' I drew a difficult breath. 'I, on the other hand, have let you and everyone down quite badly and the thought of your … disappointment in me is more than I can handle at the moment.'

He pulled me close.

I put my arms around his neck like a child. He rested his cheek on top of my head, and we sat in silence for a very long time.

Chapter Eleven

Seven days later, the Chancellor – or Dr Chalfont, as she now wished to be known – turned up to visit the Boss. They were in his office all day. I was terrified she would want to see me, and how I was even to look her in the eye, let alone speak to her, was not something I could think about. I hung about, expecting at any moment to be summoned to Dr Bairstow's office to account for my actions. I cudgelled my brains for something – anything – I could say to her, something that would be even remotely acceptable under the circumstances, and couldn't think of a damned thing. There really were no words.

The summons never came. At about four o'clock, I watched from an upstairs window as Dr Bairstow escorted Dr Chalfont to her car. They shook hands and he patted her gently on the shoulder in a way that made my eyes fill up. By the time I'd blinked the tears away, her little car was slingshotting down the drive, out through the gates, and away; and that was when I realised that whatever she could have said to me wasn't anywhere near as bad as her not saying anything at all.

And it wasn't just her. No one spoke to me. No one spoke to any of us. Sands telephoned, reporting Roberts safely delivered to his family home, and that he himself was hiding out in Rushford, at Rosie Lee's tiny house.

'A bit of a silver lining for me,' he said cheerfully. 'It's a great opportunity for her to realise how wonderful I am.'

I smiled into the phone. Just hearing his voice made me feel a thousand times better.

He burbled on. 'Listen, if you ever need a sanctuary, we're down by the medieval bridge, at the foot of the hill.'

'Thank you,' I said, touched. 'But at the moment, we're not allowed to leave the unit without the permission of a senior officer.'

He was silent for a while. 'How bad is it?'

'It's fine,' I said, lying through my teeth.

Because it really wasn't.

Leon, typically, was dealing with everything in his own fashion. The Chief Technical Officer made sure he barely saw the ex-Chief Ops Officer. He was gone when I awoke each morning, and he spent every day in Hawking, citing pressure of work. Since everyone was grounded while Dr Bairstow, Thirsk and some small anonymous government department tried to work out what to do with us, it was hard to see how much pressure there could be, but I appreciated the gesture.

Anyway, the Chief Technical Officer worked all day in Hawking. My husband returned late in the evening, climbed into bed, and curled himself around me as I lay and stared into the darkness.

The three of us, Peterson, Markham and me, were completely isolated.

Guthrie, bitterly hurt and disappointed, could barely bring himself to speak to Markham, and the rest of the section lined up behind their commanding officer. All the nasty, dirty jobs around the unit that had hitherto been shared out among them with scrupulous fairness were now detailed in their entirety to Markham. He became increasingly dirty, increasingly smelly and increasingly cheerful, confiding to us during what was by now our traditional post-dinner drink, that it pissed people off no end if, far from regarding yourself as being punished, you show them you're actually having a cracking time. That was his public face. I suspected that privately, just like Peterson and me, he was lonely, tired, and unhappy. I had no idea how his relationship with Hunter was progressing. He never said, and I never asked.

Peterson, still at least a member of the History Department, put on a brave face and uncomplainingly did everything that was asked of him. Which wasn't much. Nothing was happening – all assignments were on hold – our future was looking very shaky and people felt it was our fault. Which it was. I saw him uncomplainingly photocopying, filing, and making people's tea, and was proud of him.

Dr Dowson, hearing from somewhere that I was looking for a place to work, had smiled gently at me, and shown me to a quiet table in the Archive. It was set back in the little-used Cretan pottery section, well out of public view.

'It's a quiet table,' he announced, in case I hadn't noticed that fact. 'In the Cretan pottery section,' he'd added. 'Not used much.'

I nodded drearily and then, because I didn't want to seem ungrateful, managed a small smile.

He patted my shoulder and left me, and there I sat all day, alone in the silence, full of humiliation and resentment.

After a day or so, I realised he'd actually done me a great favour, because I wasn't dealing well with this. I didn't have Markham's cocky bravado or Peterson's patient dignity. I was a maelstrom of badly contained emotion.

Guilt, obviously, because of what we'd done.

A kind of perverse pride, because of what we'd done.

Defiance, because I was in the wrong and I knew it.

Shame and even more guilt, because of what we'd done to St Mary's and Dr Bairstow.

Fear for the future, and what it could hold for me.

A dreadful feeling of isolation, because I wasn't a part of St Mary's any longer.

Hurt, because no one from the History Department came anywhere near me.

Together with a whole raft of random, unfocused resentment just to fill in any gaps left.

I'm not good at handling emotion. I dealt with all the above by trying to ignore it. I wasn't the slightest bit successful and after I'd spent yet another afternoon with tears rolling down my cheeks and plopping on to my paperwork, I came to see what a favour Dr Dowson had done me by shoving me in this out of the way spot.

Because of what had happened to Sands, I had thought Rosie Lee might hate me, but far from it. Or no more than usual.

'He's happy,' she said, when I hesitantly enquired after him. 'But, on the other hand, he's happy wherever he is.' She paused to contemplate this phenomenon. 'He misses the place, of course, but he's not sitting around being melancholy.'

Was she having a go at me? Of course she was.

'What's he doing these days?'

'Well, at this very moment, he should be picking Benjamin up from school.' Benjamin was her son. 'They'll go to the park for an ice cream they think I don't know about, and a bit of a kick around. Then he'll take him home and they'll work on their Lego model of the proposed Mars habitat. Then I'll arrive and they'll attempt to explain the mess. I'll glare at the pair of them – for all the good it will do – then we'll have something to eat. I'll take Benjamin off to bed and David will get on with his writing.'

'His writing?'

'He's writing a book,' she said, obviously feeling her fears over her ex-boss's intelligence had been fully justified.

I remembered Sands' long and entertaining reports. His account of Viking life in Jorvik had been submitted in the form of a saga.

'Lo! In days long gone
Did the shining people-folk
Of St Mary's
Venture forth
To toil for truth's treasure
Amid the fair-faced folk
Of Jorvik.
Clerk the commander, clear eyed and calm,
Brain-beaten Bashford, bright eyed and brave,
North the normal, nettlesome and nitid.
Pale-haired Prentiss, piloting the pod.
Great warriors were they,
Stout of heart,

Supple of arm,
Strong of purpose,
Trawling for truth 'mid the tempest of Time'.

'Nitid?' I'd said. 'Seriously?'

He'd grinned. 'Why not?'

And his account of Cretan bull-jumping had had all the excitement and pace of a modern thriller. I know Dr Bairstow had enjoyed it because he'd barely deducted anything from his wages that month.

Anyway, the creativity that had occasionally landed him in trouble here was obviously being put to good use out there. Good for him. And most importantly, as Miss Lee said, he was happy.

There was more good news. One dreary, rainy morning, I saw Peterson, sorting the post. As I drew level, without looking up, he said, 'Check your personal emails.'

Back in my room, I dragged my laptop out from under the bed and switched it on to find a message from Roberts. With some difficulty, because bits of me seemed to be ballooning out of control, I sat cross-legged on the floor and read:

Hi Max,

Sands says things aren't going well for you at the moment so I thought I'd let you know. NOT foot and mouth. My dad's out hugging his cows. My mam says bloody typical, but she's laughing. And crying a bit, too. We have a bit of a knees-up planned for the weekend. Wish you could come but Sands says you're not allowed out.

Take care Max. I'll never forget what you've done and I wish I could make things right for you as you made things right for us.

Gareth.

Suddenly, the world wasn't so rainy or dreary. Roberts and his family were all right. Sands – typically – was carving out a new life for himself. Everyone was OK. It was time I was as well.

I looked at my dingy little desk with new eyes. The best thing I could do now was rub everyone's nose in it by being the most successful fundraiser ever. In the entire history of the world. I pulled out a piece of paper, drew a square, carefully coloured it in and began to scribble random thoughts. I joined these together with dotted lines. I drew boxes around some and circles around others. Activating my data table, I got stuck in.

I compiled lists. I drafted letters. At my request, Mrs Partridge initiated me into the mysteries of desktop publishing. I designed and produced leaflets. I studied local school syllabuses and looked at tailoring specific lectures. I sent out flyers. I wrote to our local TV and radio stations. I sent articles off to history and archaeological magazines, describing the work of St Mary's and the range of services we could offer. I frightened myself to death and opened a Facebook page for St Mary's. I learned to twitter. Or tweet. Actually, I never really got the hang of that. I contacted local libraries and spoke to the County Archivist. Every Friday, I bundled up a massive pile of papers and sent them off to Dr Bairstow. Every Monday morning, they came back with the word 'Approved' stamped across the top.

I spread out. Dr Dowson found me another table. Then another. Then a filing cabinet. Peterson commented that St Mary's might soon find itself working for me. We were sitting in our usual tight little group in the bar. People still didn't know how to deal with us. No one sat with us to eat, or drank with us in the bar. We had a routine. Breakfast together and map out our day. We would listen carefully to each other's plans because no one else was interested. We would make suggestions – as if we were about to spend the day doing something that mattered – and then we would bustle off, each of us pretending for the sake of the others.

Over lunch, we would tell each other how our morning had gone, chattering brightly, not catching anyone's eye, all our attention on each other. Then we'd do the same for the afternoon. And the evening as well, except we did it in the bar.

It was all a hollow show. All for the benefit of others, but we never let down our guard. Never revealed our private faces. As I'd said at the beginning, 'Don't let the bastards grind you down,' and we didn't.

We had our routine. We stuck to it.

The worst part was not commenting on the invariably grubby state of Markham. Things were really not going well for him. Sometimes he'd been fighting, although he never mentioned it. At one point we watched him trying to get to grips with his jam roly-poly with a spiral of bloodstained tissue protruding from each nostril.

He struggled through his meal, insisting everything was fine, but it wasn't, and afterwards, more to keep him out of everyone's way than anything, I took him up to Sick Bay so Hunter could check him out.

I ushered him through the doors and sat him down. Succumbing to the need for yet another bladder break, I trotted off to find the facility.

When I came out, he was sitting on the bench alone, resting his forearms on his knees, head bowed and, because he thought no one could see him, a picture of forlorn dejection. I hesitated, wondering what to do for the best, but before I could do anything, Hunter came out of the treatment room with a tray full of antiseptic wipes and gauze dressings. She stood for a moment, watching him. He looked up at her and after a moment, smiled a wobbly smile that tore at the strings of my heart.

And hers, apparently. She said, 'Hey,' very softly and took him in her arms. He wrapped his own arms around her waist and rested his head against her, his little face a picture of misery. She leaned protectively over him, gently stroking his hair and murmuring something. He closed his eyes, and for that moment, they were the only two people in the whole world. I sneaked along the corridor to the door, leaving the two of them to comfort each other.

Chapter Twelve

It had to happen, of course. Thirsk turned up. Because, thanks to the three of us, they were our overlords now.

There were two of them in the advance guard. I believe Dr Bairstow gave them the tour, introducing them to everyone. If they were impressed, then I had yet to hear of it. Not that they came anywhere near me. I heard their voices in the Library, and there was a cursory inspection of the Archive. I don't know if Dr Dowson was protecting or concealing me, but I was grateful. I sat quietly until they went away and then continued with my work.

The first I saw of them was in the dining room. The three of us were sitting at our usual table, the one at the back, out of the way, when they entered, stared around them, and sat down, waiting to be served.

I stared curiously, not liking the look of either of them very much. She was small and mousey. With her slightly protruding teeth, she reminded me of a small mammal, perpetually poised for flight. I discovered later that she was romantically inclined. She would sit in the bar every night, reading books with such titles as *The Prince and the Passion* or *The Secret Places of her Broken Heart,* or *Love's Longings*, the covers of which usually depicted a scantily clad young woman sprawled gracefully and adoringly at the feet of a muscle-bound colossus with a lunch box the size of Rushfordshire. That the heroine never caught her death of cold was explained by the city/castle/farmhouse behind them, exploding in a raging inferno which, inexplicably, neither of them appeared to have noticed.

Today Miss Mousey sat quietly, all her attention on her boss, who was eye-catching for all the wrong reasons. I disliked him on sight. For the first time, I felt a little thankful I wasn't Chief Ops Officer any longer. The thought of having to deal with him on a daily basis was not a pleasant one. He was tall and grey-haired with knobbly fingers, and he walked like a wading bird, his head and neck erect and unmoving as he thrust his legs out in front of him.

'Like a disdainful flamingo with a stick up its arse,' I said, a little more loudly than I intended.

He showed no sign he had heard, but I bet he did. I tried to tell myself I was leaving anyway and it didn't matter.

I think that by now it had dawned on him that he wasn't going to be served. I noticed Dr Bairstow making a rare appearance at one of the quiet tables, a newspaper and cup of tea in front of him. He hadn't once looked up but he knew what was going on. The fact that he hadn't strolled over with a friendly piece of advice about serving themselves was interesting.

We sat watching, quietly enjoying the scene and laying bets on how long it would take them to get the message.

'So,' I said, pouring water for Markham, whose right hand was bruised and swollen, 'do either of you know which is which?'

'That's Mr Halcombe and his assistant, Miss Dottle.'

There was a thoughtful silence and then Peterson said, 'Wouldn't it be great if his first name was Malcolm? He'd be Malcolm Halcombe.'

We had a bit of a giggle because there wasn't a lot to laugh about these days.

'*And*,' I said, grinning at them. 'If he was born in Devon, he'd be Malcolm Halcombe from Salcombe.'

Which set us off again. Oscar Wilde would have disowned us all.

We both looked at Markham, who rose magnificently to the challenge.

'And, if he's particular about personal hygiene, he'd be talcum Malcolm Halcombe from Salcombe.'

Yes, I know, but it felt so good to have something to laugh about again. I was just wiping my eyes when something rather nasty happened.

Without looking at Miss Dottle, Halcombw said abruptly, 'Get me a coffee.'

She sat frozen, turning crimson with mortification. For a moment, I thought she was going to cry. She hesitated, looking around to see who was watching.

St Mary's stared, open mouthed at such discourtesy. I mean, it's fine to call someone 'a cack-handed pillock with all the personal charisma of a sea slug', but you don't just sit there and say, 'Get me a coffee.' Who did he think he was? Dr Bairstow always served himself. I'm sure Mrs Mack would happily have served him if he'd asked, but he always looked after himself, along with the rest of us.

The room was filled with a silence that Halcombe didn't seem to notice.

Peterson, always soft hearted, pushed back his chair, but before he could move, Rosie Lee was there.

'Allow me,' she said sweetly, and disappeared in the direction of the kitchen.

St Mary's blinked and endeavoured to come to terms with the idea of Rosie Lee using her powers for good.

The silence was complete as she made her way back again with a steaming cup and saucer. Past an uncharacteristically quiet History Department. Past Dr Bairstow who had, until that moment, been enjoying a rare moment of peace and quiet. He raised his eyes as she walked past, his face unreadable. She'd once been his PA – he knew her well. Well enough to shunt her on to me at the earliest opportunity, anyway. Catching my eye, he picked up his newspaper and limped slowly out of the dining room, to all appearances unaware of the drama going on around him. Wise move.

Reaching Mr Halcombe's table, Rosie Lee placed the cup and saucer before him with the careful reverence of a holy relic,

I waited, holding my breath. If he said thank you, then there was still a chance she'd change her mind and say, 'Oh sorry, I put sugar in it and you don't, do you?' and whip it away.

He didn't. Far from thanking her, he couldn't even be bothered to look up. He was too busy making his statement. Sadly for him, he missed St Mary's making theirs.

She smiled sweetly, bobbed something that in a lesser woman might have been a curtsey, and backed off in a hurry.

He reached out his hand for his cup. If anyone was going to say anything, now was the moment.

No one said anything. It did briefly cross my mind that no matter how unhappy everyone was with us these days, at least no one had actually tried to poison us.

He sat sipping his coffee, staring around him, watching us watching him. When he finished, he replaced the cup in the saucer and patted his lips with a napkin. Seeing Rosie Lee still seated at a nearby table, he pushed the cup a little way towards her and said, 'I've finished.'

To the huge astonishment of everyone present, as if she'd been waiting for this moment, she stood up, collected his cup and saucer, smiled angelically and said, 'You're a bit of an arsehole, aren't you?'

If he was taken aback, he made a quick recovery. Shrugging his shoulders dismissively, he said, 'Nice coffee. Shame about the gob.'

She smirked. 'Oh, I don't know. You drank it, didn't you?' Holding his eye just long enough to make sure he realised what she'd done, she plonked his cup back on the table and walked away.

Abruptly, he pushed back his chair. Without even looking at Miss Dottle, he exited the room, leaving her there alone.

She sat quietly for a while, obviously unsure what to do next. I felt so sorry for her. No wonder she dreamed of romance. Personally I'd be dreaming of homicide, but most people are much nicer than me.

Peterson got to his feet, picked up his untouched cup of tea and took it to her table. He placed it gently in front of her, saying quietly, 'We tend to serve ourselves here.'

She smiled up at him and nodded her thanks. She did drink a few sips and then, obviously uncomfortable, she too got up and left.

'Well,' I said, watching her go.

Markham shrugged. 'Coffee drinker,' he said. 'What do you expect?'

There was an all staff briefing a day later. I didn't attend. Actually, it would be more accurate to say I wasn't invited. I sat in my little rabbit hole and pretended I didn't care. The upshot, as reported to me by Peterson and Markham, was that normal service was to be resumed, but that there was to be a Thirsk presence on most jumps. That would mean just Halcombe and Dottle to begin with but there would soon be many more. With rotas and schedules. St Mary's would be reduced to little more than chauffeurs.

'Apparently, there's a quota.'

'A what?'

'A quota. You know. A target.'

'I know what a quota is – are you saying they've applied one to St Mary's?'

'Yep. Three jumps a week or thirteen a month. Minimum.'

'But that's preposterous. What about pod maintenance? What about rest periods?'

'Rest periods at the end of every jump. Twenty-four hours. To be taken on site.'

'What?'

'Exactly.'

'But what about fires, plagues, battles, etc. The need to get out in a hurry. What does he think he's playing at? He's an idiot.'

'No Max, he's been quite clever. Twenty-four hours at the end of every jump and before we return to St Mary's means it's on our own time. Suppose we jump on a Monday, spend one week observing, say, the Highland Clearances, rest for twenty-four hours but return on the Wednesday. That's eight day's work for only three day's pay.'

I could hardly believe what I was hearing. Even Dr Bairstow with his reluctance to part with any sum of money higher than double figures never dreamed up anything as unfair as that.

'This guy has got to go.'

'Agreed.'

On that day, we didn't even pretend to be cheerful.

Two days later, I was sitting in the Library, compiling a list of establishments who might, at a push, be persuaded to have St Mary's come and talk to them about History. Schools, colleges, local-history societies, re-enactment groups, authors, independent programme-makers – I was casting my nets wider than one of those commercial fishing ships, from whom not even the smallest fish could hope to escape.

Dr Dowson appeared. 'Telephone call for you Max.'

I looked up. 'For me? Are you sure?'

'Oh yes. They were most insistent.'

'But ...'

'They're waiting.'

Sighing, I put down my scratchpad, wandered into his office and picked up the phone.

'Hello?'

'Max? Is that you? No, don't ask questions. Just listen.'

I did listen and then, very slowly and carefully, replaced the receiver. Laying my head on the desk, I took a minute or two to pray for patience.

The god of historians, true to form, had wandered off.

Why me?

Well, that was easy. Clerk and Prentiss were off in Etruscan Rome, lucky devils. Atherton was prepping for the Monmouth Rebellion, and North was – somewhere. It didn't really matter where – she certainly wasn't the right person for this particular crisis.

I had a quick think and then, picking up a file as camouflage, strolled casually upstairs to R&D. I needed to leave the unit, and under this new regime, I could only do that accompanied by a senior manager. Which officially, of course, he was.

Something everyone always forgot. Including, probably, Professor Rapson himself.

I explained why I needed him. He goggled and then, on my instructions, ordered us a taxi. We met it at the gates, walking slowly and casually down the long drive because Dr Bairstow doesn't miss a thing. I had no idea whether anyone else was watching us, but it seemed safe to assume I was under close observation. Professor Rapson chatted amiably about everything under the sun, waving his arms around to illustrate his points, and I could only hope that from a distance, we looked comparatively unsuspicious. Looking normal was perhaps aiming a little high.

'Well,' he said, settling himself comfortably in the back of the taxi and looking around with the air of one who doesn't get out much. 'What's all this about, then?'

I took a deep breath and said as unemotionally as I could manage, 'It would appear that Bashford, Miss Sykes and Miss Lingoss, have been arrested.'

He was relatively unsurprised. 'For what?'

'Transportation of a dead body.'

He was most indignant. 'How did they manage to lay their hands on a dead body? I've been submitting applications for years. I tell people it's for serious research and they just laugh at me. This is so unfair, Max. Why them and not me?'

I rather thought he might have missed the point slightly. While I struggled for words to readjust his ideas, he carried on. 'Is it the transportation or the dead body itself that's causing the problem? You probably have to have all sorts of licences to move them around and I'm sure they won't have had the foresight to ...'

'I'm not sure that's quite the issue here, Professor.'

'Oh. Do we have any details?'

'We do.' I said grimly. 'According to Miss Sykes, who had the sense to use their telephone call to inform *me* of this crisis rather than Dr Bairstow, it would seem that over lunch, members of both the History Department and R&D, obviously feeling that not enough damage had been done during the

William Tell incident, saw fit to resume the discussion pertaining to myths and legends. They worked their way through the pet Chihuahua who turned out to be a rat, and then Lingoss questioned whether chickens really continue to run around after their head's been chopped off. Someone said that was unlikely – imagine Bashford running around after his head had been chopped off, and then someone else said imagine Bashford running around *before* his head was chopped off, and Lingoss, in the interests of peace and goodwill, moved the conversation on to dead grandmothers on car roofs.'

'As anyone would do,' said the professor, loyally. She was one of his people, after all.

I caught the driver's eye in the rear-view mirror and said, 'Indeed,' very carefully. 'Anyway, pausing only to allocate roles – Bashford was the body, Sykes the getaway driver, and Lingoss the instigator – or the observer, as she apparently prefers to be known – they set about checking the accuracy of this particular urban legend. Bashford donned a dress and wig, made himself up to resemble what he imagined a two-day-dead corpse would look like, and they lashed him to the roof rack on his car.'

'Ingenious,' he said, missing the point as usual. 'Did they use bungee cords?'

'That detail has yet to be ascertained,' I said, nudging him back on track. 'Astonishingly, they made it as far as Rushford before the police, alerted by an avalanche of panic-stricken 999 calls, were able to pull them over. The cavalcade ground to a police-induced halt outside Boots, where a furious argument ensued over their supposed possession of a dead body.

'Matters were not improved when Bashford, in a doomed attempt to pour oil on troubled waters, climbed down off the car roof to reassure everyone. Apparently, several people fainted. The entire population of Rushford got the whole thing on their phones and our heroes made a brief appearance on the local lunchtime news: behind the one-legged jockey but ahead of the yodelling vicar. The only thing keeping them alive is Dr Bairstow's complete and utter ignorance of the phenomenon known as YouTube, which he probably imagines to be some kind of personal plumbing-related apparatus.'

Was it my imagination, or were we picking up speed?

'Our mission, Professor, should we choose to accept it, is to liberate our colleagues, smooth down Rushford's finest and get everyone back to St Mary's before tea, and certainly before anyone realises what has happened.

'What fun,' he said, bouncing in his seat. 'It's just like old times, isn't it? It's all been rather quiet recently, don't you think? So how do we set about this? Will we have to bail them out? I don't think I've brought my wallet with me.'

Since he was still in his stained and scorched lab coat and odd shoes, this didn't surprise me in the slightest.

'Or are we organising a gaol-break?' he continued with enthusiasm. 'Do we ram the station and rescue them from the wreckage. I have to say, Max, if yes, we're going to need a bigger car.'

The taxi driver gave us to understand we should get out now.

The police station in Rushford is not large. Perhaps there isn't that much crime. We stood in the tiny reception area. I had explained the purpose of our visit – twice, because they didn't seem to grasp things the first time around – while Professor Rapson immersed himself in posters about locking your car, not leaving parcels unattended, and not drinking and driving.

Of course, with my usual luck, I got the female police sergeant who'd tried to arrest me on my wedding night. The police deal with loads of people all the time. I was pretty sure she wouldn't recognise me.

'You!'

Bollocks.

'Good afternoon,' I said politely, because, of course, that always works with the police. 'I've had a telephone call about some of our people.'

She consulted a document. 'Lingoss, Bashford, and Sykes.'

'That's them,' I said, ungrammatically, but you can't do everything at once. 'Are they under arrest?'

'No,' she said, in a tone of voice that implied it was only a matter of time before they were, and probably they'd bang up the two of us as well, just because they could.

Silence fell. The professor moved on to a cheerful little poster detailing the punishments incurred for not reporting Colorado beetle.

I edged towards the sergeant and lowered my voice. 'I wonder ...'

'Yes?'

I took out my wallet. 'How much for you to keep them forever?'

She raised an eyebrow.

I raised two, because I've played poker with that cheating bunch of toe rags known as the Technical Section.

She regarded me with no expression whatsoever. Obviously, she played poker with the Technical Section as well.

I tried again. 'If you like, I'll take them away and have them shot.'

She cheered up immediately. 'That's more like it. Wait here.'

Lingoss was first through the door. Today's hair madness was green, shading through turquoise to blue. It really was a work of art. I was so lost in admiration, I missed Sykes' appearance, but no one could miss Bashford.

I've always said – when he does something, he puts his whole heart and soul into it. I was no longer surprised people had fainted. I was only surprised the whole town of Rushford hadn't fled in panic.

He wore a long black dress and his grey wig sat askew. So far so relatively normal. It was the bit in between them that had caused the panic.

He'd covered his face in a thick white paste, which was now beginning to crack and flake away. The effect was horrifying – as if his face was falling off. His eyes were surrounded by deep-purple eye shadow. I guessed the car journey had made his eyes water, and the shadow had run down his cheeks, leaving huge purple streaks. His lipstick sat alongside his mouth and ran off to one ear.

We contemplated each other in complete silence.

I turned to the sergeant. 'Never seen him before in my life.'

'Mr Bashford,' cried Professor Rapson, apparently overjoyed to see him.

'Hello, Professor,' he said cheerfully. 'Max.'

I turned to the sergeant and demanded to know why they weren't manacled to a wall.

'We needed the manacles for real criminals.'

'I could provide you with a set. No charge.'

'That's very good of you, madam, but we would prefer it if you would just take them away.'

I said pleadingly, 'Are you sure they're not under arrest?'

'For what?'

'How long a list would you like?'

'Please just take them away.'

'But – shouldn't they suffer a little first?'

'Well, they drank canteen tea. Would that do?'

'Don't you have telephone directories?'

She sighed. 'It's all electronic these days, madam. You can try clubbing people with a database, but it does turn out to be a bit of a waste of time.'

'We've got Yellow Pages by the tonne. I could let you have some of ours.'

'Won't you need them yourself?'

I eyed the miscreants. 'Of course. What was I thinking?'

'It's great here,' said Lingoss, beaming at me. 'They let us look at the cells.'

I stared reproachfully at the sergeant. 'And you didn't think to lock them in and lose the key?'

'We've already lost the key. Years ago. We generally ask people to embrace the more abstract concepts of imprisonment by envisaging the lockedness of the door and promising not to try to escape. Why are you still here?'

'I'm trying to assist in your clear-up rate. Believe me, no one would have any objections to you fitting up these three for every crime that's taken place over the last five – no, make that ten – years, and sending them down for life. This is a career-altering opportunity that might never come your way again. I urge you to seize it.'

'If it's all the same to you, madam, I'd prefer it if you just took them away and drowned them.

I sagged. 'Where's their car?'

'Around the back.' She pulled out the keys and looked at us. Bashford in diseased-zombie mode. Lingoss disrupting electronic signals with her hair. Sykes beaming angelically at the world in general. Professor Rapson apparently committing the instructions for safely crossing the road to memory – and me, neat, well dressed, mature, responsible.

I held out my hand.

She gave the keys to Bashford.

Clear case of police brutality.

We split up as soon as we entered St Mary's. The zombie and his entourage melted away in one direction and Professor Rapson and I were just signing back in again when our luck ran out. We walked slap into Halcombe, who clearly practised 'Management by Walking Around And Sticking His Nose Into Things Dr Bairstow Would Have Quietly Overlooked'.

'You ...'

He always pretended he couldn't remember my name.

'What are you doing? Have you been outside without permission?'

'No.'

He looked pleased to have caught me out in a lie. Behind him, I could see Bashford, Lingoss, and Sykes slipping quietly into the Hall.

'Allow me to offer you an opportunity to reconsider your answer.'

'OK.'

I stood, apparently lost in deep thought. And stood. And stood.

'Well?'

'Well what?'

'What are you doing?'

'Reconsidering my answer as instructed.' I frowned heavily and stared at the ceiling.

A small crowd began to gather. Bashford was hastily wiping his face.

'Have you been outside?'

'Yes.'

'So you lied.'

'No I didn't.'

'You said you hadn't been outside.'

'No I didn't.'

Seriously, I could do this all day. He really was an idiot. Even I would be the first person to say never argue with me. Dr Bairstow would have nipped this in the bud, been sarcastic at me, and sent me on my way. Perhaps Halcombe was so accustomed to Dottle's uncritical admiration that he had no idea how to handle real people. Really, I was doing him a favour.

'I asked you if you'd been outside and you said no.'

'No, you didn't.'

I thought he was going to burst. Out of consideration for Mr Strong who would be the one picking the Halcombe spleen out of the light fittings, I said, 'You asked me if I had been outside without permission and I said no.'

'And then you said yes.'

'Because you changed the question.'

'The question was about you being outside. Which you have admitted.'

'The answer was correct. It was the question that was wrong.'

I think he was unable to speak for a moment.

'You asked me if I'd been outside without permission and I said no because I did.'

'Go outside?'

'Well, yes, obviously, but I did.'

'What?'

Professor Rapson helpfully intervened. 'She did.'

155

He swelled. 'Did what?'

'Have permission. She accompanied me to Rushford.'

'For what purpose?'

He became vague. 'Colorado beetle, I seem to remember. And manacles. And electronic databases. Oh, and how to cross the road. I must say, Max, the instructions seemed very complicated. I'm sure it was much simpler in my day. Whatever happened to "At the kerb, halt. Look left. Look right. Look left again. If all is clear, then cross the road?"'

'Well,' I said, 'I think its adherents might have died out quite quickly because in this country, Professor, we drive on the left, so it's look *right*, look left, etc.'

'Really?' He seemed genuinely surprised. 'Well, that accounts for a lot, I suppose.'

Halcombe refused to be diverted. 'And Miss Maxwell's purpose in this sudden acquisition of knowledge?'

Miss Lingoss stepped forward.

'Professor Rapson doesn't usually go out on his own, and I was engaged in important scientific research this afternoon, so Miss Maxwell kindly agreed to accompany him on his quest. Thank you Miss Maxwell, I hope the task was not too onerous.'

'My pleasure, Miss Lingoss.'

We began to walk away into the Hall and that did it.

'You do not walk away from me.' His voice cracked like a whip around the Hall and people froze. If this were a Western, tumbleweed would roll slowly down the Great Hall and someone would be whistling a haunting melody.

'Good afternoon.' Dr Bairstow was limping slowly down the stairs. 'Is there some difficulty here?'

'I find Miss Maxwell is in breach of regulations. Again.'

'Very reprehensible. Well, Miss Maxwell, which particular tranche of regulations have you steamrollered this afternoon?'

'I'm not sure, sir. I've accompanied Professor Rapson into Rushford according to custom and practice, and he accompanied me in accordance with one of the confusingly numerous regulations recently imposed. I am actually quite bewildered as to where the fault lies and Mr Halcombe is about to explain it to me.'

He never got the chance. Dr Bairstow effortlessly rose above us all.

'Your only fault, Miss Maxwell, lies in not returning to your place of work immediately on your return from this excursion. St Mary's does not pay you to waste your time hanging about.'

'Yes, Dr Bairstow.'

'Miss Lingoss, kindly escort Professor Rapson back to R&D where he can immediately use his recently acquired information for the benefit of St Mary's. Andrew, my dear fellow, you look as if you would enjoy a cup of tea. Mr Bashford, wash your face. Miss Sykes, I'm not sure what you are doing, but past experience leads me to believe I shall not approve, so desist immediately. As for the rest of you ...'

But they'd scattered.

And that, folks, is how you command St Mary's.

Chapter Thirteen

Having stupidly brought myself to the idiot Halcombe's attention, I proceeded to make things considerably worse.

Slinking back to my bunker with a certain lack of enthusiasm, I addressed the mouldering heap that was my in-tray.

First up was a note from the idiot himself, instructing me to check whether we had sufficient supplies of what he referred to as Effluent Sanitiser, and the real world call Turd Tumbler, for the next few assignments and, if necessary, to order more. I could see how he'd made the connection between me and turds, but this definitely wasn't an historian area of expertise. This was a deliberate insult.

Well, two could play at that game.

Actually, at this point it occurs to me that a word of explanation might be helpful.

We have pods and in the pods are toilets. They rarely work properly and we will all go down with cholera one day but, until then, we soldier on, limiting the risk by scarfing our way through compo rations because these are well known to have an inhibiting effect on normal bowel movements. With the help of practice and meditation, I've managed to get my visits down to two a year, which is impressive, as I think everyone unconnected with the medical profession will agree.

Anyway, disposal is always a difficulty because of the chemicals and such, especially since we used formaldehyde. So Professor Rapson had directed his powerful intellect at the problem and come up with a cocktail of chemicals and enzymes that, believe it or not, breaks everything down, dries it out and leaves us with a kind of sludgy powder. We use the blue formula for flushing, pink for reducing the waste down, and green for neutralising gas and smells. Occasionally the toilet blows up and believe me, it's a real rainbow in there sometimes.

What happens to the sludge afterwards is completely beyond my ken, but the point is that we mix this coloured stuff with our brown stuff, agitate it occasionally (hence the expression Turd Tumbler) and hey presto – barring mass outbreaks of dysentery – problem nearly solved. Now the Halcombe idiot thought he'd have a laugh at my expense. Well, two can play at that game.

I fired up my data table and began my report.

Sir,

In accordance with your instructions I have conducted extensive investigations to ascertain the quantities of Effluent Sanitiser/Turd Tumbler required over the next six months and beg leave to present my findings.

For the purposes of this report I have assumed the following:

- *The length of a standard turd (let turd equal 't') is five inches, excluding the taper.*
- *The average length of assignment is five days.*
- *The average number of historians is four.*

Therefore, a throughput of one t per person per day would total 20t.

At this point, however, it should be noted that throughput figures will often be skewed by the well-known inhibiting effect of compo rations, which should be offset by:

- *The bowel-loosening effects of bad water*
- *The inadvertent ingestion of poisonous substances*
- *Sheer terror as another assignment begins the long slide south.*

Given all of the above, and assuming a standard two-pod formation, we find ourselves with the following simple equation:

Let Turd Tumbler = y
Let days of assignment = d

Let number of historians = h
Let loosening effects of bad water = bw
Let loosening effect of poison = p
Let loosening effect of sheer terror = st
Let inhibiting effect of rations = r

*Therefore, **y = d x h x (bw+p+st-r)***

Please be aware this calculation can be somewhat distorted by the gender make-up of the historians involved. Female historians tend to produce fewer and lighter t's, but urinate more frequently (let urine = u). Male historians however, while frequently exceeding their daily quota of t's, offset this by availing themselves of more informal facilities in the form of trees, rocks, and other historians for the purposes of u.

Should they be required, background notes can be attached, together with sketches of standard turd types – the sausage, the splodge, and the Mr Whippy.

Actual samples can happily be supplied upon written request.

You will be aware, however, that since I no longer have access to mission schedules or staff and pod rotas, it is impossible for me to provide you with any meaningful information and the above exercise has simply wasted both our time.

Assuring you of similar attention to detail on all your future requests.

I signed my name and every conceivable letter of the alphabet to which I was entitled, including BSc for my Bronze Swimming Certificate, copied in Dr Bairstow, not so much because he would enjoy the joke – the 'e' word was not part of his emotional repertoire – but he would appreciate it, and sent it off.

I paid for it, of course.

I was in the bar that night, with Peterson and Markham. Leon was at the other end of the room, quietly going over something with Dieter.

Ignoring me completely, Halcombe stalked to the techie table and flung down my memo.

'Please advise your wife she is here on sufferance only and as such, there are certain levels of behaviour to which she is expected to conform.'

Everything went very quiet. Heads swivelled to Leon.

I pulled out a hairpin and prepared to sally forth, but Peterson put his hand on my arm.

'Hang on a minute.'

Leon rotated his data stack again and only when he had it arranged to his satisfaction did he slowly look up.

Everyone waited for him to say something.

He said nothing. He did nothing. He simply sat very still and stared up at Halcombe.

I could see he was angry. Whether with me for putting him in this position or with Halcombe for being such a pillock remained to be seen. His blue eyes were suddenly very chilly and he held Halcombe's gaze without blinking.

I think, at this point, it began to dawn on the idiot Halcombe that he'd seriously underestimated Leon. Many do. A while ago, he led the revolt against the Time Police, travelling up and down the timeline to engage them. He fought long and hard and has the scars to prove it. Just because he doesn't make anything like as much noise as the rest of us doesn't mean he's timid. Just quiet.

The silence went on. Still he sat, unmoving, still staring up at Halcombe, who stared back. The silence lengthened. Who would blink first?

It was Halcombe. Obviously. I'd never bet against Leon, no matter how much he'd annoyed me recently.

Halcombe took a small step back and it broke the spell. Someone laughed.

Dieter had picked up the memo and scanned it. Grinning, he passed it around. I think it began to dawn on Halcombe that he'd made a tactical error. He threw us a look calculated to show everyone he was leaving of his own free will and not in any way because he'd been intimidated, turned on his heel, and walked away.

Have I said how proud I am of my husband?

All quite amusing. So far, the idiot Halcombe hadn't done a lot of damage, and his entertainment value was rising every day. Then it stopped being funny, because even an idiot can do an awful lot of harm.

He got his own back a couple of days later, announcing that either he, Miss Dottle, or both, would henceforth be present on every jump. To monitor and advise. And to prevent the south-sliding referred to in my ill-judged memo. I had a bit of a curse over that, but not as much, I suspected, as the History Department.

'Where's Dr Bairstow in all this?' enquired Markham, reading through the all-staff memo again.

'Thirsk,' said Peterson.

'What for?'

'No one knows.'

'When did he go?'

'First thing this morning.'

'Has he been sacked?' I asked, a sudden fear clutching at me, because Dr Bairstow leaving would be the end of everything. My own guess was that most of St Mary's would be out of the door with him. Especially if the idiot Halcombe became director.

'I don't think so. Something's going on. He took Major Guthrie and Chief Farrell with him.'

It was a nasty shock to realise Leon hadn't said anything to me. A very nasty shock, indeed. Was it because of my memo?

Markham stared at Peterson. 'He took all our senior officers with him when he knows we have assignments pending? And that the idiot Halcombe would be in charge?'

He shrugged. 'Apparently.'

'How long will they be gone for?'

He shrugged again.

I frowned. Our senior officers were at Thirsk. All of them. Something was definitely going on.

I got my news from Dr Dowson these days. He would bring me a mug of tea in the afternoon and sit on my desk, short legs swinging, dishing the dirt on what was happening around me.

There were two assignments pending, apparently. One was to 15th-century Venice, but the first was to Caernarfon, to witness that wily old fox, Edward I, presenting the people of Wales with the future Edward II, their first Prince of Wales.

Kings and queens move in and out of fashion but Edward II has never been popular. Son of the mighty Hammer of the Scots, his main claims to fame are losing to Scotland at Bannockburn, and annoying his wife to such an extent that she and her lover, Roger Mortimer, led a successful rebellion and deposed him.

Two separate legends surround his birth and death. The first says that his father, under some pressure to appoint a Welsh-speaking Prince of Wales to replace the one he'd recently killed, interpreted 'Welsh speaking' as 'non-English speaking', promised the people of Caernarfon a prince 'that was borne in Wales and could never speake a word of English', and dangled the newly born Edward of Caernarfon from the Queen's Tower.

There's no record of how this was received. Indeed, it's not likely it happened at all – not only was the Queen's Tower not built at the time, but Edward of Caernarfon wasn't even his father's eldest son. The story is persistent, however, and I'd always wanted to check it out.

The other, equally famous legend relates to his murder. Having failed to live up to the expectations of the people of Caernarfon in particular and Wales in general, Edward went on to fail, spectacularly, to live up to the expectations of anyone at all, managing to piss off not only his wife, but also nearly everyone in the realm, and was eventually confined in Berkeley Castle. The conditions of his imprisonment were brutal. Confined in a pit full of rotting corpses in the hope it would kill him, he once again failed to fulfil people's expectations and refused to die. The official version is that he starved to death. The more colourful version states that a group of men crept into his cell one night, pinned him down, shoved a red-hot poker up his bum, and kept it there until he died. No one has yet ascertained the truth of this one, either.

That was the point of this assignment. This is what St Mary's does. We record, document, and ensure that somewhere there's a truthful account of what actually did occur.

But not for me. Another missed opportunity. All right, when they returned from Caernarfon I would know whether or not the story was true, but that would not be anything like as good as seeing it for myself.

I cursed. And then threw my pen across the room. Dr Bairstow had known what he was doing when he ordered me to stay at St Mary's. The knowledge that people were going off without me ... that my department was functioning without me ... Sorry, I don't mean to sound like a bighead – I'm sure things probably functioned slightly better when I wasn't around, but that wasn't the point. My stapler followed the pen, burst apart and scattered staples everywhere.

The next day, the day of the Caernarfon jump, I stayed out of the way keeping busy. I reordered my files, cleaned out my drawers, fixed my stapler, dusted my desk, sorted my in-tray, watched the hands inch their way around the clock face, and went off for an early lunch.

There weren't many people in the dining room. Guthrie and Leon were still away. I was still annoyed that Leon hadn't said anything to me about that, but perhaps he thought it was a sensitive subject. Most of the History and Security Departments were in Caernarfon. There was none of the noisy chatter I'd grown accustomed to. St Mary's was a pretty dreary place these days.

The crash rocked the building.

I could hear crockery falling in the kitchen and voices raised everywhere. The alarms went off. I could hear footsteps running.

I knew what this was. Someone had called for emergency extraction. Something had gone horribly wrong with the Caernarfon assignment and this was a pod crash-landing in Hawking.

Pregnant or not, I was down the long corridor like a whippet, dodging lumps of plaster that had fallen from the ceiling. I skidded into Hawking, expecting the worst. Emergency extractions are quick, but they're not painless. That's why they're for emergencies only. I've had a few in my time and they leave their mark. Literally in some cases. Pods can materialise several feet above their plinths and believe me, a pod has the aerodynamic properties of an elephant in an iron tutu. Or they miss the plinth altogether and skid off down the hangar floor with techies having to leap for their lives. They flatten everything in their path – we've lost several flatbeds that way – and leave smoking grooves in the floor. Leon gets very annoyed about that.

Number Five, however, did not appear to have fared too badly. It was half on and half off its plinth, tilted at a precarious angle, but most importantly, I could see the door, which meant we could get in to deal with any casualties.

I looked around for the person taking charge.

Dieter was shouting instructions. Someone would be calling for the medical team. Nothing was on fire. No one was trapped under the pod with just their feet sticking out like the Wicked Witch of the East – something I knew the Technical Section was running bets on happening one day. As emergency extractions went, this one seemed quite calm. I stood quietly at the back, hoping no one would notice me since I wasn't supposed to be here, and waited to find out what had gone wrong.

The medical team crashed through the doors and approached the pod at a trot, slowing as the pod door jerked open of its own accord, so at least one person was conscious and functioning.

Halcombe appeared, jumping awkwardly through the door, followed by Clerk and Atherton, helping Prentiss and North. North was cradling her arm and cursing buckets. Ten centuries ago, her ancestors had hunted peasants for sport and their voices had evolved to be heard over hounds, horses and horns. She had no difficulty carrying on that proud tradition. Her injury wasn't severe enough to impede her fluency and her voice echoed around the concrete cavern that was Hawking.

Normally, she really, really gets on my nerves, but for some reason, today – not so much. Perhaps because the voice was directed at someone else, namely the idiot Halcombe, who was standing around trying to pretend he couldn't hear her cut-glass tones casting aspersions on his legitimacy. She's usually quite a restrained girl; not today however. And knowing how she could be when things didn't go her way, I waited hopefully for her to attack him.

She wasn't the only one – Clerk, usually one of the most good-natured people on the planet, was shouting and waving his arms, red with fury. Prentiss was joining in, the two of them shoulder to shoulder and in Halcombe's face. He made several efforts to get past them but they wouldn't let him through. The noise was tremendous: everyone was having a go at him, including the security team just now climbing out.

The medical team clambered into the pod, presumably to deal with the casualties therein, and seconds later, clambered back out again looking bewildered.

No one else emerged from the pod. I counted on my fingers – three people missing. Bashford and Sykes. And Dottle. Where the hell were they?

Clerk and the security team were making furious gestures and Halcombe was standing like a pillar of salt. No one seemed to be taking charge. I had no idea what was going on – why they'd called for emergency extraction. I didn't even know if they'd decontaminated. I looked around, but Dieter's responsibility was inside the pod, shutting things down and making them safe.

I walked slowly down the hangar, taking my time. I think I hoped that by the time I got there, things would, miraculously, have resolved themselves. They hadn't, of course. Sometimes I think the god of historians needs a good slapping.

Seeing me, Clerk, still red-faced and furious, broke off. I noted, with surprise, that Prentiss had tears of rage standing on her cheeks. Someone needed to calm things down.

The trick is not to shout. Everyone else was doing that. There was no point in me joining in as well. I said quietly, 'Mr Clerk, report.'

Halcombe opened his mouth, presumably to tell me to push off, and North, suddenly, wheeled on him, scrunched up the front of his tunic with her good hand and pushed him hard. In the silence, we all heard the thump as his head connected with the side of the pod.

'You,' she hissed, 'will be silent.'

He knocked her hand away.

I took a deep breath, pitched my voice, and said, 'Enough!'

Silence rang like a bell.

'Mr Clerk, report.'

'We have to go back, Max. He left them. This bastard ordered us to leave them.'

'Who?'

'Dottle, Bashford, and Sykes.'

'Were they injured? Trapped? Unable to get to the pod?'

'No,' said North, and contempt dripped from every syllable. 'This gutless, spineless, contemptible, despicable poltroon not only ran away, but he ordered us to do the same.'

'Why?' The word snapped out and echoed around the now silent hangar.

She turned back to Halcombe. 'Ask him. Ask him why he abandoned three people. Ask him ...' She drew breath to have another go at him.

I lifted my hand and said quietly, 'One moment please, Miss North. Allow Mr Halcombe to respond.'

He drew himself up. His reedy little voice wasn't quite steady. Was he a coward who shied away from actual confrontation? I could use that.

Swallowing, he said, 'I judged the situation to be unsafe and ordered a withdrawal. My orders were blatantly ignored, so I ordered emergency extraction.

I looked at Clerk.

'He overrode my orders, Max.'

'How? How could he do that? You were mission controller.'

He took a deep breath. 'Perhaps you don't know, all the pods have been reprogrammed, giving Halcombe the authority to override.'

I couldn't believe such stupidity.

'Are you telling me that historians are no longer in control of each assignment? That their orders can be overridden by a ...?' I dragged in a huge breath, willing myself to stay calm. 'We're St Mary's – we never leave our people behind.'

'Not any longer,' said Clerk, grimly. 'Under this idiot's regime, it would appear we are now just the sort of organisation that leaves their people behind.'

All eyes turned to Halcombe, who pursed his mouth and said primly, 'The situation was becoming dangerous. I had other lives to consider.'

I lost it. Weeks of frustration poured out of me in a torrent. I didn't shout but somehow my words carried to every corner of Hawking. 'Becoming dangerous? *Becoming* dangerous? You useless pillock. You don't even know the meaning of the word 'dangerous'. Where are your critical injuries? Where's the damage to the pod? Where's the fire? You abandoned St Mary's personnel simply because you thought the situation *might* become dangerous? Where do you keep your brains? In the same place as your balls?'

'How dare you speak to me in that manner? You will leave this unit immediately.'

After this effort to retrieve the situation, he tried unsuccessfully to push past us and get away.

No. I wouldn't be caught like that again. This had happened to me before. I was younger then and I'd meekly allowed myself to be shepherded from the building, while four men were left to die in the Cretaceous. But not this time. There's no point in making mistakes if you don't learn from them.

Now, everyone was looking at me. Dieter, for some reason, was still inside the pod. Technically, I wasn't a member of this unit any longer, but on the other hand, when the dust settled, everyone would be able to blame me.

Without turning my head, I said, 'Mr Atherton, my compliments to Dr Peterson, and could he join us at his earliest convenience.'

He looked over my shoulder. 'No need, Max.'

Peterson was striding down the hangar. People fell back to make room for him. He was amazing. He didn't raise his voice. Ignoring Halcombe as if he didn't exist, he looked around him and then quietly enquired what was going on.

I filled him in.

He turned to Halcombe and said, with no inflection in his voice. 'You left them behind.'

It was a statement, not an accusation, but Halcombe immediately began to bluster. 'I had no choice. The situation was hazardous. I judged it necessary to implement immediate withdrawal. Mr Clerk refused to obey my commands and I therefore initiated emergency evacuation.'

Which reminded me I had a bone to pick with the Chief Technical Officer whose section had presumably implemented this particular override, but that was for later. Deal with the current crisis first. Always deal with the now, and the first priority was rescue. Getting our people out. Except ... we had no senior officers to authorise that rescue.

Then ... *finally* ... the penny dropped. I stepped aside and had a bit of a think because suddenly I thought I knew why Dr Bairstow wasn't here. Or Leon. Or Guthrie. Or anyone who could take charge of this situation. Dr Bairstow wasn't director of St Mary's by accident. He was director because he was cunning and crafty and devious, yes; but mostly he was director because he saw further than most.

When Thirsk had discovered what we had done, they would immediately have informed Dr Bairstow of our transgression. It had taken us hours to get to back to Caer Guorthigirn and replace the sword and he would have used that time wisely. I could imagine him sitting behind his desk as the shadows moved across the room, plotting, planning – six moves ahead of everyone else as usual. Turning a disaster into an opportunity.

He'd been fighting off Thirsk and their attempts to establish a presence here for years. I could see him now, pulling all the threads together into one neat little package that would teach me a well-deserved lesson, give Peterson the opportunity to step from his, Dr Bairstow's, shadow, and expose Thirsk's representative for the idiot he was.

But what a risk. To take his senior staff and leave St Mary's alone and exposed to the idiot Halcombe, whom he must have known would, when push came to shove, have balls of butter.

Or was it? I was here. And Peterson. And Markham. The sudden knowledge that despite everything we had done, he still believed we could handle this between us, was like the sun coming out in my heart. Now I knew why he'd kept me at St Mary's. I might have no idea what my future held, but my present duty was certain.

I turned to Peterson, cutting across Halcombe, who was trying to issue instructions to clear the hangar. No one was listening to him. St Mary's had closed ranks. I took a moment to steady myself. Because this was the moment on which everything would pivot. This was the moment that would decide our future. Everyone was looking at me.

I said slowly and deliberately, 'Dr Peterson, sir. What are your instructions?'

He didn't get it for a moment – and then he did. Suddenly, in a way I couldn't define, he was different. Markham, standing at the back and watching very carefully, nodded at me.

It was as if the last weeks had never happened. The entire unit lifted their heads and looked to him for guidance.

He was surveying our resources, which were slim. Grey was still at Thirsk. Clerk, Atherton and Prentiss couldn't go back. You can't visit the same time twice. Ditto the security team. North was injured anyway.

That left me.

'And me,' said Markham, reading my mind.

Not for the first time I wished I had Sands and Roberts back. I did briefly consider sending for them. They could be here in a few hours, especially Sands, but with Halcombe on the premises, time was of the essence. I had to get this rescue organised and executed before he or anyone else from Thirsk could intervene and veto. Who else could I use?

There was a disturbance in the Force, and Miss Lingoss was suddenly with us. Complete with jet-black, blue and purple hair teased up on high and welded into place, defying gravity.

'I'd like to volunteer.'

She'd been a trainee historian once and, at that moment, if it would serve my needs, I would have conscripted Vortigern, the kitchen cat.

'Thank you, Miss Lingoss. Your offer is gratefully accepted.'

Peterson turned to us. 'Get yourselves kitted out. I'll find you more security back-up. Back here in ten. You can take Number Three. My authority.'

He wasn't coming with us. Dr Bairstow rarely went on assignment. As director, he was too valuable to risk. Peterson had just made the jump from historian to director. I would miss him, but I was proud of him. Plus, of course – we'd need someone to watch our backs while we were gone.

He and Markham set off for Security.

Halcombe made the mistake of shouting to his back. 'You have no authority here. I shall report this.'

He would, too. I racked my brains for a reason to keep him in Hawking, at least until I could get a rescue organised. I caught Helen's eye. She nodded and despite his protests, began to run a portable scanner over him.

I signalled to Clerk. 'Walk with me to Wardrobe please, Mr Clerk. You can brief me on the way.'

We trotted down the long corridor towards Wardrobe.

'So, Mr Clerk – what happened?'

'Well, there were crowds everywhere. All heading towards the castle.' The historian in him took over. 'Records say the baby prince was presented from the Queen's Tower, but it hadn't been built at the time and ...'

I touched his arm. 'Another time, Mr Clerk. What happened to cause the idiot to call for emergency extraction?'

He was disgusted. 'Hardly anything, Max. The bloke's a complete girl's blouse. As I said, crowds everywhere. He insisted on being at the front and of course, he hadn't a clue. Some sort of beggar jostled him and he panicked. He jumped back shouting "Leper! Leper!" and then, of course, everyone else panicked as well.'

'*Lepers*?'

'Unlikely within the town walls but ...'

'Please tell me you decontaminated before you left the pod.'

'Of course we did. Mary Jane Halcombe had us do it three times.'

'Did you get a look at the beggar?'

'I caught a quick glimpse, and she wasn't a pretty sight, but she wasn't dressed as a leper, or holding a bell or clapper, so I'm thinking it was just some sort of medieval skin complaint. Not uncommon.'

During the Middle Ages, lepers were compelled to dress in long tunics of russet, with black capes over, and a large yellow L or X prominently displayed. They carried bells or clappers to warn people of their presence and to attract charitable donations. The point being that they were easily recognisable. You didn't think you might have seen a leper. You knew when you'd seen a leper. They weren't usually allowed within town walls either, so Clerk was probably right and the woman was just a beggar, albeit one with an unpleasant skin condition. Psoriasis or eczema, maybe. Perhaps even skin cancer.

'Anyway, the crowd panicked as well.'

I nodded. I could imagine the scene. Even today, the word leper has the power to spread fear.

'The female beggar wasn't alone and some sort of punch-up started as her companions pitched in to help.'

The correct procedure would be to withdraw quietly, regroup a street or so away, and continue with the assignment.

'So what went wrong?'

'He ran.'

Of course he bloody did.

'He ran. We had to run with him, of course.'

'And he ran straight back to Number Five?'

'Yep.'

'Thus leading a great crowd of people to the pod.'

'We couldn't get in. There were people milling about everywhere. We were pushed and pulled all over the place. Eventually, I managed to get inside. Halcombe was already there. I suppose we should be grateful he didn't leave all of us behind. North turned up shortly afterwards, and while I was treating her arm, Atherton arrived. I called up Sykes and the others and they'd been shunted in the wrong direction and were on the other side of town, lying low. Halcombe was panicking. He wouldn't wait for them, overrode me, and called for emergency extraction.'

What a shambles. What a bloody, bloody shambles. What the hell were Thirsk thinking when they unleashed this idiot on us? You only had to look at the way he spoke to Dottle to realise he had the people skills of a polecat. He'd set everyone's backs up from Day One, culminating in this disastrous jump. He couldn't have made himself more ...

I stopped dead, staring into space. Clerk carried on for two or three paces and then slowly stopped.

'Max?'

I'd been stupid. I'd made some unkind jokes at his expense and called him the idiot Halcombe, but it was me who had been the idiot. Halcombe wasn't an idiot at all. Halcombe was a very, very clever man. He'd done all this deliberately. He'd seized his first chance to sabotage an assignment and now St Mary's had chalked up two successive failures. At all costs, I needed to stop him reporting back to Thirsk.

'Max?'

No time to explain. Halcombe was a threat and I needed to neuter him as quickly as possible. I mean neutralise. No, as you were – right the first time.

'Mr Clerk, I am concerned that members of this unit might have come into contact with a potentially hazardous disease.'

'But we didn't Max. Not us, anyway. Halcombe was the only one who might have had any contact and he ...'

'You're right,' I said. 'This is most worrying. I'm sure that if Dr Bairstow were here, containing the threat to Mr Halcombe would be his first priority. I want you to get yourself off to Sick Bay with all speed. My compliments to Dr Foster and inform her that Mr Halcombe is far too valuable for us to take any chances. He's to be confined in the isolation ward at least until Dr Bairstow returns and can assess the situation for himself. No visitors. No phone calls. *Total* isolation, Mr Clerk. Please make that very clear to Dr Foster.'

For a moment, he stared and then he grinned from ear to ear. 'Got it, Max. Poor sod. It's not as if life in isolation is any fun.'

'I'm sure Dr Foster will know exactly what to do under the circumstances. Off you go.'

He shot off and I made my way to Wardrobe where they were waiting for me.

Mrs Enderby had found me some sort of tent to wear. I tied up my hair and surveyed my team. Markham, Evans, Lingoss, and me. What could possibly go wrong?

Markham handed me a stun gun and pepper spray. I stuffed them into my concealed pockets. I donned my wimple, pulling the coarse, scratchy fabric straight on my shoulders, thinking about what Halcombe had done. This assignment could not have gone more wrong. Objective unachieved and now never likely to be. The pod damaged and three people lost. Well, I couldn't do anything about the first two disasters, but I could get our people back. And his person, too – Dottle. I thought about the mentality of someone who would abandon one of his own team to further his own ends, and gave a little shiver.

Mrs Enderby, fussing around, said, 'Everything all right, Max?'

'Yes. I wonder, could someone get me a com please and ask Dr Peterson if I could have a word?'

'He's waiting outside for you.'

He was indeed, looking very grave. I suspected he'd worked it out as well.

He pulled me to a quiet corner and listened while my words tumbled out, nodding occasionally.

'I propose,' I said, 'that we take him somewhere unpleasant – anywhere in the 14th century should do it – and threaten to leave him there until he tells us everything. What is his aim? Why he's really here. Everything.'

He shook his head. 'Tempting, but no. We'll get our own people back first. Dr Bairstow might not wish us to show our hand and I wouldn't want to jeopardise whatever he has planned. He might want us to keep quiet and see what Halcombe does next. Or who he reports to.'

I stared at him in admiration. 'You're even beginning to think like Dr Bairstow.'

He grinned. 'Yes, I'm expecting to go bald any minute now.' He handed me a com. 'Good thought isolating him, by the way. He knows damn well he doesn't have leprosy, but there won't be a thing he can do about it, and I've authorised Helen to initiate any treatment she thinks necessary.'

'Tim, that's .... diabolical.'

'Yeah,' he said, grinning. 'Now go and get them.'

Chapter Fourteen

We assembled outside Number Three – another one of the big pods, because, with luck, it would need to hold me, Markham, Evans, and Miss Lingoss, slightly weighed down by the two wimples and the broad-brimmed hat it had taken to control her hair, together with the rescuees: Sykes, Bashford and Dottle. We stood quietly out of the way while Dieter finished re-setting the coordinates.

Peterson stood up on the gantry, in the spot usually occupied by Dr Bairstow. He lifted his hand. I smiled back.

We filed in. No one had any bags or extra equipment. It was just us.

I seated myself and there was a pause during which the words, 'Max, you should not be doing this,' were not spoken.

'All set,' said Dieter. 'Good luck everyone.' He let himself out. The door closed behind him.

'OK everyone. Here we go. Computer, initiate jump.'

'Jump initiated.'

The world went white.

We landed on a piece of very muddy ground near the bridge leading to the East Gate. It had been raining heavily and was now raining only slightly heavily, which, for Wales, is practically a drought.

I angled the cameras around.

'Well, they haven't closed the gate,' said Markham. 'That's a good sign.'

Opening his com, he said, 'Sykes, Bashford, report.'

Nothing happened. Nobody looked at anyone else. Silence is never good.

'Sykes. Can you hear me?'

A great blast of noise filled the pod. Singing, shouting, and crashing furniture. We all stepped back and I turned down the volume.

'Bloody hell,' said Evans. 'Typical Psycho Psykes. She's started some sort of revolution. She's probably organising the resistance even as we speak. North Wales could be a free state by teatime.'

A man's voice shouted something. I heard Sykes shout something back. Not in English. That's the thing about Sykes – she might have the same sense of self-preservation as a hedgehog taking a shortcut across a motorway – but she did have the sense not to be English in a Welsh-speaking community on the day their English overlord had produced yet another son. As far as I knew she couldn't speak Welsh, but she was Scottish so it might have been Gaelic. Whatever she said, the shouter seemed satisfied and moved away.

'Are you all right?' I said, alarmed. It sounded as if a major riot was happening in a very small place.

'Oh hi, Max,' she said, showing no surprise it was me. 'Yeah, fine. We're having a bit of a party.'

Markham hastily turned away.

I said icily, 'What?'

'A party. Good old King Teddy has laid on all sorts of goodies to grease the wheels with the locals. We're all eating and drinking ourselves silly and when it's all gone we'll probably traipse off and throw stones at the castle anyway.'

There was a short silence. Markham had his back to me and Evans was staring vaguely at his feet.

I said with restraint, 'Who's we?'

'The three of us.' She broke off to shout something to someone else, pitching her voice high and rattling off tortured vowels at machine-gun speed.

'What language is that?' said Lingoss, fascinated.

'Geordie.'

We all stared at each other.

'Where are you?'

'Inaninn. Sorry, that's not easy to say. We're in an inn. Off Northgate Street, I think. There's a bush outside the door anyway. We're out the back with the horses. You can't miss it.'

'Injuries?'

'Yes. I've done something hideous to my ankle and Dottle's banged her head.'

'And Bashford?' I said, heart sinking.

'He's fine.'

'What?'

'He's fine. Not a mark on him. I think he's taking part in the "How Far Can You Throw the Pig" competition.'

I ground my teeth. 'The correct protocol is to lie low, keep quiet, and wait for rescue.'

'We are,' she said. 'We're blending in. Anyone not taking advantage of Old Teddy's catering is going to look extremely suspicious, Max. The more we eat and drink and throw pigs around, the safer we are.' Her voice resonated with injured innocence.

'Sit tight. We're on our way.' I closed the link.

I turned to Markham. 'Can you believe her?'

He stared at me, his face wooden. 'No. Unbelievable.'

I pulled out a wicker basket, popped in the small med kit, and covered it with my cloak.

'Let's go.'

The day was mild and muggy. I could smell the sea. Even over the smells of cooking and horses and wood smoke, I could smell the sea.

We entered via the East Gate. We'd chosen the East Gate because it housed the exchequer to the chancery of North Wales and was a busy place. Men scurried back and forth. Horses were being led away and fresh horses brought up. There was a good half-dozen guards that we could see, probably more that we couldn't, and none of them would be too cheerful about having to work on this feast day, but we kept our heads down and slipped through – Lingoss and Evans first then, when no alarm was raised, Markham and me.

We gathered in the wide space on the other side of the Gate and looked around.

Edward had strengthened the town walls and laid out the streets in a grid pattern. Directly ahead of us, the High Street ran down to the West Gate and the sea. The castle was away to our left, its uncompleted outline jagged against the milky grey sky. You can't miss Caernarfon Castle. It's impressive today. In 1284, still raw and unfinished, it was bloody magnificent. From the English point of view, of course.

In an effort to keep the Welsh in line, Edward had strung his castles all across Wales, but this was his capital, his place of residence – the jewel in his crown. The castle has been described as brutal and it was. A symbol of power and conquest that dominated the town. A constant reminder that Wales was a defeated country. You had to hand it to the first Edward; he subjugated the Welsh, hammered the Scots, and taxed the Irish. This was a king who made absolutely no friends wherever he went and, somewhere over there, he might well be dangling an infant off a balcony, but we had other priorities.

We looked around, getting our bearings. I saw wooden buildings leaning haphazardly over the crowded streets. A group of Grey Friars, cowls pulled over their heads, huddled out of the rain in a doorway. Over to my right, a pardoner was selling indulgences. He probably did a roaring trade so close to Northgate Street. You could lurch into one of the many hospitable establishments there, drink yourself stupid, enjoy the attentions of one or two suddenly very affectionate ladies, stagger outside again, pay to have your sins absolved, and go home to complain to your wife about the day you'd had.

On the corner, an apothecary had set up a temporary stall and was trading busily, selling off small wrapped packets of cures and medicines that might come in useful to those suffering the consequences of over-indulgence on this supposed holiday.

On the opposite corner, a small boy was selling charcoal and cords of firewood, lustily advertising his wares at the top of his voice. Nearby, a haberdasher was unrolling his wares for a group of housewives, their wimpled heads bent over a length of dark cloth. Next door, a spice merchant had set up a tiny stall, his goods carefully stacked off the cobbles, which were running with all sorts of dubious fluids. I caught a brief whiff of some unknown exotic scent.

A fowler wandered past, a brace of wild ducks swinging lifelessly from each hand. Everywhere coopers, tailors, carpenters, butchers, blacksmiths and ropemakers were extolling the virtues of their products. It was all happening in Caernarfon today. The streets were crammed with food vendors, trinket sellers, travelling musicians and all the many street traders for whom this sort of public event was just a huge moneymaking opportunity.

And, as Clerk had said, there were beggars everywhere, too. Small, sad people dressed in grey rags stood, lay or hopped, hands outstretched, perpetually murmuring requests for alms, alms, for pity's sake. None of them were lepers. No leper would ever have been allowed to roam these crowded streets. The guards would have turned them away at the gates.

'Northgate Street is just over there,' said Markham, 'According to my information it's where the prossies hang out.'

'How do you know these things?'

'I knock around with historians. It's hard not to know these things.'

On reflection, I was neither surprised that he would know, nor that Sykes and Co had ended up there.

We found the place very easily. Partly because, just as Sykes had mentioned, there was quite a large bush planted by the front door – actually it was more of a tree – but mostly because of the small group of angry men gathered outside who were trying to batter down the door.

We halted on the corner and drew back into a doorway.

'I thought it was too good to be true,' said Markham in resignation. 'With Sykes here I'm surprised the entire town isn't in open rebellion.'

I opened my com and asked, with what I thought was admirable restraint, 'What is happening here?'

'Oh, hello again, Max. Have you noticed there seems to be a spot of bother in the street?'

'What did you do?'

'Nothing.'

The shouting rose to a crescendo. Somewhere, a woman screamed. A pot shattered.

'Nothing?'

'Yes, honestly. It was two men. As I heard it, some sort of deal went wrong. Either his horse or his daughter – to be honest it wasn't clear at all – and then the shouting started, tables overturned, crockery smashed, you know how these things go, and then his friends turned up.'

'How did the deal go wrong?' said Lingoss, displaying typical R&D interest in the inessentials.

'Dunno. We weren't there, but the word on the street is that either his daughter wasn't the virgin he claimed her to be, or his horse was one of these cut-and-shut jobbies.'

'What?' I said, completely at sea.

'You know – cut and shut. You weld one half of one car on to the other half of another car and sell it on. Quickly.'

'Is that even legal?' I said, floundering even further out of my depth.

'Course not,' said Markham. 'It falls apart as soon as you go round the first bend. So I've heard,' he added quickly.

Lingoss and Evans nodded agreement.

I began to experience the familiar sensation of an assignment sliding away from me again, and made an effort to get things back on track.

'Where exactly are you?'

'We're still round the back. Sitting on the midden.'

'Why?'

'It's warm and soft.'

Lingoss nodded wisely.

'Is there back access?'

'Not where we are.'

'We can't get to you. Any chance of you coming to us?'

'Shouldn't think so,' she said cheerfully. 'I can barely walk and Dottle can't see very well.'

'What about Bashford?'

'Actually, we may have lost him.'

Oh, dear God.

'How? How have you managed to lose Bashford?'

'He went for a slash and hasn't come back.'

I took a deep breath because it's supposed to be calming. 'Why didn't he use the midden?'

'I told you. We're sitting on it.'

'What has that to do with things?'

'He said it put him off.'

'What did?'

'Us watching him.'

'Couldn't you have closed your eyes?'

'We offered. He said it would still put him off his stroke. I suggested he close *his* eyes, but apparently that doesn't work either.'

I pressed my lips together. She didn't say a word but I swear I could *hear* her beaming at me, every inch the enthusiastic, helpful historian.

'You shouldn't have let him go.'

'I had no choice. Apparently, when you have to go – you have to go.'

'And so he went.'

'Pretty much, yes.'

Markham snorted.

'But,' she continued, 'we've been talking to him the whole time and he's only just round the corner.'

'Oh, for crying out loud.' I was incensed and rightly so. The instructions are clear. Stay together in one neat package for ease of rescue. 'Stay put. Do not move. We'll get you out.'

Somehow.

'We need to split up,' I said reluctantly, because in situations like this, I like everyone to stick together, but someone needed to search for Bashford. 'Mr Evans ...'

'Roger dodger,' he said. Another one not taking this seriously at all. 'I'll find him.' He stepped away a few paces and spoke urgently into his com. That left Markham who could support Sykes, Lingoss who could guide Dottle, and me. God knows what I would do. I think that at that point I may have been slightly losing the will to live.

Evans turned back. 'He's only round the corner. He says some woman is shouting at him. About fish, he thinks, but she's shouting in Welsh, so it's not going well.'

'You speak Welsh. Go and sort it out.'

'No I don't,' he said, affronted.

'Why not? Your name's Evans.'

'I'm from Halifax. Very little Welsh spoken there.'

'Just … go and do what you can,' I said, and he disappeared.

Over the road, the assault on the inn had redoubled. Even as I watched, two of the mob trotted round the corner with a wooden bench and attempted to batter down the door. The crowd around them responded with encouragement, criticism, disapproval, and mockery. People hung from upstairs windows, showering them with the contents of pots. We pulled back out of the splash zone. There was absolutely no way in a million years we were going to get anywhere near Sykes and Dottle. The seeming leader of the gang, red faced, was screaming at his men who were heaving the heavy bench at the door. It seemed safe to assume that Edward's charm offensive with the free food and drink was not necessarily keeping the locals as quiet as he had hoped. On the other hand, this was the rough end of town and for all I knew this sort of thing happened two or three times a day. The inn door was certainly a great deal more solid than it appeared. It wouldn't last forever, though.

'We need a diversion,' I said. 'Something to disperse this crowd.'

I looked up and down the narrow street, filled with sweating men, shrieking prostitutes, a jeering mob, dogs and, just for once, inspiration failed me. Short of waving a magic wand, there was no way to disperse this little lot. The buildings were mostly of wood and thatch and I really didn't want to risk the traditional method of setting a small fire and yanking out our people in the confusion. With our luck, the entire street would go up in a blazing inferno, scores of people would die, and the subsequent riots would jump-start the Welsh resistance, which would lead to the Welsh kicking the English out of Wales forever. The subsequent resurgence of national pride would lead them to raise an army, which would sweep down on London where they would overthrow the King and his government and install their own prince, name unknown but Llewellyn seemed a safe bet, and the entire course of History would be irrevocably and fatally changed and it would be all our fault.

I realised Lingoss and Markham were staring at me in astonishment and it was possible that I might have said some of that aloud.

'I've had a brilliant idea,' said Lingoss, and before I could stop her, she'd darted into the street.

'For God's sake go with her,' I said urgently, and Markham elbowed his way through the crowd in her wake.

I heard Lingoss shout, 'Hey!' and there was a kind of collective gasp and a stunned silence fell.

Just like that. One minute a mini-riot and the next minute, complete silence. Even the dogs had shut up. What the hell had she done? I craned my neck this way and that to try to see what was happening and, suddenly, she was alone in the centre of an expanding circle and I could see exactly what she'd done.

Oh, shit.

Throughout the Middle Ages, women's hair was considered immoral and associated with temptation and sin. Only a woman of very low breeding, or a prostitute, would show her hair in public. Legally, a married woman's hair was the property of her husband. The point I'm trying to make is that you don't see much public hair. (I made a mental note to be very careful about typing that phrase in my report. Or perhaps not.) Anyway, you didn't see a lot of men's hair, either, and certainly no one had ever seen anything like this explosion of jet-black hair tastefully tipped with blue and purple. I rather liked it, but today I was in a minority of one. The effect on the good citizens of Caernarfon was astonishing. I knew they would run. The only question was whether they would run towards or away from her. I crossed my fingers for away and so, of course, they ran towards. This was Lingoss, however, a tough kid who'd looked after herself all her life. I would bet this wasn't the first angry crowd she'd run away from, but even so ...

She was already accelerating down the street when the first angry shout went up. She would have got away easily, only at that very moment, with a hollow rattling sound, a handcart came round the corner at some speed. I caught a very brief glimpse of Bashford and Evans pushing for dear life. She jinked left, and I lost sight of her. The handcart missed her by inches, but completely failed to avoid the crowd behind her. The handcart went over with a crash, shouts of Welsh abuse and bad language filled the air, and suddenly the world was full of fish.

There were fish everywhere. Some skidded slimily across the cobbles and people either trod on them, squirting bits of fish guts everywhere, or they slipped and fell, bringing down those around them. A large number of the more aerodynamic fish flew through the air, striking people impartially. No discrimination here. These fish were equal-opportunity missiles.

I stared open-mouthed, and then it got worse.

We've all heard the expression 'fishwife', usually used to denote a coarse and foul-mouthed woman. In fact, it's a bit of a cliché, but that's the thing about clichés – they're often spot on. The term fishwife came about because the women who gutted and cleaned their husbands' or fathers' catches really were coarse and foul-mouthed. This one was the Queen of Fishwives. She wanted her barrow back. Then she saw what had happened to her fish.

I caught a glimpse of Evans yanking Bashford into the shelter of a doorway, which was a very wise move because if she'd ever caught them she would have gutted them with no more compunction than she would have gutting a mackerel.

Fortunately, for them however, she was distracted by the sight of her wares strewn across the street and even more distracted by the enterprising citizens of Caernarfon taking full advantage of this opportunity for free food, and stuffing pollocks down the fronts of their tunics as fast as they could, where presumably they nestled alongside similarly named items.

With a truly terrifying bellow of rage, she launched herself upon them and since she was still clutching the vicious-looking implement with which she separated the outside of the fish from the inside of the fish, nobody hung around. I can only describe it as a small stampede.

There was a slight bottleneck at one end of the street as everyone fought their way out and then, within seconds, it was empty apart from a shoe – because there's always a shoe – stones, litter, debris, splintered wood, broken pottery, a dog cocking its leg against the now discarded bench, some rather trampled fish, and a really strong smell.

She righted the barrow one handed and gazed around her, hands on hips. I hoped to God she wasn't looking for someone to blame because, with typical historian lack of foresight, I was now the only person visible. Of Markham and Lingoss, there was no sign. Bashford and Evans were in a doorway further up the street where, if they had any sense, they would remain for the rest of their lives.

The dog finished what it was doing and trotted away. The street was so quiet I could actually hear its nails clicking on the cobbles.

She caught my eye. My God, she was a really, really big woman, bare-armed and bloodied almost to her elbows. Her massive bosom swung as she walked, probably distorting gravity. She wore a coarse sacking apron, liberally stained with fish guts, scales, and blood. Her skirts were kilted up nearly to her knees, showing bare calves and heftily shod feet. I was very conscious that I was probably the only visible person for miles around. Trying to avoid eye contact, I looked down. At my feet lay a miraculously intact flatfish. I bent awkwardly, picked it up by the tail, and held it out to her.

She stared at me, face expressionless. Her face looked as if it had been carved from a side of beef. I tried to smile and look as pregnant as possible and it must have worked because she took the fish, nodded grimly, tossed it into her handcart, and slowly trundled it back up the street and around the corner.

The sound of the wheels faded into the distance.

I took a moment to close my eyes and savour the blessed silence.

'What's going on?' said Sykes, behind me.

I damned near gave birth on the spot, took a deep breath to get my heart going again, turned slowly, and did not injure her in any way.

'Where the f– where did you come from?'

'From the inn.'

'But ...' I said feebly, 'how did you get out?'

She gestured behind her. 'Through the door.'

I felt a red mist begin to form.

'What were you doing in there?'

'Waiting to be rescued.'

'Why?'

'You told us to.'

'I told you to stay put.'

'We did stay put. For ages. And then I got bored with waiting and came out to see if you needed any help.' She surveyed the fish-related carnage.

'You said you were in the pub.'

'We were.' She pointed.

I pointed across the street to the other pub. 'With a bush by the door.'

In turn, she gestured towards to a sad-looking stick with two leaves, struggling to survive in a broken stone pot by the door behind us. 'Bush.'

Again, I pointed across the street to the other pub. 'That's a bush.'

'No, that's a vine. Not the same thing at all.'

How it would have ended, I don't know. I try to avoid arguing with her because she's short and stubborn and has no respect at all for authority. I swear I don't know how she gets through the day without someone somewhere banging her head against a wall.

She spoke into her com. 'You can come out now.'

Dottle appeared, looking sheepish and bleeding slightly from a cut over one eyebrow. Nothing serious.

Not without some trepidation, Bashford and Evans emerged from their doorway and Markham and Lingoss trotted back from wherever they'd been secreting themselves.

We attempted to pull ourselves together. Lingoss made heroic efforts to get her hair under some sort of control. Before we could shoulder Sykes, however, in the distance, I faintly heard a horn blow, followed by screams and the oh-so-familiar sound of overturning stalls.

'Nothing to do with us,' said Sykes, defiantly. 'Just so everyone's clear.'

From around the corner, came the tramp of marching feet.

'Are they coming back?' asked Dottle anxiously, surveying the fish-strewn wreckage and obviously unaware that to historians, catastrophes come not in threes, but in multiples of threes.

'No, it's soldiers.'

'Shit,' muttered Evans, looking around wildly – the traditional Security Section response to a crisis.

A troop of soldiers turned into the street.

There was nowhere to go and we had wounded. We drew back, set ourselves against the wall, and prepared to resist arrest. Again.

There were nine of them in three rows of three. Breastplates, helmets, and pikes. No swords.

'We can take them,' said Sykes with confidence.

They marched straight past us. Without even a glance in our direction. Actually, I think we all felt rather silly.

The horn sounded again and they broke into a run. In another moment, they were gone and once again, we were alone. Although given the smell where we were, that really wasn't surprising.

'What's going on?' said Bashford. I think he was a little offended. No one likes being ignored. 'Where are they going?'

'Back to the castle,' I said shortly, and anyone who knew me well would have left it at that.

'Why?' enquired Dottle.

'Because,' I said bitterly, 'there's trouble there and we all know what it is, don't we?'

'Oh my God,' said Sykes, managing to bound with excitement while standing on one leg. 'Does this mean that the King did present Edward like the story says? Is he doing it now?'

'Well, we'll never know, will we?' I said. 'Because our priority is to get back to the pod with a trio of historians stupid enough to have missed the last bus home.'

'Go,' she said. 'Go. We're fine here. Go and see what's happening.'

I was tempted. I was strongly tempted. I looked back over my shoulder at the castle, still glowering over the town. Somewhere, over there ...

Markham shook his head and I reluctantly returned to the matter in hand. He was right. If I left them and dashed off to do something more interesting I really wasn't much better than Halcombe, and being abandoned twice in one day wouldn't do Dottle any good at all.

It's bloody Sod's Law, isn't it? Suddenly we could rescue our people easily. Now we could just scoop them up and stroll back to the pod, and the reason we could do that was because everyone else had dashed off to the castle to watch the event which, I was certain, would turn out to be the motivation for the jump here in the first place. I didn't know whether to scream, spit, or swear. I'm an historian. I'm used to being where the action is, not lurking in a backstreet somewhere.

'Steady on, Max,' said Lingoss. 'Remember your condition.'

I threw her a look that should have set fire to her hair.

They were all very quiet on their way back to the pod.

We took a little time to check over the wounded. Whatever had happened in the aftermath of Halcombe's abandoning them, Dottle had obviously laid about her with spirit. She really was too good for the idiot Halcombe.

I took her aside. 'OK, let's get this wimple off and get you cleaned up a little.'

'Why?'

'Historians never go back looking scruffy. It's an image thing. No matter how bad things are, we never let people see we're not always completely on top of things.'

Pathetically hopeful, she said, 'Am I an historian?'

'Well, you're in a pod. You're wearing 13th-century clothing stained with someone else's blood. You stink of beer and horse shit. Your hair is coming down. You've split your lip and your nose is bleeding. I'd say you've nailed it.'

She glowed. Despite the crusty nose, swollen lip, and bird's nest hair, she looked quite attractive. Animation suited her. Not everyone looks as good after a punch-up, as I told her.

She sighed. 'I don't think I did a lot of good.'

'You didn't run.'

I saw her remember Halcombe.

She said quietly, 'He ran, didn't he?'

I nodded.

She picked at something dubious on her skirt. 'How could he do that? How could he just leave us?' She looked at me hopefully. 'Did he go for help?'

What could I say? How do you shatter someone's world?

I chickened out. 'I'm not sure. I only arrived in Hawking in time to be included in the rescue team.'

'Was Mr Halcombe injured?'

Why was I so reluctant to tell her? 'I don't think so, but we had to move quickly to get back here so I didn't have time to check him out.'

She wasn't stupid. 'He wasn't, was he?' She picked at her skirt a little more. 'He just ran. He left us.'

She looked around at Markham, laughing with Sykes as he applied an icepack to her ankle. 'You don't think much of us, do you?'

I smiled. 'I think you did just fine.'

She glowed. I don't think that under the Halcombe regime, a lot of praise came her way. If any at all. And then it faded again.

'I've wasted so much of my life waiting for him to notice me.'

'I wouldn't want to interfere,' I said, insincerely, 'but I think it's definitely time for a regime change.'

She nodded. 'So do you think the King did present Edward as the Prince of Wales?'

'Exactly the right question to ask,' I said. 'You should stick around at St Mary's for a while.'

Chapter Fifteen

They kept me in Sick Bay longer than anyone else – even Dottle. For once, I didn't complain. Dr Bairstow was out there somewhere. I thought I'd leave Peterson to deal with the fall-out from Caernarfon since he'd do it so much better than me. It was just possible that if I lingered here for a year or so then Dr Bairstow might have forgotten about me when I did eventually find the courage to emerge.

Fat chance.

I opened my eyes one afternoon to find him standing at the foot of my bed, silhouetted against the window – dark, sinister, and unreadable.

'Good afternoon, sir.'

'Report.'

'Not written yet, sir,' I said, trying to be crafty. I don't know why I bother.

'A verbal report will suffice.'

I sat up, marshalled my scattered wits, and gave him just the bare bones. He'd read everyone else's reports and presumably interviewed them personally, so I wasn't quite sure what he was expecting from me.

At the end, he leaned on his stick and said, 'I congratulate you on your timely actions relating to Mr Halcombe.'

I wasn't sure to which timely actions he was referring. To locking the bugger up or initiating the rescue? Whichever it was, he seemed inclined to let me live a little longer. 'Thank you, sir.'

'That this unit was able to avoid ... serious contamination is largely due to your actions.

'Thank you, sir.'

'We are all extremely relieved that Mr Halcombe was isolated before any further contamination could occur.'

O ... K ...

'I have conveyed the details of his current misfortune to Thirsk, who were most anxious he remain where he can benefit from the best medical treatment.'

I said carefully, 'And will they be sending a replacement for him?'

'Apparently not. I have assured them of my willingness to work with Miss Dottle and this has been deemed an acceptable, if temporary, solution.'

His face was unreadable. Was he saying what I thought he was saying? That Halcombe was neutralised for the near future? That Dottle would be easy to deal with? That he was – what's the word I'm looking for? Grateful?

Was he buggery.

'Regarding your subsequent actions in Caernarfon ...'

He'd know it all, of course. The riot, the wrong inn, us being up to our withers in fish, the failure to achieve our objective ... I sighed. I would have given a lot to have been able to report on Edward's presentation of his son. It was all very well the Boss generously letting me live but, at the end of the day, we'd failed.

'I understand your despondency, Miss Maxwell, but in presenting my report to Thirsk, I was able to point out that the failure of our last jump could be ascribed in no small measure to Mr Halcombe's unfamiliarity with protocols and procedures. They have, to some extent, accepted this and we have worked together to ensure such misunderstandings do not occur again.'

My head began to ache. I said gloomily, 'I wanted to go to the castle, sir, but we had injuries. Dottle had a head wound and it seemed sensible to get them all back as soon as possible.'

There was a pause while we both contemplated my unexpected use of the 's' word and then I sighed.

'It wasn't the slickest rescue in the history of St Mary's, sir. What with the street fight. And the battering ram. And the giant woman. And the fish. And Miss Lingoss' hair ...'

'To say nothing of Miss Sykes's bush,' he said.

Silence fell while I wondered if perhaps I was hearing things. I stared up at him. Not a muscle moved. There was not a flicker of expression on his face.

You can never go wrong by saying, 'yes sir,' so I said, 'Yes, sir.'

He nodded and limped from the room.

After he'd gone, Helen wandered in muttering to herself, sat in the window seat, and lit a cigarette. Having unexpectedly survived Dr Bairstow, I got cocky. I'd been dying to talk to her, and here was the opportunity.

Last Christmas we'd had a bit of an unofficial crisis and the three of us, Markham, Peterson and I had had to shoot off to Ancient Egypt. As you do. We'd ended up having to dunk Markham in the Nile. For his own good, of course, but that was when Peterson had mentioned his Special Question. The one he was going to ask Helen.

Once, I'd have scoffed at the thought, but now Leon and I were married. Was it possible – was it actually possible – that he and I were setting such a wonderful example of marital bliss that others might be contemplating the same thing?

Well, anything's possible. The law of averages says that somewhere in the world there must be a competent politician, an honest banker, an England footballer who knows what to do with the ball inside the penalty box – that last one comes from Leon; don't ask me what he's talking about – and now meet Farrell and Maxwell, the poster children for marital stability.

I thrust this and other scary thoughts to the back of my mind and said, 'Has Peterson said anything to you?'

'He says lots of things to me. Some days you just can't shut him up.'

'No, I mean about – anything?'

'Such as?'

'Well I wondered – he said something once and I thought ...' I tailed away, afraid of saying too much.

She threw her cigarette end out of the window. Someone shouted a protest.

'For God's sake, Bashford. You're standing up to your knees in discarded dog ends. Where did you think they came from? Did you think they sprang up from the ground like serpents' teeth? Idiot!'

She shut the window with a bang and said shortly, 'No, he hasn't said anything. And in his position at the moment, he's not likely to, is he?'

So she knew what I was on about.

I risked life and limb. 'Well, *you* could always talk to him.'

I didn't think she'd attack a patient – you know, Hippocratic Oath and all that – but I wasn't 100 per cent certain so I gripped the bedclothes and got ready to move quickly should I have to.

To my enormous surprise, she said quietly, 'No. I couldn't do that to him. It would injure his pride and at this moment that's all he has left. I can't take that away from him.' She looked at me. 'Can I?'

I shook my head. She was right.

She smiled. 'He's an idiot, of course, but I understand.'

So did I. I think.

She leaned her head against the window and we both sat in silence until Hunter came in to tell her that Professor Rapson had scalded himself making toast and could she come at once please.

I was discharged that evening. I picked up my bag, headed for the stairs and freedom, and then stopped. Looking back over my shoulder, I could see the place was deserted. I turned back and walked down the corridor to the isolation room.

It's a big four-bed room with a large viewing aperture – or window, as those of us who aren't Mr Strong call it. I stood and looked through into the ward.

Halcombe lay on the bed, reading a newspaper. He was dressed in St Mary's sweats and looked a complete pillock. Or if you want to push a bad joke even further – pollock.

I stood very still, but we all have a sense that tells us when we're being watched.

He looked up and for what seemed like a very long time, we just stared at each other. Neither of us moved and then, at the optimum moment, just as I was considering walking away, he gave a small, smug smile, and returned to his newspaper.

I turned and left, the memory of that smile burning a hole in my mind.

I clattered down the stairs, reviewing my 'Awkward Interviews' list. So far – so good. I'd survived both Drs Bairstow and Foster. Now for the most difficult of them all.

I knew Leon had returned from Thirsk because he'd been to visit me. We'd been very polite to each other because we both knew we needed privacy for our next conversation. He'd enquired after my welfare. I'd enquired after his and then we sat in silence, not because we had nothing to say to each other, but because we had too much.

Using the back stairs, I made my way to our room. Once there, I showered and changed and sat quietly, waiting for Leon. Who had some explaining to do.

He came in about an hour later, still wearing his orange jumpsuit and looking tired and dirty. I left him to have a shower in peace. I even got him a beer out of the chiller, because I'm a good wife and he's lucky to have me.

He settled himself in the other chair, cracked the beer, and we looked at each other.

The silence went on and on. This was ridiculous. If one of us didn't make a move soon, then this kid was going to be saddled with parents who never spoke to one another. I decided I would let him speak first and then we would discuss things quietly and rationally.

Finally, he said, 'You just couldn't stay out of a pod, could you?'

Quiet and rational flew straight out of the window and headed south for the winter. The words were out before I could stop them.

'Well, if you hadn't been stupid enough to put a non-historian override on our pods, I wouldn't have had to, would I?'

'I was instructed to do so.'

I felt my temper beginning to rise. 'By that idiot Halcombe? What were you thinking?'

'I was thinking of obeying instructions. An unfamiliar concept for you, I'll grant, but one the rest of us mastered some time ago.'

I snapped, 'Yes, well your slavish adherence to the rules nearly got a couple of historians and a civilian killed last week. I hope you're proud.'

He regarded me stonily.

'More or less proud than someone whose flagrant disregard for the rules brought disgrace on this unit, ruined careers, and was responsible for inflicting Thirsk on us in the first place? Tell me Max – more or less proud?'

There. It was out. The first time he'd levelled direct criticism. We'd papered over the cracks and now not only had those cracks reappeared, but the wall had fallen down and was about to bring the house down with it.

Lemming like, I hurled myself off the cliff. 'I'm a little surprised at the current levels of hypocrisy ricocheting around this room. From you of all people. I don't remember all this criticism when I stole your pod and yanked Bashford and Grey out of Colchester. I don't remember Dr Bairstow complaining then. Or Guthrie. Or you. It was all, "Oh well done, Max. Good job, Max."'

He started to speak and I cut across him.

'I hear a lot of talk about whether stealing the sword was doing the right thing for the wrong reason, or vice versa, but the fact is we did the right thing for the right reason. Don't you understand? Roberts' community was dying. Because of something we did. Did you expect us to stand by and do nothing? Or should we just have stood back, recorded, and documented as we always do? Yes, we interfered, but we'd already done that when we passed on the location of the sword.

And Dr Bairstow interfered when he passed that information to Thirsk. And Thirsk interfered when they stole the sword. They're the guilty party because it wasn't theirs to take. It was a gift to the people of Caer Guorthigirn. It wasn't us who stole the sword. We're the ones who put it back.'

In any argument, it's always vitally important to have the last word. I turned on my heel and stormed out, slamming the door behind me with such force that I heard plaster drop somewhere. For some reason, the sound made me even more furious, which I wouldn't have thought possible.

Leon and I don't have many rows. There's been the odd tiff concerning squeezing toothpaste tubes – squeezing from the bottom is a sure sign of a sick mind, believe me. Or over who snores the loudest – it's me, but a polite spouse wouldn't mention that. But now I needed to get away before guilt, righteous indignation, disappointment and more guilt all collided in one lethal explosion and I did him a serious injury.

A quick tip. If you're going to storm out then it's a good idea to make sure you have somewhere to storm to. I was halfway down the stairs before I realised it was late at night and I'd left my bed behind, which only added to my resentment. I'd done nothing wrong. I actually hadn't done anything wrong. On the contrary, I'd saved St Mary's staff from the consequences of Leon's folly and now I was the one without a place to lay my head. I made a mental note to be much more strategic about this sort of thing in the future.

I strode through the Hall, some sort of autopilot taking me to the Archive, I suppose. I could at least get a couple of hour's work done and after that, maybe, curl up in one of the armchairs in the Library.

I was halfway across the room before I realised I hadn't switched on the lights. The stairs and the Hall were dimly lit and people were always working in the kitchen, but the Library should have been dark and it wasn't.

I stopped, turning my head to locate the source of the light. There – in the far corner. Someone had left an active data stack.

I frowned. That shouldn't happen. For those of us absent-minded enough to forget to exit the system properly after we'd finished – which was most of us – there was an automatic shutdown after an hour.

I pulled out a chair, meaning to shut the thing down properly so that whomever it belonged to wouldn't lose their work, but I couldn't find the login, which was odd. There was nothing to identify the user.

Rotating the stack, I looked for a clue, but there was nothing. I looked over my shoulder. I shouldn't be doing this. Access to anything other than the basic admin systems was forbidden to me, so, of course, I had a good look. I made myself comfortable and started at the top. I just skimmed the first part, and then thought, shit! I went back to the beginning and, with my heart thumping, read everything very slowly. I found a sheet of paper and a pen and made a few notes, including coordinates.

When I'd finished, I tried to go back again for a second reading but it wouldn't let me, and, as I tried to force it, with no warning at all, the data stack collapsed into a meaningless jumble and then disappeared altogether. I was back in the dark.

Curiouser and curiouser.

I sat back in my chair, folded my arms, sank my chin on my chest, and had a bit of a think.

Chapter Sixteen

I met Peterson and Markham at breakfast the next morning. We sat at our usual table. Looking across the room, I could see a blushing but delighted Dottle sitting at the historians' table, wearing her bruises like a badge of honour. It was always possible that if we strolled over we would be asked to join them, but there had been no word of reinstatement. Or, to be fair, of dismissal either. We were in a kind of no man's land. So we stayed apart, taking a perverse pride in maintaining our isolation. Which suited me, because I had a Secret and a Plan.

'Need to talk to the pair of you,' I said, spreading a thick layer of chunky marmalade on my even more thickly buttered toast.

'You are talking to the pair of us, said Markham logically. 'What's up?'

'Something happened last night.'

'Yeah, we heard,' said Peterson. 'I was just dropping off when someone apparently detonated a bomb further down the corridor. I thought the ceiling was coming down again. You and Leon have a row?'

'Never mind that now,' I said, suddenly realising I hadn't thought of Leon once throughout my very long and busy night. 'I've had a brilliant idea.'

Neither of them groaned, which I appreciated. Pouring myself another cup of tea and making sure no one could overhear, I pulled out my piece of paper. 'King John.'

Markham nodded. 'Brother of the more famous Richard. Robin Hood. Magna Carta'

'That's the one, but you missed something out. He's the king who lost something in The Wash.'

'What – you mean – like a sock?'

'No,' I said, carefully, and talked them through my idea.

At the end, they sat in silence, thinking.

'But whose was the data stack?' persisted Markham. 'There must have been a user ID. You can't build a stack without one.'

'Blank,' I said, although I had a very good idea. Only three people possessed the technical expertise to build a stack without an ID and I was pretty sure it wasn't Dieter or Polly Perkins, the head of IT. Which just left ...

We'd had a row. I'd stormed out. Straight down to the only other place I could currently call mine, to find an open data stack almost as if it was meant for me to find. Was I being manipulated? Or was I just kidding myself?

'What's Dr Bairstow going to say about all this?' said Markham.

Peterson poured himself another cup of tea. 'I suspect he'll either be so incensed at our actions that we'll be decapitated on the spot or he'll forgive us instantly. I don't think there'll be any middle ground.'

We all nodded. Make or break time. An opportunity for triumph. Or disaster so complete there would be no coming back from it.

'Well, I'm in,' said Markham. 'I'm not spending the rest of my life scraping everyone else's hairy slime out from under my fingernails.'

I put down my suddenly unwanted toast.

'Me too,' said Peterson. 'We can't go on like this. We need either to make things better or make them so bad they chuck us out. Either way we'll know where we stand. Let's do this. Agreed?'

'I'll put together a proper briefing,' I said. 'Can you both get away this afternoon?'

'Probably, said Peterson.

'What about you?' I looked at Markham.

'I'm cleaning out the grease traps,' he said. 'Trust me, no one will come anywhere near me for weeks.'

'Good. Tim, can you ask around – discreetly, of course – just in case this was a legitimate piece of work and someone, somehow, just forgot to shut it down.'

He nodded. 'I can do that.'

'OK,' I said, feeling my heart lift with the familiar surge of excitement. God, I'd missed this. 'Everything exactly as normal and then meet in my room at 14:30.'

They grinned at me. I grinned back.

I pottered through my morning. It was perhaps fortunate that I worked alone. I was pretty sure my attempts to look normal would have demonstrated a crying need for psychiatric assistance. I took what I needed from the Library shelves, went back to my own desk, and got stuck in. I made up a proper mission folder and worked as if it were a legitimate jump.

After an hour or so, I had to scoot off for yet another bladder break, and when I got back, Dottle was waiting for me.

I stiffened, trying to see past her to my desk. Had I left anything incriminating hanging around? No. The King John material seemed to be covered by my Rushford Agricultural Show folder.

'I just wanted to say thank you,' she said in a small voice. 'Will you say thank you to the others for me?'

'Of course,' I said. 'But why don't you tell them yourself?'

She looked down. 'I don't like to ... I mean ...'

'They would appreciate it,' I said.

She blushed again.

'I saw you sitting at the historians' table at breakfast.'

'Yes, people have been ... very kind.'

'People usually are,' I said.

There was a silence as, not for the first time I guessed, she compared St Mary's behaviour with that of the idiot Halcombe. I looked at her. She wasn't the same person as last week. She would always be shy and quiet, but these days there was a new confidence about her. She held herself differently. I suspected that when Halcombe was eventually released from Helen's enthusiastic anti-leprosy regime, he would find his world had changed. I was certain hers had.

'Well,' she said, suffering the usual shy person's difficulty in extricating herself from any situation, 'again, thank you very much.'

'You're welcome,' I said, trying not to twitch with impatience, because this was important to her. 'Can I ask, what are your plans for the future?'

'I'm not sure yet, but I do intend to look for something different.'

'Well,' I said, 'and please don't faint with terror or anything, but you could do worse than make an appointment with Dr Bairstow and ask for his advice.'

She blinked, but I was sure I was right. 'He's not a monster and he's certainly not a bully. If he can't help he'll certainly point you in the direction of someone who can.' Kalinda Black, our liaison officer at Thirsk, was my bet.

'All right,' she said, edging away. Without even a glance at my desk, I was pleased to note. 'I'll do that. Goodbye.'

'See you later,' I said, waited until she'd disappeared, and then pulled out King John again.

Less than three hours later, I had what I needed.

We lunched as normal, not that that was easy, and then made our separate ways to my room.

Markham made the tea and I locked the door, hoping Leon wouldn't suddenly take it into his head to finish early. He never had before and there was no reason why he should now, but it did strike me that being in a locked room with Markham and Peterson could take some explaining away. We began.

'OK,' I said. 'It's October 1216 and King John is in deep shit. He's lost his father's massive Angevin empire and is in the process of losing his English kingdom as well. He's ill with dysentery. He's had to sign Magna Carta. And now, on top of all that, he's about to lose the Crown Jewels.'

'According to contemporary accounts, he's travelling to Bishop's Lynn – it's been upgraded to King's Lynn today – and he falls ill. Understandably by now, he's quite paranoid, so he decides to move to Newark Castle where he thinks he'll be safer. Attempting to cross The Wash, which was much more extensive than today, he crosses at Wisbech, fording the Wellstream. His baggage train doesn't make it. It's unclear whether John was present or not. All we know is that by the end of the day, it was all gone. And not just the Crown Jewels. There's a quantity of stuff left to him by his grandmother, the Empress Mathilda, including a number of her husband's crowns, holy relics, portable altars, and the famous Sword of Tristram. All lost, and John, for whom this was probably the last straw, dies just a few days later.

'There's a lot of discussion about this. Whether, for instance, John was present at the disaster or not; or whether, desperate for cash to pay his troops, he stole the jewels himself to break up or pawn, and losing them in The Wash was just his cover story. There's no doubt they vanished, however. None of them were ever mentioned in the Rolls – that's the royal inventory – from that date onwards.'

I continued with mounting excitement. 'If we could just get our hands on even a tiny portion of what was lost ... The total value has been estimated at £70 million. I have to sit down even to think about such a sum, although according to Dr Bairstow on a bad day, that's what it costs to run St Mary's for an afternoon.'

'All right,' said Peterson, 'but now we have a problem. We're not official any longer. What do we do with this stuff once we have it? Without the official backing of St Mary's, we could be classed as looters.'

'Never mind that,' said Markham. 'The issue we should be addressing is who do we get to recover it afterwards? Thirsk? Because I have to say I'm not thrilled about risking life and limb just to benefit the plonkers who inflicted Halcombe upon us.'

'And the Chancellor got the boot,' I said, because I still felt guilty about that.

Peterson grinned. 'So let her discover it then.'

There was a silence as we all thought about that.

'Well, why not?' he said. 'We keep this strictly in-house. We bury it somewhere in St Mary's grounds. Up in the woods, perhaps, where it's not going to be discovered by accident.'

'That makes it very clear that St Mary's is involved,' nodded Markham.

'And the Chancellor won't need to beg permission to dig. Dr Bairstow will give it happily.'

I wasn't too sure. 'You don't think it will look a little suspicious? Being found here?'

'I don't see why,' said Peterson slowly. 'There's no reason why something lost in the 13th century shouldn't eventually end up here. It's perfectly possible that someone discovered it afterwards, brought it here and buried it for safekeeping, and then died.'

'Taking the secret with him to his grave,' said Markham, with relish.

'It will just be one of those unresolved mysteries. And the Chancellor could bring in her own team. She could even include a few people from Thirsk for neutral observation.'

'Will she do it, do you think?'

'What? Would Dr Evelyn Chalfont pass up an opportunity to hand those bastards their own arses in public? How hard should we think about that?'

I nodded. He was right. 'OK. That's settled then. Tomorrow, first thing, we'll meet up in the woods and do a recce. It shouldn't take us long to find somewhere suitable and note the coordinates.'

'All right,' said Peterson. 'Let's do it.'

We planned the recce for dawn, making our separate ways to the old barn, and meeting there. Mindful of the need for plausible behaviour, I got up early, handed Leon a frigid mug of tea – I mean I was frigid, not the tea – and told him I was off to use the Library before anyone else could get in there. Which was mostly true, because I don't lie to Leon, but there's no doubt that being married is a bit of a bugger if you're up to no good.

Letting myself out of our room, I crept around the gallery to the huge alarm of Evans who, far from patrolling the building and keeping us all safe through the night, was sitting in a small alcove having a crafty fag and reading the *Sunday Sport*.

'It's official,' he said, flourishing the paper at me. 'The PM and the Cabinet are being controlled by aliens from an underground spaceship just outside Saffron Walden.'

'Well, that accounts for a lot.'

'No, it's true. Look.'

He handed me his paper, folded back to show a picture of one scientist handing this top-secret information to another. You could tell they were scientists because they were wearing white coats. And you could tell they were passing info because one was handing a briefcase to the other. And you could tell it was top-secret info because the briefcase was helpfully labelled Top Secret.

I unfolded the paper and read it. Yes, he was right. Apparently, for the last two hundred years, successive governments had been controlled by tentacled aliens who come from small star just north of Alpha Centauri, and who are operating from their spaceship just outside Saffron Walden. Just off the B184. Between Littlebury and the golf club. Their sworn purpose being to brainwash world leaders and reduce them to ineffective puppets with minimal brain function. So mission accomplished, then.

I handed him back his paper. 'Any fall-out from Caernarfon?'

He shook his head. 'Major Guthrie just glared at me, and everyone else moaned about the smell of fish, so no. You?'

I shook my head.

'Where are you off to?' he said, belatedly remembering his professional responsibilities.

'Early morning run,' I said, looking him in the eye.

He stared at me for a long time, taking in my inappropriate footwear, my lack of water, my pregnant condition.

Turning to the back pages of his chosen literature, he said, 'Peterson and Markham said they'd meet you behind the barn. Don't keep them waiting.'

We found what we thought would be an appropriate spot in a large clearing just off the path that led up to Pen Tor, well out of sight of St Mary's. Well out of sight of everything, actually.

Markham stood with his hands on his hips and looked around. 'It's a clearing now, but suppose there's some socking great oak tree growing here eight hundred years ago.'

'Not important. The important thing is that the clearing exists now and can be easily excavated. Whatever is growing here eight hundred years ago will just have to be dealt with.'

I sat on a fallen log while they triangulated the position and when they'd finished, we all sat in the early morning sunshine and listened to the birdsong.

'This is never going to work,' said Markham, uncharacteristically gloomy.

I thought of the serendipitous data stack. 'Yes it will. Trust me.'

Having settled on our burial site, we had to decide which pod to take. Not that there was really any choice. It would have to be Leon's own personal pod, hidden from prying eyes in the paint store. We'd never get away with taking one of the regular ones. There was never a time of day when Hawking wasn't occupied.

I stockpiled the food and drink. People kept staring as I helped myself to yet more sandwiches, but that's one good thing about being pregnant – you can get away with all sorts of bizarre behaviour. Markham acquired the digging equipment. Again, people were so used to seeing him covered in dirt and clutching some kind of ferocious-looking implement, that they never looked twice.

We settled on the middle of the afternoon. Never choose midnight if you're up to something dodgy. Creeping through a building at midnight is just asking for trouble. Not that we thought there would be any. With luck and careful planning, we would be there and back again before teatime. At some point, I did wonder about the ease with which we were pulling this off, and I was right – it *was* all too easy, because just as we were setting off down the dim corridor that led to the paint store, one of the shadows moved, revealing itself to be Miss Dottle. We all looked at each other.

'This is what comes of saving civilians,' said Markham, exasperated. 'No good deed goes unpunished.'

Now what were we to do? The existence of Leon's pod was an unofficial secret. I'm pretty sure most of the Technical Section knew about it, and most historians too, but Dottle, despite everything I'd said, wasn't one of us. This wasn't something we wanted Halcombe knowing about. Or anyone.

We looked at each other and I shook my head. Keeping the existence of Leon's pod quiet was far more important than our hare-brained attempt to reinstate St Mary's.

I turned back to her, smiled sweetly, and prepared to get rid of her. Chance would have been a fine thing.

'I want to go with you.'

'Go where?'

'England. 1216.'

Shit. Shit, shit, shit.

'No, sorry,' I said, 'I'm not with you.' I gestured at Markham and his implements. 'We're actually on our way to ...' I stopped, temporarily at a loss.

'Empty the ...' said Markham, similarly stricken.

Peterson smiled down at her.

She blushed hotly, saying, 'I know what you're up to.'

His smile never faltered. 'And what would that be?'

'England 1216. And don't bother to deny it.' She turned to me. 'I saw the file on your desk.'

'What?' I moved subtly into fighting mode. Was that why she'd been there? Had she been spying for Halcombe? I felt so stupid. I'd believed every word she said.

'No, no,' she said hastily, putting up her hands in a placatory gesture. 'I wasn't spying. Honest. I went to thank you. You were just going out of the door when I arrived. I called after you, but the door banged and I don't think you heard me. I went to scribble you a quick note and saw the file.' She blushed even more furiously; any minute now, she was going to burst into flames. 'I didn't think you'd want anyone seeing it so I pulled the flyer for the Rushford Show over it.' She drew herself up. 'I know you're up to something. I've been watching you. I want to be involved.'

Peterson said gently, 'The best way to help us is to go back to the main building and pretend you never saw us.'

She shook her head. 'I want to come.'

He tried again. 'I don't think you understand how dangerous ...'

Markham said, 'Don't want to rush anyone, but this lot's heavy and someone's going to be walking past in a minute. Can we get a move on?'

'You must understand,' I said desperately. 'What we're doing is not legal. Our careers are already in ruins. Yours isn't.'

'I don't want a career. I want to do this.'

No she didn't. If she knew what we were up to, she'd run a mile. She'd never have the balls for this. I wasn't sure I had the balls for this.

I'd underestimated her. She drew herself up and stuck out her tiny chin.

'Either you take me with you or I go straight to Halcombe right now and tell him what you're up to. He'll have the three of you out of here faster than ...' She paused, but lacking the historian's traditional colourful turn of phrase, was unable to think of anything that would impress us. 'If you want to proceed you have to take me with you. If I don't go – no one goes.'

She set her mouth in a grim line. It was like being threatened by a wet hamster.

'I blame you,' said Markham to me. 'Next time we just leave her in Caernarfon, OK?'

I looked at him. This was Markham-speak for yes, she can come.

I sighed and turned back to her. 'You do as you're told.'

'Of course,' she said, wide-eyed.
I knew that look.

Chapter Seventeen

We got it wrong. We got it all completely wrong. To this day, I can't understand why we're not dead.

For a start, John didn't just drop the crown jewels in The Wash and run away. I'd held out the faint hope that it would be a case of just a few wagons being bogged down and spilling their load, which would enable us to take advantage of the confusion, quietly pocket a few items, and make our escape. Of course, it wasn't that easy. Nothing's ever that easy for us.

We landed as close as we could to the assumed sight of the catastrophe and that was the first thing that went wrong.

We touched down and the pod tilted. Dottle, who didn't have her pod legs yet, staggered, and everyone looked accusingly at Peterson who held up his hands and said defensively, 'Not my fault.'

One of the hydraulic legs extended, which did no good at all. We were still at an angle. The computer said, 'Warning. Unstable surface. Recommend immediate ...'

Peterson told it to shut up and it subsided with an offended chirp. We all hung on to the console, holding our breath, waiting to see if we would tilt any further. So long as we didn't fall door-side down, we could still clamber out, although that's a little undignified and does nothing to enhance our professional image.

We didn't tilt any further. Everyone drew in the breath they hadn't realised they were holding.

'Right,' I said, briskly. 'Let's have a look, shall we?'

We squinted at the screen.

'Is it still night?' asked Dottle, uncertainly.

'No. According to us it's several hours after dawn.'

'Then why can't we see anything?'

'That's a very good question,' said Peterson thoughtfully.

We waited for his very good answer. In vain.

'Come on,' I said. 'We can't sit here all day. Let's find out what's happening. Miss Dottle ...'

'I'm coming with you,' she said, alarmed.

I sighed. 'Under normal circumstances I would allow that, but I don't think these are normal circumstances. You can see the pod is unstable. We can't just go off and leave it. We need you here.'

She blinked rapidly. Was she going to cry? 'But I want to come with you.'

'Look,' said Tim gently. 'You can see we have a problem with the pod. You insisted on coming along and you're in a position to do some real good here, because if you weren't with us today then I would have to risk life and limb by telling Max she should be the one to remain with the pod, because she's pregnant and someone must. Fortunately for us, because Max isn't very reliable, we have you instead. You insisted on coming – but the downside is that you have to do as you're told.' He stepped back and looked at her face. 'Are you afraid to be alone?'

'No,' she said, stoutly and probably inaccurately. 'I'll be fine. And if anything does go wrong – which I know it won't – I do know that whatever happens, someone will come and rescue *you*.'

There was a very slight emphasis on the last word, and I remembered her boss had abandoned her. I wondered briefly what it must be like suddenly to realise that the person to whom you have given your devotion isn't worth it.

'Secondly,' continued Peterson, 'we might have to exit in a hurry. And not for the first time, I might add, so we need you to watch the screen. If you see us galloping towards you, get the door open and be ready.'

'Ready for what?'

'For whatever we're running away from to have a go at you too.'

Having thus reassured her, he turned to me and Markham. 'Are we all set?'

We nodded.

'Right, see you in a bit ...' he hesitated. 'It's Lisa, isn't it?'

Oh, Tim. Everyone knows if you give a stray a name then you have to keep it forever.

She nodded, scarlet-faced again.

He thumped her cheerfully on the shoulder. She staggered. 'Right. See you in a bit, Lisa. Have the kettle on.'

There was a storm coming. We could feel it in the air.

'Well,' said Peterson. 'Now we know why it was so dark.'

Huge black clouds were massing overhead, lit with that lurid, dirty yellow glow that never bodes well, meteorologically speaking. A strong wind blew in our faces, pushing warm air ahead of it. We were in for a huge storm.

I looked around us. We'd scrambled ungracefully from the pod, splashed through eighteen inches of brackish water, and gained the comparative safety of a large tump of reedy grass.

In its own way, the landscape was quite beautiful. A vast expanse of salt marsh rolled away in every direction. Every now and then, the clouds would rip apart and all the channels and deep pools would gleam with brilliant light. Mudflats glistened so brightly they dazzled the eyes. Then the clouds would roll back together and the sullen darkness would descend again. On a still day, this area must be home to hundreds, if not thousands, of wading birds and wildfowl, but not today. Today, apart from the wailing wind, the landscape was lifeless. Channels of water twisted between isolated tussocks of coarse grass. There were no trees as far as I could see. Faintly, in the distance, I could hear what I assumed was the boom of breakers, crashing upon the shore. I could smell the sea, mud, and brackish water. Lots of brackish water.

We weren't given any time to stand and stare. Markham nudged me and nodded over my shoulder. I turned.

This was the next thing we got wrong. As I said, I thought it would just be a case of a few wagons, sinking slowly into the quicksand as horses and drivers jumped to safety. I don't know why I thought that. I never learn. My job takes me all over the place – sorry, used to take me all over the place – and the one thing I always forget is that nothing is ever as we think it will be.

The baggage train was colossal. I couldn't see the end. Widely spaced carts snaked across the marshes, winding their way around the boggy bits, seeking a safe crossing. Covered wagons, open wagons, men on horseback, men on foot, spare horses, packhorses, soldiers, it just went on and on. Of course, this wasn't just the Crown Jewels. This must be all his household goods: wardrobe, supplies, equipment – almost everything he owned.

We stared, open-mouthed at such madness. Gold is not light. Treasure is heavy. How on earth could John have expected this lot to cross these salt marshes safely? Every turn of the wheel must cause the wagons to sink more deeply into the mixture of soft sand, soil, and water. It was folly. Massive, massive folly.

The next thing to be ascertained – was John with them? Or had he ridden on to Swineshead, to treat his dysentery with peaches and new cider? Note to dysentery sufferers: don't do that. It doesn't work. Go to the chemist instead. Or better still, the nearest hospital. Best of all – don't catch it in the first place. According to Clerk, who's had it once, and Bashford who's had it twice – dysentery is a bitch.

'I reckon it's all of a mile long,' said Markham, dragging me back from thoughts of bloody stools. 'What was he thinking? I mean, I know he was a bit of a bastard, but seriously, what was he thinking?'

'He's desperate,' said Peterson, peering through his binoculars. 'He's lost England's continental empire. The French are occupying a large part of south-east England. The Welsh are revolting. The Scots are marching down from the north. He needs to pay his army. What would you do?'

All the time that we were talking, the wind had been rising. We weren't dressed as contemporaries, having reckoned that swanning into Wardrobe and asking to be kitted out in 13th-century gear would have been a bit of a giveaway. So Peterson and Markham wore their usual jumpsuits with body warmers, and I was in jeans, sweatshirt and body warmer – all in extra-large. Possibly we could have looked more professional. The wind whipped at my hair. I rammed in my hairpins and trusted to luck.

'Can we get any closer?' said Markham. He surveyed the scene. '*Should* we get any closer?'

Another good question. I looked down. Black water swirled around my ankles. I could feel pressure building in my head. There were no friendly gleams of light in the sky now.

'They've stopped,' said Markham, referring to the train. 'They're not going to attempt the crossing.

I didn't blame them. I didn't blame them in the slightest. Except that I suspected they had no choice but to continue. Presumably they had guides who could take them along safe paths, but surely there was no safe way they could turn this little lot around. Their choice was to stand still and withstand the worst of the storm or push on with as much speed as they could muster, cross at the point indicated by their guides and head for safety.

They chose to push on. If it was any consolation, there was no correct choice that day. Whether they stayed put or attempted the crossing, this baggage train was doomed.

Which, of course, was why we were here.

'We don't get involved in this at all,' I said, zipping my body warmer all the way up to my chin. Unfamiliar words to an historian. 'We wait here, see what happens, and then seize any opportunities that might come our way. All right?'

They nodded. We crouched in the wet and waited.

But not for long.

The storm came on quickly, blowing in from the sea. The sound of crashing breakers was much louder now. The sky darkened further. I saw flashes of lightning in the clouds. Thunder rumbled in the distance.

I heard Dottle's voice in my ear. 'Are you all right out there?'

'Yes,' said Peterson untruthfully. 'We're fine,' and as he spoke, the rain started. Big heavy raindrops, driven nearly horizontal by the wind. We huddled together and waited.

Unbelievably, the baggage train picked up the pace. Soldiers ranged up and down the column, shouting at the drivers to pick up speed. Disjointed words floated towards us on the wind and were as quickly whipped away again. Mules and horses were becoming nervous. I could hear drivers shouting and whips cracking. Gaps began to open up as some wagons moved faster than others. Some drivers attempted to manoeuvre around the slower-moving vehicles, steering off the path, which upset the guides. We could hear shouts of warning and curses. Horses reared in their harnesses and then the inevitable happened. A wagon tipped over, dragging the horses with it. The driver jumped down. The two soldiers with him began to cut the horses free. They kicked their way to their feet, rearing and plunging. Other horses became fretful. The shouting increased.

'Here we go,' said Peterson softly. 'Eyes on the prize, people.'

Panic was spreading throughout the train. Drivers jumped down and ran to their horses' heads. Still the rain hammered down and the wind blew solidly. Canvases flapped, spooking the horses even more. Lightning forked across the sky and thunder boomed overhead, making me jump.

I heard Peterson say, 'You all right in there, Lisa?'

'Yes.' Her voice was surprisingly firm. 'You?'

'We might need a towel when we get back, but we're all fine here.'

I was too fat to crouch for long, but I knelt, wiping the water from my eyes with my sleeve, desperately trying to make out what was going on. The leading wagons were now only a hundred yards or so away and I could barely see them. I was pretty sure no one could see the lop-sided hut half in and half out of a bog and the three idiots crouching in the mud. We were safe. From discovery anyway. Sadly, the weather is an equal-opportunity bastard.

'Listen,' said Markham suddenly. 'That's not thunder.'

We stood up, braced ourselves against the wind, and looked around.

A long, low, continuous rumble filled the air. Beneath my feet, the ground quivered. Surely not an earthquake? I looked down. The water was visibly higher. Our little reedy island was slowly disappearing.

'Back to the pod,' shouted Markham, grasping my arm.

'What? Why?'

'Storm surge. Move.'

'But the wagons ...'

He put it in terms an historian could understand. 'Something's coming and it will kill us all. Move.'

We didn't have to fight our way back. The wind was behind us and we nearly flew back to the pod. Dottle, still unfamiliar with the controls, didn't have the door open ready.

I shouted, 'Door,' and we crashed inside.

She was holding a towel, which she shyly offered to Peterson. He thanked her politely and refused to catch anyone's eye.

I scrambled into the seat, wiped the water from my eyes, angled the cameras, and tried to see what was going on.

And that was when we realised how badly we'd got things wrong. And why there was never going to be the slightest chance of us 'rescuing' the Crown Jewels and reinstating the good name of St Mary's. And just how much trouble we were in. Because, like the hundreds of men and horses out there, we were about to be overtaken by the weather.

Things were much quieter here inside the pod. Rain hammered on the roof, we could still hear the shrieking wind, and occasionally our pod would tremble, but out there was a nightmare from hell.

All semblance of order had gone from the baggage train. Horses were rearing and plunging. Mounted soldiers were abandoning their duty and striking off across country, their horses splashing through pools of muddy water as fast as they could go. Much good it would do them. Some drivers tried to turn their wagons and now it was just chaos. Drivers in the leading wagons whipped up their horses and made for the ford, trusting to luck to cross the estuary in time although how they could see through the wind and rain was a mystery.

There was no chance for anyone. There was no chance – as we belatedly realised – for us, either.

I could see something dark on the horizon, growing larger every second. I peered through the grey sheet of rain. A wave of dirty water was roaring across the fenland. Not fast and not high – I've seen bigger bores on the Severn – but completely unstoppable, sweeping up everything in its path. Black, muddy, foaming water. I saw a dead dog turning over and over in it.

Terrified horses screamed and tried to bolt. Men jumped from the tangled wagons and ran as fast as they could, splashing through the mud, falling over unseen obstacles, desperately trying to outrun the oncoming water. No one – nothing – stood any chance at all. It was coming.

And then it was here.

The wave hit with tremendous force. I saw one wagon upended, wood splintering in all directions. The horse, still trapped between the traces, cartwheeled high through the air, legs flailing, screaming with terror. It hit the ground with an appalling smash that must surely have broken its back. I caught a final glimpse of its head, straining above the water, of rolling, terrified eyes and then it was gone. All around us, wagons tumbled over and over, colliding, breaking up, and shedding their loads. Caskets and trunks burst open, spilling their contents. Everything was being swept away in the torrent.

There was no possible way we could salvage any of this. Men, wagons, horses, gold, silver, crowns, altarpieces, precious jewels, none of it would ever be seen again. Everything would be scattered across miles and miles of empty countryside, to be buried or swept away. All of it lost forever.

I had thought we could just wait until the storm had subsided and help ourselves to whatever was still lying around, but there was no chance. From the crowns of the Holy Roman Emperor to the smallest gold coin, by this time tomorrow, it would be buried under feet of mud and debris. In our time, it must be fifty feet down and scattered over miles and miles and miles of Fenland.

We'd gambled and lost.

There was no time for despair. We were next. I had visions of us being washed all the way across country to Birmingham.

'Brace yourselves,' I shouted, sliding out of my seat. Peterson pulled Dottle to the floor and we all hung on to the seat column. Down here, the carpet smelled strongly of mud and stagnant water. Things hit us. Hard. Wagons. Carts. Dead horses. I could still hear the occasional scream as men were washed past. Something thudded into the side of us and the pod moved slightly, came to rest, and then moved again. I suspected pods had all the buoyancy of a stone monolith, so this wasn't good at all. We came to rest somewhere else, lurched violently and then we were on the move again.

'Bloody hell,' said Markham, twisting to look up at the screen. 'It's like bloody Noah's ark. This is a bit of a bugger, Max. We should get out of here.'

Normally, I would argue, but what was the point of staying? We would be wasting our time here. The sea was pouring across the land. There would be nothing left. Nothing to show what had happened here. He was right. I pressed my cheek into the carpet and thought seriously about spending the rest of my life in this position. We'd had just this one chance and we'd got it wrong. It seemed so clear now. If there had been the slightest chance of salvaging any of the treasure, then it would have been done at the time. The fact that nothing – not even a wagon wheel – was ever discovered should have been a bit of a clue. I'd really lost the plot with this one.

I heard Dr Bairstow's voice again. 'One day Max, you will go too far.' I'd accepted the blame when we'd stolen Arthur's sword but, internally, I'd been sure I'd done the right thing. Now I had to accept it. I was the one who had talked them into this. I was the one who had stolen a pod and set off on yet another illegal jump. Do I never learn? Success might – just might – have rendered our actions slightly acceptable, but to break the rules and fail ... And to fail so spectacularly as well ...

There was no coming back from this one. I was finished. We all were. I tried to burrow my face into the rough carpet. It's supposed to be indestructible. The carpet I mean. Maybe some of it would rub off on me. I felt a hot tear trickle down my cheek and soak into the harsh pile.

Peterson heaved himself up and sat at the console. 'Hang on. I've had a brilliant idea.'

'Whatever it is, you'd better make it quick,' said Markham, as we collided with something else. The pod jolted and tilted.

Peterson was banging keys and pulling up data.

I wiped my face and struggled to my feet. 'What can I do?'

He pushed me into the seat. 'Help me with these coordinates.' We lurched again and began to tip. 'Quick.'

I bent to my task as we were washed across East Anglia. Dottle and Markham stayed quiet and let us get on with it.

'No time to check them,' said Peterson. 'Just get them in.'

I banged in the coordinates. 'Done.'

'Let's go.'

I said, 'Computer, initiate jump.'

'Jump initiated.'

The world went white.

Chapter Eighteen

I'm embarrassed to admit I'd completely forgotten about Miss Dottle, and when I heard the faint moan, for a moment I wondered who it could possibly be.

Markham helped her up.

'No, no I'm fine. I think I might have sprained my wrist, but it's not serious.'

Peterson gave her the seat. She blushed again and Markham grinned at me.

'Tim, where are we?'

He grinned, mischief dancing across his face. At that moment, he looked like a wet and muddy ten-year-old.

'Can't you guess?'

'No,' I said through gritted teeth, because I was well down the road to self-recrimination and despondency and slightly miffed that no one else was coming with me.

'We're in Bishop's Lynn,' he said cheerfully, shutting things down.

'And this is good because ...?'

'Because it's yesterday.'

I stared at him for a moment and then woke up. 'The baggage train is still here. In Lynn.'

'Yes.'

'They haven't set off yet.'

'No.'

'The storm hasn't happened yet.'

'No.'

'You're going to try and steal something before they set off?'

'Yes.' He glanced at the read-outs. The baggage train will set off in a few hours to make the low tide and we have twelve hours before we turn up at the Wellstream on our original jump. Should be more than enough time. Let's have a look at what we have to work with, shall we?'

Suddenly, I wasn't soaking wet, freezing cold and full of self-pity. Well, I was, but I had other things to think about now. More important things.

'Where are we?'

He angled the cameras. 'Some sort of courtyard.'

'Right,' I said. 'Let's think about this and make sure we get it right this time. Do we look for John or the baggage train?'

'The baggage train will be easier to find,' said Markham. 'You can't hide that number of wagons and horses.'

'But,' said Dottle, and stopped.

'But what?' said Peterson.

She shook her head.

'No, go on.'

'Well,' she said nervously, bright red again. 'If I was the King, I wouldn't want to be separated from my treasure. Would you?'

We thought about it.

'Good point,' said Markham. 'Certainly not the most valuable pieces. So where would a king stay?'

'The biggest and best inn in the place.'

'Not necessarily,' I said. 'He might be inflicting himself upon the Bishop, out at his manor at Gaywood.'

'Or, he might be at St Margaret's Priory, attached to the church.'

'Yes,' said Markham thoughtfully. 'When Henry IV travelled, he always preferred to stay in religious establishments. He reckoned the standard of hospitality was much higher than your average inn.'

Peterson stared at him. 'How do you know these things?'

'I keep telling you, I knock around with historians. Things rub off.'

'More like flake off in your case,' said Peterson.

We stared at Markham suspiciously and then thought about things some more.

'No,' said Peterson, eventually. 'If he's fleeing the French prince, then he's going to want the safety of town walls around him, isn't he? I would.'

True.

I roused myself. 'We need to have a look around. It's a big town for the day, but not that big. We'll find them soon enough.' I looked around. 'Miss Dottle, I'm putting you in charge of the getaway again. We may have to leave in a hurry, so be ready.'

'Why, what's going to happen?'

'No idea,' said Markham cheerfully, 'but something will.'

We slipped out into a warm wet night. Even if I hadn't known there was a massive storm on the way, I would have known there was a massive storm on the way, if you know what I mean. The air was close and oppressive. The pressure began to give me a headache. People often talk of the calm before the storm. This is how it feels.

Thinking about it, there can't be many people in this world who have been walking around in clothes soaked in a rainstorm twelve hours before it actually happens. I couldn't help wondering uneasily if we weren't causing some kind of temporal conundrum here. If the Time Police turned up, we'd have a hell of a lot of explaining to do. I tried to think of a rule we hadn't broken recently, and failed. No I didn't. No running in the corridors. I hadn't been able to run anywhere for some weeks now. So that was all right then. I'd hold off the Time Police with my immaculate corridor-traversing technique.

We groped our way along the wall. There were no torches anywhere and of course, we had no night vision. I could only hope my eyes became accustomed to the dark because right now, everything was just black on black.

We were in a small courtyard, backing on to a big, sprawling two-storeyed building. I could feel paving of some kind beneath my feet. Dark walls reared up around us. Looking back, the pod was quite invisible.

There was no moon – or rather, the moon was obscured by thick, heavy clouds which hung, seemingly, only just overhead, strangely bright against the black sky.

In the distance, a dog barked and that set off a few more. Someone shouted, a door banged, and they fell silent.

It was so quiet. The whole place was silent. This was Bishop's Lynn, a busy place, and the King was in town. Why wasn't it lit up like a firework factory? Where were the last-minute repairs to harness and wagons? Why weren't blacksmiths working the night round?

Had John imposed a curfew? We knew that he was ill. He was suffering from dysentery, which is never any fun. He would be dead in a few days. Now I came to think of it, Henry V died of dysentery as well.

Where was I? Yes – sick king. All right, he might have gone to bed early, but would everyone else? There were large numbers of soldiers here tonight. At the very least, the ladies of quickly and easily bought affection should be doing a roaring trade. Tonight, they were probably hiring themselves out by the minute.

We set off. Single file, walking in the shadow of the high walls. Markham, me, then Peterson. We ghosted gently down the street.

Ghostly we might have been, but they very nearly bloody caught us.

Just as we were oozing silently around the corner, a number of dark shadows oozed just as silently towards us. I froze. We all froze. Always the best thing to do in a crisis. I felt a pressure on my arm and carefully eased my weight backwards against the wall. We stood motionless, hardly even daring to breathe, trying to see what was going on because obviously we weren't the only people up to no good here.

I heard whispering, sibilant in the darkness and then, a faint, flickering light. Someone was lighting a torch.

I eased my weight onto my back foot and silently lifted the other, placing it down with extreme caution. I knew Peterson and Markham would be doing the same. Someone was bringing a torch and we couldn't afford to be seen. There was no one else on the streets. A curfew had definitely been imposed. Something was up.

Markham had his hand on my shoulder. I crept backwards, trailing my hand along the wall as we retraced our steps back to the pod and safety.

Except that they followed us. Not knowingly of course, but they followed us every inch of the way. We couldn't shake them off.

I heard a faint crunch as Peterson, leading the way, walked into the pod. I heard the slither of his hands as he felt his way towards the door. Dottle – definite historian material – had learned from her previous error and had it open ready. We squeezed back inside and the door closed behind us.

'Well,' said Peterson, exhaling hard. 'That was close. Two minutes earlier and they'd have had us. Anyone else getting the feeling this jump isn't meant to be?'

I was peering at the screen. The torch had been thrust into a sconce in the far wall and threw out a very faint light. Four men stood at the entrance to the courtyard. Minutes passed and none of them moved. They just stood. Silent and unmoving. The whole thing was rather eerie.

'What's going on?' whispered Dottle.

'Shh...' I said, although God knows why. No one could possibly hear us.

Whatever they were looking or waiting for happened out of range of our cameras. With no given signal that I could see, they split up. One crossed the courtyard and opened a small door. Two disappeared back into the street and the one remaining in the entrance waved his arm.

Someone, somewhere, must have been keeping watch, because the very next minute, a column of some half-dozen men appeared in the entrance and then walked swiftly across the courtyard, vanishing through the little doorway in the same eerie silence. The shapes were difficult to make out because the one flickering torch caused shadows to jump and leap across the walls. I was certain they were hooded and masked but strangely, their feet were bare. Of course – for silence.

Whatever was going on, once again, St Mary's was right in the middle of it.

'What on earth ...?' said Peterson.

'Assassins?' queried Markham.

'There's no point – he's dying. He'll be dead in a week.'

'Yes, but they don't know that.'

What the hell was going on?

Suddenly it all became clear. The men reappeared, every one of them carefully bearing a casket, or a small trunk, or a bundle of some kind. They paused in the courtyard and then the man at the entrance gave some sort of signal and they all vanished soundlessly out into the night.

I had it. I knew what was happening. The words tumbled out in my excitement. 'Oh, my God – he is. He's stealing them. John's stealing the Crown Jewels. He'll say they were lost. They were never lost. He's going to hide them here somewhere and then tomorrow, very publicly, and very ostentatiously lose them. He's planned all this. He's going to try to escape his creditors, his enemies, everyone. It's brilliant, and if the devious bastard hadn't buggered it all up by dying, he'd probably have got away with it.'

And we were right in the middle of it. I wasn't sure whether this was a good or bad thing. Shadowy figures moved around the courtyard. Armed guards patrolled the street outside. Now what? I sank back into the seat, stared at the screen and tried to think.

It was all happening. Right here. Right now. Right in front of us. There must be some way we could turn this to our advantage. There must be.

Markham and Peterson were pulling out bedding to use as makeshift cloaks.

'And none of this stuff is ever found?' demanded Markham, pulling a blanket over his head.

'Well, no one looks for it here. Why would they? We've just seen it all washed away forever.'

'So there's the possibility that it's all still here?'

'Not all of it, obviously. Just the small, valuable, portable stuff.'

'So,' said Markham. 'This means they're out there now, concealing this treasure somewhere nearby?'

'Yes,' I said impatiently, heading towards the door.

'Where are you going?'

'To steal the Crown Jewels, of course.'

'No,' said Peterson. 'No. Sorry Max, but no. It's all very well for you to risk life and limb in an historian kind of way, but not against armed men busy carrying out the biggest jewel theft of all time. Your repertoire of devious tricks will not avail you here. They'll skewer you as soon as they clap eyes on you. Stay here and keep the motor running.'

I couldn't believe it. 'But ...'

'No,' said Markham, following him towards the door. 'This is no time for girl power. You two stay here, run the hoover round, put the kettle on, and have everything nice for when the men get back.'

He was out of the door before I could rip his arms off.

They were good. I stared at the screen and try as I might, I couldn't make them out, and I knew they were there. Somewhere.

I guessed they were edging their way around the wall, but where they were going and what they were going to do when they got there, I hadn't a clue. I wouldn't mind betting they didn't either.

I remembered I was an historian. All right, a disgraced historian, but nevertheless ... I activated the night vision, set everything to record and then, because there wasn't anything else I could do, I paced. Up and down. Up and down. Returning every few steps to peer uselessly at the screen again.

Dottle wisely got out of the way.

Men came and went, bearing bundles or small trunks. They couldn't possibly move it all so it would be the small, easily carried and most valuable items that would be taken. That would not meet a watery end in The Wash tomorrow. I kept checking the recorders and angling the cameras. Everything was working perfectly well, but I had to do something.

Then another small group of dark figures appeared. The one at the end, shorter than the others, was struggling with a heavy casket. He set it down and ostentatiously eased his back. His companions manoeuvred themselves past him. No one stopped moving, not even for one moment. What a shame John couldn't organise his country as well as he could plan a jewel heist. He was in the wrong job.

As the last figure disappeared out of the gate, Markham picked up his casket, staggered slightly for the benefit of anyone watching, and stepped into deep shadow.

Nothing happened. No one shouted a demand to know what he thought he was doing.

I signed to Dottle who switched off the lights and I got the door open. The smell of wood smoke flooded in on the night air. We stood either side of the door and waited. My God, we were stealing the Crown Jewels. We were in the same league as John Lackland and Colonel Blood.

Markham struggled through the door. Dottle took one end of the casket and they set it down. I closed the door. The casket was heavy. I could tell by the way that it thumped to the floor. Dottle turned the lights up – just a fraction so as not to affect his night vision, and I asked him where was Peterson.

'He was just behind me.'

I flew to the screen. There he was. He was slipping out of the building, carrying something long and thin. If this was part of the regalia, then it might well be some sort of sceptre.

Things weren't so easy for him. Two other men appeared behind him, carrying a trunk between them. Right on his heels. There would be no slipping into the shadows for him. I felt my breath catch in my throat.

Tim's brilliant. He doesn't know the meaning of the word panic.

He stepped out of the line and without any attempt at concealment, crossed the courtyard towards us. Markham went to the door and stood with his hand on the manual control, waiting for my signal. Waiting for the first sign of trouble.

Quite openly, Peterson approached the pod. He propped his bundle upright against the wall and grinned cheerfully up at the camera he knew was hidden there. He fumbled a moment and then, still grinning, relieved himself against the pod, splashing it everywhere. Leon was going to go ballistic.

I'll admit I was surprised, but only because he usually pees on me. The other two men trudged on, backs bent, out of the entrance, and just for a quick second, the courtyard was empty. Dottle hit the lights again. Markham got the door open and we yanked him inside before it was even half-open.

We stood motionless, heads tilted, listening for a shout or some kind of alarm, but one man appeared in the doorway, another one in the entrance, they passed each other without speaking, and it looked as if we'd got away with it. Slowly, we unfroze and began to breathe again.

'We can't jump until they finish,' said Peterson. 'And just pray they do before the sun comes up and people start moving around.'

'They will,' said Markham, confidently. 'They'll want to be finished and gone before first light.'

'Yes, but we have to be gone in a few hours,' I said. 'So lots to worry about still.'

Even as we spoke, the last man was out through the arch. Unseen hands closed the little door. Someone removed the torch from the wall. Silence and stillness fell. I heaved a sigh of relief. The whole thing had taken no longer than twenty minutes from start to finish. If we'd waited even another few minutes we'd have lost our chance.

'Well,' said Markham, surveying our loot. 'We'd better see what we've got.'

I made them wash their hands and we all covered our hair. We always do this. Whatever we recover is always subject to rigorous scrutiny and we can't have experts casting doubt on the stuff we've gone to so much time and trouble to 'rescue', simply because someone has shed modern epithelia and hair all over it.

We laid the blankets over the muddy floor and investigated.

Markham's big heavy leather casket turned out to contain another smaller casket.

'It's not locked,' he said, frowning at the catch. 'Not that that would have been a problem.'

He eased open the lid, said, 'Shit,' and sat back on his heels in awe.

'Oh my God,' said Peterson.

Dottle's eyes were huge. Without thinking, she reached out to touch it.

Peterson gently grasped her wrist. 'Be careful. Your fingerprints might ruin everything.'

She blushed again and nodded.

'This must be from the Empress Mathilda's collection,' I said. 'I wonder if it was hers. Her own personal property.'

It was a crown. My first crown – and judging by the expressions on everyone else's faces, their first crown too.

We didn't touch it. We left it in its casket, crawling around on the floor so we could appreciate it from every angle.

Before anyone faints with excitement, I should say now that it wasn't the Imperial Crown of the Holy Roman Empire, with its distinctive hoop. That would have been too much, even for us, but it did have the traditional octagonal shape. Long golden pins held the eight plates together. Rounded and polished stones had been embedded in the gold plates and held in place with exquisitely fine wire. It was quite small – maybe made for a woman's head – which made sense since this particular piece had come to John through his grandmother, the Empress Mathilda.

We stared and stared at this beautiful object winking and glowing in the light.

'Shit,' said Markham again, which really just about summed up everything. We nodded, then closed the lid and packed the casket carefully inside the larger one and unwrapped the slender bundle.

If the crown had impressed us, the contents of the bundle just blew us away.

'Dear God,' said Peterson, and put his head in his hands.

'What?' said Dottle in alarm. 'What's the matter?'

We were looking at a sword.

We stared at it in silence. A long, long silence. Something, somewhere clicked itself on, I heard a hum and then whatever it was clicked itself back off again. Still we stared.

'What's wrong?' said Dottle, her voice beginning to rise. 'For God's sake, tell me.'

Peterson sat back and closed his eyes. I felt tears rolling down my cheeks. I know, but I was pregnant. Cut me some slack, please.

Markham cleared his throat and said, 'What is that?'

Peterson opened his eyes. He turned to me and gripped my hands. He had to swallow several times before he could speak and I couldn't speak at all.

His eyes shining, he said hoarsely, 'It's the Sword of Tristram. This is the Sword of Tristram, I'm sure of it. Look, there's the verse inscribed on the blade, just as described. Max, we've done something ...'

He stopped. He was right. I wasn't sure if we'd done something wonderful or something terrible.

Whether by good luck or bad, we'd pinched one of the very few items that definitely, definitely could be traced back to John's accident in The Wash. The crown was wonderful – but a crown is just a crown. It didn't have Property of the Holy Roman Empire inscribed anywhere on it, but this was the Sword of Tristram. Known. Documented. Lost in The Wash. I keep saying that and Markham says it makes it sound like an odd sock, but you know what I mean.

In the silence, I heard him get up and put the kettle on.

Chapter Nineteen

I think we all felt better after a mug of tea. I know I did. I'd turned the heaters up full blast so we were warmer now too, albeit a little steamy.

'He's a clever bugger,' said Markham in admiration, sprawled on the muddy floor clutching his mug. From one clever bugger to another, this was high praise.

Yes, John lost his baggage train in The Wash. Ninety per cent of it, anyway, but the remaining ten per cent – the really good stuff – never made it that far and was currently being hidden in the near vicinity. Very well hidden, since none of it was ever found again. Did he take the secret with him to his grave? If only he hadn't died, it would probably have worked. A nice injection of cash just as he needed it. Unfortunately for him, he did die, and who now knew what happened to that other ten per cent? Was it all still buried out there somewhere, just waiting for someone to find? Someone like us, for example?

But not tonight. We had what we came for. Let's not be greedy.

'Now what?' said Dottle, sitting, big-eyed in the corner.

'We need to go,' I said. 'When the sun comes up people are going to be curious about the sudden appearance of a small stone shack in the corner of the courtyard.'

'And even more curious about its sudden disappearance,' said Peterson, hauling himself to his feet. 'Come on. Treasure to bury. Jobs to save. Reputations to reinstate. Let's get cracking. Max, I'll need you to double-check my calculations. Get this wrong and we'll really be in trouble.'

'Why?' said Dottle.

Peterson scribbled on a piece of paper and shoved it in front of her. 'This is us. Our order of events is as follows: 12th April from 08:00 to 09:00, we're at the Wellstream watching the baggage train being lost. Yes?'

She nodded.

'We jump back – which admittedly we didn't plan to do but we're historians and we can adapt – so we jump back to midnight on the 11th April, steal a few things and depart around,' he glanced at the chronometer, 'around 02:00.'

She nodded again.

'Then we jump to the present location of St Mary's to hide this little lot for future discovery. We need to leave a safety margin so let's say we arrive at ...' he punched a few keys, '02:30.'

She nodded again.

'We must – must – finish hiding this little lot and be out of there before, at the very latest 07:30.'

'Why?'

'Because at 08:00 we're floundering around in the mud and watching the baggage train. We can't be there *and* at St Mary's.'

'Why not?'

'You can't have the same people in the same time twice.'

'Why? What would happen?'

'No one is quite sure, but everyone agrees it wouldn't be good. Not good at all. Not good for the timeline and especially not good for those trying to be in two places at the same time. Therefore, I don't care what anyone says – we're out of this by 07:30, job done or not. Is everyone clear on that?'

We got busy. Markham and Dottle cleared things away; Tim and I calculated and laid in the coordinates.

The world went white.

We were back at St Marys, but still in 1216, and let me say now that the woods of 1216 are considerably less friendly than the woods of today. Peterson was angling the cameras, but the view everywhere was exactly the same. Dense, tangled undergrowth and thickly growing trees. So much for our carefully chosen clearing.

And it was pissing down. The storm, so deadly in East Anglia, had mellowed to heavy rain here. Not that it mattered. We were still soaking wet.

'What's down there?' asked Dottle, trying to angle the cameras. 'Is there a St Mary's?'

'In 1216?' I said, vaguely. 'I'm not sure. I don't think it's even a priory yet. There might be a few huts but that's it. And on a night like this, no one's going to be out anyway. We'll be fine,' I added with typically misplaced confidence.

It was a vile night. The storm here was considerably less severe than in East Anglia, but conditions weren't pleasant at all. The rain lashed down. The wind was heaving the branches around. The primitive smell of wet earth and leaves hit me in the face and for one moment, I was back in the woods on the way to Arthur's Cave. In the distance, I could hear barking – a warning for us to take care. I doubted whoever was living down there would venture out on a night like this, but there was no point in taking chances.

'Are there wolves?' said Dottle, looking about her in some alarm.

Actually – that was a very good question. Yes, there were. Especially in this part of the country. John himself had offered a reward of ten shillings (a very great deal of money in 1216) for every two wolves killed and Edward I would order the complete extermination of all wolves in the counties bordering the Welsh Marches. Gerald of Wales wrote of how the wolves of Holywell devoured the corpses left in the wake of Henry II's Welsh campaign. I really wished I hadn't just remembered that.

'No,' I said, 'just village dogs,' and refused to catch Peterson's eye.

We stood in the doorway and peered out into the dark woods.

Markham was angling a soggy piece of paper. 'Ten paces that way.' He set off, forcing his way through the undergrowth. We followed, clutching spades, forks, and a pickaxe.

'So where exactly do we put it?'

He halted. 'Any place we can get a bloody spade in the ground. Not you Max. I'm in enough trouble without having to explain to Leon why we turned his pregnant wife into a navvy. You're the timekeeper and in charge of refreshments.'

There was no arguing with him and actually, I didn't want to. It was bloody hard work. They cleared the undergrowth first then Peterson hacked at the soil with the pickaxe and Markham dug. Occasionally they swapped over. Every now and then, Dottle had a go as well.

The digging seemed to take forever. The rain lashed down the whole time, sometimes washing the soil back in faster than they could dig it out. The bottom of the hole was filled with muddy water. They slipped and slithered and dug and dug.

'It's going to need to be deep,' said Peterson, stopping to wipe his face and rest his back. 'As far as I know this woodland is undisturbed until the present day but pigs root for truffles, dogs bury things and then dig them up again for reasons which escape everyone, trees blow over in storms ...'

'Earthquakes ... sea monsters .... Ice Ages ...' said a muffled voice. Markham was standing in a hole nearly as deep as he was.

'So not that deep then,' said Peterson, grinning at me.

I leaned over to look and my foot slipped in the mud. I would have joined him if Peterson hadn't grabbed me. 'Steady on. We don't want two of you in there. Markham's the official depth marker.'

'I have depth too, you know,' I said indignantly, because I don't like being useless.

'No you don't. Nor height. Plenty of width though. Is there any more tea?'

'Yes, pull out the portable depth marker and all of you come inside and take a few minutes.'

I can't begin to describe the state of the interior. Mud. Muddy water. Discarded towels. Footprints. Handprints. Clods of earth from our boots. The smell of wet leaves and wet earth. I closed the door behind them, shutting out the wind, rain, and animals that might not be wolves. They gulped down their tea and flexed their aching shoulders.

'How are we doing for time?'

'Not so bad, and it's going to be much easier filling in than digging out. Come on.'

We huddled in the doorway looking out at the rain slanting through the torchlight. Something howled.

'They sound very close,' said Dottle, looking around nervously. 'Are you sure they're not wolves?

'We're not in a sleigh being chased through the snow, for God's sake,' said Peterson, and I didn't think this was the moment to tell them about Gerald of Wales. 'Max, can you keep an eye out?'

I did. I took a torch and, as best I could in all the twisted undergrowth, patrolled a wide circle around them. At every moment, I expected to see glittering eyes in the undergrowth, but I couldn't see a thing except wet bushes, darkly glistening tree trunks, and lashing rain. According to the sounds I was hearing, they were quite close. All around me. Whatever they were. Not wolves, I told myself firmly. A pack of feral dogs, probably, living in the wild wood. Because in 1216, all the woods were wild. Unmanaged. Thick. Tangled. The home of outlaws. And wolves. You met some nasty things in the wild wood. I picked up a handy piece of wood. Yes, and one of those nasty things was me.

I forced my way back to the others. Peterson was just handing the carefully re-wrapped leather casket and bundle down to Markham, still standing in the bottom of what looked to me like an abyss.

I shouted over the noise of the wind and rain. 'How much longer?'

'We just have to fill in the hole.'

'Hey!' shouted a disembodied voice.

'And get Markham out, of course.'

'Hey!'

'Possibly the other way around.'

I said quietly, 'Tim, we should go as soon as possible.'

'What's the problem? Have you seen something?'

'No. But I am hearing things.'

He peered through the wind and rain. 'Me too.'

'And me,' said the hole.

I handed my branch to Dottle. 'Back to the pod. Usual instructions.'

She didn't bother to argue. She was getting the hang of this. She set off, using the branch to widen the path.

I said to Peterson, 'What can you hear?'

He shrugged. 'I can hear a talking hole. Isn't that enough?'

'Let's get him out. Quick as we can.'

We heaved out the massive lump of mud formerly known as Markham and I stood, flashing the torch around and keeping watch.

No need to tell them to hurry – they were heaving the soil back as fast as they could go, shovelling for dear life.

I pushed my hair back off my face, wiped the rain out of my eyes, and willed myself to stay calm. My job was to keep them safe. Keep them safe while we implemented my stupid scheme that was supposed to get us all out of the trouble I'd got us into in the first place. I was going to say 'get us out of the hole we'd dug for ourselves', but suddenly it wasn't the time for stupid jokes. Every hair on the back of my head was standing on end. A primal response to a primal predator. We had to get out of here and we had to get out of here now.

With a huge effort, I refrained from telling them to hurry, because they were hurrying. They were shovelling the earth as fast as they could go. I could hear their breath coming in short pants. Peterson was stamping it down like a madman. All my instincts were telling me – screaming at me – to get out of there as fast as we could. Because something was coming. Something moved in the undergrowth. I flashed the torch and for a moment, eyes gleamed.

'Done,' panted Markham, pulling the undergrowth back to try and disguise the raw earth.

'Come on,' I said. 'Don't run.'

We formed the traditional St Mary's clump, watching each other's backs, and forced our way back towards the pod. I went first with the torch. Markham and Peterson backed along behind me. We tripped and stumbled our way through the wood. Behind and to one side, something glided with us. I didn't dare flash the torch around. The pod was only paces away.

The door was shut.

'Shit,' said Peterson. 'Miss Dottle, could you open the door, please.'

At the same time, I said, 'Door.'

The door, which had started to open, jerked closed.

Something was behind us.

I shouted, 'Door,' and again, the door opened fractionally and then closed again.

This is what happens when you bring amateurs along. We were both trying to open the door at the same time. The first command opened the door and the second, given a fraction of a second later, was closing it again.

Peterson opened his com. 'Miss Dottle, leave the door alone.'

I opened my mouth to say Door yet again and something hit me from behind. For a moment, I thought my last moment had come and waited for the smell of wet wolf, the yellow eyes in my face and the teeth at my throat, but it was Markham, shoving me against the side of the pod. He stood in front of me, clutching a tree branch. Something dark moved, uttering a low, liquid growl that lifted the hairs on my neck.

I kicked the door and shouted, 'Dottle, step back from the door. Don't touch anything.' I took a deep breath and said as calmly as I could, 'Door.'

The door slid open. I didn't take any chances, shoving my hand in the gap to keep it open. Markham pushed Peterson first, and then me. We both fell through the door and I landed on Peterson, probably nearly crushing the life out of him.

Markham threw his branch at whatever it was that was out there and followed us in. The door closed behind him.

Peterson was threshing around. 'Get off me, will you. I can't breathe.'

I lifted my head. 'Listen sunshine. The number of times you've peed on me, the least you can do is let me use you as a landing strip occasionally.'

Markham heaved me to my feet and we all stood, panting. Listening. Apart from our own breathing, the familiar faint hum, and a quiet click as a read-out changed, there was nothing.

Dottle was in tears. 'I'm sorry, I'm so sorry; I didn't know what to do. I kept trying to open the door and it kept closing again. I kept hitting the door switch as you said, and it wasn't working, and I didn't know what to do, so I just kept hitting it and ...'

'It's OK,' said Peterson, wiping his face and getting his breath back. 'We're all safe and sound now. It's OK.'

We tried to tidy ourselves and the pod, but it was hopeless. Every towel was sodden and muddy. The floor was swimming. The locker doors, the console, everything was covered in muddy smears. The place stank. You can't be washed away in some sort of storm surge, go on to dig a hole in a muddy wood while surrounded by hostile indigenous wildlife, and expect to look good at the end of it. We couldn't even say we'd carried out the Great Jewel Heist of 1216 because King John had done that.

'We were merely the jackals snapping at his heels,' said Markham, earning himself no friends at all in a confined space.

We did our best, however, smearing mud all over the few places that hadn't previously looked like a swamp and then it was time to go. I think we would all have liked to put off that moment for as long as possible. We had no idea what we would be going back to, and we'd done the walk of shame once, but our time was up. We had to go.

I did the business.

The world went white.

Obviously, we couldn't keep this one quiet. For a start, there was the state of us when we got back. We looked as if we'd stood under the Victoria Falls for a week and then been involved in some sort of mudslide.

Helen went ballistic – and not just with me this time. Everyone was exposed to her displeasure. It was good to see the load spread evenly for a change.

Peterson had strained his bad arm and shoulder. He was confined to bed for the rest of his life. He looked exhausted and didn't argue, which, I think, worried her more than anything. Markham physically was OK, but very quiet. Apparently, he didn't even try to goose Hunter, which caused her some concern.

I was in and out of the scanner all evening – when I wasn't being yelled at. I protested I hadn't actually done any digging, but no one took the slightest bit of notice.

'Please,' I said, eventually, just to shut them up. 'I don't feel very well. Can I go to bed?'

Silence. Medical people converged on me like heat-seeking missiles.

'What did you just say?' said Helen.

'I don't feel very well. I'm cold. I'd like to have a bath and go to bed.'

I was freezing cold. My head hurt. My chest hurt. I just wanted to sleep.

I spent an hour up to my nose in a hot bath. When I came out, Dottle was fast asleep which was just as well, because I was much too tired to talk.

And, if truth be told, more than a little scared about what was going to happen next.

Chapter Twenty

Dr Bairstow sent for me directly after breakfast. Dottle had been discharged. Peterson and Markham, exhausted, were still asleep. So, just me then. I thought about this as I made my way to his office.

At least this time he instructed me to sit down.

Everything was just as it had been. There was no sign of the recent Halcombe infestation. What was going on?

He stared at me for a long time. I made myself stay calm and return his stare. I hadn't actually been in his office since that day. Mrs Partridge sat behind him as she always did. She kept her eyes on her scratchpad. I was getting no clues from either of them.

He kept it short. 'Report.'

I kept to the facts as I knew them. I said nothing about anonymous data stacks. I said nothing about stealing Leon's pod. I'm not sure I even mentioned Peterson and Markham, although he must have known they'd been with me. Nothing about Dottle, either. I outlined the mission objective, described what had happened as unemotionally as I could, and ended with the burial in the woods. Then I shut up and, without actually saying so, gave him to understand the whole thing was now up to him.

He stared at his desk for a while, then got up and limped to the window, looking out over the South Lawn. I stared at his back, oscillating between hope and fear. Finally, he heaved a sigh and came to sit back down again. We looked at each other.

He said faintly, 'The Sword of Tristram?'

'We think so sir, yes.'

'And possibly the crown of the Holy Roman Emperor?'

'One of them, sir, yes.' I said, not wanting to overstate things.

'Buried in our woods.'

'We certainly hope so.'

'You noted the spot?'

'We did, sir. All ready for you to inform Thirsk.'

Silence did not so much fall as plummet. Taking my heart and hopes with it.

He sat back in his chair. 'No,' he said firmly.

I could hardly believe my ears. Had we done all this for nothing? Had I just made things worse? I swallowed hard. 'I'm sorry, sir – what?'

'No.'

I took a deep breath, sat forwards, and prepared to argue to the death. I had nothing to lose. If the worst came to the worst, I'd grab a spade from somewhere and, pregnant or not, go and dig the bloody stuff up myself. At least there wouldn't be any wolves this time. 'But sir ...'

'No,' he said again. 'Not Thirsk. They are not, at the moment, among my favourite people.'

He had favourite people?

Almost as if talking to himself, he continued. 'They turned on us. They turned on their Chancellor. Setting aside your illegal actions, your improper use of a pod, your disobedience, your irresponsibility, and your thoughtless stupidity – subjects to which, do not doubt, we will frequently be returning – this will be an astounding find. More than astounding. We have, in the past, enabled them to make a number of spectacular discoveries which have considerably enhanced their prestige in the academic world. None of that could have been achieved without us and yet, at the first opportunity, they cut us adrift to fend for ourselves. And not just us, but the very able Chancellor whose foresight in backing St Mary's has been instrumental in their success. I am not an unforgiving man,' he added unconvincingly, 'but on this occasion, I see no need to involve Thirsk in any way. We are perfectly capable of handling the discovery of these artefacts for ourselves.'

'We tend not to preside over our own discoveries, sir,' I said cautiously, hoping I was nudging him in the right direction. Towards Dr Chalfont. On the grounds of ...'

'I don't intend that St Mary's should discover these items. After your recent behaviour, I wouldn't let you excavate one of Mr Strong's compost heaps,' he said, returning to his customary tone. 'I think we should rub their noses in it by inviting Dr Chalfont to preside over the find. And, possibly, Professor Penrose as well. You can never have too many academics to muddy the waters. I shall telephone her at once to discover whether she will provide her own team or whether she wishes St Mary's to do the donkey work. Then, after the dust has settled, accolades awarded, benefits reaped and fame and fortune enjoyed, then, and only then, might I allow myself to contemplate the possibility of permitting St Mary's to enter, once again, into some sort of partnership with the University of Thirsk. Under renegotiated terms, of course. I expect Dr Chalfont will be delighted to assist me in that area.'

He sat back, smiling the satisfied smile of someone settling the score in such a manner that it would probably remain settled until the end of time. I would bet good money that Dr Chalfont was sitting by the phone and expecting his call any minute now.

'Awesome, sir,' I said, giving credit where it was due and reserving a little for myself as well.

I was convinced of it now. Dr Bairstow had engineered the whole thing. Well, not us stealing Arthur's sword perhaps, but he'd certainly been behind all subsequent events. I could picture the scene. He'd been notified of our transgression and, unable to do anything about it, he'd simply, in the words of a famous military leader I couldn't call to mind at that moment, tied a knot and gone on.

Faced with the ever-present threat of Thirsk's interference, he'd turned a disaster into an opportunity to discredit them. I wondered how he'd managed to engineer things so we got Halcombe. I could imagine him vehemently protesting. I could hear him saying, 'No, not Halcombe. He's not the man to fit in at St Mary's.' And because that was exactly what Thirsk wanted, they'd fallen for it. And Dr Bairstow had let him get on with things, with the result that Helen had Halcombe in isolation and his loyal lieutenant had defected to the enemy.

'What about the id ... what about Mr Halcombe, sir?'

He smiled coldly, his resemblance to a merciless bird of prey increasing with every second. 'Oh, while Mr Halcombe would appear to be on Thirsk's payroll, I'm almost certain he is taking his instructions from someone else.'

I sat up straighter. 'Who?'

He said nothing because he always expects us to work things out for ourselves. I thought furiously.

'The same people who got to Hoyle?'

'Yes, I think so, don't you?'

Some months ago, during my fortunately brief stint as Training Officer, we'd had an assignment go wrong and we'd finished up at the Battle of Bosworth. One of my trainees, a somewhat unbalanced young man, had allowed an obsession to overcome him, been manipulated into hijacking a pod, and attempted to pervert the course of History. He'd died, but not before he'd told us of some shadowy presence that had tried to use him to disgrace St Mary's. It would seem they hadn't given up.

I was about to ask if Thirsk had been aware of this, but second thoughts answered that question for me. Of course not. They'd been used. They would not be happy about it. The corridors of our former employers would run thick with blood, blame, and retribution.

And St Mary's was now in a position to replace what, on the face of it, was a rather dull iron sword whose provenance could never be proved, with the fabulous, genuine, easily identifiable Sword of Tristram. And a crown belonging to the Holy Roman Emperor. And we'd saved Miss Dottle from a fate slightly worse than death. Bloody hell, we're good.

I shuffled forwards on my chair. I had to know. Other than Mrs Partridge, no one else was here. No witnesses.

'Sir, did you engineer all of this?'

He looked down his beaky nose. 'No, of course not. You and you alone were responsible for your disgraceful behaviour at Thirsk. I merely took advantage of an unfortunate situation to make sure everyone got exactly what they wanted. Thirsk got their permanent presence here, and what a double-edged sword that has turned out to be for them. Because of that, Dr Chalfont will almost certainly be restored to her rightful position as Chancellor. Indeed, it is my hope that her imminent discovery will lead to her position being considerably strengthened.'

His chair creaked as he leaned forwards and said in a softer tone, 'And you, Max have, I hope, learned a valuable lesson.'

I blinked back a sudden tear, nodded, and said in a small voice, 'I have, sir.'

He sat back and said briskly, 'Then we need say no more about it. I shall inform all departments that you have been reinstated as Head of the History Department.'

I took a deep breath. 'Actually, sir, if you don't mind – no.'

'No?'

'Sir, Mr Clerk has done an excellent job. It's not fair on him. I don't have long to go and I have one or two small funding projects I'd like to finish. I'll put in for my last jump if I may, and then, if you don't mind, on the agreed date, I'll sally forth and multiply.'

He nodded. 'As you wish.'

I felt about a hundred years younger as I walked out of his room. I would have liked to have felt about a hundred pounds lighter as well, but that doesn't happen when you're pregnant. Which I was. Very pregnant. Definitely time to put together my last jump, but first, I had a bridge to mend.

He was in our room, sitting at the table, frowning at his data stack.

I was very conscious of being in the wrong – and given the state of his pod he had a more than legitimate grievance, and so I made a huge effort to be conciliatory.

'I think we were both to blame.'

He shut down his data stack. 'All right, shall we agree to split things 50/50?'

I was outraged. 'No! More like 70/30.'

'I think you're being too hard on yourself.'

'No, that's not what I meant.'

'Well, tell me what you did mean.' He sat back, smiling, encouraging, sympathetic, reasonable, calm, everything I hate. He knows I can't deal with that.

I struggled to find the words, through mounting exasperation. 'I mean ... That is ... You were the one who ...' and conscious that I was still tired, that I still had 13th-century mud under my fingernails, that I was still pregnant, that it was vitally important I remain composed and make my case calmly and reasonably, and that he was Leon – husband and hero – I began to cry.

He pushed himself up from the table, but I waved him back.

He regarded me with some concern. 'Max, you never cry. Are you feeling all right? Should I take you back to Sick Bay?'

I sniffed and wiped my nose on my sleeve – yes, I know, not an attractive habit – and groped for the tissue that was bound to be in one of my pockets somewhere. 'No, no. I'm OK. One good blow and I'll be fine.'

A pause. 'What are we talking about here?'

So, there we were, all on track for a happy ending. Except for the idiot Halcombe, of course. Helen was still enthusiastically doing everything she could to prevent him developing leprosy.

'Still undergoing multi-drug treatment,' she said, in answer to my query, 'Daprone, clofazimine, rifampicin…'

'For how long?'

'Twelve months should do it. Maybe two years.'

I stepped back. 'What? We don't want him here all that time.'

'We haven't got him here all that time. I'm shunting him off to some obscure military hospital somewhere.'

'But he doesn't *have* leprosy.'

She shrugged.

'But surely he must know he doesn't have it. He knows he was making it all up.'

'Well, he can hardly come out and say so, can he? What could he say: Oh I wanted to sabotage the assignment and I thought leprosy was a good way to go, but I'm fine now?' She gestured at the frankly terrifying battery of equipment surrounding a glum-looking Halcombe, and at Nurse Hunter, suited, booted, handling him with a pair of tongs and, by the looks of it, enjoying every minute.

'And as a member of the medical profession,' she added virtuously, 'it is my duty to take every precaution to safeguard the welfare of my patients.'

First I'd heard of that, but now was probably not the time to mention it.

'But doesn't he know – leprosy isn't that infectious?'

'Then he's a victim of his own ignorance, isn't he. Silly ass.' She walked off.

I'm telling you now – don't ever mess with St Mary's.

Chapter Twenty-one

I thought I'd better put in for my last jump before fate intervened and everything went tits up again. Always quit while you're ahead.

Our last jump is supposed to be something special. It's usually a personal choice – a chance to see a favourite event or person, or as I said to Leon, an inadequate reward for years of unremitting toil and sacrifice. I could still hear him laughing from the bathroom.

I'd spent some time thinking about where and when. Until recently, of course, a last jump hadn't seemed a likely possibility but now, suddenly, it was all back on again. I spent an hour or so, running through old favourites – Carthage, Persepolis, Babylon, Hastings, and so on. These were exciting possibilities and well worth a look, but last jumps don't always go according to plan. On Kal's last jump, we had encountered Jack the Ripper and he'd proved surprisingly difficult to get rid of. My previous last jump – it's complicated, don't ask – the one to Agincourt, had gone about as badly as anything could go.

And then, from nowhere a memory popped into my head. A memory of sitting on the grass at Caer Guorthigirn and thinking about giant stones dancing across the landscape.

Out of consideration to Leon, I ought to choose a destination where nothing could possibly go wrong, and where better? The site was uninhabited and it wasn't as if the stones were likely to uproot themselves and chase us down the road, were they?

Leon and I weren't supposed to jump together, so I opted for Markham and Peterson, both of whom, after everything that had happened recently, deserved a nice day out.

'Where are we going?' enquired Markham, absent-mindedly scratching himself.

'What are you doing?' enquired Peterson, moving away. 'Have you got mange again?'

'No!' he said, hurt.

We regarded him suspiciously.

He stared right back, visibly struggling not to scratch.

I cleared my throat for attention. 'Right – my last jump.' I brought up an image on the screen.

'Wow!' said Peterson. 'Cool.'

'Yes, I thought so too,' I said smugly.

Markham blinked. 'What the hell is that?'

'Stonehenge.'

'No it's not. I've been to Stonehenge. It's huge. Big stones on top of other big stones. This is just ...' he tailed away.

'Just what?'

'Just ... stones.'

'Yes,' said Peterson, scathingly. 'The clue's in the name. *Stone*henge.'

I intervened before things could deteriorate further. 'There were many Stonehenges. The version we see today with the trilithons is quite modern.

Markham sighed. 'Only an historian could describe something dating from 2000 BC as quite modern.'

Never mind saving him from Peterson. I was going to thump him myself.

Correctly anticipating my expression, he sat up straight. 'Sorry. Carry on.'

'As I would have been saying, had I been allowed to get on with it, there were many phases of Stonehenge. I've requested and been granted permission to jump there, but Thirsk, possibly proffering an olive branch, have offered to fund an in-depth look at early Stonehenge. Sometime between 2600 and 2100 BC, when it was smaller than it is today.

I started bringing up images.

'Stonehenge has evolved over thousands of years and there were several construction phases. The first, a circular bank-and-ditch enclosure, dates from around 3100 BC.

'The next phase is somewhat vague – a timber structure may have been erected around this time, but during the third phase, which is when we're going, two concentric circles were built. At least, popular opinion has it they were circles. Excavations show they were in fact horseshoe shaped and whether that was deliberate or whether the circles were unfinished is another of the things we'll be investigating. The horseshoe shape has always been important, especially to the ancient world. It's the last letter of the Greek alphabet. Both Greeks and Romans hung horseshoes on their walls for luck, a superstition that continues to this day. Hanging a downward pointing horseshoe on your bedroom wall makes men more virile and women more fertile. Theories say the shape describes the route of the sun. So, are they simply unfinished circles or some kind of protective symbol?'

'Protection from what?' asked Markham.

'Let's see if we can find out. After this phase, the big Sarsen stones were introduced and Stonehenge begins to take on the shape we know today.'

'The modern phase,' said Markham, straight-faced.

Peterson turned to him. 'There is evidence of cremated bones being buried at the bottom of some of the Aubrey Holes. Wouldn't it be fascinating if some of them were yours?'

'No,' said Markham.

I intervened again. 'A nice, simple jump. Another surveying job.'

'Because the last one went so well,' muttered Markham.

'What is the matter with you?' said Peterson. 'Has Hunter given you the boot again?'

'No, of course not. She knows how lucky she is. In fact, she's always banging on about me having to go and see her in Sick Bay.'

'Why?'

He shuffled uneasily. 'Don't know. So how long are we on site for?'

'As long as it takes,' I said briskly. 'A week probably. As well as a survey of the henge, I want an overview of the entire area. It's not known as the Sacred Landscape for nothing. There's barrows, tumuli, Woodhenge, Silbury Hill – you name it – it's all there. It will be winter so we'll have all the time in the world to do a proper job. Get yourselves kitted out and meet me tomorrow outside Number Eight.'

'Why winter?' said Markham, mournfully.

'Well, other than during the solstice, the site's likely to be deserted. The ground's far too hard to dig – all building work will have ceased. Everyone will very sensibly be at home, huddled around the fire.'

'Except us.'

'Except us, obviously. Undisturbed and able to get on with things.'

'What's the weather likely to be?' enquired Peterson, bashing away at his scratchpad.

'Well, the general trend was towards milder weather, but around 2200 BC, major volcanic eruptions disrupted the North Atlantic weather patterns and winters became bitterly cold, so I'm not sure what we'll get.'

'It's Salisbury Plain,' said Markham gloomily. 'It'll be raining.'

'You don't know that.'

'It's always raining on Salisbury Plain. When I was in the army, I spent what seemed like years there, running pointlessly in one direction and then back in another direction and then off in a completely different direction. It was like rugby but with bombs instead of balls. Thank God, I barely remember any of it, but the bit I do remember is that it always rains on Salisbury Plain. Great, grey, icy sheets of it, coming at you sideways ...'

'Yes, all right. We get the picture. Three sets of wet weather gear then.'

'Excellent idea. What will you two be wearing?'

They made it special for me. Dr Bairstow met me in the Great Hall and offered me his arm. We walked slowly down the long corridor, the rest of the History Department trailing along behind, laughing and cracking terrible jokes.

The techies applauded as we approached Number Eight. I looked up. Nearly everyone in the unit was crammed on to the gantry, watching and waving. I waved back.

Leon handed me into Number Eight where Peterson and Markham were already waiting. He didn't say anything. We'd said it all the night before, curled up together in our room, watching the moon cast shadows on the walls as the soft breeze fluttered the curtains, and we made plans for our future.

He ran a professional eye over the console. 'Everything's all laid in. Even an historian won't be able to get this one wrong.'

Markham snorted. 'You underestimate them.'

Leon took my hand. 'Take care.'

'Of course,' I said, slightly indignantly. Why does everyone think I don't?

His gaze swept around the pod, alighting on the other two musketeers. No words were spoken, but it was very clearly understood that the consequences of not safely bringing back either the pod or me would be serious. Probably in that order, too. He might be a husband at night, but during the hours of daylight, he was a techie to his fingertips.

Not that anything could go wrong on this jump. The landscape would be empty. Monotonous, even. As far as I knew, earthquakes rarely happened on Salisbury Plain. The mammoths and dinosaurs were all dead. Glaciers no longer gouged their way across the landscape. As Markham said, stowing his gear in a locker, even an incendiary historian couldn't accidentally set Stonehenge alight, because not only was there nothing to burn, but the continual, incessant, never-ending rain would ensure we couldn't get a flame even if we took one of Professor Rapson's homemade flame throwers.

'He does seem to have a bee in his bonnet about Salisbury Plain,' said Peterson, watching him bang the locker doors closed.

'He does seem to be scratching a lot,' I said.

He looked up to see us watching him. 'What?'

'Nothing,' we said.

'Sit down Max,' said Peterson, indicating the right-hand seat.

'Are you driving?' I said, suddenly alarmed.

'Of course. You're the guest of honour. Now, close your eyes.'

'Is this so I won't see you bounce us all the way into Somerset?'

He sighed. 'No, it's so that when you open them, the first thing you will see is Stonehenge at sunrise.'

I was touched. 'Tim, that's lovely. Thank you.'

'Good luck everyone,' Leon said, smiled for me alone, and left the pod.

The door closed behind him.

'Everyone sitting comfortably?' said Peterson. 'Then I'll begin.'

The world probably went white. I had my eyes closed.

We barely bumped at all. I was impressed. I could hear them both fussing around, muttering to each other. 'Don't open your eyes yet.'

'All right,' I said, swallowing down my impatience.

'There we go. Open your eyes, Max.'

I opened my eyes, blinked, and blinked again.

They'd dimmed the lights in the pod so I could appreciate the full beauty of the scene outside.

Stonehenge at sunrise, but not the modern Stonehenge, with the familiar jumble of stones standing like jagged teeth against a wide sky. This was an early version. Tim moved out of the way and I leaned forward to see. I could just make out the dark bluestones, rearing up out of the early morning mist. The huge sarsens were not yet in place. Instead of the famous trilithons, the smaller bluestones stood in lonely splendour. A wonder of light and shade in the early morning light.

We'd landed exactly where I'd planned. Just about a hundred yards from the northeast entrance. Our idea was to approach Stonehenge from the Avenue, as our ancestors had done, to see what they would have seen. And it was breath-taking.

There had been a hard frost overnight and what would have been a wide, white panorama bisected by blue shadows had been transformed into a golden glowing landscape as the sun rose higher into the sky. It wasn't the winter solstice or any kind of astronomically important date but even so, to watch the long, dark shadows sweeping across the silent landscape was very special.

'Are we getting all this?' I said, suddenly alarmed because I'd allowed myself to be carried away by the view.

'Of course,' said Peterson, pulling our gear out of the lockers. 'Do you want to stop for tea first or shall we get cracking?'

Markham was peering at the screen. 'It's not raining. Are you sure we're in the right place?'

'Good point,' said Peterson. 'I'm always confusing Stonehenge with the palace of Versailles. Should we check the coordinates again?'

I struggled, trying to thrust my arms into my heavy-weather jacket, wind a scarf around my neck, and assemble everything I needed, all at the same time. 'Everyone ready?'

Raining it might not have been, but it was cold. Bloody cold. We scrambled up onto the roof and stood in the freezing silence, maps, charts, and scratchpads scattered at our feet, orienting ourselves, turning slowly, trying to take it all in at once.

'Wow,' said Markham softly, and he was right. 'All these lumps and bumps…'

'Barrows and tumuli you mean?'

'Yeah …'

'All of which we will be endeavouring to map.'

'Yeah …'

'There's so much more here than we thought,' said Peterson, staring around in the hushed stillness, his breath puffing in the cold.

'Yes. A lot of it will be ploughed over in the centuries to come, or will be eroded or destroyed,' I said. 'But at the moment it's a real landscape of the dead.'

'It's bloody amazing,' said Markham, putting the Security Section's spin on things.

'Right.' I said, scrabbling at my scratchpad with gloved fingers. 'First things first. As in the words of the song, we'll walk up the Avenue to Stonehenge, approaching the north-east entrance. I want to check out the Station Stones and the two barrows within the henge. We'll count and plot the positions of the bluestones. Keep your eyes open for any evidence that they're uncompleted circles. Then we'll move on to the Aubrey Holes and from there to the ditch and bank which are the oldest components. Let's go.'

We jumped down. Well, they jumped down and I scrambled ungracefully down after them, much to their amusement. I noticed they stood well back.

'No, I'm fine. I can manage.'

'Actually Max, we were concerned you would fall.'

'Oh,' I said, slightly mollified. 'That was thoughtful.'

'Because let's face it, if you fell on Markham you'd kill him.'

I stamped back inside the pod.

We gathered our gear together, loading up with total stations, portable laser distance meters, spare batteries, our 3D scanner, cameras and recorders, and something to eat and set off, our feet crunching on the frosty grass. Looking back, I could see our footprints. We were the only people here. The only living people, that is.

We walked slowly up the Avenue, turning occasionally to absorb the full impact of the huge silence around us. Despite the weak sunshine, the air was bitterly cold. There were no birds in the sky. The air was completely still. Apart from us, nothing was moving. There was not so much a sense of age as of agelessness. Of something that had already been here for a very long time.

The Avenue was bordered on each side by the traditional bank and ditch. The frost lay thick at the bottom of the ditches where the sun rarely reached at this time of year.

We paused just inside the entrance, between what today is the Slaughter Stone and its now-disappeared partner. The sun was well risen by now, although it had had no effect on the frost. The icy stones twinkled at us. The whole effect was, as Markham had said – bloody amazing.

We were seeing something that had vanished four thousand years ago. The whole world is familiar with Stonehenge as it is today , but no one for all that time had ever seen this. Just us. God – I love this job!

Peterson and Markham stayed behind me as I recorded everything, rotating slowly to get the full effect. I didn't want any of our frosty footprints to mar this perfect shot. I got the four Station Stones, the North and South Barrows and the horseshoes of bluestones, all perfectly aligned and upright. Finally, I snapped off the recorder. 'OK guys, let's get cracking.'

We had a plan of action. Using the 3D scanner, Peterson would scan the stones. Making multiple scans from different directions, he'd create an image of every surface.

Markham had the hand-held laser scanner to plot the position of each individual stone, its measurements and its relationship to the others.

I was in charge of the cameras and recorders. I'd get details of the colours and textures. All this mass of information would form a point cloud, and the computer would turn it all into a stunning, full-size, navigable 3D holo. Thirsk were going to love this. I could just see Dr Bairstow's face as he presented it to them. Closely followed by his massive invoice.

I moved slowly from stone to stone, dictating as I went and cursing as the biting cold made my eyes stream. I was looking for tool markings or carvings of any kind, screwing up my eyes in the brilliant light.

A slight breeze got up, making my cheeks tingle. I pulled my jacket more closely around me and began to examine the bluestones, gently touching each one as I passed. Touching History. And avoiding standing in their shadows. You can call it superstition if you like, but not until you've stood, alone, in a stone circle four thousand years ago and heard strange noises in the wind. *Then* you can call it superstition. If you dare.

My circle complete, I wandered again into the centre and stood looking around me, taking it all in. I could see our footprints in the frosty grass, criss-crossing the circle. The wind sighed softly through the stones.

We stopped for lunch, taking it outside the henge by unspoken consent. For some reason, none of us wanted to eat inside. You don't sit down and start scarfing ham sandwiches in Canterbury Cathedral and this was exactly the same.

The afternoon was shorter than we expected. Only an hour or so after we'd eaten, the sun hid behind the clouds moving up from the horizon and I found I was shivering.

'Come on,' said Peterson. 'There's no time limit on this job. Let's call it a day and see what we've got so far.'

After the Arctic temperatures outside, the inside of the pod was warm and full of light. We dumped our gear, shrugged out of our heavy clothes and began to download the info. I plugged my recorder into the screen as Peterson rummaged through the meal trays. We pulled the heating tabs and sat down with a hot meal to view what we had so far.

'Tomorrow,' I said to Markham, 'we'll measure the bank and ditches. Tim, can you make a start with the Aubrey Holes. When we've finished here, we'll move across country to see what we can see.'

'I want to walk the Cursus,' said Peterson, mouth full of treacle tart. 'It's older than Stonehenge, you know.'

'You will,' I said. 'We've plenty of time on this.'

After we'd finished, we cleared away and went outside for a look at Stonehenge under the stars.

The night was clear and very, very cold. 'It's going to be another lovely sunny day tomorrow,' said Markham, demonstrating why it was so fortunate for the world of weather forecasting that he'd taken up a career in security.

I looked up at the stars. Today, with light pollution everywhere, we're used to just a few faint dots in an orange night sky, or, if we're lucky, the odd constellation or two, but this – this was amazing.

Arching overhead, brilliant in the night sky, a whole galaxy floated by. The Milky Way stretched from horizon to horizon. I tried to pick out the constellations I knew – Orion with his belt and the one I always called The Milk Saucepan. I should be able to find the North Star, something I'd learned to do in basic training. Ian Guthrie had spent hours trying to install the rudiments of night-time navigation in me, but there was no chance tonight. Polaris was only one brilliant star among many. So many stars. Some were big and bright and solitary; others were grouped in clusters so dim and distant they looked like stellar dust sprinkled across the sky.

This was what our ancestors saw when they looked up. When they saw pictures in the sky. Gods, heroes, fabulous animals – they all whirled overhead in some intricate celestial dance. I was sure if I stood in the right place at the right time and said the right words, I would hear the Music of the Spheres. Tonight was a night for wonder. And mystery. And magic.

Dark against a star-filled sky, the stones cast long shadows. I stared, entranced, at a black and silver landscape under a black and silver sky, imagining I could hear the stones whispering their secrets to one another as they drove their roots deep into time itself.

It's on nights such as these that the Wild Hunt streams across the sky in relentless pursuit of their human prey. Time out of mind they've hunted their quarry across this landscape; pursued them to the edge of sanity and beyond. Once caught, their victims, doomed and damned, would be dragged back to the Hollow Hills, never to be seen in this world again. The only protection for humans is to stay indoors, bolt the door and shutter the windows. Whole families would huddle around the hearth, keeping up the fire and praying to their gods as Herne the Hunter and the rest of that furious host swept across the starlit skies.

I shivered, and not because of the cold, either. I wouldn't want to be here alone. Not at night, anyway. Stones have long memories.

I looked around the desolate plain and listened to the lonely wind. I even looked up to the sky, half convinced I could hear the baying hounds and thunder of hooves as Herne and his huntsmen galloped overhead. This was an eerie landscape. Haunted even before the arrival of man. Back in the Ancient Days. Before History began.

I shivered again.

'Me too,' said Peterson. 'Let's get back inside. Busy day tomorrow.'

We woke early the next morning, all ready to get going again.

'What a lovely sunny day,' said Peterson sarcastically, staring at the enormous clouds building in an already overcast sky. 'Let's go outside and listen to the wind shriek.'

We wrapped up well and set off towards Stonehenge again, walking directly into the icy wind. My ears throbbed.

'This is bracing,' said Peterson, cheerily.

I stopped just inside the entrance and looked around me. This was not the same place as yesterday. Today there was no golden sunshine. No specks of light glinted off the icy stones. Today the bluestones were dark and sullen. Something tightened at the base of my skull. Something had changed. Were the stones closer together? Did they reach towards us like fingers? I shivered.

We – the three of us – have been rattling around History for years now. Admittedly, things haven't always gone according to plan and sometimes that's no bad thing, because as historians, you get to develop a kind of sixth sense. It's that little tickle at the back of the brain that defies all the evidence of eyes and ears and says, 'Something's not quite right.' It's the triumph of experience over optimism. The prudent historian heeds this tiny tickle.

I think we've established that the 'p' word doesn't really apply in my case, but contrary to all the evidence so far, I'm not completely stupid. I stood still, turning my head from left to right, trying to identify the reason for this flickering unease.

There was nothing. Nothing I could see that would account for my sudden feeling of disquiet but even so ... We may be modern and urban these days, but when we really need them, the instincts of our ancestors are not that far away.

I stood, listening to the wind's song in the stones.

A single snowflake drifted down and landed on my sleeve. Then another. And another. I looked up and saw many more, swirling above my head, light against the darkening sky.

Peterson and Markham were on the other side of the henge, unpacking their gear. I trudged across the iron-hard ground.

'I don't like the look of this, guys. We can't work in this weather. Let's get back and wait it out.'

Obediently, they began to pack up again.

'Nothing changes, does it,' said Markham, chattily, shouldering his backpack. 'Anything more than three snowflakes brings the entire country to a complete standstill.'

'We can leave you outside if you like,' said Peterson. 'All the more room for Max and me.'

'You don't want to set a precedent. If she gets any bigger then you'll be joining me outside.'

I poked him. 'You do know I'm standing right here, don't you? And that I have sharpened hairpins and I'm not afraid to use them.'

'Just saying,' he said.

We pulled up our scarves, turned our faces to the snow-laden icy blast, and set off for the pod. There was always tomorrow.

I don't often dream. Well, no, that's not true. I probably dream as much as other people do, but many of my dreams are best not remembered.

I remember this one. This one was vivid. Intense. Terrifying. And very memorable.

The night was clear and bright. Stars crackled with cold in the night sky. I stood alone in the centre of the henge. I dreamed I heard a horn sound, faint but crystal-clear. Something was coming and suddenly I was very, very afraid. I tried to get away, but the pod had gone. Peterson and Markham had left me. There was nowhere to run to. A single thought pounded through my brain. Get out of the circle.

I turned and ran – past the two rings of bluestones, towards the entrance. Where the Slaughter Stone had stood, two tall figures barred the way. I wheeled away. Back the way I had come. I would scramble over the ditch and the bank. Escape that way.

I couldn't get out. The same tall black figures stood where the Aubrey Holes had been. All fifty-six of them. Once there had been stones here. Now they were gone, but do stones have ghosts?

I shouted, 'Let me out,' and in my dream, I spoke in some strange tongue that I understood at the time but could never remember afterwards.

In the manner of stones, they stood, unmoving.

The world began to slide away from me. I looked up and saw the White Horse of Uffington running wild among the stars.

Something was coming. Something was coming for me.

I ran and ran, zigzagging backwards and forwards around the circle, but I couldn't get out. They wouldn't let me out until finally, I sprawled, panting on the ground. A voice in my head said, 'Don't look up.'

I clung to a tuft of grass, knuckles white in the starlight. I don't know why I did that. Whether it was a primitive urge to earth myself, to escape the merciless sky gods and seek the protection of Mother Earth, Gaia herself, I don't know.

'Don't look at them. Let them pass.'

Now, seemingly coming up through the ground, I could hear hounds baying, horns sounding.

They were here.

I turned my head slightly and looked up. Who wouldn't? And I was in good company. Pandora. Orpheus. Lot's wife. They all looked. Of course, it never ends well, but they looked just the same. And now, so did I.

The hunt hurtled across the sky. This was not some gentle phantom host, pale and ethereal. These were monsters, bursting from the clouds, pounding the sky with their hooves. Things with beaks urged on horses whose hooves struck blue sparks from the sky. Harsh, discordant horns echoed amongst the stones. I heard them urging each other on with voices from the underworld. Whips cracked blue lightning. Some rode goats, crouching on their backs and clinging to their horns.

At the front tore a huge figure, horned like a stag and riding a giant boar. Sweat and foam trailed long streamers from them both. The cold, crackling night air was suddenly full of the nostril-searing smell of urine and blood and fear.

They all followed hounds too big to be of this world. Great slavering beasts whose eyes flickered a deep and bloody red and from whom no prey could ever escape.

'Don't look at them. Don't let them see you.'

Then – suddenly – they saw me.

'Wake up, Max.'

I opened my eyes to find Leon standing beside the bed. The dream flew away on wisps of wind.

I smiled drowsily at him and snuggled down further into the glorious softness. After the icy cold of Stonehenge, this was just wonderful.

'Come on, Max. Time to wake up.'

I struggled with my usual morning dysfunction, mumbling, 'I am awake.'

He was holding a mug of tea. I blinked up at him, trying to focus. 'Oh, that's nice. Thank you.'

He put the mug down on the bedside table. I felt the bed tip as he settled himself beside me. I snuggled against him, enjoying his solid, comfortable warmth. He put his arms around me and I felt my eyelids droop again. My bed was warm and soft. Leon was here. There was tea. Today was a good day for a bit of a lie-in. 'Mmm, this is nice. Can you pass me my tea, please?'

'You can't have your tea until you wake up.'

I smiled and buried my head deeper into his shoulder, saying sleepily, 'I am awake.'

'No, you're not, Max. You're not awake. And if you don't wake up right now then you never will.'

I had no idea what he was on about and I was so warm and comfortable. I said drowsily, 'Don't understand.'

'I'm trying to tell you. You must wake up. This instant. You're dying Max.'

'What ...?'

He shook me hard. 'MAX – WAKE UP!'

I struggled to open gummy eyes. I was comfortable. I was floating in delicious warmth. Why did he want me to get cold all over again?

Blinking and squinting, I managed to focus. I couldn't see very clearly. A black figure crouched beside me, half hidden in the swirling snow. It *was* Leon – but he was older. His hair was almost completely silver and he wore it brushed back from his forehead. He had a fresh scar on one cheekbone and another smaller one on his chin. One of the big blasters was slung across his back. He wore body armour. He had a battered look about him. Snow was settling in his hair and on his shoulders. I struggled to make out what was going on. Why was he here? Why wasn't I in bed? Why did he look so different?

My lips felt stiff and cold. I mumbled, 'Leon?'

He heaved me to my feet. 'Come on. Up you get,' and I realised I'd been almost buried in snow. He brushed me down with one hand, holding me upright with the other. 'You were lost in the snowstorm.'

He crouched again and I realised the two snowy lumps at my feet were Peterson and Markham. He heaved Markham out of the snow and slapped his face a couple of times. 'Wake up! Open your eyes!'

Markham staggered slightly, 'Wha…? Where'm I?'

'Asleep in the snow,' he said tightly. 'Give me a hand.'

We all pulled out Peterson, who stood swaying.

'Listen to me, all of you' he shouted, over the noise of the wind. 'I can't stay, but you must get back to the pod. Get out of the cold.'

He turned us around. 'You were going in the wrong direction. The pod's over there. Less than one hundred yards. Stay together. Go now, before you freeze to death.'

'How did you ...?'

He touched my face with his gloved finger. 'Good to have seen you again, Max. I've missed you.'

What did that mean? Was I ... not around for some reason? Was I dead?

He paused, bent his head, and kissed me very quickly, and that was when I knew he was real, because his lips were as cold as mine were.

'Leon, wait. What did you mean?'

He was already stepping back into the swirling snow. No, he was becoming part of the swirling snow.

His voice drifted back on the wind. 'Get back to the pod.'

Then he vanished completely, leaving us alone.

I was shivering uncontrollably. The last thing I wanted to do was turn into that icy wind again. I remembered the comforting warmth of the snow. Then I remembered Leon.

Beside me, Markham's legs sagged.

'No,' I said sharply, pulling his arm. 'Back to the pod. Back to the pod or we're dead.'

He mumbled something. I linked an arm with him, he did the same with Peterson, and we struggled into the wind.

It wasn't far. Fifty yards – no more. We had been nearly there. Why hadn't we made it? I struggled to reassemble memories that were flying further and further apart with every second.

Markham muttered something.

'What?' I shouted, above the wind.

He lifted his head. 'Rescued by a bloody technician. The shame of it.'

'If you feel you can't live with it, we can always leave you here.'

And then we were at the door.

We took care of each other, helping each other strip off our soaking gear and wrapping ourselves in thick, warm blankets. I kicked the heaters up to full blast, and Peterson rummaged in the rations pile for hot soup. We sipped slowly, warming our hands on the mugs. I inhaled the glorious rich smell of oxtail soup.

Finally, Markham said, 'Was that Leon?'

I nodded.

'Why wouldn't he stay?'

'Just a guess,' I said slowly, 'but I think he was on his way to somewhere else.'

'He looked older,' said Peterson.

I nodded again.

'Well,' said Markham, 'tell him I owe him a pint.'

We waited two days and three nights for the snow to stop and then we gave up. The world outside was just a featureless landscape. Everything was white. Barrows and tumuli were just so many lumps in the snow. The outer stones on the north-east side were almost completely covered in long smooth drifts of windblown snow. The temperature stayed below freezing and chilled the blood no matter how much clothing we wore. Stepping outside entailed cracking the icy crust which had formed over the surface of the snow. It was as if someone had dumped the contents of the North Pole on to Salisbury Plain.

'Told you,' said Markham, packing up his gear. 'Never mind Death Valley or the Namib Desert. Never mind whether it's then or now – Salisbury Plain is the most inhospitable spot on the planet.'

No one disagreed.

Chapter Twenty-two

So that was my last jump. Not the spectacular success I would have wanted to finish on, but at least we all survived. I might have looked somewhat bedraggled on my return because Leon, waiting for me outside the pod as he always did, took one look and said quietly, 'Max. Enough.'

I didn't even think about arguing with him.

We all spent a day in Sick Bay.

Markham recklessly presented Hunter with a very short list of all the areas of his body he claimed were suffering from frostbite and should be massaged with warm oil before irreparable damage set in, and subsequently spent the remainder of the day hiding out in the women's ward.

'I'm claiming sanctuary,' he announced. 'Like that bird at Ephesus. You know. Wossername.'

'Arsinoe,' said Peterson. 'Legend says she had her hands cut off so she couldn't keep a grip on the altar. Do you really want to give Hunter ideas?'

'He'll be lucky if it's just his hands,' I said, and there was a thoughtful silence.

They had the tact to take themselves off when Leon turned up. He sat on the bed because I think he's the one person at St Mary's not terrified of Dr Foster, and we smiled at each other.

We talked about my leaving date, the cottage in the village, everything under the sun. I told him about seeing an older version of him at Stonehenge, and how he'd saved my life. All our lives. And that Markham owed him a beer. The only thing I didn't mention was the sentence that was running round and round my head until I wanted to scream.

'Good to see you again, Max. I've missed you.'

I tried to push it aside. It could mean anything. It could mean that he'd missed this younger version of me but I didn't think that was it. It could mean that we weren't together any longer. It could mean he'd left me. Or I'd left him. It could mean I was dead.

And, finally, came my last few weeks at St Mary's. We'd signed the lease on the cottage in the village and ferried most of our bits and pieces to our new home. It was a pretty place, not large, but directly opposite the pub which more than made up for the lack of a third bedroom. It would be our home for six months, and afterwards – I had no idea. I had no idea whether I would return to St Mary's or not. I think I was just drifting through the days … waiting …

I did very little during my final weeks, ignoring Peterson's comment that I'd done very little *before* my final weeks, but it was pleasant to slow down and take some time just to talk to people. I spent a wet afternoon sitting with Mr Strong in his cosy cubbyhole in the basement, drinking tea and munching my way through an entire pack of chocolate digestives. He told me some very interesting stories about Dr Bairstow and the early St Mary's. I listened carefully and took mental notes.

I had afternoon tea with Dr Bairstow and Mrs Partridge. She laid out the best china – the good stuff with the pretty floral pattern. I was honoured.

And, of course, I had to endure the increasingly frequent antenatal check-ups.

Helen didn't mince her words. 'I can't believe it Max, You're overweight ...'

'I prefer the expression underheight.'

'Your diet's appalling ...'

'Brown food is good for you.'

'You've been terminally constipated for most of your life and especially the last nine months, and yet, unbelievably, you and young Farrell are sound and healthy. What are your plans?'

'Well, I'm pretending not to notice they're organising my leaving do. Or that the History Department have clubbed together and bought baby furniture. Or that Wardrobe has made a huge number of little baby jumpsuits, tactfully in both blue and orange. Or that R&D have made a rocking horse … Are you listening?'

She was rummaging in a drawer, paused awkwardly and then thrust a package at me. 'Here.'

'What's this?'

She looked away. 'Just a small present. You might never notice it among all that other grand stuff.'

'Can I open it?'

'If you want to. It's nothing special.'

She was wrong. It was very special. I gently pulled the paper apart so Leon and I could open it together later, to reveal a soft lemon blanket, carefully edged in matching ribbon.

'Helen, it's beautiful. Where did you get it?'

She hastily lit a cigarette. 'I ... knitted it.'

'You can knit?' I said, in much the same tones as people might say, 'You sided with the Fascists?'

'Why not?' she said, puffing smoke out of the window.

'I don't know. I just never thought ...'

The only thing I knew about knitting was that old women did it as they sat at the foot of the guillotine watching the heads roll. Personally, I would have thought that was a bit of a splash zone, but knitters are obviously made of stern stuff. Clearly, one of Helen's ancestors had sat there, shouting out the score as she flapped her needles, and now her descendent had harnessed that need to witness violence, pain, and fear, and become a doctor.

'Well, it's beautiful, Helen. Thank you.'

'You're welcome. Why are you still here?'

I spent a couple of days in the Library, writing up my overdue reports, tidying things away, and chatting with Dr Dowson.

And spending a lot of time with Leon. We didn't do a lot, just sitting quietly, enjoying the peace and just for once, having the time to talk. We sat in our room, or walked around the gardens, or lazed away the afternoon under the willows by the lake. In the evenings we would sit in the bar for what wasn't always a quiet drink.

One evening, we entered the bar to find a small crowd in one corner, where, it turned out, Markham was proudly displaying the reason for his constant scratching. Apparently, and no one was quite sure how he'd managed it, he had ringworm.

'Does it move?' asked Bashford, giving it a prod.

'What?'

'Does it move? Does it wriggle around under your skin? Will it burst out of your chest?'

'No, no, and no.'

'Well that's disappointing. Exactly what does it do then?'

'Don't know. I suppose I could teach it to do tricks.'

'It's massively contagious,' said Helen, appearing from nowhere.

'What?' said Bashford, stepping back in a hurry.

'It will multiply overnight and its offspring will spread throughout your entire body. They will burrow into your vital organs. They will infiltrate and consume your brain, excreting it out through your ears. They will eat your eyeballs from the inside out. You will be riddled with pus-filled sores. Gangrene will set in, resulting in multiple amputations. You will be racked with excruciating pain and die in screaming agony.'

Markham was suddenly at the epicentre of an expanding circle.

'It's probably too late to save you, but you'd better report for treatment anyway.'

'What for?'

'To get rid of it, of course.'

He clutched himself protectively. 'Not Oscar!'

'You named your ringworm Oscar?'

'Of course.'

'In God's name, why?'

'He's a boy. You surely didn't expect me to call him Janet.'

'Treatment! Go! Now!'

He scuttled off.

Peterson grinned up at her. 'Really? I didn't think ringworm was that serious.'

'It's not. I just couldn't resist. It was a little joke. I thought I'd show my human side.'

And so my last day arrived.

I rolled out of bed, showered and dressed. I took my time partly because today I could, but mostly because at this stage of my pregnancy, I didn't have a lot of choice. I pottered around our room, conscious of more than a little sadness. I don't know why – it wasn't as if I would never see any of them again. Our position opposite the pub would make us a convenient crashing place for those who had left their legs in the bar.

I sat on the bed, slowly combed and plaited my hair and pictured happy domestic scenes. Playing with the baby in our bit of garden. It would be midwinter, but I'm an historian and never let boring facts get in the way of a good fantasy. Leon bustling around the kitchen producing something delicious while I drank wine and watched him. Sunday mornings in bed with tea and toast crumbs everywhere.

Of course, it wouldn't be like that at all. It would be a screaming hell-hole of wet nappies, a crying baby, and tired and frustrated parents. Our cottage would cease to be cosy and become cramped. Leon would find excuses not to come home, staying later and later at work, until finally he would sleep at St Mary's, and we would drift further and further apart. Then one day we would decide it wasn't working and it was time to go our separate ways, and I'd spend the rest of my life cursing myself for having abandoned my principles and embraced domesticity. I would die old and alone, in a cardboard box in a shop doorway somewhere. Boots, probably, or Dorothy Perkins.

You see, this is what comes of having so much hair. If I had a bob, I'd have stopped at the Sunday morning tea and toast crumbs and shot happily off for breakfast. Never grow your hair past shoulder length.

My last afternoon was lovely. I was gossiping with Mrs Enderby when someone telephoned me to go down to the Hall. Everyone was gathered there. I clattered down the stairs demanding to know why I was the only person actually working and informing Dr Bairstow that the place was going to the dogs.

He ignored this provocation. There were speeches, presents, terrible jokes, and embarrassing stories and I did a really bad job of not crying in public. I looked at the little pile of gifts and thought about the solitary girl who'd stamped up the drive all those years ago with equal amounts of qualifications and attitude. I'd had no idea what I was getting into – and that applied to more than just the job.

I looked up to find Dottle standing before me, smiling nervously. She thrust a package at me. 'I made this for your baby.'

'Well, thank you.'

I set down my glass and unwrapped the package. She'd made a small, pale blue teddy with endearingly lopsided cross-stitched eyes. I smiled down at it.

Every child should have a bear to watch over them. Even I'd had one. Until he was lost. I searched and searched but I never found him. These days, I had Bear 2.0, a treasured possession – a gift from Leon, brought to comfort me in dark times. I shook myself a little. Now my child would have a bear as well. I would settle him at the foot of the cot where he could sprawl, wonky and unbalanced – just like the rest of us. He would watch over my child as Bear had done for me.

'Thank you, Lisa.'

She was scarlet. 'It's the least I could do,' and scurried off.

Mrs Mack served champagne. I allowed myself a few celebratory sips, quite enjoying myself until Markham told me the celebrations were about having finally got rid of me. I tried to sulk but that's actually quite tricky when you're grinning from ear to ear.

Leon and I wandered from group to group. I was sipping tonic water from a champagne glass – which doesn't make it taste any better, believe me – and saying goodbye to everyone.

Mrs Enderby put her arms around as much of me as she could manage and gave me a big hug.

I said goodbye to everyone, carefully packed everything in a box, and escaped upstairs to pick up the last of my stuff from my old office. Rosie Lee was there. Yes, I was surprised too, but I suppose if it came to a toss-up between working and going downstairs and being nice to people then working came an easy first.

Most of my stuff was long gone, but I pulled the last few things out of my bottom drawer. There was a bottle in there – in the event of an emergency, drain contents, smash bottle, and tidy the body away afterwards. I left it for Clerk. He'd need it.

I packed up the last remnants of my working life, adding it to the gifts already in the box. Dottle's teddy peered cheekily over the top.

Miss Lee watched me in silence and then, just as I was picking up my little cardboard box and preparing to depart, she said, 'Here,' and put a package in front of me.

I said, 'What's this?' and she rolled her eyes at my stupidity.

'It's for you,' she said. 'Everyone buys presents for the baby, but no one ever buys anything for the person who's about to do all the work. I thought I would.'

'Oh,' I said, touched. Now I came to think of it, she was right. Although I wasn't going to tell her so because that wasn't a precedent I wanted to set, but she was right. I'd been laden with little knitted bootees, shawls, toys, teddies and so on, because suddenly, you stop being a person and become a mother and the two are not the same at all. For some, of course, it's a voluntary and welcome transition. For others – not so much.

She turned away to her desk and I pulled off the paper. Inside was one of those mugs with 'World's Greatest Boss' written on it.

I looked over at her, her back defiantly towards me, ears bright red. It was important I didn't say too much.

'Thank you.'

Still with her back to me, she nodded.

I took a deep breath. 'After ... you know ... when we're settled ... it would be nice if you and David ... and Benjamin, of course ...'

She nodded again. I nodded back, realised she couldn't see me because I was still standing behind her, and cursed myself for an idiot. Intellectually speaking, being pregnant had done me no good at all.

'Well, I'll see you soon, I hope.'

She turned, her arms full of files. Every inch the busy assistant. My heart went out to Clerk. She was going to eat him alive. Her flush had faded to acceptable levels. 'Good luck.'

I nodded and let myself out of the door.

I strolled slowly around the gallery, listening to the clamour down in the Hall. Historians and alcohol. Always a volatile mix.

Leon met me at the top of the stairs. 'What's in the box?'

'Just a few last-minute things.'

'Do you want me to take them with the rest?'

'No, it's OK. It's not heavy.'

'Are you coming with me?'

How to explain I wanted to leave as I arrived? Alone.

'Actually, do you mind if I walk?'

He smiled and I realised I didn't have to explain anything. 'No, not at all. There isn't much room in the car anyway. I'd probably have had to put you on the roof rack and I really don't think we want to start all that again. I'll see you in about half an hour.'

He disappeared. I stood for a moment, looking down into the Hall. I'd said my goodbyes. I didn't want to do it all again. Never ruin a good exit. I turned away. I'd nip down the back stairs, come out in the car park, catch one last glimpse of the horses in their paddock, stroll around the side of the building, down the drive and into the village. A nice walk in the late afternoon sunshine, and then into our cottage for our first proper meal together.

It was a good feeling. I rested the box on top of my suddenly convenient bump and set off. Past Peterson's office, past Wardrobe, and down the back stairs. There were memories everywhere. Over there was where Dr Dowson and Professor Rapson had nearly come to blows over the correct way to cook rabbit shit. Here was where Guthrie had led the charge against the Time Police. Down that corridor was the storeroom where Bitchface Barclay had told me what I'd done at Troy, and where she'd cruelly ripped apart Bear 2.0 and left him for me to find. I reached the back door, failed to open it one-handed, and set down my box. I got it open, wedged it with my foot because it was on a spring, awkwardly reached down for my box, and a voice I hadn't heard for a long time said, 'Good afternoon.'

Chapter Twenty-three

I was frozen, still bending to reach my box. This could not be happening. This was impossible. How could this be? I hadn't seen or heard from him for so long that I'd forgotten all about him. I think we all had, and now, when I least expected it, here he was. Again.

I could feel the blood draining from my face. I was going to faint. I closed my eyes.

'Careful,' he said. 'We don't want any accidents, do we? Just take a moment. Breathe deeply. That's it. Take your time.'

Not for one moment was I lulled by this consideration. My eyes flew open and I found myself looking down the barrel of some sort of gun.

He looked the same as ever. Thinning hair brushed back. His face was a little bonier, and the scars on his face looked older and whiter, but physically he looked just as he always did. Except for his expression. I'd seen him threatening, screaming, furious, desperate, cold and calculating, triumphant, but I'd never ever seen him calm, polite, and smiling. Personally, I preferred cold and calculating.

'What do you want, Ronan?'

'Yes, you see, I could make some hurtful remark about it being very obvious what I want, but we'd only start off on the wrong foot again, and the whole afternoon would just go straight down the tubes. Then one or other of us would end up either badly injured or dead, and it's all so unnecessary when a little common courtesy will make this an enjoyable experience for both of us. Don't you agree?'

'What do you want?'

His expression didn't change but his eyes did. Suddenly his gun was under my chin.

'I told you. A little common courtesy.'

Keep him talking. Keep him here. All right, most of St Mary's was in the Great Hall drinking their heads off without me – but surely, someone would be along in a minute. I knew this wasn't an often-used back door but even so, surely Mr Strong would want to check his cleaning materials, or inspect something ... or someone would ...

'If you would care to step through the door and turn to your left, please.'

I shook my head. 'No.'

'Yes, anticipating a little difficulty in this area, I've taken the precaution of bringing – this.' I felt a prick against my neck.

'What is that?'

'A tranquiliser gun. Filled with weed killer from your very own supplies. Just through that door over there. How thoughtful. Off you go now.'

Slowly, very slowly, I inched out through the door. It was only as I stepped out into the car park that the full realisation dawned on me. There was no one to help me. The area was deserted. Leon had long gone. I was being kidnapped and no one would know. How long before Leon became worried? Quite some time – he'd think I was still here having a good gossip. Then he'd telephone St Mary's and they'd look around, not find me and then they'd organise a full-scale search. They'd find the little box of possessions I'd carefully left behind for them to discover, but they wouldn't find me. Because I wouldn't be here. Because standing directly in front of me was a pod. Battered and scruffy, with half the casing blown off on one side, but a working pod nevertheless, and once I stepped inside I was lost. A sudden gust of wind felt cool on my face and I suddenly realised I was sweating.

I stood very still.

'I do understand your natural reluctance, but I'm afraid you have very little choice in this matter. Walk into the pod, please.'

I rolled my eyes around but no one was in sight. No one at all. Other than a few birds and a car passing in the distance there was no sound, either. This was the barely used back of a building especially selected for its remote location.

He nudged me again and I realised I'd come to a halt. I started to think again. I was heavily pregnant. In every sense of the word. I weighed half a ton. If I just stood still, what could he do?

'Stick you with weed killer, you idiot,' said a voice in my head. 'Remember the standard operating procedure. Keep your head down, your mouth shut and await rescue.'

I tried to delay. 'What do you want?'

'I'll tell you once you're inside. You really shouldn't be standing about in your condition. Go on. In you go.'

He was still calm. Still polite. If I didn't know who he was, I wouldn't be concerned at all. I did know who he was, however, and I was very concerned. Actually, I was so terrified I could barely move my legs. This was very, very bad. I was in a lot of trouble here. More trouble than I'd been in for a long time. No – more trouble than I'd ever been in before, because now it wasn't just me at risk.

I'd been hot – now, suddenly, I grew very cold.

He pushed me in the back and I took a reluctant half step forwards. He pushed again. I took another, praying, not just to the god of historians, but any benevolent deity who happened to be passing, that someone would appear from somewhere. A complete waste of time. It was Friday. Alcohol was being consumed somewhere else. I was leaving so I'd handed in my com and I've never had a mobile phone. There was no chance of any sort of rescue of any kind. I was on my own.

He said softly, 'Door,' and the door slid open.

I halted on the threshold and considered my options. That didn't take long.

'I don't want to kill you,' he said softly. 'I really don't, but I will if I have to. Into the pod please.'

Again, that prick in the neck.

What could I do?

Nothing. I stepped into the pod.

'A little further, please.'

Another step. The door slid shut behind me.

Leon and I were once pursued by the Time Police. Not for very long, thank goodness, but for long enough for me to realise how difficult life is for those attempting to survive outside their own time. Everyone has a place in the world. You might not like it, but that's your place and it fits you perfectly. It's where you're supposed to be. Try moving out of that place, out of your own time, and life becomes very difficult. Without membership of a family, or guild, or tribe, without letters of introduction or recommendation, without ID cards or a credit record – life becomes nearly impossible. Ronan was a fugitive. He'd been on the run for years. I would have expected the state of his pod to reflect that fact. Yes, it was battered and well used, and there was more duct tape around than Leon would have been happy about, but it was clean, neat and smelled no worse than any other pod I'd ever been in.

I think, subconsciously, I'd been hoping for some sort of mechanical failure. Or that his pod was unstable and the safety protocols would cut in, but there was no hope. This pod was, apparently, in full working order. I felt my shoulders drop with disappointment.

'Please,' he said. 'You've had a long day. You should sit down.'

I must have looked surprised at this consideration because he smiled. I was not reassured.

'Yes, I can well imagine your astonishment, but things really will proceed so much more quickly and smoothly if you can just accept that I don't want to kill you – far from it – and sit down and make yourself comfortable. I really, really don't want anything to happen to you.' He smiled again. 'Or your child.'

'What do you want, Ronan?'

'I want you. And your child of course. And now I have you. If you could just excuse me for one moment, please. Computer. Execute pre-programmed jump.'

'Jump executed.'

Before I could do anything about it, the world went white.

We landed with a bit of a bump. Nothing serious. It would have been one of Peterson's better efforts.

'Well,' he said, coming to sit in the other seat, but still holding the gun. 'Here we are at last.'

'Where? Where are we?'

I was scanning the read-outs. Some weren't working. I suspected some might have been giving false readings because there were no sets of coordinates that I recognised.

'Oh, I'm not going to tell you that. I think it can only add to your experience if you don't know when or where you are. Imagine the fun you'll have discovering that for yourself. Would you like some tea?'

He really was a very clever man. If he'd shouted, raged, and waved his gun around, then I'd have fought back and it would all have gone very badly. For both of us, I'd like to think, but when your kidnapper fusses around the place asking if you're warm enough and how many sugars you take, it's quite difficult to feel threatened.

I told him three because I needed the energy, and he seemed genuinely amused.

'Isn't that rather a lot?'

'No. You can never have too much sugar.'

'Especially if you're planning to throw your tea all over the console in the hope of disabling the pod. That was the plan, wasn't it?'

I was getting my breath back. Two could play at this polite kidnapping game.

'Yes, it was. Well spotted. Although I was hoping it wouldn't be the tea that would be the problem but the sugar. IT once told me if I ever spilled tea on my keyboard to swill it under the tap as quickly as possible. It can't do any more harm and possibly might save the keyboard.'

He nodded. 'It's the sugar that does the damage. I once lost an entire mission plan when I knocked over a mug of coffee. I was extremely annoyed about that, I can tell you.'

Keep him talking. 'We have cup holders in our pods.'

'No! Really? What a very good idea. It would appear Leon Farrell does have some uses after all.' He sat back, smiling. Holding the gun ...

I began to feel I was losing my grip on things. I was sitting in a pod with a renegade historian and murderer from the future and we were discussing minor IT mishaps over a cup of tea. Ronan, however, was a very clever man and I was here for a reason. And, in addition to being clever, he was vicious, ruthless and he hated me. Don't lose sight of that, Maxwell. Don't let him fool you. Sit quiet. Ask questions. The longer I was in here, still comparatively safe, the more chance I had of ... of ... thinking of something that would get me home.

On the face of it, the odds didn't look good. He hadn't made himself tea. He sat, just that little bit too far away from me, the dart gun on the console where he could get to it if need be.

Leaning back, but never taking his eyes from me, he said, 'I've given up trying to kill you, Max. You have more lives than a sack full of cats. I've revised my strategy a little and I think you'll agree I've come up with a winner.'

He paused so I could be impressed. I said nothing, nursing my empty mug in my lap, because according to Ian Guthrie, everything can be a weapon.

'My plan is that you stay alive for as long as possible, because you will hate every moment of the life you will lead here. This place really is the arse end of nowhere, Max, and every day will be a squalid struggle to keep yourself and your child alive. Believe me, the things you will do will both surprise and appal you. There will be no depths to which you will not sink.

'Which brings me to the point of today. I can see that you're puzzled, so let me clarify. I've brought you back here today, to this lovely time and place, for you to give birth.'

I had the strangest feeling my blood had turned to ice. I could do nothing but stare at him as the impact of his words sank in. It may have looked as if I was uncomprehending, but my mind was working furiously. I knew what he had planned and it was very, very bad. In fact, it couldn't be worse. This was not some plan to kill me – something with which I could grapple and potentially overcome. His plan was that I should live – and for as long as possible – because he wanted my child to be born here, and once it was – once it was born here, wherever here was – then I was lost. We were both lost. Because if she or he was born here then they became a contemporary, and even if Leon and every single member of St Mary's came roaring over the horizon, once my child was born here, it could never leave this time.

'Exactly,' he said, having watched me come to this conclusion.

'They'll find me,' I said, with a confidence I was far from feeling.

'I'm counting on it,' he said. 'But will they find you in time, eh? You don't have long to go, do you? A day or two at the most. Will they have found you by then, do you think? I don't think so. And then it will be decision time, won't it? Who stays and who goes home? The child stays, of course. No question of that – didn't you just fight a bloody battle with the Time Police over that very issue. They'll be watching you like a hawk in future. You'll never get away with that again. So what will you do? It might die if it stays here, but it'll definitely die if you try to get it out. So will you stay too? I think we both know the answer to that one. You'll stay, and begin your endless, bitter struggle for survival.

'And that's the bit I'm really looking forward to, Max. Watching to see exactly what you will do to keep yourself and your child alive until your rescuers appear. However long that takes. How low will you sink? What will you do for a bowl of unidentifiable slop if you haven't eaten for a week? Or a piece of worm-ridden bread carelessly tossed into a gutter for you to grovel after? How many hours will you spend on your knees in some filthy alley somewhere, performing for a group of laughing men you suspect have no intention of paying you anything? Your looks won't last long here, I can tell you that for nothing. In three months' time, you'll be giving yourself away for anything you can get.

287

'And then, just picture the scene: a pod materialising out of nowhere – your dream come true – and all those clean, well-fed, glossy friends of yours bursting out of the door, all eager to save their colleague, and they won't even recognise you. They'll run straight past that boney bag of rags – the one with her legs permanently open to catch any passing trade. The one with the wailing kid hanging off her empty tit. That will be you, Maxwell. What you have become. Can you imagine the looks on their faces?

'And then what? Because that's when the fun really starts. For me, anyway. Oh, I'll grant you, Leon Farrell will hide his disgust – doesn't he just piss you off sometimes? It must be like being married to a noble horse. What of Noble Leon? Will he stay with you? I wouldn't be too sure of the answer to that, if I were you.'

'Good to see you again, Max. I've missed you.'

'And finally you, my lovely Max. How much will you love this child of yours – the reason for what I can assure you is going to be a pretty dreadful life? How tempted will you be? Imagine one night – you're hungry. It's hungry. You're both cold. It won't stop whining. On and on. Driving you insane. If only it would die. And it might. It *could*. Just a little pressure ... here ... and problem gone. Really, looking at the scabby little runt, it's a kindness, don't you think? And you'd be free. Free to return to St Mary's when they turn up for you. Free to make up some story about the tragic loss of your child. Because you wouldn't want people to know, would you Max? You wouldn't want Noble Leon knowing you'd murdered your own child to ensure your escape.'

He sat back. The console was covered in spittle from the violence of his words. His scars showed white against his livid skin. His eyes were bulging with the fury I had known would not be that far beneath the surface.

I was beyond speech. Beyond thought. I should have taken advantage of his temporary loss of control, but I couldn't. I was overwhelmed. Completely overwhelmed. Not just by the tidal wave of words, but the hatred behind them, and the vividness with which he'd portrayed my future. I couldn't move. I could barely breathe.

We sat in silence, contemplating his words while the console ticked over in the background. He was the first to rouse himself.

'Now, I know you have plenty to say to me, but shall we pause for a moment and readjust our thoughts. Are you feeling thirsty yet?'

I stared at him. Wild ideas flew through my mind. Smash the mug and attack him with one of the jagged pieces. Throw myself at him and do whatever damage I could. It would be considerable, I'd make sure of that. Even if I just threw him to the floor and fell on top of him, it might wind him long enough for me to ...

To roll over like a beached whale, rock myself to my feet and lumber to a console that wouldn't accept my instructions. Come on Maxwell, you can do better than that. Then my brain caught up with my ears.

'Why would I feel thirsty?'

'Well – and don't think I don't feel badly about this because I do know pregnant women aren't supposed to take drugs – I slipped a little something in your tea. Just a little beta-blocker thing. Just to slow you down a little. Relax – well, you probably are already, aren't you? Sit back and let everything just wash over you and then ...'

'You're wasting your time.' I said, trying not to feel relaxed. This was surely just psychological. Like when people say, 'Max you're looking tired,' and suddenly I feel as if I could sleep for a week. I tried to sit up and look alert.

Somehow, he'd got the mug off me without me noticing. When had that happened? I saw another mug held in front of me.

I shook my head. I couldn't afford any more drugs. 'No.'

'I would if I were you. This could be the last cup of tea you get to enjoy for a very, very long time. If not forever. Take it.'

I shook my head again.

'Well, I think in a couple of hours, you'll be sorry, but suit yourself.'

The mug disappeared.

Something seized my arm. 'Up you get.'

I tried to make myself as heavy as possible.

'Now stop that. You'll need to find yourself water and somewhere safe to spend the night and you can't do that if you're skulking in here. Be sensible – the sooner you're out there, the sooner you can start your lovely new life.'

Something heaved me to my feet. I swayed. Not deliberately.

'This way.'

I heard the door open and hot sunshine flooded into the pod.

'Where is this place?'

'Well, I have to say I think even a travel agent would have to describe it as a complete shithole. There's no wealth here. No trade routes. No nothing. Just a handful of badly built huts filled with desperate people trying and mostly failing to survive. The infant mortality rate is dreadful. There's barely any water. It's baking hot during the day and bitingly cold at night. The only excitement is when the slavers turn up – every three or four years – and take away anyone they think they can make a profit from. When I say that's usually only three or four men and never any women, then you'll understand just how bad – how truly awful – life is here. Welcome to your new home.'

By now, I was approaching the threshold, blinking in the sunlight. I felt him put his hand on the small of my back to give me one last shove. I had nothing to lose. I threw myself backwards, hoping, I think, that I could at least crush the life out of him.

He stepped aside and I crashed heavily to the floor, hurting my back.

'Get up.'

I could feel him trying to grab my arm to drag me outside.

As best I could, I curled into a ball, tucking in all my extremities so he'd have nothing to grab hold of.

He seized my hair and tried to drag me. There was no way that was going to work, but it was so excruciatingly painful that

I instinctively put up my hands to try and pull his hands away. He released my hair and seized a wrist.

I grabbed for one of the seat columns, meaning to hang on for grim death.

'Let go or I'll break your fingers. How long do you think you'll last without working hands?'

It was a psychological moment. If I let go – if I accepted that I was going to be forced outside, like it or not – then he'd won. It would be like giving in. I was determined not to do that. I would fight every inch of the way. I tightened my grip.

He covered my body with his own. I couldn't move. I could barely breathe. That funny pain stabbed again. I heard his voice in my ear. 'How about in your eye?' and felt the prick of the dart on my eyelid.

I let go.

He grabbed my ankle and pulled me to the door. I scrabbled for a grip on something. Anything. I tore my fingernails clawing at the carpet. I kicked out with my other leg, but nothing would stop him. I twisted so I was on my back. He was grunting with effort. I kicked again and my foot connected with something. I heard him hiss with pain and he kicked back.

A huge burning spasmed in my left knee, which went numb.

'Stupid bitch. Do you want me to cripple you as well?'

I was being dragged outside. Desperately I tried to cling to the doorframe, but couldn't get a grip. I was being pulled face down through the dust. My top rode up and I could feel stones and rough vegetation scratching my stomach. I scrabbled again, screaming and cursing him, digging in my fingers, trying to stop this. Because I was fighting for my life. And that of my child.

All too soon, it stopped, and I was coughing and choking in the dust, trying to think ... What could I do ...?

I'd missed my chance. His voice came from some distance away.

'I'll be back soon. I'll bring you a present and perhaps, if you're nice to me, I'll let you have it. Goodbye Max.'

I rolled over and pushed myself up.

The pod sat some twenty feet away, door shut. Invulnerable. There was nothing I could do.

I knew he was watching me. I gave him two fingers and then, because he wasn't worth so many, just the one. I could imagine him laughing.

Then the pod was gone. Dust swirled in the vacuum. I was alone.

Chapter Twenty-four

I'm not ashamed to say I panicked. That's one of the few advantages of being an historian. You can go from nothing to flat-out panic in about one third of a nano-second and I did. Ignoring the pain in my knee, I ran hither and thither. Don't ask me why. I ran to where the pod had been. Maybe I thought it had been fitted with a camouflage device and he was still here, invisible, watching me. Extracting every last ounce of revenge.

He wasn't, but that didn't stop me. I limped around, shouting for him to come back and face me. I cursed him with all the bad language I knew. In every language I knew. I shouted for Leon. Tears ran down my cheeks, and all the time, the brazen sun blazed down and I wasted precious effort and energy running around and achieving nothing.

Eventually, not looking where I was going, I tripped over something and fell heavily, sprawling on my face in the dust. I don't know how long I lay there, gasping and sobbing until, finally exhausted, I subsided into hiccupping sobs.

I think it was at this point that the cruelty of Ronan's revenge was brought home to me. I might survive. I probably would. But what of my baby? What of my hopes for a life with Leon? All my plans for the future? None of that would happen now. Could ever happen. With one simple action, he'd ruined my life. And the life of my child. And Leon's.

'Good to see you again, Max. I've missed you.'

Was that what Leon had meant? That I was here and he was there and this was the end of our life together.

I know I lay in the dust for a very long time until, conscious of the heat of the sun on the back of my head, I sat up, wiped my face, pushed my hair behind my ears, and started to think properly.

Lifting my head, I looked around me. I was on a small plateau overlooking a wide, barren, cracked plain that had once been a lake bed. I could see the ridges where water had once flowed. The last remnant, a tiny stream, meandered through a sludgy marsh that I could smell from all the way up here.

Some attempt had been made to dam the stream and the muddy water had oozed sideways to form a small, dark pool apparently devoid of life. There were no reflections of blue sky in the water. No glints of light as the sun caught wind-blown ripples. No birds floated serenely or waded in the shallows.

Some thirty or forty mud-brick huts squatted miserably in the sun. There was no shade, no trees, no wind, although the thick dust piled up on the south and east sides of the huts spoke of vicious winds when they did come, hot from the desert, bringing drought, famine and more misery in their wake. I could see what I took to be a well at what I took to be the centre of the village. I could only guess at the quality of the water. If it hadn't dried up. The streets, such as they were, were filled with rubbish and debris just left lying around. There was no livestock, no dogs trotting busily about their business, no cats basking on the roofs, no washing hung over walls and bushes, no children played. It looked dirty, squalid, and desperately, desperately poor.

What catastrophe had led to the lake drying up, I had no idea. I do know that about seven thousand years ago the world underwent a great climate change. The one that led to the transformation of the Sahara from fertile green plains to harsh desert. Something similar might have occurred here, although on a smaller scale. Why were people still here? Might there be old people here who remembered the days before the desert? Were they desperately hanging on in the hope that one day the rains would return? Or were they just too afraid, too apathetic, too poor, or too stubborn to seek a new place for themselves?

I've seen some shitholes in my time, but nowhere had I ever seen a place exude such an air of hopelessness and despair. At what point had the inhabitants given up? When had survival, not living, become the priority?

I wriggled into the shade of a rock, tried to make myself comfortable, and made a few decisions. Starting with staying away from that squalid little settlement for as long as I could. Of course, it was always possible they would take me in and share their meagre resources with me, but it was more probable that they would not, either driving me away with stones and curses, or using me as unpaid labour for the rest of my very short life. I would take a day or two to suss things out. Once I found water – and I would – there would be no rush.

Survival is a state of mind. Yes, all right, water, shelter and food are useful too, but as Ian Guthrie kept reminding us during training, it's your attitude that will save your life. I would need the sort of attitude that doesn't turn over a rock and say, 'Oh yuk! Big squidgy caterpillar!' but, 'Oh wow – a caterpillar! And a big green one, too! They're really tasty! I'll be eating well tonight!' Because everything can be eaten. You don't turn up your nose at anything that is even remotely edible. Insects, for instance, are a valuable source of protein. I would learn to scavenge. I would do whatever it took to survive.

I could keep myself warm. Guthrie had taught us how to make a fire without matches, and how to take rocks from around the fire and place them at our backs and feet to stay warm during the coldest night.

I felt a surge of optimism. I could do it. I could survive. I had to survive, because this was my life now. St Mary's was over. Everything was finished and I couldn't afford to waste time on regret. Or bitterness. Or self-pity. From now on, every moment would be devoted to survival. I was determined not to lead the life Ronan had mapped out for me.

I certainly wasn't going to rush headlong down to the village below. I would observe, take my time, and keep myself and my child safe. I leaned back against the rock and breathed deeply, easing my aching back. Stay calm. Just stay calm, Maxwell. You're not dead yet.

But how long before I wished I were?

Somewhere, high above me, an eagle screamed. I looked up and my attention was caught by a tiny patch of green, high on the rocky slope to my right. A scrubby tree or maybe a few bushes. Whatever it was, green was good. Might there be water up there? Even a trickle would be wonderful. Now that I was calmer, I was conscious of a throbbing knee, raw throat, and raging thirst. Wherever I went, I had to get out of the sun and up was as good a direction as any. I would take things slowly. I'd be fine. Turning my back on the desolate plain below, I set off.

An hour later, I wasn't sure I'd made the right decision. It's not easy climbing a steep, rocky slope when you can't see your own feet. My knee still hurt. And my back. I struggled and scrambled, wondering if it would have been better to have taken my chances down below. Several times, I lost sight of the bushes and had to struggle hard with the despair that sat like lead at the back of my mind, all too eager to overwhelm me should I let it.

I sat on a convenient rock and tried not to pant. In my head, Major Guthrie told me to keep my mouth closed. Whether that had been survival training or just exasperation on his part I couldn't remember, but it was good advice. I put my hands on my bump and said, 'How you doing in there?'

The lack of an answer only served to emphasise the deep, hot silence all around me.

A green-tailed lizard scuttled past, paused as it saw me, and then continued on its way. As I followed it with my eyes, I heard it. Just the very faintest sound. A faint and far off trickle of water. I was right. There was water up here.

I turned my head this way and that until I was certain of the direction and then set off. It wasn't easy. I had to detour round larger rocks and then I picked up what looked like a path. I could see goat tracks. Well, I assumed they were goat tracks. Nothing else could survive up here.

There. There it was. A tiny trickle of water emerging from beneath a rock, and by the first piece of good luck I'd had that day, falling a few inches into a hollowed out rock that formed a small basin. I fell to my knees and cupped my hands.

The water was icy cold. I remembered to sip slowly. Actually the basin was so tiny that I had little choice, but the taste was wonderful. I sipped and sipped. I splashed my face and the back of my neck. The ground I was kneeling in was wet and deeply pockmarked with goat hoof prints, so the water was good – if a little goaty.

I began to feel more cheerful. It was possible that I could survive. More than that – I could thrive. Animals and birds would come to drink. I could set traps. And there would always be those delicious fat green caterpillars. It would bloody well serve Ronan right if he turned up again, all ready for a good gloat, and I was king. Or queen, of course. I would have him executed. He would die horribly. It would take days. Up yours, Ronan. You should have killed me when you had the chance.

The pain exploded inside me like a huge, deep, red-hot furnace, radiating outwards, pushing all thought out of my head. I toppled sideways onto the ground, drew up my knees, and yelled, 'Aaaggghhh.' It didn't stop. It went on and on, building in waves, pushing, pushing, and searing my insides. Because I just wasn't in enough trouble already, was I?

I tried to remember all those antenatal lectures from Helen. God, I wish I'd listened. Since it had never occurred to me that I'd have to do this on my own, I'd decided I'd just concentrate on my bit and let everyone else get on with things down at the business end. That didn't seem like such a good idea now. I tried not to hold my breath. I tried to ignore the instinct to fight against it. Go with the flow. Embrace my inner agony. Bollocks, it hurt. It bloody, bloody hurt like hell. Leon Farrell was never coming near me again as long as I lived.

I rolled over on to my hands and knees and things eased a little. I tried to remember my breathing. In and out was the best I could do at the moment. Gradually, but not anything like gradually enough, the pain subsided. I flopped back onto the ground and tried to think.

What to do? Where to go?

My choices were limited. Whether I wanted to go down to the village or not was now immaterial. There was no way I'd make it back down the hillside and it would be dark in a few hours anyway. I should move away from the water. All sorts of things would turn up to drink in the night. All sorts of predators. It would help if I knew when or where I was, but wolves seemed a good bet. And bears. Mountain lions. Jackals. Wild dogs. Carnivorous goats. All of those and more would be attracted to the scent of blood, the cries of a woman giving birth and the wail of a new-born infant.

I allowed myself a quick sob of self-pity. I had solved one problem only to have another fling itself at me. I could really have done with even one day, just to suss things out a little, get the lie of the land and now – when I needed it least ...

I should time the contractions. I didn't have a watch so I started to count in my head. Shakily, I pulled myself to my feet. I had hours yet. The pains would build slowly. No need to panic ye –

The next one hit me like a ten-tonne truck.

What? No! This wasn't right. It couldn't be much more than five minutes since the last one. It wasn't supposed to go like this. It was supposed to –

I dropped to my knees again, gritting my teeth. Sweat stung my eyes. Remember to breathe. Try to go with the pain. Wait for it to go away. Which it did, rolling away again, leaving me breathless, weak, and desperate.

Because I had to find somewhere safe. And soon, because I didn't know when or where I was. Because I was lost. Completely and utterly lost. Lost in time and space. Lost somewhere in History. I could be anywhere. Anytime. Now, when I needed it least, I was overwhelmed by a terrifying, dizzying downward spiral of panic that robbed me of the ability to think or to move. The words ran through my head: They'll never find me. I'm going to die here and no one will ever know. Leon will never know what became of me. Will he think I left him? That I ran away without even telling him I was leaving? No one at St Mary's will ever see me again and I'll never see them. I'll never see anyone again. I'll die here, either in agonising childbirth, or of hunger, or of exposure, alone, and something will eat me, and my bones will be scattered and no one will ever know what happened to Maxwell and her baby.

And Leon will have lost another child.

That thought kicked me like a mule and fortunately, at the same time, another burst of agonising pain put a stop to that nonsense. It's really quite difficult to feel sorry for yourself when it feels as if a white-hot drill is boring its way through –

A bright red ball of light soared into the air, exploded with a crack, and hung, fizzing in the air.

What the f…?

Initially, I thought it was St Mary's. Well, who else could it be?

The answer turned up immediately. The Time Police.

Of course, it was the Time Police.

Some time ago, I was involved in covering up the fact that St Mary's had removed a contemporary from his own time during the Trojan War. The Time Police turned up to arrest us all. We fought back. People died. Theirs and ours. We patched up some sort of peace, but it's a very wary peace. A little while ago I lied through my teeth to Captain Ellis and his squad when they turned up to investigate an alleged anomaly in Rouen, 1431. We were as guilty as hell, but mainly thanks to Sykes exercising her superpower of vomiting at will, we got away with that as well. But it's not an easy relationship. We don't trust them and they certainly don't trust us. They are, in general, the harbingers of doom.

I've never been so pleased to see harbingers of doom in my entire life. An amplified voice boomed, 'Dr Maxwell. Please identify yourself and your location.'

That's another thing about the Time Police. The word subtle is not in their vocabulary. They're focused, driven, and do whatever is necessary to get the job done, and I was guessing their job was to find me. Because I was an idiot. I'd once spent weeks being chased up and down the timeline by these very people and I'd completely forgotten about their unparalleled ability to track down their targets. I'm tagged. We all are. For this very purpose. The St Mary's tracking equipment is crap.

From bitter experience we've learned it's quicker and easier to jump up and down shouting, 'Over here, idiots,' than wait for one of our tag readers to pick us up. For the Time Police, however, with their futuristic weapons and advanced tech, finding me would be a stroll in the park.

Obviously, St Mary's had discovered I was missing, and lacking any sort of clue to my whereabouts had called in the Time Police, who had found me with one hand metaphorically tied behind their metaphorical backs.

Again, the hills were alive with the sound of the Time Police doing what they did best.

'Dr Maxwell. Advise us of your location.'

The words bounced off the valley walls. I was willing to bet if there ever had been anyone in the village below they weren't there now. They probably thought their gods were speaking to them. It's interesting to think that every major religion that claims to have heard the voice of their god might well have heard nothing more than the Time Police ordering some unfortunate to surrender at once, or be zapped with one of their sonic thingies. I took a moment to wonder whether they could actually be responsible for parting the Red Sea, told myself not to be so bloody stupid, and staggered to my feet. I struggled a little way back down the goat track, leaned on a rock, and squeaked, 'Here. I'm here.'

You'd have had to have the hearing of a bat to have heard me, but somehow they did. I could hear the sound of men cursing as they tripped and stumbled over loose rocks until, finally a few minutes later, they appeared. Armoured, although not helmeted; guns at the ready. I brushed myself down, tucked my hair behind my ears, and stood as straight as I could because I'm an historian and image is everything.

The one in front stopped dead and wiped his sweating face. Things could have been worse. It was Captain Ellis. The nearest thing I had to a friend in the Time Police.

'Was it Ronan?'

I nodded.

'Still here?'

I shook my head. 'Long gone.'

He looked around him. 'For God's sake, Max. What are you doing all the way up here?'

'Sound tactical thinking. I'm sure Sun Tzu or Scipio or Nelson always advocated occupying the high ground.'

'Nelson was a sailor, you idiot. What would he know about high ground?'

'Well, he scrambled all over Emma Hamilton and she was a big girl.'

He was joined by four other men, all hot and panting.

'Only four of you? What happened to the might and majesty of the Time Police?'

'There are three other teams out scouring the area for you.'

'That brings back happy memories.'

He ignored that.

One of his men fumbled with his pack. 'Are you all right, Dr Maxwell? Do you need any water?'

And at that moment, with an exquisite sense of timing that I would never have expected from the somewhat lackadaisical god of historians, my waters broke. I don't think any of us knew where to look. This was not turning out to be a good day and it was going to get worse.

I doubled up again, but this pain was different. There was an urgency about it. I put both hands on a rock and began to pant.

My world was suddenly full of panicking men.

'We need to get her down the hill. Back to the pod.'

'How? Look at the size of her.'

'I … heard … that.'

'Max, is there anything you can do to slow things down?'

'Don't … think so.' I disappeared into my own private world of pain again, surfacing a minute or so later to find them deep in some sort of technical discussion and apparently oblivious to my suffering.

'Aaaggghhh,' I said, just to speed things up a bit.

'We're going to make a seat for you. Can you sit upright?'

I nodded confidently, pretty sure that I couldn't, but not seeing any other way.

He put his hand on my shoulder. 'We'll get you home, Max.'

I nodded, words being beyond me at that moment. I was going home. Maybe there would be a happy ending after all. Aren't Time Policemen wonderful?

'Not necessarily,' said the voice in my head. 'Have you considered that they may not be here to save you, but to ensure this infant stays in his own time?'

I caught my breath. That was true. If the kid was born now – and every indication was that it would be, then there was no way they would let it leave. It would have to stay. And I would stay with it.

I've never liked these bastards.

And it was coming. Coming now. The urge to push was overcoming my ability to pant.

I had no idea labour could go so quickly. Helen had given me to understand it would last for hour after agonising hour. Days even. A long, drawn-out period of blood and pain, culminating in the violent expulsion of an infant who would occupy my every waking moment and never give me a moment's rest until I sank, prematurely old and exhausted, into the longed for peace and quiet of the grave. She's not in great demand at antenatal clinics.

I squinted up at the sky, estimating I'd only been at it for about an hour. Surely, there was plenty of time yet.

They'd used their weapons to make a basic chair on which, not without some trepidation, I sat. I rested a hand on each of their shoulders, they took the probably considerable strain, and off we lurched.

We did not hang around. The ground was rough with loose stones threatening to trip us every inch of the way. They did their best but we nearly fell several times and once we actually did. Fortunately, although not for him, I fell on one of them. I wasn't given any time to recover or even to complain. In a flash, the two of them had hoisted me back up again and set off at an even faster pace, which was just as well. It had taken me an hour or so to climb up and even I could tell we didn't have

302

another hour. Big deep pushing pains were coursing through my body with hardly a pause.

Captain Ellis went first, picking the best path, and then my two officers carrying me. Another followed behind – presumably to pick me up in case I fell off backwards – and one ranged about us in case of trouble.

There was no effort at concealment. They were the Time Police and they didn't give a rat's arse for historical accuracy. They got the job done – whatever that job was. Today that job was me. I knew their brief would be flexible. Get me back to my own time before I gave birth. If they failed with that objective, then their next was to ensure the infant stayed in this time – whenever this was. I must remember to ask. What they would do with me was a bit of an unknown. I wondered briefly if I should inform them that if anything happened either to me or his child, then Leon would hunt them to the ends of the earth and beyond, but they had enough on their plates at the moment. Besides, I needed my breath for other, more important things.

The next pain, following hard on the heels of the previous one, was particularly bad. Despite all my best efforts, I lurched and yelled, 'Aaaggghhh' which was echoed by the poor sod on the left, as I inadvertently clawed his neck, and the guy on the right who lost his footing and went down heavily on one knee. I more or less fell off, but managed to stay on my feet. I put my hands on my knees and panted for dear life. They milled around, another officer took the place of the one with the wonky knee, and off we went again.

It was going to be close. I could see their pod, a squat black affair. It wasn't that far off, but neither was I. I slipped from their makeshift chair and dropped to all fours. The urge to push was overwhelming. There was no way I could withstand it. I fell sideways, drew up my knees and pushed, sobbing, 'I can't. I can't go on. It's coming now.'

Two men seized me, hauling me up, and not gently either. I had the bruises for days afterwards. They draped my arms around their necks and they ran. There was nothing I could do. My feet barely touched the ground. We slipped and slithered down the last hundred feet or so. I was screaming, I know that, begging them to put me down.

'Hang on, Max, for God's sake,' shouted Ellis from somewhere behind me. 'You *must* hold on. Just a few more minutes.'

I didn't have a few more minutes. I didn't have any time at all. An odd bit of my mind, bored with this current crisis, took a second to wonder at which moment a child is officially born. When the head appears? When the whole child is expelled? When it draws its first breath? When the cord is cut?

I sunk my chin on my chest and cried, 'Nnnngggg' just by way of a change.

Ellis shouted something and they increased their pace, galloping headlong towards the pod.

It was being born. I could feel it. I tried to twist myself free, but they had me in a grip of steel and I wasn't going anywhere except towards the pod at top speed.

I heard someone shout, 'Door', and then we were inside.

'Quick, get her clothes off.'

Someone tugged at my shoes. I felt my trousers being yanked down.

I said, 'Hey,' and someone else said, 'Sorry about this, Max,' but I was pretty much past caring.

I brought my knees up and connected heavily with someone's chin. Even over the noise I was making I heard his teeth snap together.

And there it was. I could feel it happening. Now. I curled myself for one final almighty effort …

'Nnnngggg.'

'Bloody hell, it's coming. What do we do?'

And then everything happened at the same time. Voices shouted around me.

'Give me the med kit.'

'Get that door shut.'

Someone took my hand. I seized it and gripped hard.

'Aaaggghhh.'

No, that wasn't me. That was the unfortunate bloke whose thumb I'd just dislocated.

'Door!'

'Aaaggghhh.'

Yes, that one was me.

'Aaaggghhh,' because here it came. Now. I clenched my teeth and pushed.

'Bloody hell, Max. No! Not yet! Stop!'

Yeah, like that was going to happen.

'Look out.'

'Computer ...'

'Aaaggghhh.'

'Initiate ...'

'Aaaggghhh.'

'... Jump.'

'Aaaggghhh.'

The last word was lost in my final scream, the wail of a newborn infant and the thud of our heavy landing and in which order they came is a secret I will take to the grave.

I was surprised at the landing. I thought they'd be better than that. Although, as Captain Ellis complained to me later, one of his men had a badly sprained knee, one had bitten through his tongue and was in some discomfort, and one had a dislocated thumb, so perhaps there was some excuse. Anyway, I was home.

My home anyway.

I struggled to sit up and see my baby.

Someone said, 'That's not right.'

'What?' I said, panicking as only an experienced historian and new mother can do. 'What's not right? What's happening? Tell me.'

'My bloody thumb,' said the voice. 'Look at it, it's ...'

I never found out what it was, because the door opened and Helen stood on the threshold with Hunter behind her, carrying a med kit.

'Move,' she said, and quite honestly, our big rufty-tufty Time Policemen couldn't move quickly enough, clustering together at the door.

I said weakly, 'Helen …'

'Yes,' she said, 'just a minute.' She and Hunter bent over something.

'Helen …'

There was an orange explosion at the door and Time Policemen flew in all directions. Like skittles. Leon was with us.

He fell into the pod, dropped to his knees beside me, and said, 'Max.'

I put my arms around his neck and whispered, 'Leon.'

He put his arm around my shoulders, gently supporting me and wriggled himself alongside. I leaned gratefully against him, feeling all his solid warmth around me. His heart was racing and the hand holding mine was not steady. Neither was his voice.

He said, 'Max,' again and his voice broke. I clutched his hand because I couldn't speak either.

And then I remembered. 'Helen – what's happening? It's not crying.'

'Not all babies cry.'

'Why isn't it crying?'

'I suspect it's very sensibly sussing out its surroundings before making any sort of sound. Obviously a strong sense of self-preservation its mother would do well to emulate.'

'Is it all right?'

'It's fine as far as I can tell,' she said casually, with no sense at all of the importance of the question. 'If you can just wait quietly for one moment ...'

She and Hunter bent over the baby and did things I couldn't see. I clung to Leon who clung back again.

'Here you are,' she said finally, lifting something very loosely wrapped in a sterile cloth.

She placed the baby – my baby – our baby – gently into my arms.

I stared, awestruck. It was very quiet around the pod. Everyone was staring.

'Well,' said someone quietly. 'Will you look at that.'

'It's a boy,' said Leon, hoarsely, touching his head with one finger.

'It certainly is,' I said. 'He's going to be popular with the girls.'

Leon sighed. 'Right, that settles it. Tomorrow morning, like it or not, you get your eyes tested.'

I squinted. 'Are you saying she's a girl?'

He sighed. 'No, he's a boy. A perfectly normal little boy. He's just not hung like the National Gallery.'

'I don't understand.'

'That's his cord.'

'We'll give you some privacy for a moment,' said Helen. 'Apparently, thanks to Max, there are other casualties.' She and Hunter left the door open so they could keep an eye on things while they treated the Time Policemen I'd managed to injure during the birthing process.

'My tongue hurth like hell,' someone was saying thickly.

'Not a lot I can do,' said Hunter. 'Suck ice cubes and wait for the swelling to go down. It will. It's stopped bleeding already. No hot drinks for a while, obviously.'

He made an anxious noise.

'No, beer should be fine.'

In the distance, I could hear Helen telling someone not to be such a wuss. He had another knee, didn't he?

I lay back against Leon as we stared at our baby. I watched tiny fingers fasten around his thumb and felt tears begin to fall. I looked up at Leon, and there he was – wife in one arm and baby in the other, his eyes shining and at that moment, the happiest man on the planet.

A sudden shriek of pain made us both jump.

'Call yourself a Time Policeman,' said Hunter, scornfully. 'That was pathetic.'

'That was bloody agony.'

'Oh, don't be such a wimp. I've put your thumb back in. There's a woman in there who's just had a baby and you don't hear her whinging.'

'Yeah? Try putting that back in and see what sort of a fuss she makes then.'

Their voices died away and we were left alone.

Just the three of us.

I knew there were still problems out there.

I knew – Captain Ellis knew – they all knew – Matthew had been born between times. We'd jumped from there, but not yet landed here. Did that count?

Would they make us go back? The shadows in the corners deepened. My feet grew cold.

And Halcombe. He was still here, supposedly incubating leprosy, but we couldn't keep him locked up forever.

And the Sword of Tristram and the Holy Roman Crown were still buried up in the woods awaiting discovery and St Mary's rehabilitation.

And Dottle, slowly extricating herself from Halcombe's influence. I knew she wanted to stay. Could a place be found for her?

And what about Tim and his Special Question?

And what of that unfamiliar Leon who swooped in, saved us all and then swooped back out again?

One hell of a 'To Do' list.

Captain Matthew Ellis appeared in the doorway. 'They're going to move you up to Sick Bay now. Sorry, Max, but we need our pod back.'

We all surveyed the mess. It looked as if a major battle had been fought in here.

He knelt alongside. 'Just look at this little fellow, Max.' He turned to look at me and said quietly, 'Lucky baby. Five seconds earlier and he'd have been in trouble.'

I felt a great tidal wave of relief surge through me. He was a good man.

Leon held out his hand. 'I can't thank you enough.'

Ellis took it. 'No need to thank me at all. Have you thought of a name yet?'

'Yes,' said Leon, unexpectedly. 'With your permission, he's Matthew Edward Farrell.'

There was a short silence.

'I should be tremendously honoured.' He stroked a tiny hand with his finger. 'Hey there, Matthew. Welcome to the world.' He turned back to us, but looking at me. 'So that's a happy ending then.'

'So it would seem,' I said, looking at him. 'Thank you, Matthew.'

He smiled. 'My pleasure. No, hold on. What should I say? Oh yes – an honour and a privilege.'

'And I'm sorry about your crew. I had no idea they were so fragile. You should employ more girls.'

'We used to, but they made the boys cry.'

'I know the feeling,' said Leon.

He shrugged. 'One sprained knee, one swollen tongue, one dislocated thumb – considering St Mary's past record, I think we got off lightly this time.'

Chapter Twenty-five

I've never slept so much in my life. It was as if a lifetime of disturbed nights, broken sleep patterns, and bad dreams suddenly teamed up and presented their bill all at the same time. If I so much as leaned back and closed my eyes for a second, I would fall asleep, opening my eyes some time later, smiling groggily at Leon or whoever happened to be present, before falling asleep all over again. Leon claimed I once nodded off in the middle of lunch, which didn't seem very likely, but I wasn't awake long enough to argue.

I missed large chunks of Matthew's first week, but since, like me, he was out like a light himself for a lot of the time, so did he. Helen refused to worry, telling Leon bluntly that his life was never likely to be this peaceful again, and to make the most of it.

For the three of us, the days drifted by in a little pink bubble of peace and happiness. I had no idea what was going on outside of Sick Bay – what was happening with Ronan, the Time Police, whatever – and neither did I care enough to ask. People dropped in to say hello and were gone again when I woke up. Dr Bairstow called to offer his congratulations and, as he said, to inspect the latest member of his unit. Seen close together, I thought I saw a certain resemblance – they certainly had the same amount of hair but, possibly fortunately, I fell asleep before I could point this out.

On the fourth day, Markham danced into the ward, eyes alight with mischief and grinning his head off.

Leon, sitting with Matthew in the window seat, enquired placidly what was going on.

'Just a heads up,' he said. 'There's going to be shouting. I didn't want you to be too alarmed.'

'What have you done now?'

'As at this moment – nothing at all. However, I'm about to sacrifice myself for the common good. Well, Peterson's good, actually. This could be the last time you ever see me.' He posed dramatically. 'Farewell, my friends. It is a far, far better thing that I do ...'

'When did you ever read *A Tale of Two Cities*?' demanded Leon.

'Chicken pox.'

We waited, but that seemed to be it.

I could hear Hunter approaching, talking to someone.

He drew himself up. 'Here goes. Never let it be said a Markham flinched in the face of peril ...' and slipped out of the door.

Staggering artistically towards the nurses' station, he called hoarsely for help. Sadly, far from relinquishing her post to go to his aid, Hunter merely sighed and enquired what was the problem this time.

He opened and closed his mouth a few times, apparently unable to speak.

She looked up, irritated. 'What?'

He uttered a few disjointed words in a croaky sort of voice.

She put her hands on her hips. 'What are you supposed to be? The Hoarse Whisperer?'

Wisely, he gave that up and staggered again. 'I think I'm going to faint.'

Still she showed no signs of moving from the station. 'Put your head between your legs.'

'You'd think she would have learned by now,' murmured Leon.

Markham grinned angelically. 'I'm sure I'd feel so much better if I could put my head between ...'

She was out from behind the desk in a flash, but this was Markham and he was already accelerating away. I could hear the sound of her shouting dopplering away into the distance and then a door slammed.

Leon and I looked at each other. 'What was that all about?'

We were about to find out.

Peterson appeared, paused by the empty station, and looked around him, a picture of furtive unease. Actually, a picture of well-dressed, furtive unease. He'd ditched his blues and was wearing a smart jacket and trousers. I would swear he'd had his hair cut. Squaring his shoulders, he smoothed down his hair, straightened an unfamiliar tie, and entered Helen's office.

I sat stunned. Oh my God – Tim's Special Question. This was it.

Leon turned to me. 'Is this what I think it is?'

I nodded.

'What are his chances of success do you think? Or even his chances of survival?'

I shrugged. 'I honestly have no idea. I suppose it depends on whether she's had a cigarette recently.'

'Which reminds me ...' he said, handing me a sleeping Matthew and climbing up on the table.

'What are you doing?'

'Checking the batteries. The two most precious things in the world are here in this room at this moment. In the very likely event of St Mary's going up in flames, I want as much warning as possible.' He began to inspect the smoke detector.

Matthew and I watched with equal levels of disinterest: he because he was asleep, and me because the silence from Helen's office was far more interesting. I went to get up.

'You're not going out there,' said Leon, without even looking. 'Just because our proposal was a public event doesn't mean theirs should be too.'

I was going to argue but at that moment, out of nowhere – I don't know how he does it – Markham slithered back into the room.

'Hey,' he said breezily and then blinked at the sight of Leon standing on the table. 'Am I interrupting a suicide pact? What's going on?'

'I was about to ask you the same thing,' I said.

'Do you two want to be alone? Should I leave?'

'Not before you tell me what's happening.'

'Can't tell from here. They have the door closed. There's no shouting though, which I usually find is a Good Thing.'

'And a bit of a Rare Thing in your case, I should imagine,' said Leon, replacing the cover to the smoke detector. 'What have you done with Hunter?'

'Laughing her head off in the rest room.'

'Really? What did you do?'

Markham ignored him, pulling over my fruit bowl, and helping himself to my tangerine.

I took the tangerine off him in exchange for Matthew.

'Wait,' he said, holding him like an unexploded bomb in a nappy. 'Is it safe to touch him? Is it like terrapins?'

'What on earth are you talking about?' said Leon, from up near the ceiling.

'You know – you mustn't touch them because of giving them germs. Or possibly the other way around. I forget.'

Leon shook his head. 'The thinking processes of the Security Section never fail to baffle and bemuse me.'

'Says the man standing on a table,' he replied, jiggling Matthew up and down. 'Who's a pretty boy, then?'

'He's a baby – not a parrot.'

He sniffed. 'What's that awful smell? It's not me is it?'

'He's filling his nappy,' said Leon, jumping down, apparently satisfied that should St Mary's ignite, we would at least have a fighting chance of escaping. 'He's only four days old and he's already been more times than his mother has in her entire life.' He removed Matthew from Markham's arms and took him away.

The continuing silence worried me. I stared through the door towards Helen's office. 'Do you think she's shot herself? Has she shot him? What's going on in there?'

'Of course she hasn't shot herself,' said Markham scornfully. 'She's a doctor. It's far more likely she's shot someone else. Halcombe would be my first choice.'

I settled back down with a sigh of relief. 'Good for her. Sometimes the medical profession really comes through.'

'Nobody's shot anyone,' said Leon, voice of reason, dispeller of happy fantasies and nappy changer. 'Although I can understand the necessity for desperate measures at the thought of spending the rest of your life shackled to an historian.'

'Pity,' said Markham with regret. 'Shooting Halcombe would have solved so many problems. I'm sure doctors shoot their patients all the time. We could all swear it was an accident.'

I nodded. 'And help bury the body afterwards. Well, not me, obviously, because I'm on light duties, but I'd be happy to urge the rest of you on with word and gesture. We'd have to do it behind Leon's back of course, because he never lets me have any fun. Husbands!' I threw him a scathing look.

He grinned amiably, seemingly ignorant of the lowly position of husbands in the scheme of things.

'You do realise,' I said, 'that with Leon and me shackled together until the end of time, and if Helen does say yes and Tim survives the shock, then that just leaves you and Hunter. Can we expect a happy announcement any time soon?'

We both looked at him expectantly, but without a great deal of hope. The precise nature of his relationship with Hunter was a mystery to everyone.

He put his hands in his pockets, looked out of the window, sighed, and turned back into the room again – mischief written all over his face.

'No need, really. We've been married for years.'

And then he was out of the door before either of us was able to utter a word.

THE END

Jodi Taylor

The Chronicles of St Mary's

Also by
Jodi Taylor

The Nothing Girl

A Bachelor Establishment

For more information about **Jodi Taylor**

and other **Accent Press** titles

please visit

www.accentpress.co.uk

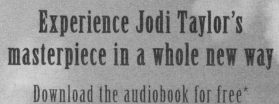
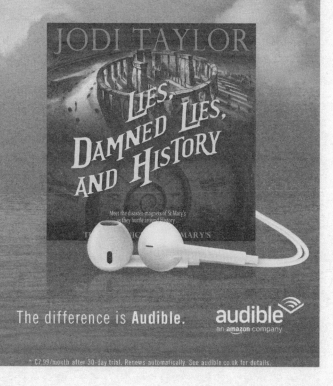